Stephen Crane: Stories and Tales

Stephen Crane:

Stories and Tales

Edited by Robert Wooster Stallman

NEW YORK

VINTAGE BOOKS

1955

CONTENTS

INTRODUCTION

LUCKLESS in everything else, Crane had the great luck—phenomenal among writers—to write two works of art having major importance in American letters and to write them both before he was twenty-two. Though he died when he was but twenty-eight, he left behind him more than enough perfections to place him solidly among the half-dozen major artists of American fiction in the nineteenth century—not in the first rank with Hawthorne and Melville and Henry James but, counting work for work, in the second rank with Poe and Howells and Twain. Not counting his detective fiction, Poe is at his best in but a couple of short stories and one novel, *The Narrative of A. Gordon Pym.* Crane perfected more works than either Poe or Twain. He first broke new ground with *Maggie: A Girl of the Streets,* the then sordid realism of that work initiating the literary trend of the next generation. *Maggie* is a tone painting rather than a realistic photograph of slum life, but it opened the door to the Norris-Dreiser-Farrell school of sociological realism. The sensational success of *The Red Badge of Courage* (a best-seller in England and in America, it outsold Zola and Tolstoy and even Kipling) brought him into instantaneous and meteoric renown. In *The Red Badge,* an impressionistic painting notable for its bold innovations in technique and style, and in *The Open Boat,* that flawless construct of paradox and symbol, Crane established himself among the foremost engineers in the techniques of modern fiction. *The Open Boat* (1897) is a perfect fusion of the impressionistic realism of *Maggie* (1893) and the symbolic realism of *The Red Badge of Courage* (1895). The two main technical movements of modern fiction—realism and symbolism—have their beginnings here in these achievements of Stephen Crane.

Crane is frequently spoken of as the most legendary figure in American letters since Edgar Allan Poe. "A genius as singular as Poe" and "destined from the first to be a present-day Poe"—Hamlin Garland concluded after meeting him—"a singular and daring soul, irresponsible as the wind." A whole mythology of bizarre tales, some of them not entirely untrue, surrounds his elusive and enigmatic personality, and it is difficult to distinguish the real Crane from the mythical Crane when so much of the factual is itself fantastic. The fantastic pursued him beyond the grave in the fact that after he died his widow—an extraordinary woman and a faithful wife—returned to her former trade in Jacksonville, Florida, where as the madam of a bawdyhouse she presided over a mansion modeled on Brede Place, the semi-medieval residence of the Cranes in England.[1] Crane, by nature overgenerous, had a trigger-quick love for the underdog—Bowery bums and streetwalkers—and an immense capacity for friendship. His friendship was shared by the literary great—Conrad, Henry James, H. G. Wells, Ford Madox Ford, William Dean Howells, Hamlin Garland, and others. Conrad affectionately attended him during his fatal illness, and Henry James, waiting upon him with oversolicitous devotion, treated him as though he were another Keats—a pet lamb in a sentimental tragedy. He lived violently and he died young, but even while he lived, the real Crane was being converted into the conventional legend of the artist —luckless, penniless, creative only when fever-ridden or drunk. There is this folk version of the wayward genius, under which Crane's myth-making personality has been likened to Poe's, and there is the more classical version of the "stricken boy," the genius who dies young—Chatterton, Keats, Schubert, Beardsley.

The Crane portrait hangs, as it were, between calumny and idolatry; seen from this latter point of view (viz. Ford Madox Ford's) we get a sentimentalized impression: "I took him at once to be a god—an Apollo with starry eyes."

---

[1] See Chapter xxx of *The St. Johns* by Branch Cabell and A. J. Hanna (1943). What they report is probably legend, not fact.

The reputation of Crane is as contradictory as the man himself. Not fame alone but scandal attached to his name, and by 1896 he was "the most thoroughly abused writing man" in America. To champion a woman of the streets and get into a tangle with the police was bad taste in the 1890's, and Crane's unearned ill repute among certain editors and his scandalous reputation with the public contributed to the neglect into which his works fell after 1900. An author who shows "bad taste" in his life cannot show "good taste" in his writings—it is the same moral whip that is even today used against Poe and Byron. The abuse of Crane's name came solely from the American press, and in 1897 he settled in England because of it.

There seem so many of them in America who want to kill, bury and forget me purely out of unkindness and envy—and my unworthiness, if you choose. All the hard things they say of me affect me principally because I think of mine own people —you and Teddie and the families. It is nothing, bless you. Now Dick Davis for instance has come to like the abuse. He accepts it as a tribute to his excellence. But he is a fool. Now I want you to promise to never pay any attention to it, even in your thought. It is too immaterial and foolish. Your little brother is neither braggart or a silent egotist but he knows that he is going on steadily to make his simple little place and he can't be stopped, he can't even be retarded. He is coming. [Letter to William, October 29, 1897.]

But there was another reason for Crane's going to England. He had reason to fear malicious gossip about his marriage to, or his living with, a woman who had once been associated with a "house of joy."

He had suffered out the public indifference to *Maggie* (as late as 1930 that book remained practically unknown in America), but critical ridicule heaped on *The Black Riders*—published just before *The Red Badge,* and preferred by Crane as his "more ambitious effort"—must have added to his embitterment.

Fame descended upon Crane in 1896, in January, when he was living with his brother at Hartwood, Sullivan County, New York, and a few months before he died he wrote from England to an American editor, Joseph O'Connor: "I have only one pride—and that is that the English edition of 'The Red Badge of Courage' has been received with great praise by the English reviewers. I am proud of this simply because the remoter people would seem more just and harder to win." [2] No man of his generation was more admired and loved or received greater critical recognition, but that was in another country.

The chief impetus for Crane's American success was provided by British praise, and the tumultuous reception accorded *The Red Badge* by the British journals was first heralded at home by Harold Frederic's London dispatch to the *New York Times* on January 26, 1896: "Stephen Crane's Triumph—London Curious About the Identity of America's New Writer." (Crane wrote Hitchcock about it: "delighted with Frederic's letter in the Times.") Then, once America got wind of it, but not until then, his book early the next year "swept the country," leading the bestseller lists by March and April in sixteen cities and going through fourteen American printings that year. At home derision and heated contention accompanied the praise, the American press taking offense at being told that Crane had been "first praised in England." What a controversy *The Red Badge* stirred up! What critical warfare it ignited! The *Critic* in January 1897 counterblasted against the *Daily News* that Crane had been reviewed "from Maine to California before a single English reviewer had received the book," and it reminded these ignorant English editors that some half-dozen other authors had also been first "discovered" or "boomed" here in America. Behind the blurred truth, however, it was exactly as the *Daily News* asserted: "After English praise, the author's countrymen reconsidered their verdict." The book did pretty well for the first three months, but at first it sold very slowly. "Mr. Hitchcock tells me," Crane wrote in a letter of December 24, 1895, "that the book does not sell much in New York. It has gone to about 4,500, though, and many of them have been sent west." He remarked to a friend: "Oh, of

[2] Published in the *Rochester Post-Express*, April 18, 1900, p. 4; reprinted in part in the *Literary Digest*, June 23, 1900.

course, I should be glad if everybody, Canadians, Feejees, Hottentots, wild men of Borneo, would buy *The Red Badge*—four copies of it—but they won't; so what's the use of thinking of the reader?"

"Who is this man Crane, anyway?" The question was asked in the editorial offices of the *Philadelphia Press,* where in December 1894 *The Red Badge* was making its first appearance—serialized from December 3 to 8. "Well, if he keeps this up, we'll all know him in a few years." Appleton brought out the book-length version early in October 1895, and two months later (during the week of November 30) Heinemann published it in England. The Muse on Publisher's Hill showed prophetic wit in putting *The Red Badge of Courage* into Heinemann's "*Pioneer* Series of *Modern* Fiction." Or again in crowning the first American edition with a gilt top! The flash and blast that the book made, the shock and excitement, the sensation it produced were at once "unprecedented and irresistible." As Conrad, H. G. Wells, Mencken, and Hergesheimer testify, it detonated on the public—to use Conrad's trope— with "the impact and force of a twelve-inch shell charged with a very high explosive." What caused the explosion, particularly upon his more perceptive readers, was the explosive style of the book, Crane's own bombardment of similes and metaphors.

Sentimental critics have shed literary tears over Crane's early death, but his death at twenty-eight resulted in no loss to literature. He had exhausted his genius. By 1900 the whirligig of taste had replaced Crane with Frank Norris, and the *Bookman*—reviewing *McTeague,* which had appeared the year before—piously admonished Norris "to walk humbly" amidst "the warning of Mr. Crane's obvious failure to meet the expectations he excited." Hamlin Garland, shifting away now from his former praise, wrote in *Roadside Meetings* (p. 206) that Crane "was too brilliant, too fickle, too erratic to last. He could not go on doing stories like *The Red Badge of Courage.*" But this is misleading and it ignores the fact that Crane went on doing not more *Red Badge*'s but other kinds of stories just as

good or, in *The Open Boat*, better. Two opposite points
of view, both of them mistaken, argue that (1) his last
works show "no diminution of literary powers" and (2)
that he died young "without fulfilling his wonderful promise." It seems to be the occupational disease of critics to
concern themselves more with an author's future promise
than with his present achievement, and consequently no
American author "succeeds" because he inevitably "fails."
As for Crane's failure to live up to the fulfillments that
his work "promised," he excited no expectations but those
he fulfilled in the works that excited them. It is not true
that he "expended himself" with the creation of *Maggie*
and *The Red Badge*, not yet; but after his initial achievements—*Maggie*, a little later *The Red Badge*, *George's
Mother*, and then *The Open Boat*—he wrote no more
than a half-dozen first-rate tales, and in poetry, after *The
Black Riders*, there was the same falling off, the late work
sharply declining from the early. He produced too much,
he kept repeating himself, and he never developed. His
writings fill twelve volumes—eighty-six sketches and tales,
five brief novels, three volumes of verse, and a mass of
journalistic stuff (one hundred and twenty-eight articles).
The greater part of all this work is second-rate. The artist
had succumbed to the journalist (for example, *Active
Service, The O'Ruddy, Great Battles of the World*), though
some of the pure Crane shone even at the end of his comet-
like career. As Sherwood Anderson said: "Suppose he did
put a pretty little patent-leather finish on some of his later
tales. Take him for what he was—his importance."

What killed Crane was not literary neglect—he died, so
the popular notion has it, "tragically young," "a boy,
spiritually killed by neglect"—but rather his own will to
burn himself out, his Byronic craving to make his body
"a testing ground for all the sensations of life." He aimed
not to live very long (thirty-five at best, he wrote Nellie
Crouse), and knowing that his time was short, he had no
time to lose. *He lived in desperation against time.* Like
F. Scott Fitzgerald, who wrote (to quote Malcolm Cowley)
"in a room full of clocks and calendars," Crane feared

time if he feared anything. (It is curious that he should describe his mother in terms of time: "She spoke as slowly as a big clock ticks and her effects were impromptu.") He died at the same sinister hour as Fitzgerald, three in the morning. His life was again like Fitzgerald's in this: though filled with adventure, it was neither thrilling nor romantic, but actually somewhat banal. "Even his war adventures," as H. L. Mencken says, "were far less thrilling in fact than in his florid accounts of them." [3] What D. H. Lawrence remarked about Melville is true also of Crane: "The artist was so much greater than the man."

Crane was intense, volatile, spontaneous—what he wrote came unwatched from his pen. He wrote as he lived, and his life was shot through with ironies. Seeing life from a water-soaked dinghy, as it were, the sea tossing him about this way and that, he saw it as an angry or indifferent sea —"the grim waves menacing" and "most wrongfully and barbarously abrupt." If he won any "grace" from that cold voyage it was, I think, the artist's gift of ironic outlook, that grace of irony which is so central to his art. Irony is Crane's chief technical instrument. It is the key to our understanding of the man and of his works. He wrote with the intensity of a poet's emotion, the compressed emotion that bursts into symbol and paradox.

2

Crane wasted his genius. Under the mistaken notion that only those who have suffered shipwreck can become its interpreters, he expended himself in a search for experience. Willfully and needlessly he risked his life—among bandits in Mexico, under shellfire in Cuba and Greece as war correspondent, and off the Florida seacoast as a filibustering seaman in the disaster that befell him when he survived shipwreck only after suffering thirty hours at sea in a ten-foot dinghy. It was natural that Crane should want to see actual warfare after writing about it, and four years later as war correspondent in the Greco-Turkish War he tested the psychological truth of his imagined picture.

[3] In *A Mencken Chrestomathy* (1949), p. 497.

"My picture was all right!" he told Conrad. "I have found it as I imagined it." But at what a cost! Exposures endured in Cuba wrecked his health and impaired his art. Nothing vital came from his war experiences. His imagination, as one friend said, "worked better in a room than on a battlefield." [4] And the pity of it all is that it could have been otherwise. He could have lived in one of his brothers' homes and done his writing there; he could have retreated from life to calculate it from a distance as Hawthorne and James did. Instead, he chose to get as close to life as possible. Garland, meeting him in McClure's office one day, said to him earnestly:

Crane, why don't you cut loose from your associations here? Go to your brother's farm in Sullivan County and get back your tone. You don't look well. Settle down to the writing of a single big book up there, and take your time to do it.— Impulsively thrusting out his hand to me, he said—I'll do it.—Alas! He did not. He took a commission to go to Greece and report a war. On his return from Greece he went to Cuba.[5]

Writing from London in 1897 to his brother William, Crane said: "My idea is to come finally to live at Port Jervis or Hartwood. I am a wanderer now and I must see enough but—afterwards—I think of P. J. & Hartwood."

He wanted to get at the real thing, and so he stood all night in a blizzard in order to write *Men in the Storm;* to get at the real thing he spent a night in a Bowery flophouse in order to write *An Experiment in Misery;* to get at the real thing he traveled across the Western prairies, and out of it he got *The Blue Hotel* and *The Bride Comes*

---

[4] C. Lewis Hind in *Authors and I* (1921), pp. 73–4. The same opinion is given by H. G. Wells, Hamlin Garland, and others.

[5] *Roadside Meetings,* pp. 203–4. Beer states that Crane could have retreated to his brother's home "and stayed as a pensioner until, somehow, he had established himself with a public. But Crane's independence had a bent almost savage and ungracious." *Hanna, Crane, and The Mauve Decade,* pp. 277–8. (All references to Beer are to this volume.) Crane's niece argues *contra* Beer that Crane's brothers were not oversolicitous about him: "My Uncle, Stephen Crane," *American Mercury,* 31 (January 1924), 24. This article fills in the situation but does not change the fact that, while his brothers may not have been oversolicitous about him, still they would have taken him in as they had before. There was no necessity for Crane's sleeping in Bowery flophouses. He went to them by choice.

to Yellow Sky; out of Mexico he got *Horses—One Dash!*
and other sketches; and out of Cuba and Greece impressions of war for *Wounds in the Rain,* stories like *Death
and the Child,* and the novel *Active Servic*e. But was there
any need for Crane to experience a blizzard in order to
write *Men in the Storm?* Would not an imaginary rather
than an actual blizzard have served just as well, the germinal idea of the story being a *symbolic* storm—the storm
of social strife? Familiarizing himself with New York
tenement life certainly was not necessary for the germinal
idea of *An Auction,* in which he depicts the social shame
of a poor couple whose household goods are auctioned off
amidst the derisive mockery of a parrot and a gaping
crowd. No personal experience of Bret Harte's country
was needed to write parodies of Bret Harte's Californian
tales—in *Moonlight in the Snow, Twelve O'Clock,* and
A Self-Made Man. Much of Crane's anecdotal material
might just as well have originated in other people's experience, and in fact some of it did—for example, the incident used in *The Lone Charge of Francis B. Perkins* was
taken from Ralph Paine.

In his quest for and immersion in experience, Crane
stands at the headstream of what has been defined as the
dominant American theme and literary trend [6]—exempli-
fied in Hemingway, Anderson, and Thomas Wolfe, who
put the same premium on personal experience. Consider-
ing how much personal experience he had to draw upon,
he put it to very little significant use. At his best he used
not the experienced event but the event distilled for its
thematic potentialities. The exception is *The Open Boat,*
but here—as with Conrad in *Heart of Darkness,* which is
taken straight from life—the personal experience served
simply as the canvas for the re-created picture. The only
work Conrad ever wrote immediately after an actual experience on the spot was *The Idiots* (*Life and Letters,* I,
164). *The Open Boat* was an immediate transcript of personal experience, but it is personal experience transformed
into an impersonal and symbolic representation of life—

[6] See Philip Rahv's *Image and Idea* (1949), p. 8.

the plight of mankind tossed upon an indifferent sea. The calculated design and significance of the story can be explained by no source other than the conceiving imagination of the artist. Crane excels in the portrayal of mental turmoil, and for this psychological realism his creative imagination required no first-hand experience. *The Open Boat* and *Horses—One Dash!* are his most directly autobiographical tales, but most of his fiction is only remotely autobiographical. Contacts with reality, for Conrad and Crane alike, provoked hints for characters, details of locality, and the like; but it is seldom that Crane presents minute descriptions of people or scenes, and details of locality are not photographically recorded. The locality of *The Blue Hotel* has symbolic import and could have been painted with no first-hand knowledge of it. He could have written *The Blue Hotel* without leaving New York City. The fight that he witnessed and tried to stop during an incident in Lincoln, Nebraska, became the fight depicted in *The Blue Hotel,* but the germinal idea for the story might just as well have had a literary source. *The Blue Hotel* has been called "a Hemingway story," but in germinal conception it follows Robert Louis Stevenson's formula: a certain scene and atmosphere suggest the correlative action and persons for that particular locality, and they are so used as to express and symbolize it. The atmosphere of the old blue hotel, the psychic quality of its screaming blue, impels and foreshadows the action that expresses it—the murder of the Swede.

Crane's two greatest works—*The Red Badge of Courage* and *The Open Boat*—represent two opposite methods of creation: from imagined experience and from actual experience. In contradiction to his theory that the artist can write about life only after first experiencing it, Crane reproduced the immediacies of battle in *The Red Badge of Courage* long before he had seen and suffered actual shellfire. The single marvel he wrung from personal experience was *The Open Boat,* and the marvel of it is that he manipulated the whole experience into art without altering the facts. Yet a paradox is here established, for the masterpiece that he salvaged from his expense of greatness could have been conceived without the personal experience—as *The Red Badge of Courage* is there to testify.

They all insist—said Crane, referring to the reviewers of his *Red Badge*—that I am a veteran of the civil war, whereas the fact is, as you know, I never smelled even the powder of a sham battle. I know what the psychologists say, that a fellow can't comprehend a condition that he has never experienced, and I argued that many times with the Professor. Of course, I have never been in a battle, but I believe that I got my sense of the rage of conflict on the football field, or else fighting is a hereditary instinct, and I wrote intuitively; for the Cranes were a family of fighters in the old days, and in the Revolution every member did his duty. But, be that as it may, I endeavoured to express myself in the simplest and most concise way. If I failed, the fault is [not] mine.[7]

Discovery that the author had been born six years after Appomattox provoked "universal surprise." Harold Frederic, discussing this question in his *Times* article on Crane, pointed out *why* it is that the best accounts of battles have been written by novelists who never saw warfare, and the least realistic accounts by trained correspondents who were on the spot. Between them, Frederic found, "The line between journalism and literature obtruded itself." This same point holds true of most of the war tales Crane wrote after he himself had witnessed a battle; there is very little difference between the war tales written before he had experienced war and the war tales written after his experience of it except that the later ones are often more journalism than literature. Frederic, himself a novelist and a journalist, put his finger on the paradox of art:

It seems as if the actual sight of a battle has some dynamic quality in it which overwhelms and crushes the literary faculty in the observer. At best, he gives us a conventional account of what happened; but on analysis you find that this is not what he really saw, but what all his reading has taught him that he must have seen. In the same way battle painters depict horses in motion, not as they actually move, but as it has been agreed by numberless generations of draughtsmen to say that they

[7] Letter to John N. Hilliard, written from England. Reprinted in *New York Times, Supplement,* July 14, 1900, p. 466.

move. At last, along comes a Muybridge, with his instantaneous camera, and shows that the real motion is entirely
different.[8]

Comparison between Crane's description of war and a
painter's was noted in the New York *World* the next
month (February 1896): Zola, "rather than Mr. Crane, is
the Verestchagin of literature."

The critical point to make about the notion that artists
cannot reproduce the actualities of life without first experiencing them is that the exact obverse is, in fact, the
truth. "I decided that the nearer a writer gets to life, the
greater he becomes as an artist." Yet Crane's own art was
at its greatest when he wrote at some distance from the
reality he had experienced or when, on the other hand, he
wrote out of no personal experience at all. His best works
do not vindicate or support the creative principle that
generated them.

What are the proper uses of personal experience?
Thomas Wolfe, learning from wasted experience, tried to
find the answer—too late to be of use to him. "And now
I really believe that *so far as the artist is concerned* [italics
mine], the unlimited extent of human experience is not
so important for him as the depth and intensity with which
he experiences things." [9] And *imagines* things! The depth
and intensity of the artist's personal experience does not
distinguish him *as* artist. Fitzgerald likewise exploited personal experience, sometimes shamefully, but he was an
artist who knew how to convert it into an imaginative
construct. Mark Twain's explanation for not continuing
to write novels was that "capital"—personal experience—
was not sufficient by itself.

3

There is an ironic contradiction between Crane's art and
his theory of art. There is, furthermore, a duality in his
theory. He argued for personal experience as the basis of

[8] *New York Times, Supplement,* January 26, 1896, p. 22.
[9] *The Story of a Novel,* in *The Portable Thomas Wolfe* (1948),
p. 586.

art, but he also argued for imaginative experience. At the same time he also believed that the greater the obstacles an artist had to overcome—the harder the conditions he had to meet—the greater his art would be. In the letter in which he says that he wrote *The Red Badge* "intuitively," he explains: "It was an effort born of pain, and I believe that it was beneficial to it as a piece of literature. It seems a pity that this should be so—that art should be a child of suffering; and yet such seems to be the case." [1] Crane (unwittingly) echoed Keats—and with the same inconsistency; for Keats, too, believed in Inspiration and simultaneously held that art is not born without pain. It is difficult to reconcile Crane as Inspirational Artist with the calculated design of *The Red Badge,* every impression in it being preconceived. His casual remarks about art, as one writer says, have an offhand air "designed to deceive his readers into believing that for him art was a matter of no great moment, that creation was a natural function, hardly worth comment or appraisal." [2] Like Conrad and Chekhov, Crane spoke of the artist as being "nothing but a powerful memory that can move itself at will through certain experiences sideways, and every artist must be in some things powerless as a dead snake." Chekhov said that a writer should depend solely upon memory, he should never keep a notebook. "When he died the drawer of his writing-table was found to be stuffed with notebooks." I am quoting here Edwin Mitchell, whose *Art of Authorship* (1935) was first to announce the existence of a Stephen Crane Notebook.[3] According to Crane's niece, manuscripts were often returned by publishers with the

[1] Letter to John N. Hilliard in *New York Times, Supplement,* July 14, 1900, p. 466.
[2] *The Art of Stephen Crane,* unpublished Cornell University dissertation by Jean Elizabeth Whitehead (1944), p. 71.
[3] Photostat copy of Crane's Notebook is in my possession, the gift of Mr. H. B. Collamore. The Notebook, pocket size, contains first drafts of unpublished sketches and articles, scraps of description and dialogue, and the opening pages of *A Desertion.* One of Crane's notes is a quotation from Emerson: "Congratulate yourselves if you have done something strange and extravagant and have broken the monotony of a decorous age."

demand: " 'Take the swear words out of it, and we will publish it.' His reply was unvarying: 'I can't, as that is how such men talk.' He had a passion for truth, and felt that to make such a change would not be sincere." [4] Crane did a good deal of revising, however, and he revised even after his work had been published. My point is that as soon as an author corrects so much as a comma he is no longer a purely inspirational creator. As for Crane's moral megrim that revisions are "dishonest" and "insincere," that scruple too contradicts the view of the artist as a conscious architect, and Crane *was* such an artist. As Yeats aptly put it: "The correction of prose, because it has no fixed laws, is endless; a poem comes right with a click like a closing box." [5]

Crane's poems came just that way. "Personally I like my little book of poems, *The Black Riders,* better than I do *The Red Badge of Courage.* The reason is, I suppose, that the former is the more ambitious effort." [6] Crane was at his *most* inspirational in writing his poems; "ambitious effort" is contradictory. And though he preferred his poetry to his fiction, he said elsewhere about *The Black Riders:* "Some of the pills are darned dumb, anyhow." As another instance of self-contradiction, he concealed whatever moral meaning his stories intended—"I let the reader find it for himself." But, like Conrad, Crane put little stock in the reader's perceptiveness, and according to his friend Herbert P. Williams, "he does not think to trust the imagination of any one who reads."

—Trust their imaginations? Why, they haven't got any! They are used to having everything detailed for them. Our imaginations are defunct for lack of use, like our noses. So whether I say a thing or suggest it, I try to put it in the most forcible way.—

[4] Edna Crane Sidbury: "My Uncle, Stephen Crane," *Literary Digest,* 4 (March 1926), 250.

[5] *Letters to Dorothy Wellesley* (1940), p. 24.

[6] Letter to John N. Hilliard (1897). Again, in a letter written late in 1895 and published the next year in *Leslie's Weekly,* Crane said: "I suppose I ought to be thankul to *The Red Badge,* but I am much fonder of my little book of poems, *The Black Riders.* The reason, perhaps, is that it was a more ambitious effort."

Singular declaration, this, for a man whose books appeal chiefly to men of powerful imagination.[7]

While no systematic point of view can be extracted from Crane's remarks and written commentaries, he subscribed to one theory again and again, Hamlin Garland's "veritism." But even this theory does not account for his art.

The creed of veritism which Garland preached—the theory that art is founded on personal experience and copies reality—Crane echoed when, not long before his death, he told a friend: "You can never do anything good aesthetically—and you can never do anything that's any good except aesthetically—unless it has at one time meant something important to you." And in an early letter (1895), taking issue with one of Henry James's critical tenets, he said: "What, though, does the man mean by disinterested contemplation? It won't wash. If you care enough about a thing to study it, you are interested and have stopped being disinterested." He told Reginald Kauffman: "I could never do what I didn't feel like doing—not even writing." In *Crumbling Idols* (1894), which Crane most likely read, Garland advised young writers: "Write of those things of which you know most, and for which you care most. By doing so you will be true to yourself, true to your locality, and true to your time" (p. 35). While Crane was still at college (he was not there very long), he told a school chum who wanted to write but could not "get down the real thing":

Treat your notions like that—he said, scooping up a handful of sand and tossing it to the brisk sea-breeze—Forget what you think about it and tell how you feel about it.—And then years later, when this same aspiring writer queried Crane whether he would now revise the advice he had given him that day on the beach, Crane said emphatically—No. You've got to feel the things you write if you want to make an impact on the world.[8]

And so, "to make an impact on the world," he studied the demi-world of New York: he spent several nights in

[7] "Mr. Crane as a Literary Artist," *Illustrated American*, July 18, 1896, p. 126.

[8] Arthur Oliver quoting Crane in "Jersey Memories—Stephen Crane," *New Jersey Historical Society*, 16 (1931), 454–5, 460.

a Mills Hotel "in search of material." His training as a newspaper reporter accounts in part for the theory he believed in. Such contacts with life set him apart from William Dean Howells. The very places Crane went slumming in—Bowery saloons, flophouses, and police stations —Howells prudishly avoided even when he was a reporter: "abhorrent contacts" he called them (in *Years of My Youth*).[9] At the other extreme was Jack London, who championed "the exalting of the life that is in me over Art, or any other extraneous thing." For Crane, on the contrary, life was but fuel for his kiln.

Crane's infrequent comments on art amount to no more than the standard of *truth and sincerity* that Conrad and Henry James and Howells promulgated. Truth is the sum of James's critical theory; fidelity is the chief tenet in Conrad's code of the artist. Their art, however, always was several jumps ahead of their theory, and contradicted it. They are not realists. Their art does not copy reality; it is impressionistic and symbolic. "Realism" to Howells and Henry James and Conrad meant truth and fidelity to the facts of experience, and almost everything that Crane wrote was motivated by this principle. It was an ethical-and-æsthetic principle, and Howells had announced it in his 1891 volume, *Criticism and Fiction:*

> I confess that I do not care to judge any work of the imagination without first of all applying this test to it. We must ask ourselves before we ask anything else, Is it true?—true to the motives, the impulses, the principles that shape the life of actual men and women? This truth, which necessarily includes the highest morality and the highest artistry—this truth given, the book cannot be wicked and cannot be weak; and without it all graces of style and feats of invention and cunning of construction are so many superfluities of naughtiness. . . . In the whole range of fiction I know of no true picture of life —that is, of human nature—which is not also a masterpiece of literature, full of divine and natural beauty. (P. 241.)

[9] As Van Wyck Brooks mentions in *A Chilmark Miscellany* (1949), pp. 236–7, Howells had "a morbid horror of the sordid and ugly; and this squeamishness had grown on the tender-minded Howells with his life in Venice and later in Cambridge and Boston."

Art, said Garland in *Crumbling Idols,* is an individual thing. It's a question of "one man facing certain facts and telling his individual relations to them." It is a question of conscience, of artistic integrity. You will find Conrad and Henry James dealing with this theme not only in their prefaces, but also in their fiction. The artist must create his vision with the utmost fidelity to what Conrad called "the image of truth abiding in facts" (*Life and Letters,* I, 280). Crane expressed the same conviction: "To keep close to my honesty is my supreme ambition. . . . This aim in life struck me as being the only thing worth while. A man is sure to fail at it, but there is something in the failure." Again: "a man is born into the world with his own pair of eyes and he is not at all responsible for his vision—he is merely responsible for his quality of personal honesty." [1] That, too, rings with Howells's voice. Writing is a test of moral courage, he told Crane. "A writer of skill cannot be defeated because he remains true to his conscience." In Lowell's remark to Howells, Hawthorne comes to mind: "After all, the barriers are very thin. They are paper. If a man has his conscience and one or two friends who can help him, it becomes very simple at last." Crane had plenty of friends, and they all believed in his genius. Genius for Crane amounted to *inspiration* ("I write what is in me"), and *truth* to life and *honesty* of conscience or *sincerity* of purpose.

The one thing that deeply pleases me in my literary life [he wrote an editor shortly after the publication of his *Red Badge of Courage*]—brief and inglorious as it is—is the fact that men of sense believe me to be sincere. "Maggie," published in paper covers, made me the friendship of Hamlin Garland and W. D. Howells, and the one thing that makes my life worth living in the midst of all this abuse and ridicule is the consciousness that never for an instant have those friendships at all diminished. Personally I am aware that my work does not amount to a string of dried beans—I always calmly admit it.

[1] Letter to Joseph O'Connor, literary editor of the *Rochester Post-Express,* published in the *Post-Express* April 18, 1900. Reprinted in "Some Letters of Stephen Crane," *New York Times, Supplement,* July 14, 1900, and in the *Academy,* August 11, 1900, p. 116.

But I also know that I do the best that is in me, without regard to cheers or damnation. [Letter to O'Connor, written 1898?]

Sincerity was Garland's idol, and truth and beauty were somehow one. "If we insist on sincerity, the question of dignity will take care of itself. Truth is a fine preparation for dignity, and for beauty as well" (*Idols*, p. 35). So Zola seemed to Crane "a sincere writer" and Stevenson "insincere." And that was that. Purely subjective criteria. But then, Crane was not a critic and did not profess to be. "My judgment in the case is not worth burning straw," Crane once wrote, "but I give it as portentously as if kingdoms toppled while awaiting it under anxious skies." [2] Crane was even less of a critic than myself, said Conrad. "Criticism is very much a matter of vocabulary very consciously used; with us it was the intonation that mattered. The tone of a grunt could convey an infinity of meaning between us." Once in a while, however, Crane got off some good grunts. Of Stevenson, whom he parodied in *The O'Ruddy,* he exclaimed to Ford Madox Ford: "By God! when Stevenson wrote 'With interjected finger he *delayed* the action of the *timepiece,*' meaning [as Ford explains it] 'he put the clock back,' Stevenson put back the clock of English fiction one hundred and fifty years!" Crane was conceited by streaks, more often modest than not, and quite unpredictable.

From Howells and Garland, Crane received not only personal encouragement and public praise, but also a creed to go by. Garland as a young man making his first visit to the East had been befriended by Howells and, in turn, he became Crane's greatest benefactor. The copy of *Maggie* that Garland sent Howells went unread until Crane wrote him "a heartbreaking note to the effect that he saw I didn't care for his book. On this I read it, and found I did care for it immensely." [3] He was so impressed, that in the *New York Press* (April 15, 1894) "The

[2] Quoted by Beer in his Introduction to Vol. VII of the *Work,* p. xiv.

[3] Letter from Howells to Mrs. Stephen Crane, in the *Academy,* 59 (August 1900), 123.

Greatest Living American Writer" called it "a remarkable book. There is so much realism of a certain kind in it that unfits it for general reading, but once in a while it will do to tell the truth as completely as Maggie does."

Garland's 1893 review of *Maggie*—of immense value to Crane because it was his first—applauded the author for writing about *the life he had lived* and for writing about it *truthfully,* not mincingly as others had done. In *Maggie* and *George's Mother* Crane had already written the novel Howells was asking for: the novel of social and moral intent which adjusts "perspectives" by portraying—in Emerson's words—not "the great, the remote, the romantic," but "the familiar and the low." (Emerson, implicit in Howells's creed, is traceable throughout much of Crane's writings.) "I had no other purpose in writing *Maggie* than to show people as they seem to me. If that be evil, make the most of it." [4] *Maggie* was "evil" because it exposed—without the custom-built moralizing of the contemporary novel—what it was forbidden to expose. Howells, as Crane quoted him in the *Times,* said that "a novel should never preach and berate and storm." Crane said the same thing a few years later:

Preaching is fatal to art in literature. I try to give to readers a slice out of life; and, if there is any moral lesson in it, I do not try to point it out. I let the reader find it for himself. [5]

And then (echoing Howells) he added: "As Emerson said, 'there should be a long logic beneath the story, but it should be carefully kept out of sight.' " Howells's insistence that "A man should mean something when he writes" is echoed in Crane's insistence of May 1895 about *The Black Riders:* "But I meant what I said." In *Maggie* he meant what he said, and what he meant was "to show that environment is a tremendous thing in this world, and often shapes lives regardlessly."

Howells was not shocked by *Maggie* (it shocked Rich-

[4] Letter to Catherine Harris dated November 12, 1896. Quoted in Beer, pp. 312–13.

[5] Letter to John N. Hilliard (1897).

ard Watson Gilder, who rejected it for the *Century*), but
he thought its realism too realistic and he advised the
young man to remove the profanities, "which I thought
would shock the public." Howells was often squeamish
about getting the whole truth—"perhaps it is better not
to recognize the facts." De Forest's novels were too grim,
and Howells shuddered. The realism he got in Crane and
Frank Norris was more than he had bargained for. His
own brand, the "romance of the commonplace," seemed
to the new century all too namby-pamby, "kittenish" (as
Mencken calls it). And Garland, finding Crane's philosophy too pessimistic ("a realist or verist is really an op-
timist"), cooled off. What he wrote after 1900 was not
inspired by the program of realism he had formerly pro-
fessed.

Crane did not start out as a writer in the Howells-
Garland camp, and during his career he changed styles
several times. *The Monster* is not in the style of *The
Open Boat* nor the style of *The Sullivan County Sketches*.
The first change came in 1892, shortly after he completed
The Sullivan County Sketches ("How I wish I had dropped
them into the wastebasket!"). It began when he suddenly
"renounced the clever school in literature":

You know [he wrote to Lily Brandon on February 20, 1896]
when I left you [1892, autumn], I renounced the clever school
in literature. It seemed to me that there must be something
more in life than to sit and cudgel one's brains for clever and
witty expedients. So I developed all alone a little creed of art
which I thought was a good one. Later I discovered that my
creed was *identical* [italics mine] with the one of Howells and
Garland and in this way I became involved in the beautiful war
between those who say that art is man's substitute for nature
and we are the most successful in art when we approach the
nearest to nature and truth, and those who say—well, I don't
know what they say . . . they fight villianously and keep
Garland and I out of the big magazines. Howells, of course, is
too powerful for them.
If I had kept to my clever Rudyard-Kipling style, the road
might have been shorter but, ah, it wouldn't be the true road.
The two years of fighting have been well-spent. And now I am

almost at the end of it. This winter fixes me firmly. We have proved too formidable for them, confound them.[6]

Crane says that he "developed all alone a little creed of art," but it is more than probable that he knew Howells's *Criticism and Fiction* some time after its publication in 1891. His acknowledgment to Howells for his "re-adjustment" in critical outlook is not made in this letter, but it is made in his inscription written in a presentation copy of *Maggie*: "as a token of the veneration and gratitude of Stephen Crane for many things he has learned of the common man and, above all, for a certain re-adjustment of his point of view victoriously concluded some time in 1892." Crane was very much in Howells's debt. The resemblance between his creed and Howells's has been denied by Crane's latest biographer (cf. John Berryman's *Stephen Crane*, p. 54), but Crane's confession of faith—"identical"—pins it down. The creeds of Crane and Howells *are* identical, both in social philosophy and in æsthetic principle.

4

What makes Crane of such exceptional critical interest is the great range and number of comparisons with other artists, echoes, and parallelisms that suggest themselves to any critic who has studied the man and his art. The range of cross-references extends from Flaubert and Hawthorne to Mark Twain and Rudyard Kipling, or—in terms of his influence on twentieth-century fiction—beyond his contemporaries Frank Norris and Theodore Dreiser to Dos Passos and Hemingway. While Crane's influence can be documented by a formidable catalogue of specific echoes in later American fiction, it persists more significantly in less subtilized form—that is, his naturalistic outlook in modern novels of slum life, his concept of the soldier as Everyman in modern novels of war. Maggie's brother (as

[6] Quoted in Melvin Schoberlin's Introduction to *The Sullivan County Sketches* (Syracuse University Press, 1950), p. 19. Reproduced here by permission of the Syracuse University Library and Melvin Schoberlin.

other critics have pointed out) is a forebear of Studs
Lonigan, and Crane in several of his stories (*An Episode
of War* is one example) foremirrors Hemingway. Modern
American literature has its beginnings in Mark Twain and
Stephen Crane. Crane in his use of dialect and in his
stories of childhood links with Twain, Kipling, and Booth
Tarkington. Crane's own Tom Sawyer is Jimmie Trescott
(in *Making an Orator*), and his *Sullivan County Sketches*
and *Whilomville Stories* had their inspirational source in
Twain's *Roughing It* and *Life on the Mississippi* (Crane's
favorite book). More important is the kinship they estab-
lish in the history of American literature: they each
brought new subject-matter into fiction and perfected the
techniques for manipulating it. Technically, *The Red Badge
of Courage* stands in legitimate comparison with *Huckleberry Finn*. They have the same form—namely, repetitions
of ironic episodes—and they deal with heroes in quest of
selfhood. In *Huckleberry Finn* every episode is built upon
the themes of death and deception or betrayal, and the
same themes or leitmotivs are central in *The Red Badge*.

The numerous artists who collect or radiate around
Crane form, as it were, a literary cartwheel. The spokes
that compose it include: the legendary Poe and Robert
Louis Stevenson, the adventurer and sketch-writer Robert
Cunninghame Graham, the realists Howells and Garland,
the naturalists Norris and Dreiser, the impressionists Chekhov and Katherine Mansfield and Conrad and Henry
James, and the writers on warfare, including Tolstoy, Zola,
Ambrose Bierce, J. W. De Forest, Rudyard Kipling, and
Henri Barbusse. Kipling's war tales and poems paved the
way for Crane's *Red Badge;* his soldier hero, as British
reviewers detected, seemed not unrelated to Tommy At-
kins. Crane's earliest style was Kiplingesque, as in some
of *The Sullivan County Sketches* (for example, *Killing
His Bear*), and something of Kipling's influence infected
certain later pieces such as *The Quest for Virtue, God Rest
Ye, Merry Gentlemen,* and *Kim Up!*—one of his very
last tales. Kipling's subject is similar to Crane's and Conrad's. The key to the whole work of Kipling, as Edmund

Wilson defines it, is that "the great celebrant of physical courage should prove in the long run to convey his most moving and convincing effects in describing moral panic." Kipling was one of the three or four influences that Crane admitted, though not always publicly. "If I had kept to my clever Rudyard-Kipling style, the road might have been shorter but, ah, it wouldn't be the true road." Kipling's ballads, read to Crane by Irving Bacheller, brought forth a burst of excitement. Chance made their careers run similarly too. Both became celebrities while still youths: Kipling in 1887, when he was twenty-two, and Crane—"a sort of American Kipling"—when twenty-four. Both had been journalists before becoming authors, and both wrote about warfare they had never seen. By further coincidence, their greatest recognition came only after their books had reached England, and both suffered their greatest abuse here in America—Kipling, hurt and bewildered, fled from Vermont. Kipling might have expressed the same sad and bitter note that Crane felt, the same lament:

Now that I have reached the goal [he wrote in a letter from England three years before he died] I suppose that I ought to be contented; but I am not. I was happier in the old days when I was always dreaming of the thing I have now attained. I am disappointed with success, and I am tired of abuse. Over here, happily, they don't treat you as if you were a dog, but give everyone an honest measure of praise or blame. There are no disgusting personalities.[7]

It was Conrad who first identified similarities between Crane's artistic temperament and his own and who first identified *The Red Badge of Courage,* with its psychological inquiry into the moral problem of conduct, with his own *Nigger of the "Narcissus."* (Crane's enthusiasm for this story led him to seek out Conrad in England and thereby become his friend and later his neighbor.) Conrad might have noted further similarities had he known Crane's *An Experiment in Misery* and *Maggie,* for the short story carries the Conradian theme of Solidarity (the theme also of *The Open Boat*), and *Maggie* the Conradian theme of

[7] Letter to John N. Hilliard, reprinted from the *New York Times, Supplement,* July 14, 1900, p. 466.

Fidelity—*Maggie* being a study in infidelity or betrayal.
Crane and Conrad are closely akin not only in temperament, but also in artistic code and in thematic range and
ironic outlook or tone. Both treat the subject of heroism
ironically and both contrive for their heroes, usually weak
or defeated men, unequal contests against outside forces,
pitting them against the sublime obstacles of hostile or indifferent nature. *The Open Boat* epitomizes this subject for
Crane, *Typhoon* for Conrad.

The Red Badge of Courage is readily identifiable with
Lord Jim, but their differences are, I think, more instructive. Whereas Lord Jim has an innate capacity for heroism,
Henry Fleming has it thrust upon him by chance and at
the wrong moment. For Crane, as *The End of the Battle*
testifies, heroism is not a predictable possession, but an
impersonal gift thrust upon man with ironic consequences.
The whole intention of his fable *A Mystery of Heroism*
is to explode the myth of heroism. The soldier Collins
does a heroic deed, but, as in Kipling, it is "the heroism
of moral fortitude on the edge of a nervous collapse."
Collins runs under shellfire to get water at a well and once
there he is a hero, "an intruder in the land of fine deeds,"
but once there the poor hero is cut off (both literally and
symbolically) from his fellow men, and the emptiness of
his vainglorious triumph is symbolized by the bucket from
which the wasted water spills as he nervously makes his
way back to the men. Crane's characters are always common, insignificant, and virtually nameless persons; no
Crane character is heroic, none is a leader, none is an
ideal. When compared with Conrad's, Crane's concept of
man's nature seems shallow. It is neither penetrating nor
magnanimous.

5

Crane stands in close kinship to Conrad and Henry James,
the masters of the impressionist school. Edward Garnett,
in 1898, hailed Crane as "the chief impressionist of the
age," adding that "Mr. Crane's talent is unique." All three
aimed to create (to use Henry James's phrase) "a direct

impression of life." Their credo is voiced by Conrad in his celebrated Preface to *The Nigger of the "Narcissus"* —it is "by the power of the written word, to make you hear, to make you feel—it is, before all, to make you *see*." Their aim was to immerse the reader in the created experience so that its impact on him would occur simultaneously with the discovery of it by the characters themselves. Instead of panoramic views of a battlefield, Crane paints not the whole scene but disconnected segments of it, all that a participant in an action or a spectator of a scene can possibly take into his view at any one moment. Crane is a master at creating illusions of reality by means of a fixed point of vision, through a specifically located observer.

From their position as they again faced toward the place of fighting, they could of course comprehend a greater amount of battle than when their visions had been blurred by the hurling smoke of the line. They could see dark stretches winding along the land, and on one cleared space there was a row of guns making gray clouds, which were filled with large flashes of orange-colored flame (*The Red Badge of Courage*, p. 333).

"None of them knew the colour of the sky"—that famous opening sentence of *The Open Boat* defines the restricted point of view of the four men in the wave-tossed dinghy, their line of vision being shut off by the menacing walls of angry water. Busy at the oars, they knew the color of the sky only by the color of the sea, and "they knew it was broad day because the colour of the sea changed from slate to emerald-green, streaked with amber lights, and the foam was like tumbling snow." Everything is keyed in a state of tension—even their speech, which is abrupt and composed of "disjointed sentences." Crane's style is itself composed of disjointed sentences, disconnected sense-impressions, chromatic vignettes by which the reality of the adventure is evoked in all its point-present immediacy.

Crane's style has been likened to a unique instrument that no one after his death has ever been able to play. *The Red Badge of Courage* seems unprecedented and non-comparable. But Chekhov, who was almost of an age with

Crane, and a little later Katherine Mansfield, who adopted the method of Chekhov, were both masters of the same instrument. In its episodic structure and impressionistic style Chekhov's *The Cherry Orchard* suggests a parallel to *The Red Badge of Courage*. All three artists had essentially the same literary aim and method: intensity of vision, objectivity in rendering it. All three aimed at a depersonalization of art: they aimed to get outside themselves completely in order "to find the greatest truth of the idea" and "see the thing as it really is"; to keep themselves aloof from their characters, not to become emotionally involved with their subjects, and to comment on them not by statement, but by evocation in picture and tone. "Sentiment is the devil," said Crane (and in this he echoed Flaubert).

A great stylist, Crane puts language to poetic uses, which is to use it reflexively and symbolically. *The works that employ this reflexive and symbolic language constitute what is permanent of Crane.*

Crane's language is the language of symbol and paradox: the wafer-like sun in *The Red Badge;* or in *The Open Boat* the paradox of "cold, comfortable sea-water," an image that calls to mind the poetry of Yeats, with its fusion of contradictory emotions. This single image evokes the sensation of the whole experience of the men in the dinghy, but it suggests furthermore another telltale significance, one applicable to Stephen Crane. What is readily recognizable in this paradox of "cold, comfortable sea-water" is that irony of opposites which constituted the personality of the man who wrote it. It is the subjective correlative of his own plight. The enigma of the man is symbolized by his enigmatic style.[8]

[8] Portions of this Introduction first appeared in the Introduction to the Modern Library edition of *The Red Badge of Courage,* copyright 1951 by Random House, Inc., and used here by courtesy of Random House, Inc. *Stephen Crane: an Omnibus,* published by Alfred A. Knopf in 1952, reproduces for the first time portions of the earliest known manuscript of *The Red Badge of Courage* and presents first American publication of the final handwritten manuscript; it also presents the first collection of Crane's letters. The introductions and notes in the present book are reproduced from *Stephen Crane: an Omnibus.*

PART I

Bowery Tales

INTRODUCTION

CRANE was born with printer's ink in his veins: both his parents were writers and two of his brothers were newspaper reporters. His ancestry comprised clergymen and soldiers, and his literary work (as Clarence Peaslee first pointed out) shows the hereditary influence of these two professions: "the one furnishing the basis of style, the other of incident." [1] At school Crane took a course in the Bible, but homework for that course must have come easy for him, as his father was pastor of the Methodist church and his mother, a newspaper reporter on church affairs and lecturer on Temperance and Woman's Rights, was the daughter of Reverend George Peck, at one time editor of the *Christian Advocate* (the official organ of the Methodist Episcopal Church), and the niece of Bishop Jesse Peck, one of the founders of Syracuse University. His father, editor of various church periodicals, was a learned divine and "a writer of rare ability, adorning his discourses with a style of rich beauty." Stephen got from his parents not only a natural bent for writing but a marked predilection for casting his ideas, incidents, and sometimes even his style in Biblical form. Several of his parable poems deal with Christ; *The Red Badge of Courage* is shot through with religious symbolism; and scriptural allusion and metaphor occur in *Maggie, George's Mother, An Experiment*

[1] "Stephen Crane's College Days," *Monthly Illustrator,* 13 (1895–7), 27–30.

in Misery, and *The Open Boat.* The only thing he found to
praise in a story sent him by a young writer for his criticism was its religious motif, and he singled it out—"You
will never hold the cross toward me"—with the comment:
"That, I think is very effective."[2] Another woman once
asked him what Hamlin Garland looked like, and his
answer was: "Oh, like a nice Jesus Christ."

Crane's father was a noted wit, and the comic charac-
terizes much of Crane's writings. Reverend Jonathan
Townley Crane had such a sense of humor that his congre-
gation proposed to publish a book of his witticisms.
Stephen wrote stories when but eight years old; at sixteen
he was doing newspaper reporting for his mother's column
in the *New York Tribune,* ghost-writing for his elder
brother, Townley, the *Tribune's* New Jersey correspondent,
and sometimes writing up stuff for his brother Wilbur, also
with the *Tribune.* Crane was born, so to speak, on Park
Row.

For three summers (1888–90) Townley, in charge of a
news bureau for several newspapers, had Stephen write up
"Shore News" about resorts along the New Jersey coast,
collecting space-rate for it as though it were his own. In
the spring of 1891—Stephen was then a freshman at Syracuse University—he was hired by Willis Johnson as city
correspondent for the *Tribune.* He had spent the fall term
at Lafayette College, but he preferred baseball to mining-
engineering, and in theme-writing he got zero; so he trans-
ferred in January to Syracuse University and arrived at
the Delta Upsilon Fraternity "in a cab and a cloud of
tobacco smoke." Here, too, he lasted just one term.[3] Ath-
letic but also literary, an omnivorous reader, he used to
retreat to the cupola of the chapter house and, smoking
his prized water-pipe, read or write sketches.[4] The most

[2] See letter to Miss Walker, pp. 653–4.
[3] See letter p. 627.
[4] Crane is reported to have placed some of these sketches in the
Detroit Free Press, but neither these sketches nor the "first fiction"
Crane said he wrote for the *Tribune* at eighteen have ever been traced.
The only known piece published under Crane's name before 1892 was
a story called *The King's Favor,* which appeared in the Syracuse *Uni-*

important thing that happened to him at the university was his writing a story about a streetwalker.

Crane got his "artistic education" (as he put it) on the Bowery. But at nineteen when he wrote this draft of what was to become *Maggie: A Girl of the Streets,* he knew very little about the Bowery, slum life, and prostitutes. *Maggie,* it has always been taken for granted (by Hitchcock, Starrett, and others), is a record of what Crane observed as a newspaper reporter in New York. But he was not a New York reporter until 1892, and he had already written his study of slum life months before exploring the scene of his novel. Garland in his *Arena* review said "it is written by one who has lived the life. The young author . . . has grown up in the very scenes he describes." But that is inaccurately put, for *Maggie* was composed before personal experience. So too with *George's Mother* and *The Red Badge of Courage:* after he invented them he tested them for their truth to life and injected into their plots some personal espisodes experienced during the progress of composition. "The vaunted Crane realism," as Harvey Wickham pointed out, "was never of the photographic sort. Thus the only incident which really happened [in *George's Mother*] was George's amazing lunch—a charlotte russe and a beer." George and his mother were drawn from two relatives of Wickham, "Crane transposing them to the slums, preserving only the characters—a plausible and worthless young man with an indulgent and credulous parent." Wickham's relative, whose real name was Frank, actually gave "George's lunch," and Crane watched him consume it in a Fourteenth Street resort opposite Tammany Hall.[5] Disputing Beer's opinion that Crane had invented the plot of *Maggie,* Frederic Lawrence (in a letter written

---

versity Herald in May 1891. His first appearance in a professional magazine was in *Cosmopolitan Magazine* with *A Tent in Agony,* published in December 1892. Five of his Sullivan County sketches were published in the *Tribune* during the summer of this year.

[5] "Stephen Crane at College," *American Mercury,* 7 (March 1926), 291–7. Wickham, a college friend of Crane, corrects Beer in this article. Beer had suggested (1923) that the characters in *George's Mother* were nothing more than a coarsened Stephen Crane and his mother.

in 1923) claimed that both *Maggie* and *George's Mother* were drawn "from our own observations and adventures." Crane of course knew the Bowery intimately and had considerable experiences with prostitutes, but not until he had written one or two drafts of *Maggie*.

Robert Davis has described for us one of Crane's encounters with Bowery streetwalkers: a girl they met one night was asked by Crane, when he spotted her as she crossed the street: "A stranger here?"

—Well, suppose I am a stranger. Can you show me anything?—
—Yes—replied the author of *Maggie*.—I can show you the way out, but if you prefer to remain—Crane made another gesture with his felt hat and bowed with an air of magnificent finality.
The girl suddenly found an extra button at the throat of her coat and fastened herself in. The light seemed to go out of Stephen Crane's eyes as though some one had turned down a lamp from within.
—You shouldn't hang out here, kid—said Maggie in a throaty voice.—You look cold. You can't stand it. This fat guy can.—[9]

It looks like an episode right out of his own book!

It is impossible to say where Crane got the stuff and craft of *Maggie*. Either he invented the plot or he took it from Zola's *L'Assommoir*. It is not certain, however, that he read that book. Crane said he began *Maggie* at twenty and "finished it when I was somewhat beyond 21." He also said he wrote it "in two days before Christmas," and his niece reports that he wrote it "at our house in two or three nights." According to Berryman, Crane had "unconscious aggressions" to discharge against his mother and so he chose "the subject of *Maggie*, his first work, following immediately upon his mother's death," and he represented his mother there as Maggie, a fallen woman. But the facts inconvenience that theory, for *Maggie* was conceived as early as April or May 1891, months before his mother died (December 7). The draft Crane wrote "in two days

[9] *Work*, II, xviii–xix.

before Christmas" was a second draft. "One day in the summer of 1891," says Willis Johnson (day editor of the *Tribune* and a friend of the Crane family), "he brought me a big bundle of manuscript, and asked me to read it and tell him what to do with it. I found it to be not a Sullivan County sketch, but a tale of the slums of New York, the first draft of *Maggie: A Girl of the Streets.*" Johnson was impressed by Crane's "mastery of the speech and manners of the denizens of the New York slums, *although he had spent little time in that city and had enjoyed little opportunity for observation of its ways.*" [7] As Crane made trips to New York from his brother's place at Lake View that fall and explored the Bowery with his friend Wallis McHarg in January, Johnson must be correct in saying that he first saw the manuscript—at least some fragment of the novel—in the summer of 1891. Frank Noxon testifies that Crane's fraternity brothers at Syracuse saw the manuscript. Crane wrote this first draft of *Maggie* at the Delta Upsilon house. Sheets of it, carelessly left scattered about his front-corner room, were "picked up and read by droppers-in." [8] His fraternity brothers, says Clarence Peaslee, advised him about the plot of *Maggie*. He told them about it, "putting it in various lights and constructions, and then asking which was more effective."

After writing a story—another friend, R. G. Vosburgh, tells us—he would put it away for two or three weeks, and work on something else until his mind was thoroughly clear for a fresh consideration of it. When the story was taken out for revision it would be turned over to his friends for criticism, and Crane would argue with them about the objections they would make. He often accepted suggestions for changes but it always seemed as though these changes were those he had already decided upon himself before they were mentioned by others. This was also characteristic of the discussions of *The*

[7] "The Launching of Stephen Crane," *Literary Digest International Book Review*, 4 (April 1926), 289.

[8] "The Real Stephen Crane," *Step Ladder* [Chicago], 14 (January 1928), 4–9.

Red Badge of Courage. He convinced himself; others might help him, but he arrived at his own conclusions.[9]

That summer, and again in 1892, Crane beachcombed Asbury Park for the *Tribune*. Early in 1892 he worked for the *Herald*, but he was fired in February, and in August the *Tribune* fired him and Townley for an article in his brother's column ("On the New Jersey Coast") which gave offense not only to *Tribune* readers, but also to its owner and editor, Whitelaw Reid, then running for the vice-presidency of the United States. It jeopardized the election of his boss. Visiting Hamlin Garland a few days after the Sunday it appeared (August 21), Crane told him he had lost his job. "You see, I made a report of a labor parade the other day, which slipped in over the managing editor's fence." The paraders of the Junior Order of United American Mechanics were insulted by the *Tribune*'s corrosive account: "probably . . . the most awkward, ungainly, uncut and uncarved procession that ever raised clouds of dust on sun-beaten streets." The throng that watched them march got ridiculed too, and even the town: "Asbury Park creates nothing. It does not make; it merely amuses." Crane's article was not calculated to please either the marchers or their employers, and if the marchers thought there was some praise for them ("The visitors were men who possessed principles"), that was only because they were not used to finding irony in a newspaper column.

It belonged in the novel this bright college boy was writing, but as a budding journalist the ironic was quite misplaced. So, too, was his contempt of these galley-slaves of capitalistic oppressors: "They merely plodded along, not seeming quite to understand, stolid, unconcerned and, in a certain sense, dignified—a pace and a bearing emblematic of their lives. [Crane had a symbolic bent even here!] They smiled occasionally and from time to time

---

[9] "The Darkest Hour in the Life of Stephen Crane," *Book Lover*, 2 (Summer 1901), 339. For further discussion of Crane's creative process see my Introduction, pp. xv–xxi above and *passim*; and *Stephen Crane: an Omnibus*, pp. 203–13, 217–24.

greeted friends in the crowd on the sidewalk. Such an assemblage of the spraddle-legged men of the middle class, whose hands were bent and shoulders stooped from delving and construction, had never appeared to an Asbury Park summer crowd, and the latter was vaguely amused." But not Crane. Garland asked him what he expected by writing such a thing, and Crane smiled with bitter reflection—"I was so hot at the sight of those poor misshapen fools shouting for monopoly that I gave no thought to its effect upon my own master. I don't know that it would have made much difference if I had. I wanted to say those things anyway." (Crane's picture of the Asbury Park parade seems echoed in his description of the workingmen in episode 7 of *Maggie*.) The *Tribune* got a telegram from the United American Mechanics informing Reid that his newspaper had better eat its words or he had better retire as candidate. "You'd hardly think," Crane told Arthur Oliver, "a little innocent chap like me could have stirred up such a row in American politics. It shows what innocence can do if it has the opportunity!" [1] "What innocence can do" is the crux of *The Bride Comes to Yellow Sky;* what innocence must do is the crux of *The Red Badge of Courage*. Innocence thwarted and betrayed by environment is the sum of *Maggie*. Innocence debased and deluded is *George's Mother*.

So Crane got a theme for fiction out of this experience. It was the turning-point in his career, Willis Johnson thought, for it was he who advised Crane to give up newspaper work, not to waste his talent competing with penny-a-liners. It would have been the turning-point had Crane taken Johnson's advice. But the typesetting rooms where Crane had spent much of his spare time as an undergraduate had inspired him to become a journalist, and he was determined to stick to that profession. "I could never do what I didn't feel like doing—not even writing," he told a friend, "but as I felt more often and more intensely like

[1] In "Jersey Memories—Stephen Crane," *New Jersey Historical Society Proceedings*, 16 (1931), 459–60. The quotation preceding this one is taken from "Stephen Crane, ex-'94," by M. Ellwood Smith, in the *Syracusan*, 10 (December 1, 1917), 4.

writing than anything else, I thought I'd better try newspaper work." [2] William Dean Howells, beginning like
Crane as a typesetter, turned his back on journalism; but
Crane wanted to study "unvarnished" human nature and
he liked to experience things and not just write about
them, and so he became a space-paid reporter rambling
through the Bowery and trudging from one editor's office
to another trying to place an occasional article at five dollars a column. One of the editors who hired him (Ed
Marshall, later famous as a war correspondent in Cuba)
said that Crane's article on tenement-house fire panics "was
one of the best things that he or any other man ever did."
Crane himself thought that some of his short sketches of
New York city street life were among his best things, and
he intended to have them published "in book form under
the title 'Midnight Sketches.' " (They were collected, most
of them, under that title in Vol. XI of the collected
Work.) Some of these sketches perished beneath the scis-
sors of Crane's editors. There was one called "Sixth Avenue" which would have provoked libel from advertisers
in the *New York Press,* and after Curtis Brown crossed
out the offending phrases, another editor threw it away
as not exciting enough (*Contacts,* page 260). In the spring
of 1893, at the time of beginning *The Red Badge of
Courage,* he wrote sketches of East Side children (one of
these was *An Ominous Baby*), but he could not sell them
until the next year. Neither could he sell *The Reluctant
Voyagers* and *The Pace of Youth* when they were written.
Through Garland he got a commission from the Wilson
Newspaper Syndicate to write a story about New York
lodginghouses, and so Crane and one of his artist friends
spent a night and two days (according to Vosburgh) as
tramps on the Bowery. Seen there in March, he was
pointed out as an eccentric wasting his time in Bowery
dives, "the outcast son of an Episcopal minister."

But the outcast in *An Experiment in Misery* is not
Stephen Crane. "Mrs. Howells was right," Crane wrote in

[2] Reginald Kauffman in *Modern Culture,* October 1900, pp.
143–5.

1896, replying to Miss Catherine Harris's letter about *Maggie*, "in telling you that I have spent a great deal of time on the East Side and that I have no opinion of missions. . . . In a story of mine called *An Experiment in Misery* I tried to make plain that the root of Bowery life is a sort of cowardice. Perhaps I mean a lack of ambition or to willingly be knocked flat and accept the licking." To the young man in the story the noise of the city was "the confusion of strange tongues, babbling heedlessly; it was the clink of coin, the voice of the city's hopes, which were to him no hopes." Environment—"*unholy* atmospheres"—is the antagonist, but the young man does nothing to change it. In the flophouse the naked bums take "splendid poses, standing massively like chiefs."

An Experiment in Misery, like *Maggie,* combines irony and pity. There are tracings here of the same leitmotivs—"unholy atmospheres"—and the same imagery—"wreathed in a red grin"—that Crane reused in *The Red Badge of Courage,* and in touching upon the theme of solidarity *An Experiment in Misery* anticipates *The Open Boat.* But in this earlier piece Crane has not patterned the imagery or made it consistently metaphorical, and details that might have been converted to evoke symbolic overtones are wastefully misspent. The opinion that *An Experiment in Misery* is "far more important than the more famous and accessible *Red Badge of Courage* or such stories of mere physical accident as *The Open Boat,*" as Ludwig Lewisohn would have it, can be dismissed without further comment. (*The Monster,* another social study, has also received undeserved acclaim. I don't think it needs to be demonstrated that *The Monster* is not a unified structural whole.) *An Experiment in Misery,* as Edward Garnett aptly noted, reveals in its "nervous audacity of phrasing . . . the quality of chiaroscuro of a master's etching." That Crane had always been "an ardent admirer of fine paintings" (as a college friend mentions) is evident in his language, in the brush-strokes of his style. The subject of *George's Mother,* so the *Book Buyer* (1896) complained, "seems more suitable for drawing in shades of gray, while

Mr Crane's brushes are full of red and yellow paint." And *Maggie* shows the same "blinding glare of primary colors" as *The Red Badge of Courage*, "a panorama of illumination."

The Men in the Storm, written at the same time as *An Experiment in Misery* (March 1893?), is filled with "social calculation." Homeless wanderers, some down-and-outers and Bowery bums, stand in a blizzard at the closed doors of a charitable house. They are waiting (symbolically) for "the open door"—for a social change. "Oh, let us in fer Gawd's sake!" Across the street is a stout and well-clothed rich man, with "a beard like the Prince of Wales. He stood in an attitude of magnificent reflection. He slowly stroked his moustache with a certain grandeur of manner, and looked down at the snow-crusted mob." Crane here *evokes by picture* his criticism of the rich. Flaubert's *Madame Bovary*, which Crane had no doubt read, employs the same technique of submerged commentary: for example, the picture of the Comte de Vaubyessard's ball (Chapter i, page viii). Similarly, at the end of the story Crane's description of the blizzard is loaded with a significance that is pictured, not stated: "The snow beat with merciless persistence *upon the bowed heads of those who waited*." It is a snowstorm of social strife that beats down on the men. "A street lamp on the curb *struggled to illuminate,* but it was reduced to impotent blindness by the swift gusts of sleet crusting its panes."

The Men in the Storm is a far more richly packed piece of symbolism than *An Experiment in Misery*, but it is spoiled by some passages of direct statement: "There were men of undoubted patience, industry, and temperance, who in time of ill-fortune, do not habitually rail at the state of society, snarling at the arrogance of the rich, and bemoaning the cowardice of the poor, but who at these times are apt to wear a sudden and singular meekness, as if they saw the world's progress marching from them, and were trying to perceive where they had failed, what they lacked, to be thus vanquished in the race." That is bad writing and bad artistry.

The *Press* printed *An Experiment in Misery* the next April, and Garland mailed both *An Ominous Baby* and *The Men in the Storm* to the *Arena* (published there in 1894) with a note to the editor to be generous because "the author is hungry." It was Garland who had suggested that Crane should study East Side life. "I remember talking with him about 'the bread lines,' which regularly formed each night at certain bakeries which gave away their stale bread, and at my suggestion he went down one winter's evening [in a March blizzard, 1893], joined one of these lines, and made a study which he afterwards called *The Men in the Storm,* a fine sketch. . . . And yet in spite of my aid and these promising activities, he remained almost as needy as ever. Thin and seedy, he still slept on the floor—according to his own story, smoking incessantly and writing in any possible corner." Depressed, Crane soberly told Garland one day: "I'd trade my entire future for twenty-three dollars in cash." In 1896 Crane inscribed a copy of *George's Mother:* "To my friend Eddie in memory of our days of suffering and trouble. . . ."

Nothing Crane had written was published in 1893 except *Maggie*. Like Hawthorne's first novel, it was published at the author's expense (William Crane gave him one thousand dollars) and under an assumed name: "Johnston Smith." Crane first made it "Johnson Smith," these being the two most numerous names in the city directory, but finally inserted the "t" in the former name so that (as Crane whimsically explained it to Willis Johnson) "neither Mr. Podsnap nor Mrs. Grundy might suspect him of being the guilty author!" He planned to wait, so he told somebody else, "until all the world was pyrotechnic about Johnston Smith's *Maggie* and then I was going to flop down like a trapeze performer from the wire and, coming forward with all the modest grace of a consumptive nun, say, I am he, friends!" Beer, quoting this last, says that few of Crane's friends had read the manuscript. But the fact is that most of his friends had read it— Noxon and Peaslee, Harvey Wickham, Louis Senger and his cousin Linson in Crane's room, Corwin Linson in his studio, and others elsewhere. Garland, getting a copy of the paper-bound, mustard-colored pamphlet in his mail, immediately wrote to accuse Crane of being the author, and soon afterwards he came and "confessed his crime." The printer, too, played it safe. He refused his name to the book. It was too frank and might get him into trouble. The frightened printer probably made "about $700 out of me. . . . A firm of religious and medical printers did me the dirt." Ironically enough, it was a religious house. "Will made me get the thing copyrighted. I had not even that much sense." So he sent one dollar and a typewritten title-page to the Librarian of Congress on January 19, 1893, for copyrighting the as yet unpublished book. This title-page bore Crane's name but omitted "Maggie" from the title. It was William who had christened it a couple of months before (in November, says Beer): "Maggie: A Girl of the Streets." He had persuaded Stephen that characters in a novel ought to be given names. In revising *The Red Badge of Courage,* however, his procedure was just the reverse. While he followed his brother's advice during composition of the first drafts of *The Red Badge,* when he came to revise the final handwritten manuscript he recast the names of his soldiers and reduced them to anonymity.

Maggie was published this spring (1893), and Garland reviewed it in the June issue of the *Arena.* "The three months which have passed have been months of very hard work to S. Crane. . . . I wrote a book." So Crane informed Lily Brandon. Beginning *Maggie* at Syracuse and finishing it at Lake View in December 1891, he then revised it in March 1892, and then he recast it for the fourth time during the winter of 1892–3. On the 23rd of March he took the manuscript to Richard Watson Gilder, who thought *Maggie* too "cruel" for the *Century.* Johnson sent Crane to Ripley Hitchcock at Appleton and Co., who told Johnson: "That boy has the real stuff in him." He rejected *Maggie,* but accepted *The Red Badge of Courage* two years later and then, because that novel was a sensational success, he got Appleton to reissue *Maggie;* and so it appeared for the first time between hard covers in June 1896. An English edition of *George's Mother* appeared that same month, and later that year Heinemann published *Maggie* with "An Appreciation" by William Dean Howells. Crane, correcting the proofs and writing a preface for Appleton, asked Hitchcock to "watch for bad grammatical form and bad spelling. I am too jaded with Maggie to be able to see it." But he "carefully plugged at the words which hurt. Seems to me the book wears quite a new aspect from very slight omissions. . . ."

2

George's Mother, not published until 1896 (issued one week before *Maggie*), was begun in 1893 and completed late in 1894. Crane wrote Garland on November 15, 1894: "I have just completed a New York book that leaves *Maggie* at the post. It is my best thing. Since you are not here, I am going to see if Mr. Howells will not read it." Howells, interviewed by Crane for the *New York Times* in October 1894 ("Fears Realists Must Wait"), must have had *George's Mother* in mind when he said: "I like to see the novelists treating some of the other important things of life—the relation of mother and son. . . . The other [i.e., the relation of man to maid] can be but fragmentary." Reviewing "New York Low Life in Fiction" for the New York *World* two years later, he praised Crane's honesty with the reader for what we would today call his social realism: the pathos of the underprivileged "rendered without one maudlin touch." Whereas *Maggie* is a full study, *George's Mother* "is the study of a situation merely: a poor, inadequate woman, of a commonplace religiosity, whose son goes to the bad. The wonder of it is the courage which deals with persons so absolutely average, and the art that graces them with the beauty of the author's compassion for everything that errs and suffers."

George's Mother had its title changed several times after Howells first saw the manuscript. It was "A Woman without Weapons" when the *Bookman,* in May 1895, referred to it by that title as one of Crane's manuscripts now in

the publisher's hands. Upon publication, *George's Mother*
was reviewed by Harry Thurston Peck in the *Bookman*
for July, but he was no more perceptive than Howells in
seeing what the novel is really about. He was right, however, in his conjecture about the date of its composition:
"from a consideration of the internal evidence, we should
say that its first draft must belong to the time when he
wrote and published *Maggie*. Judged by the qualities of
style and strength we should, in fact, pronounce it to be
even earlier, and probably one of Mr. Crane's first attempts
at serious composition; for it is altogether crude and un-
satisfactory." Howells's verdict, made that same month in
the New York *World,* placed *Maggie* and *George's Mother*
above *The Red Badge of Courage,* and in *Harper's Magazine* almost two decades later he reckoned from his Editor's Easy Chair that *The Red Badge* was the best seller
of its day "possibly because it was his worst book." It was
Howells's critical creed that influenced Crane to recon-
struct *Maggie,* an influence that he acknowledged—"a certain re-adjustment of his point of view victoriously concluded some time in 1892." It is not improbable that
Howells's opinion of *The Red Badge* had something to do
with Crane's own feelings about it: "People may just as
well discover now that the high dramatic key of *The Red
Badge* cannot be sustained. I don't think *The Red Badge*
to be any great shakes but then the very theme of it gives
it an intensity that a writer can't reach every day." Garland said the same thing, but he waited until Crane was
dead and buried before he printed it—in the *Saturday
Evening Post* for July 28, 1900.

Garland in the *Arena* (June 1893) thought that *Maggie*
"fails of rounded completeness. It is only a fragment." But
"It is the voice of the slums. . . . His book is the most
truthful and unhackneyed study of the slums I have yet
read, fragment though it is." And that was why he thought
it important. "It is important because it voices the blind
rebellion of Rum Alley and Devil's Row. It creates the
atmosphere of the jungles, where vice festers and crime
passes gloomily by, where outlawed human nature rebels

against God and man." Rupert Hughes, in *Godey's Magazine* (October 1895), echoed Garland and argued that to
write books that arouse "sympathy for the unfortunates
who must fill the cellar of the tenement we call life . . .
is far better even than to be artistic." Evidently the ladies
of Port Jervis did not see it that way, for they didn't think
it proper to permit Stephen Crane into their homes (Beer,
page 389). The latest opinion on *Maggie* (1951) is that
it is "a short, murky novel." [3]

Howells, not agreeing with Garland in this, thought
Maggie and *George's Mother* superior to *The Red Badge
of Courage* "as pieces of art," and then, grounding his
verdict on his own canon, added that "as representations
of life their greater fidelity cannot be questioned." No
wonder Crane felt obliged to test the imagined reality of
The Red Badge by experiencing the real thing, as though
that would prove its worth! Crane's social studies won
Howells's praise because they squared with his creed. "Mr.
Crane has the skill to show how evil is greatly the effect
of ignorance and imperfect civilization." Present-day Marx-
ian and sociological critics judge novels on the same
ground: novels should deal with the fundamental realities
of American life. In *The O'Ruddy* Crane, who began as
a social critic, ended as a romanticist, and even as the
realist of slum life he kept repeating himself. Two years
before he died his coauthor for this last novel prophesied
that Crane "was most likely to produce the great American novel" (Robert Barr in the *Bookman*, July 1900).
Perhaps he had already written it. According to Ben Hecht,
Maggie and *George's Mother* constitute "the great American novel."

3

All Crane stories end in irony. Some end in a minor note,
like *Maggie* and *George's Mother*—"not with a bang but
a whimper." Every Crane story worth mentioning is designed upon a single ironic incident, a crucial paradox or

[3] John T. Winterich, Introduction to Folio Society edition of *The
Red Badge of Courage*, p. 14.

irony of opposites. All of them are built out of anecdotal
material, and all are concerned with virtually the same
problem—the moral problem of conduct. It is the same
in Conrad. In method of construction, however, Crane's
closer affinities are with Chekhov. They were among the
first to eliminate plot. Crane constructs his stories, like
Chekhov, by building up to a crucial moment of impasse
and collapse. A Crane story consists of that moment when
the characters confront the inescapable impasse of a situation by which they are boxed in, and then—the moment
of spiritual collapse—"nothing happens," and they are left
with a sense of loss or insignificance or defeat, futility or
disillusionment.

Crane is a master of the contradictory effect. The scene
of Maggie at the theater (episode number 8) epitomizes
the design of the whole story: illusions and ideals shattered by realities. Crane's Maggie is a Bowery version of
Flaubert's Emma Bovary. Maggie at the theater and Emma
at the opera parallel each other in ironic intent and structural purpose. Not logic but mood defines the relationship
between the various episodes of *Maggie. The Red Badge
of Courage* and *The Open Boat,* like *Madame Bovary,* are
constructed of alternating moods, each built-up mood of
hope or illusion being canceled out by contradictory moods
of futility, disillusionment, or despair. This method of the
double mood was Flaubert's major technical innovation.
It is the form of Joyce's *Portrait of the Artist as a Young
Man* and of *Dubliners* (notably *The Dead*), and almost
all of Katherine Mansfield's and Chekhov's short stories
are in this form. It is the form of Melville's masterpiece,
Benito Cereno, and of Hawthorne's Kafka-like parable, *My
Kinsman, Major Molineux.* Crane constructs his stories
to effect a single mood (*The Upturned Face* is one example), or by a series of moods with each unit composed of
a contrast. *Maggie,* a sentimental melodrama that borders
upon travesty, concludes with the orgy of melodramatic
emotion which Maggie's mother gives vent to over the
death of the daughter whom she has brutalized and driven
into the streets. The final turnabout is a parody of pious

sentiment—"Oh, yes, I'll fergive her! I'll fergive her!" The grotesque buffoonery of this mock lamentation is comic enough, but tragedy underlies it in the theme that all is sham, even between mother and daughter.

George Kelcey in *George's Mother* is his mother's ideal, and she is deluded. (It is significant that Crane at first called this novel "A Woman without Weapons.") Her whole life sacrificed to his well-being, she anticipates the time when her son shall become "a white and looming king among men." She worships him with all the devotion of a sweetheart, and with the blind devotion of a religious fanatic she dies still believing in him. Like Crane's own mother, Mrs. Kelcey is a member of the W.C.T.U. and is filled with religious zeal. Her great grief is that her son refuses to attend prayer-meetings. These conventicles are her shrine, and a "smiling saloon" is George's. Each one has found a place of refuge from the world's harsh realities, where the chosen few congregate and are saved. For George it is whisky that is prophetic. In a ritual of emptying and refilling of glasses, he holds communion with his coreligionists behind the closed doors of little back rooms at night. He partakes too much and loses his job as a consequence, whereupon his friends forsake him. Sometimes he dreams "of the indefinite woman and the fragrance of roses that came from her hair," but she too forsakes him. The forsaken mother, broken and deranged, is tormented by visions. "She was staring off at something sinister." The devils of sin she had warred against all her life have at last overpowered her. It is the demon world making final onslaught against that visionary hope she worshipped as her son. He too has been possessed and destroyed. She tried to save him, but when he entered the chapel that one time he resentfully consented to accompany her there, "he felt a sudden quaking. His knees shook. It was an awesome place to him." And in the chamber of death where his mother cries to him unheeded, there too he quakes, becoming so nervous "that he could not hear the chatter from the bed, but he was always conscious of the ticking of the little clock out on the kitchen shelf."

The ticking clock signifies life dissipated and unconverted. It is "emblematic of the life of the city." City and church, George and his mother—they are counterparts.

The conflict between George and his mother is summed up in Crane's symbolic picture of city and church. The conflict between them (reality versus illusion) is symbolically pictured in Part XI:

In a dark street the little chapel sat humbly between two towering apartment-houses.

The city overpowers the church.

A red street-lamp stood in front. It threw a marvellous reflection upon the wet pavements. It was like the death-stain of a spirit.

The red street-lamp shines; the church is humble. George is "the death-stain of a spirit."

Farther up, the brilliant lights of an avenue made a span of gold across the black street. A roar of wheels and a clangour of bells came from this point, interwoven into a sound emblematic of the life of the city.

In Part XVII the ticking clock replaces the clangor of bells. George belongs to the noisy world of brilliant lights.

It seemed somehow to affront this solemn and austere little edifice. It suggested an approaching barbaric invasion. The little church, pierced, would die with a fine illimitable scorn for its slayers.

The little church signifies Christ—"pierced." George not only turns his back on the church but, ironically, immediately after experiencing it, goes to the Devil—and faster than ever before.[4]

---

[4] George's Mother was discussed in similar terms by the Critic in June 1896, and I have drawn some phrasings from this review and others, including the Academy and the New York Press reviews of the same year. Nothing has been written on George's Mother since then that even approximates exegesis, and no insight whatsoever is exhibited in what few commentaries Crane's critics have written about this work from 1896 to the present.

THE MEN IN THE STORM

THE blizzard began to swirl great clouds of snow along the streets, sweeping it down from the roofs, and up from the pavements, until the faces of pedestrians tingled and burned as from a thousand needle-prickings. Those on the walks huddled their necks closely in the collars of their coats, and went along stooping like a race of aged people. The drivers of vehicles hurried their horses furiously on their way. They were made more cruel by the exposure of their position, aloft on high seats. The street cars, bound up-town, went slowly, the horses slipping and straining in the spongy brown mass that lay between the rails. The drivers, muffled to the eyes, stood erect, facing the wind, models of grim philosophy. Overhead, trains rumbled and roared, and the dark structure of the elevated railroad, stretching over the avenue, dripped little streams and drops of water upon the mud and snow beneath.

All the clatter of the street was softened by the masses that lay upon the cobbles, until, even to one who looked from a window, it became important music, a melody of life made necessary to the ear by the dreariness of the pitiless beat and sweep of the storm. Occasionally one could see black figures of men busily shovelling the white drifts from the walks. The sounds from their labour created new recollections of rural experiences which every man manages to have in a measure. Later, the immense windows of the shops became aglow with light, throwing great beams of orange and yellow upon the pavement. They were infinitely cheerful, yet in a way they accentuated the force and discomfort of the storm, and gave a meaning to the pace of the people and the vehicles, scores of pedestrians and drivers, wretched with cold faces, necks, and feet, speeding for scores of unknown doors and entrances, scattering to an infinite variety of shelters, to places which the imagination made warm with the familiar colours of home.

There was an absolute expression of hot dinners in the pace of the people. If one dared to speculate upon the destination of those who came trooping, he lost himself in a maze of social calculation; he might fling a handful of sand and attempt to follow the flight of each particular grain. But as to the suggestion of hot dinners, he was in firm lines of thought, for it was upon every hurrying face. It is a matter of tradition; it is from the tales of childhood. It comes forth with every storm.

However, in a certain part of a dark west-side street, there was a collection of men to whom these things were as if they were not. In this street was located a charitable house where for five cents the homeless of the city could get a bed at night, and in the morning coffee and bread.

During the afternoon of the storm, the whirling snows acted as drivers, as men with whips, and at half-past three the walk before the closed doors of the house was covered with wanderers of the street, waiting. For some distance on either side of the place they could be seen lurking in the doorways and behind projecting parts of buildings, gathering in close bunches in an effort to get warm. A covered wagon drawn up near the curb sheltered a dozen of them. Under the stairs that led to the elevated railway station, there were six or eight, their hands stuffed deep in their pockets, their shoulders stooped, jiggling their feet. Others always could be seen coming, a strange procession, some slouching along with the characteristic hopeless gait of professional strays, some coming with hesitating steps, wearing the air of men to whom this sort of thing was new.

It was an afternoon of incredible length. The snow, blowing in twisting clouds, sought out the men in their meagre hiding-places, and skilfully beat in among them, drenching their persons with showers of fine stinging flakes. They crowded together, muttering, and fumbling in their pockets to get their red inflamed wrists covered by the cloth.

New-comers usually halted at one end of the groups and addressed a question, perhaps much as a matter of form, "Is it open yet?"

Those who had been waiting inclined to take the questioner seriously and became contemptuous. "No; do yeh think we'd be standin' here?"

The gathering swelled in numbers steadily and persistently. One could always see them coming, trudging slowly through the storm.

Finally, the little snow plains in the street began to assume a leaden hue from the shadows of evening. The buildings upreared gloomily save where various windows became brilliant figures of light, that made shimmers and splashes of yellow on the snow. A street lamp on the curb struggled to illuminate, but it was reduced to impotent blindness by the swift gusts of sleet crusting its panes.

In this half-darkness, the men began to come from their shelter-places and mass in front of the doors of charity. They were of all types, but the nationalities were mostly American, German, and Irish. Many were strong, healthy, clear-skinned fellows, with that stamp of countenance which is not frequently seen upon seekers after charity. There were men of undoubted patience, industry, and temperance, who, in time of ill-fortune, do not habitually turn to rail at the state of society, snarling at the arrogance of the rich, and bemoaning the cowardice of the poor, but who at these times are apt to wear a sudden and singular meekness, as if they saw the world's progress marching from them, and were trying to perceive where they had failed, what they had lacked, to be thus vanquished in the race. Then there were others, of the shifting Bowery element, who were used to paying ten cents for a place to sleep, but who now came here because it was cheaper.

But they were all mixed in one mass so thoroughly that one could not have discerned the different elements, but

for the fact that the labouring men, for the most part, remained silent and impassive in the blizzard, their eyes
fixed on the windows of the house, statues of patience.

The sidewalk soon became completely blocked by the
bodies of the men. They pressed close to one another like
sheep in a winter's gale, keeping one another warm by the
heat of their bodies. The snow came upon this compressed
group of men until, directly from above, it might have
appeared like a heap of snow-covered merchandise, if it
were not for the fact that the crowd swayed gently with
a unanimous rhythmical motion. It was wonderful to see
how the snow lay upon the heads and shoulders of these
men, in little ridges an inch thick perhaps in places, the
flakes steadily adding drop and drop, precisely as they fall
upon the unresisting grass of the fields. The feet of the
men were all wet and cold, and the wish to warm them
accounted for the slow, gentle rhythmical motion. Occasionally some man whose ear or nose tingled acutely from
the cold winds would wriggle down until his head was
protected by the shoulders of his companions.

There was a continuous murmuring discussion as to the
probability of the doors being speedily opened. They persistently lifted their eyes toward the windows. One could
hear little combats of opinion.

"There's a light in th' winder!"

"Naw; it's a reflection f'm across th' way."

"Well, didn't I see 'em light it?"

"You did?"

"I did!"

"Well, then, that settles it!"

As the time approached when they expected to be
allowed to enter, the men crowded to the doors in an
unspeakable crush, jamming and wedging in a way that,
it seemed, would crack bones. They surged heavily against
the building in a powerful wave of pushing shoulders.
Once a rumour flitted among all the tossing heads.

"They can't open th' door! Th' fellers er smack up agin
'em."

Then a dull roar of rage came from the men on the outskirts; but all the time they strained and pushed until it appeared to be impossible for those that they cried out against to do anything but be crushed into pulp.

"Ah, git away f'm th' door!"

"Git outa that!"

"Throw 'em out!"

"Kill 'em!"

"Say, fellers, now, what th' 'ell? G've 'em a chance t' open th' door!"

"Yeh damn pigs, give 'em a chance t' open th' door!"

Men in the outskirts of the crowd occasionally yelled when a boot-heel of one of trampling feet crushed on their freezing extremities.

"Git off me feet, yeh clumsy tarrier!"

"Say, don't stand on me feet! Walk on th' ground!"

A man near the doors suddenly shouted: "O-o-oh! Le' me out—le' me out!" And another, a man of infinite valour, once twisted his head so as to half face those who were pushing behind him. "Quit yer shovin', yeh"— and he delivered a volley of the most powerful and singular invective, straight into the faces of the men behind him. It was as if he was hammering the noses of them with curses of triple brass. His face, red with rage, could be seen, upon it an expression of sublime disregard of consequences. But nobody cared to reply to his imprecations; it was too cold. Many of them snickered, and all continued to push.

In occasional pauses of the crowd's movement the men had opportunities to make jokes; usually grim things, and no doubt very uncouth. Nevertheless, they were notable —one does not expect to find the quality of humour in a heap of old clothes under a snowdrift.

The winds seemed to grow fiercer as time wore on. Some of the gusts of snow that came down on the close collection of heads cut like knives and needles, and the men huddled, and swore, not like dark assassins, but in a sort of American fashion, grimly and desperately, it is true, but yet with a wondrous under-effect, indefinable and mystic, as if there was some kind of humour in this catastrophe, in this situation in a night of snow-laden winds.

Once the window of the huge dry-goods shop across the street furnished material for a few moments of forgetfulness. In the brilliantly lighted space appeared the figure of a man. He was rather stout and very well clothed. His beard was fashioned charmingly after that of the Prince of Wales. He stood in an attitude of magnificent reflection. He slowly stroked his moustache with a certain grandeur of manner, and looked down at the snow-encrusted mob. From below, there was denoted a supreme complacence in him. It seemed that the sight operated inversely, and enabled him to more clearly regard his own delightful environment.

One of the mob chanced to turn his head, and perceived the figure in the window. "Hello, look-it 'is whiskers," he said genially.

Many of the men turned then, and a shout went up. They called to him in all strange keys. They addressed him in every manner, from familiar and cordial greetings to carefully worded advice concerning changes in his personal appearance. The man presently fled, and the mob chuckled ferociously, like ogres who had just devoured something.

They turned then to serious business. Often they addressed the stolid front of the house.

"Oh, let us in fer Gawd's sake!"

"Let us in, or we'll all drop dead!"

"Say, what's th' use o' keepin' us poor Indians out in th' cold?"

And always some one was saying, "Keep off my feet."

The crushing of the crowd grew terrific toward the last. The men, in keen pain from the blasts, began almost to fight. With the pitiless whirl of snow upon them, the battle for shelter was going to the strong. It became known that the basement door of the foot of a little steep flight of stairs was the one to be opened, and they jostled and heaved in this direction like labouring fiends. One could hear them panting and groaning in their fierce exertion.

Usually some one in the front ranks was protesting to those in the rear—"O-o-ow! Oh, say now, fellers, let up, will yeh? Do yeh wanta kill somebody?"

A policeman arrived and went into the midst of them, scolding and berating, occasionally threatening, but using no force but that of his hands and shoulders against these men who were only struggling to get in out of the storm. His decisive tones rang out sharply—"Stop that pushin' back there! Come, boys, don't push! Stop that! Here you, quit yer shovin'! Cheese that!"

When the door below was opened, a thick stream of men forced a way down the stairs, which were of an extraordinary narrowness, and seemed only wide enough for one at a time. Yet they somehow went down almost three abreast. It was a difficult and painful operation. The crowd was like a turbulent water forcing itself through one tiny outlet. The men in the rear, excited by the success of the others, made frantic exertions, for it seemed that this large band would more than fill the quarters, and that many would be left upon the pavements. It would be disastrous to be of the last, and accordingly men with the snow biting their faces writhed and twisted with their might. One expected that, from the tremendous pressure, the narrow passage to the basement door would be so choked and clogged with human limbs and bodies that movement would be impossible. Once indeed the crowd was forced to stop, and a cry went along that a man had been injured at the foot of the stairs. But presently the slow movement began again, and the policeman fought at the top of the flight to ease the pressure of those that were going down.

A reddish light from a window fell upon the faces of the men when they, in turn, arrived at the last three steps and were about to enter. One could then note a change of expression that had come over their features. As they stood thus upon the threshold of their hopes, they looked suddenly contented and complacent. The fire had passed from their eyes and the snarl had vanished from their lips. The very force of the crowd in the rear, which had previously vexed them, was regarded from another point of view, for it now made it inevitable that they should go through the little doors into the place that was cheery and warm with light.

The tossing crowd on the sidewalk grew smaller and smaller. The snow beat with merciless persistence upon the bowed heads of those who waited. The wind drove it up from the pavements in frantic forms of winding white, and it seethed in circles about the huddled forms passing in one by one, three by three, out of the storm.

AN EXPERIMENT IN MISERY [1]

IT WAS late at night, and a fine rain was swirling softly down, causing the pavements to glisten with hue of steel and blue and yellow in the rays of the innumerable lights. A youth was trudging slowly, without enthusiasm, with his hands buried deep in his trousers pockets, toward the downtown places where beds can be hired for coppers. He was clothed in an aged and tattered suit, and his derby was a marvel of dust-covered crown and torn rim. He was going forth to eat as the wanderer may eat, and sleep as the homeless sleep. By the time he had reached City Hall Park he was so completely plastered with yells of "bum" and "hobo," and with various unholy epithets that small boys had applied to him at intervals, that he was in a state of the most profound dejection. The sifting rain saturated the old velvet collar of his overcoat, and as the wet cloth pressed against his neck, he felt that there no longer could

[1] This story had a different beginning and ending in the version appearing in the New York Press for April 22, 1894. They are reprinted here for the first time. In its original version the story began this way:

Two men stood regarding a tramp.

"I wonder how he feels," said one, reflectively. "I suppose he is homeless, friendless, and has, at the most, only a few cents in his pocket. And if this is so, I wonder how he feels."

The other, being the elder, spoke with an air of authoritative wisdom. "You can tell nothing of it unless you are in that condition yourself. It is idle to speculate about it from this distance."

"I suppose so," said the younger man, and then he added as from an inspiration: "I think I'll try it. Rags and tatters, you know, a couple of dimes, and hungry, too, if possible. Perhaps I could discover his point of view or something near it."

"Well, you might," said the other, and from those words begins this veracious narrative of an experiment in misery.

The youth went to the studio of an artist friend, who, from his store, rigged him out in an aged suit and a brown derby hat that had been made long years before. And then the youth went forth to try to eat as the tramp may eat, and sleep as the wanderers sleep.

be pleasure in life. He looked about him searching for an
outcast of highest degree that they two might share miseries, but the lights threw a quivering glare over rows and
circles of deserted benches that glistened damply, showing
patches of wet sod behind them. It seemed that their usual
freights had fled on this night to better things. There were
only squads of well-dressed Brooklyn people who swarmed
toward the bridge.

The young man loitered about for a time and then went
shuffling off down Park Row. In the sudden descent in
style of the dress of the crowd he felt relief, and as if he
were at last in his own country. He began to see tatters
that matched his tatters. In Chatham Square there were
aimless men strewn in front of saloons and lodging-houses,
standing sadly, patiently, reminding one vaguely of the
attitudes of chickens in a storm. He aligned himself with
these men, and turned slowly to occupy himself with the
flowing life of the great street.

Through the mists of the cold and storming night, the
cable cars went in silent procession, great affairs shining
with red and brass, moving with formidable power, calm
and irresistible, dangerful and gloomy, breaking silence
only by the loud fierce cry of the gong. Two rivers of
people swarmed along the sidewalks, spattered with black
mud which made each shoe leave a scar-like impression.
Overhead, elevated trains with a shrill grinding of the
wheels stopped at the station, which upon its leg-like pillars
seemed to resemble some monstrous kind of crab squat-
ting over the street. The quick fat puffings of the engines
could be heard. Down an alley there were sombre curtains
of purple and black, on which street lamps dully glittered
like embroidered flowers.

A saloon stood with a voracious air on a corner. A sign
leaning against the front of the doorpost announced "Free
hot soup to-night!" The swing doors, snapping to and fro
like ravenous lips, made gratified smacks as the saloon
gorged itself with plump men, eating with astounding and
endless appetite, smiling in some indescribable manner as

the men came from all directions like sacrifices to a hea-
thenish superstition.

Caught by the delectable sign, the young man allowed
himself to be swallowed. A bartender placed a schooner of
dark and portentous beer on the bar. Its monumental form
upreared until the froth atop was above the crown of the
young man's brown derby.

"Soup over there, gents," said the bartender affably. A
little yellow man in rags and the youth grasped their
schooners and went with speed toward a lunch-counter,
where a man with oily but imposing whiskers ladled
genially from a kettle until he had furnished his two
mendicants with a soup that was steaming hot, and in
which there were little floating suggestions of chicken. The
young man, sipping his broth, felt the cordiality expressed
by the warmth of the mixture, and he beamed at the man
with oily but imposing whiskers, who was presiding like a
priest behind an altar. "Have some more, gents?" he inquired of the two sorry figures before him. The little
yellow man accepted with a swift gesture, but the youth
shook his head and went out, following a man whose
wondrous seediness promised that he would have a knowledge of cheap lodging-houses.

On the sidewalk he accosted the seedy man. "Say, do
you know a cheap place to sleep?"

The other hesitated for a time, gazing sideways. Finally
he nodded in the direction of the street. "I sleep up there,"
he said, "when I've got the price."

"How much?"

"Ten cents."

The young man shook his head dolefully. "That's too
rich for me."

At that moment there approached the two a reeling man
in strange garments. His head was a fuddle of bushy hair
and whiskers, from which his eyes peered with a guilty
slant. In a close scrutiny it was possible to distinguish the
cruel lines of a mouth which looked as if its lips had just
closed with satisfaction over some tender and piteous mor-

sel. He appeared like an assassin steeped in crimes performed awkwardly.

But at this time his voice was tuned to the coaxing key
of an affectionate puppy. He looked at the men with
wheedling eyes, and began to sing a little melody for charity. "Say, gents, can't yeh give a poor feller a couple of
cents t' git a bed? I got five, an' I gits anudder two I gits
me a bed. Now, on th' square, gents, can't yeh jest gimme
two cents t' git a bed? Now, yeh know how a respecterble
gentlem'n feels when he's down on his luck, an' I—"

The seedy man, staring with imperturbable countenance
at a train which clattered overhead, interrupted in an ex-
pressionless voice: "Ah, go t' hell!"

But the youth spoke to the prayerful assassin in tones
of astonishment and inquiry. "Say, you must be crazy!
Why don't yeh strike somebody that looks as if they had
money?"

The assassin, tottering about on his uncertain legs, and
at intervals brushing imaginary obstacles from before his
nose, entered into a long explanation of the psychology of
the situation. It was so profound that it was unintelligible.

When he had exhausted the subject, the young man
said to him: "Let's see th' five cents."

The assassin wore an expression of drunken woe at this
sentence, filled with suspicior of him. With a deeply pained
air he began to fumble in his clothing, his red hands
trembling. Presently he announced in a voice of bitter
grief, as if he had been betrayed: "There's on'y four."

"Four," said the young man thoughtfully. "Well, look-a
here, I'm a stranger here, an' if ye'll steer me to your
cheap joint I'll find the other three."

The assassin's countenance became instantly radiant with
joy. His whiskers quivered with the wealth ot his alleged
emotions. He seized the young man's hand in a transport
of delight and friendliness.

"B' Gawd," he cried, "if ye'll do that, b' Gawd, I'd say
yeh was a damned good fellow, I would, an' I'd remember
yeh all m' life, I would, b' Gawd, an' if I ever got a chance
I'd return the compliment"—he spoke with drunken dig-

nity—"b' Gawd, I'd treat yeh white, I would, an' I'd allus remember yeh."

The young man drew back, looking at the assassin coldly. "Oh, that's all right," he said. "You show me th' joint—that's all you've got t' do."

The assassin, gesticulating gratitude, led the young man along a dark street. Finally he stopped before a little dusty door. He raised his hand impressively. "Look-a here," he said, and there was a thrill of deep and ancient wisdom upon his face, "I've brought yeh here, an' that's my part, ain't it? If th' place don't suit yeh, yeh needn't git mad at me, need yeh? There won't be no bad feelin', will there?"

"No," said the young man.

The assassin waved his arm tragically, and led the march up the steep stairway. On the way the young man furnished the assassin with three pennies. At the top a man with benevolent spectacles looked at them through a hole in a board. He collected their money, wrote some names on a register, and speedily was leading the two men along a gloom-shrouded corridor.

Shortly after the beginning of this journey the young man felt his liver turn white, for from the dark and secret places of the building there suddenly came to his nostrils strange and unspeakable odours, that assailed him like malignant diseases with wings. They seemed to be from human bodies closely packed in dens; the exhalations from a hundred pairs of reeking lips; the fumes from a thousand bygone debauches; the expression of a thousand present miseries.

A man, naked save for a little snuff-coloured undershirt, was parading sleepily along the corridor. He rubbed his eyes and, giving vent to a prodigious yawn, demanded to be told the time.

"Half-past one."

The man yawned again. He opened a door, and for a moment his form was outlined against a black, opaque interior. To this door came the three men, and as it was again opened the unholy odours rushed out like fiends, so

that the young man was obliged to struggle as against an
overpowering wind.

It was some time before the youth's eyes were good in
the intense gloom within, but the man with benevolent
spectacles led him skilfully, pausing but a moment to de-
posit the limp assassin upon a cot. He took the youth to
a cot that lay tranquilly by the window, and showing him
a tall locker for clothes that stood near the head with the
ominous air of a tombstone, left him.

The youth sat on his cot and peered about him. There
was a gas-jet in a distant part of the room, that burned a
small flickering orange-hued flame. It caused vast masses
of tumbled shadows in all parts of the place; save where,
immediately about it, there was a little grey haze. As the
young man's eyes became used to the darkness, he could
see upon the cots that thickly littered the floor the forms
of men sprawled out, lying in death-like silence, or heaving and snoring with tremendous effort, like stabbed fish.

The youth locked his derby and his shoes in the mummy-
case near him, and then lay down with an old and familiar coat around his shoulders. A blanket he handled
gingerly, drawing it over part of the coat. The cot was
covered with leather, and as cold as melting snow. The
youth was obliged to shiver for some time on this affair,
which was like a slab. Presently, however, his chill gave
him peace, and during this period of leisure from it he
turned his head to stare at his friend the assassin, whom
he could dimly discern where he lay sprawled on a cot in
the abandon of a man filled with drink. He was snoring
with incredible vigour. His wet hair and beard dimly glistened, and his inflamed nose shone with subdued lustre
like a red light in a fog.

Within reach of the youth's hand was one who lay with
yellow breast and shoulders bare to the cold draughts. One
arm hung over the side of the cot, and the fingers lay full
length upon the wet cement floor of the room. Beneath
the inky brows could be seen the eyes of the man, exposed
by the partly opened lids. To the youth it seemed that he
and this corpse-like being were exchanging a prolonged

stare, and that the other threatened with his eyes. He drew back, watching his neighbour from the shadows of his blanket-edge. The man did not move once through the night, but lay in this stillness as of death like a body stretched out expectant of the surgeon's knife.

And all through the room could be seen the tawny hues of naked flesh, limbs thrust into the darkness, projecting beyond the cots; upreared knees, arms hanging long and thin over the cot-edges. For the most part they were statu-esque, carven, dead. With the curious lockers standing all about like tombstones, there was a strange effect of a graveyard where bodies were merely flung.

Yet occasionally could be seen limbs wildly tossing in fantastic nightmare gestures, accompanied by guttural cries, grunts, oaths. And there was one fellow off in a gloomy corner, who in his dreams was oppressed by some fright-ful calamity, for of a sudden he began to utter long wails that went almost like yells from a hound, echoing wail-fully and weird through this chill place of tombstones where men lay like the dead.

The sound, in its high piercing beginnings that dwindled to final melancholy moans, expressed a red and grim trag-edy of the unfathomable possibilities of the man's dreams. But to the youth these were not merely the shrieks of a vision-pierced man: they were an utterance of the mean-ing of the room and its occupants. It was to him the pro-test of the wretch who feels the touch of the imperturbable granite wheels, and who then cries with an impersonal eloquence, with a strength not from him, giving voice to the wail of a whole section, a class, a people. This, weav-ing into the young man's brain, and mingling with his views of the vast and sombre shadows that, like mighty black fingers, curled around the naked bodies, made the young man so that he did not sleep, but lay carving the biographies for these men from his meagre experience. At times the fellow in the corner howled in a writhing agony of his imaginations.

Finally a long lance-point of grey light shot through the dusty panes of the window. Without, the young man could

see roofs drearily white in the dawning. The point of light
yellowed and grew brighter, until the golden rays of the
morning sun came in bravely and strong. They touched
with radiant colour the form of a small fat man who
snored in stuttering fashion. His round and shiny bald
head glowed suddenly with the valour of a decoration. He
sat up, blinked at the sun, swore fretfully, and pulled his
blanket over the ornamental splendours of his head.

The youth contentedly watched this rout of the shadows
before the bright spears of the sun, and presently he slumbered. When he awoke he heard the voice of the assassin
raised in valiant curses. Putting up his head, he perceived
his comrade seated on the side of the cot engaged in
scratching his neck with long fingernails that rasped like
files.

"Hully Jee, dis is a new breed. They've got can-openers
on their feet." He continued in a violent tirade.

The young man hastily unlocked his closet and took out
his shoes and hat. As he sat on the side of the cot lacing
his shoes, he glanced about and saw that daylight had
made the room comparatively commonplace and uninter-
esting. The men, whose faces seemed stolid, serene, or ab-
sent, were engaged in dressing, while a great crackle of
bantering conversation arose.

A few were parading in unconcerned nakedness. Here
and there were men of brawn, whose skins shone clear and
ruddy. They took splendid poses, standing massively like
chiefs. When they had dressed in their ungainly garments
there was an extraordinary change. They then showed
bumps and deficiencies of all kinds.

There were others who exhibited many deformities.
Shoulders were slanting, humped, pulled this way and
pulled that way. And notable among these latter men was
the little fat man who had refused to allow his head to be
glorified. His pudgy form, builded like a pear, bustled to
and fro, while he swore in fishwife fashion. It appeared
that some article of his apparel had vanished.

The young man attired himself speedily, and went to his

friend the assassin. At first the latter looked dazed at the sight of the youth. This face seemed to be appealing to him through the cloud-wastes of his memory. He scratched his neck and reflected. At last he grinned, a broad smile gradually spreading until his countenance was a round illumination. "Hello, Willie," he cried cheerily.

"Hello," said the young man. "Are yeh ready t' fly?"

"Sure." The assassin tied his shoe carefully with some twine and came ambling.

When he reached the street the young man experienced no sudden relief from unholy atmospheres. He had forgotten all about them, and had been breathing naturally, and with no sensation of discomfort or distress.

He was thinking of these things as he walked along the street, when he was suddenly startled by feeling the assassin's hand, trembling with excitement, clutching his arm, and when the assassin spoke, his voice went into quavers from a supreme agitation.

"I'll be hully, bloomin' blowed if there wasn't a feller with a nightshirt on up there in that joint."

The youth was bewildered for a moment, but presently he turned to smile indulgently at the assassin's humour. "Oh, you're a damned liar," he merely said.

Whereupon the assassin began to gesture extravagantly and take oath by strange gods. He frantically placed himself at the mercy of remarkable fates if his tale were not true. "Yes, he did! I cross m' heart thousan' times!" he protested, and at the moment his eyes were large with amazement, his mouth wrinkled in unnatural glee. "Yessir! A nightshirt! A hully white nightshirt!"

"You lie!"

"No, sir! I hope ter die b'fore I kin git anudder ball if there wasn't a jay wid a hully, bloomin' white nightshirt!"

His face was filled with the infinite wonder of it. "A hully white nightshirt," he continually repeated.

The young man saw the dark entrance to a basement restaurant. There was a sign which read "No mystery about our hash!" and there were other age-stained and

world-battered legends which told him that the place was
within his means. He stopped before it and spoke to the
assassin. "I guess I'll git somethin' t' eat."

At this the assassin, for some reason, appeared to be
quite embarrassed. He gazed at the seductive front of the
eating-place for a moment. Then he started slowly up the
street. "Well, good-bye, Willie," he said bravely.

For an instant the youth studied the departing figure.
Then he called out, "Hol' on a minnet." As they came
together he spoke in a certain fierce way, as if he feared
that the other would think him to be charitable. "Look-a
here, if yeh wanta git some breakfas' I'll lend yeh three
cents t' do it with. But say, look-a here, you've gotta git
out an' hustle. I ain't goin' t' support yeh, or I'll go broke
b'fore night. I ain't no millionaire."

"I take me oath, Willie," said the assassin earnestly, "th'
on'y thing I really needs is a ball. Me t'roat feels like a
fryin'-pan. But as I can't get a ball, why, th' next bes' thing
is breakfast, an' if yeh do that for me, b' Gawd, I say yeh
was th' whitest lad I ever see."

They spent a few moments in dexterous exchanges of
phrases, in which they each protested that the other was,
as the assassin had originally said, "a respecterble gentlem'n." And they concluded with mutual assurances that
they were the souls of intelligence and virtue. Then they
went into the restaurant.

There was a long counter, dimly lighted from hidden
sources. Two or three men in soiled white aprons rushed
here and there.

The youth bought a bowl of coffee for two cents and a
roll for one cent. The assassin purchased the same. The
bowls were webbed with brown seams, and the tin spoons
wore an air of having emerged from the first pyramid.
Upon them were black moss-like encrustations of age, and
they were bent and scarred from the attacks of long-for-
gotten teeth. But over their repast the wanderers waxed
warm and mellow. The assassin grew affable as the hot
mixture went soothingly down his parched throat, and the
young man felt courage flow in his veins.

Memories began to throng in on the assassin, and he brought forth long tales, intricate, incoherent, delivered with a chattering swiftness as from an old woman. "—great job out 'n Orange. Boss keep yeh hustlin', though, all time. I was there three days, and then I went an' ask 'im t' lend me a dollar. 'G-g-go ter the devil,' he says, an' I lose me job.

"South no good. Damn niggers work for twenty-five an' thirty cents a day. Run white man out. Good grub, though. Easy livin'.

"Yas; useter work little in Toledo, raftin' logs. Make two or three dollars er day in the spring. Lived high. Cold as ice, though, in the winter.

"I was raised in northern N' York. O-o-oh, yeh jest oughto live there. No beer ner whisky, though, 'way off in the woods. But all th' good hot grub yeh can eat. B' Gawd, I hung around there long as I could till th' ol' man fired me. 'Git t' hell outa here, yeh wuthless skunk, git t' hell outa here, an' go die,' he says. 'You're a hell of a father,' I says, 'you are,' an' I quit 'im."

As they were passing from the dim eating-place, they encountered an old man who was trying to steal forth with a tiny package of food, but a tall man with an indomitable moustache stood dragon-fashion, barring the way of escape. They heard the old man raise a plaintive protest. "Ah, you always want to know what I take out, and you never see that I usually bring a package in here from my place of business."

As the wanderers trudged slowly along Park Row, the assassin began to expand and grow blithe. "B' Gawd, we've been livin' like kings," he said, smacking appreciative lips.

"Look out, or we'll have t' pay fer it t'-night," said the youth with gloomy warning.

But the assassin refused to turn his gaze toward the future. He went with a limping step, into which he injected a suggestion of lamb-like gambols. His mouth was wreathed in a red grin.

In City Hall Park the two wanderers sat down in the little circle of benches sanctified by traditions of their class. They huddled in their old garments, slumbrously conscious of the march of the hours which for them had no meaning.

The people of the street hurrying hither and thither made a blend of black figures, changing, yet frieze-like. They walked in their good clothes as upon important missions, giving no gaze to the two wanderers seated upon the benches. They expressed to the young man his infinite distance from all that he valued. Social position, comfort, the pleasures of living were unconquerable kingdoms. He felt a sudden awe.

And in the background a multitude of buildings, of pitiless hues and sternly high, were to him emblematic of a nation forcing its regal head into the clouds, throwing no downward glances; in the sublimity of its aspirations ignoring the wretches who may flounder at its feet. The roar of the city in his ear was to him the confusion of strange tongues, babbling heedlessly; it was the clink of coin, the voice of the city's hopes, which were to him no hopes.

He confessed himself an outcast, and his eyes from under the lowered rim of his hat began to glance guiltily, wearing the criminal expression that comes with certain convictions.[2]

[2] The original version included the following final part:

"Well," said the friend, "did you discover his point of view?"

"I don't know that I did," replied the young man; "but at any rate I think mine own has undergone a considerable alteration."

STEPHEN CRANE.

MAGGIE: A GIRL OF THE STREETS

I

A VERY little boy stood upon a heap of gravel for the honour of Rum Alley. He was throwing stones at howling urchins from Devil's Row, who were circling madly about the heap and pelting him. His infantile countenance was livid with the fury of battle. His small body was writhing in the delivery of oaths.

"Run, Jimmie, run! Dey'll git yehs!" screamed a retreating Rum Alley child.

"Naw," responded Jimmie with a valiant roar, "dese mugs can't make me run."

Howls of renewed wrath went up from Devil's Row throats. Tattered gamins on the right made a furious assault on the gravel-heap. On their small convulsed faces shone the grins of true assassins. As they charged, they threw stones and cursed in shrill chorus.

The little champion of Rum Alley stumbled precipitately down the other side. His coat had been torn to shreds in a scuffle, and his hat was gone. He had bruises on twenty parts of his body, and blood was dripping from a cut in his head. His wan features looked like those of a tiny insane demon. On the ground, children from Devil's Row closed in on their antagonist. He crooked his left arm defensively about his head and fought with madness. The little boys ran to and fro, dodging, hurling stones, and swearing in barbaric trebles.

From a window of an apartment-house that uprose from amid squat ignorant stables there leaned a curious woman. Some labourers, unloading a scow at a dock at the river, paused for a moment and regarded the fight. The engineer of a passive tugboat hung lazily over a railing and watched. Over on the island a worm of yellow convicts came from

the shadow of a grey ominous building and crawled slowly
along the river's bank.

A stone had smashed in Jimmie's mouth. Blood was bubbling over his chin and down upon his ragged shirt. Tears
made furrows on his dirt-stained cheeks. His thin legs had
begun to tremble and turn weak, causing his small body
to reel. His roaring curses of the first part of the fight had
changed to a blasphemous chatter. In the yells of the
whirling mob of Devil's Row children there were notes of
joy like songs of triumphant savagery. The little boys
seemed to leer gloatingly at the blood upon the other
child's face.

Down the avenue came boastfully sauntering a lad of
sixteen years, although the chronic sneer of an ideal manhood already sat upon his lips. His hat was tipped over his
eye with an air of challenge. Between his teeth a cigar-
stump was tilted at the angle of defiance. He walked with a
certain swing of the shoulders which appalled the timid. He
glanced over into the vacant lot in which the little raving
boys from Devil's Row seethed about the shrieking and
tearful child from Rum Alley.

"Gee!" he murmured with interest, "a scrap. Gee!" He
strode over to the cursing circle, swinging his shoulders in
a manner which denoted that he held victory in his fists.
He approached at the back of one of the most deeply
engaged of the Devil's Row children. "Ah, what d' hell,"
he said, and smote the deeply engaged one on the back of
the head.

The little boy fell to the ground and gave a tremendous
howl. He scrambled to his feet, and perceiving, evidently,
the size of his assailant, ran quickly off, shouting alarms.
The entire Devil's Row party followed him. They came to
a stand a short distance away and yelled taunting oaths
at the boy with the chronic sneer.

The latter, momentarily, paid no attention to them.
"What's wrong wi'che, Jimmie?" he asked of the small
champion.

Jimmie wiped his blood-wet features with his sleeve.

"Well, it was dis way, Pete, see? I was goin' teh lick dat Riley kid, an' dey all pitched on me."

Some Rum Alley children now came forward. The party stood for a moment exchanging vainglorious remarks with Devil's Row. A few stones were thrown at long distances, and words of challenge passed between small warriors. Then the Rum Alley contingent turned slowly in the direction of their home street. They began to give, each to each, distorted versions of the fight. Causes of retreat in particular cases were magnified. Blows dealt in the fight were enlarged to catapultian power, and stones thrown were alleged to have hurtled with infinite accuracy. Valour grew strong again, and the little boys began to brag with great spirit. "Ah, we blokies kin lick d' hull damn Row," said a child, swaggering.

Little Jimmie was trying to stanch the flow of blood from his cut lips. Scowling, he turned upon the speaker. "Ah, where was yehs when I was doin' all deh fightin'?" he demanded. "Youse kids makes me tired."

"Ah, go ahn!" replied the other argumentatively.

Jimmie replied with heavy contempt. "Ah, youse can't fight, Blue Billie! I kin lick yeh wid one han'."

"Ah, go ahn!" replied Billie again.

"Ah!" said Jimmie threateningly.

"Ah!" said the other in the same tone.

They struck at each other, clinched, and rolled over on the cobble-stones.

"Smash 'im, Jimmie, kick d' face off 'im!" yelled Pete, the lad with the chronic sneer, in tones of delight.

The small combatants pounded and kicked, scratched and tore. They began to weep, and their curses struggled in their throats with sobs. The other little boys clasped their hands and wriggled their legs in excitement. They formed a bobbing circle about the pair.

A tiny spectator was suddenly agitated. "Cheese it, Jimmie, cheese it! Here comes yer fader," he yelled.

The circle of little boys instantly parted. They drew away and waited in ecstatic awe for that which was about to happen. The two little boys, fighting in the modes of four thousand years ago, did not hear the warning.

Up the avenue there plodded slowly a man with sullen eyes. He was carrying a dinner-pail and smoking an apple-wood pipe. As he neared the spot where the little boys strove, he regarded them listlessly. But suddenly he roared an oath and advanced upon the rolling fighters. "Here, you Jim, git up, now, while I belt yer life out, yeh disorderly brat." He began to kick into the chaotic mass on the ground. The boy Billie felt a heavy boot strike his head. He made a furious effort and disentangled himself from Jimmie. He tottered away.

Jimmie arose painfully from the ground and, confronting his father, began to curse him. His parent kicked him. "Come home, now," he cried, "an' stop yer jawin', er I'll lam the everlasting head off yehs."

They departed. The man paced placidly along with the apple-wood emblem of serenity between his teeth. The boy followed a dozen feet in the rear. He swore luridly, for he felt that it was degradation for one who aimed to be some vague kind of soldier, or a man of blood with a sort of sublime licence, to be taken home by a father.

II

Eventually they entered a dark region where, from a careening building, a dozen gruesome doorways gave up loads of babies to the street and the gutter. A wind of early autumn raised yellow dust from cobbles and swirled it against a hundred windows. Long streamers of garments fluttered from fire-escapes. In all unhandy places there were buckets, brooms, rags, and bottles. In the street infants played or fought with other infants or sat stupidly in the way of vehicles. Formidable women, with uncombed hair and disordered dress, gossiped while leaning on railings, or screamed in frantic quarrels. Withered persons, in curious postures of submission to something, sat smoking pipes in obscure corners. A thousand odours of cooking food came forth to the street. The building quivered and creaked from the weight of humanity stamping about in its bowels.

A small ragged girl dragged a red, bawling infant along the crowded ways. He was hanging back, baby-like, bracing his wrinkled, bare legs. The little girl cried out: "Ah, Tommie, come ahn. Dere's Jimmie and fader. Don't be a-pullin' me back." She jerked the baby's arm impatiently. He fell on his face, roaring. With a second jerk she pulled him to his feet, and they went on. With the obstinacy of his order, he protested against being dragged in a chosen direction. He made heroic endeavours to keep on his legs, denounced his sister, and consumed a bit of orange-peeling which he chewed between the times of his infantile orations.

As the sullen-eyed man, followed by the blood-covered boy, drew near, the little girl burst into reproachful cries. "Ah, Jimmie, youse bin fightin' agin."

The urchin swelled disdainfully. "Ah, what d' hell, Mag. See?"

The little girl upbraided him. "Youse allus fightin', Jimmie, an' yeh knows it puts mudder out when yehs come home half dead, an' it's like we'll all get a poundin'." She began to weep. The babe threw back his head and roared at his prospects.

"Ah," cried Jimmie, "shut up er I'll smack yer mout'. See?" As his sister continued her lamentations, he suddenly struck her. The little girl reeled, and, recovering herself, burst into tears and quaveringly cursed him. As she slowly retreated, her brother advanced, dealing her cuffs.

The father heard, and turned about. "Stop that, Jim, d'yeh hear? Leave yer sister alone on the street. It's like I can never beat any sense into yer wooden head."

The urchin raised his voice in defiance to his parent, and continued his attacks. The babe bawled tremendously, protesting with great violence. During his sister's hasty manœuvres he was dragged by the arm.

Finally the procession plunged into one of the gruesome doorways. They crawled up dark stairways and along cold, gloomy halls. At last the father pushed open a door, and they entered a lighted room in which a large woman was rampant.

She stopped in a career from a seething stove to a pan-covered table. As the father and children filed in she peered at them. "Eh, what? Been fightin' agin!" She threw herself upon Jimmie. The urchin tried to dart behind the others, and in the scuffle the babe, Tommie, was knocked down. He protested with his usual vehemence because they had bruised his tender shins against a table leg.

The mother's massive shoulders heaved with anger. Grasping the urchin by the neck and shoulder she shook him until he rattled. She dragged him to an unholy sink, and, soaking a rag in water, began to scrub his lacerated face with it. Jimmie screamed in pain, and tried to twist his shoulders out of the clasp of the huge arms.

The babe sat on the floor watching the scene, his face in contortions like that of a woman at a tragedy. The father, with a newly ladened pipe in his mouth, sat in a backless chair near the stove. Jimmie's cries annoyed him. He turned about and bellowed at his wife. "Let the kid alone for a minute, will yeh, Mary? Yer allus poundin' 'im. When I come nights I can't get no rest 'cause yer allus poundin' a kid. Let up, d'yeh hear? Don't be allus poundin' a kid." The woman's operations on the urchin instantly increased in violence. At last she tossed him to a corner, where he limply lay weeping.

The wife put her immense hands on her hips, and with a chieftain-like stride approached her husband. "Ho!" she said, with a great grunt of contempt. "An' what in the devil are you stickin' your nose for?" The babe crawled under the table, and, turning, peered out cautiously. The ragged girl retreated, and the urchin in the corner drew his legs carefully beneath him.

The man puffed his pipe calmly and put his great mud-died boots on the back part of the stove. "Go t' hell," he said tranquilly.

The woman screamed, and shook her fists before her

husband's eyes. The rough yellow of her face and neck flared suddenly crimson. She began to howl.

He puffed imperturbably at his pipe for a time, but finally arose and went to look out the window into the darkening chaos of back yards. "You've been drinkin', Mary," he said. "You better let up on the bot', ol' woman, or you'll git done."

"You're a liar. I ain't had a drop," she roared in reply. They had a lurid altercation.

The babe was staring out from under the table, his small face working in his excitement. The ragged girl went stealthily over to the corner where the urchin lay. "Are yehs hurted much, Jimmie?" she whispered timidly.

"Not a little bit. See?" growled the little boy.

"Will I wash d' blood?"

"Naw!"

"Will I—"

"When I catch dat Riley kid I'll break 'is face! Dat's right! See?" He turned his face to the wall as if resolved grimly to bide his time.

In the quarrel between husband and wife the woman was victor. The man seized his hat and rushed from the room, apparently determined upon a vengeful drunk. She followed to the door and thundered at him as he made his way downstairs.

She returned and stirred up the room until her children were bobbing about like bubbles. "Git outa d' way," she bawled persistently, waving feet with their dishevelled shoes near the heads of her children. She shrouded herself, puffing and snorting, in a cloud of steam at the stove, and eventually extracted a frying-pan full of potatoes that hissed. She flourished it. "Come t' yer suppers, now," she cried with sudden exasperation. "Hurry up, now, er I'll help yeh!"

The children scrambled hastily. With prodigious clatter they arranged themselves at table. The babe sat with his feet dangling high from a precarious infant's chair and gorged his small stomach. Jimmie forced, with feverish rapidity, the grease-enveloped pieces between his wounded lips. Maggie, with side glances of fear of interruption, ate like a small pursued tigress.

The mother sat blinking at them. She delivered reproaches, swallowed potatoes, and drank from a yellow-brown bottle. After a time her mood changed, and she wept as she carried little Tommie into another room and laid him to sleep, with his fists doubled, in an old quilt of faded red-and-green grandeur. Then she came and moaned by the stove. She rocked to and fro upon a chair, shedding tears and crooning miserably to the two children about their "poor mother" and "yer fader, damn 'is soul."

The little girl plodded between the table and the chair with a dishpan on it. She tottered on her small legs beneath burdens of dishes. Jimmie sat nursing his various wounds. He cast furtive glances at his mother. His practised eye perceived her gradually emerge from a mist of muddled sentiment until her brain burned in drunken heat. He sat breathless.

Maggie broke a plate.

The mother started to her feet as if propelled. "Good Gawd!" she howled. Her glittering eyes fastened on her child with sudden hatred. The fervent red of her face turned almost to purple. The little boy ran to the halls, shrieking like a monk in an earthquake. He floundered about in darkness until he found the stairs. He stumbled, panic-stricken, to the next floor.

An old woman opened a door. A light behind her threw a flare on the urchin's face. "Eh, child, what is it dis time? Is yer fader beatin' yer mudder, or yer mudder beatin' ye fader?"

III

Jimmie and the old woman listened long in the hall. Above the muffled roar of conversation, the dismal wailings of babies at night, the thumping of feet in unseen corridors and rooms, and the sound of varied hoarse shoutings in the street and the rattling of wheels over cobbles, they heard the screams of the child and the roars of the mother die away to a feeble moaning and a subdued bass muttering.

The old woman was a gnarled and leathery personage who could don at will an expression of great virtue. She possessed a small music-box capable of one tune, and a collection of "God bless yeh's" pitched in assorted keys of fervency. Each day she took a position upon the stones of Fifth Avenue, where she crooked her legs under her and crouched, immovable and hideous, like an idol. She received daily a small sum in pennies. It was contributed, for the most part, by persons who did not make their homes in that vicinity. Once, when a lady had dropped her purse on the sidewalk, the gnarled woman had grabbed it and smuggled it with great dexterity beneath her cloak. When she was arrested she had cursed the lady into a partial swoon, and with her aged limbs, twisted from rheumatism, had kicked the breath out of a huge policeman whose conduct upon that occasion she referred to when she said, "The police, damn 'em!"

"Eh, Jimmie, it's a shame," she said. "Go, now, like a dear, an' buy me a can, an' if yer mudder raises 'ell all night yehs can sleep here." Jimmie took a tendered tin pail and seven pennies and departed. He passed into the side door of a saloon and went to the bar. Straining up on his toes he raised the pail and pennies as high as his arms would let him. He saw two hands thrust down to take them. Directly the same hands let down the filled pail, and he left.

In front of the gruesome doorway he met a lurching figure. It was his father, swaying about on uncertain legs. "Give me deh can. See?" said the man.

"Ah, come off! I got dis can fer dat ol' woman, an' it 'ud be dirt teh swipe it. See?" cried Jimmie.

The father wrenched the pail from the urchin. He grasped it in both hands and lifted it to his mouth. He glued his lips to the under edge and tilted his head. His throat swelled until it seemed to grow near his chin. There was a tremendous gulping movement and the beer was gone. The man caught his breath and laughed. He hit his son on the head with the empty pail.

As it rolled clanging into the street, Jimmie began to scream, and kicked repeatedly at his father's shins. "Look at deh dirt what yeh done me," he yelled. "Deh ol' woman 'll be t'rowin' fits." He retreated to the middle of the street, but the old man did not pursue. He staggered toward the door. "I'll paste yeh when I ketch yeh!" he shouted, and disappeared.

During the evening he had been standing against a bar drinking whiskies, and declaring to all comers confidentially: "My home reg'lar livin' hell! Why do I come an' drin' whisk' here thish way? 'Cause home reg'lar livin' hell!"

Jimmie waited a long time in the street and then crept warily up through the building. He passed with great caution the door of the gnarled woman, and finally stopped outside his home and listened. He could hear his mother moving heavily about among the furniture of the room. She was chanting in a mournful voice, occasionally interjecting bursts of volcanic wrath at the father, who, Jimmie judged, had sunk down on the floor or in a corner.

"Why deh blazes don' cher try teh keep Jim from fightin'? I'll break yer jaw!" she suddenly bellowed.

The man mumbled with drunken indifference. "Ah, w'at's bitin' yeh? Wa'a 's odds? W'a' makes kick?"

"Because he tears 'is clothes, yeh fool!" cried the woman in supreme wrath.

The husband seemed to become aroused. "Go chase yerself!" he thundered fiercely in reply. There was a crash against the door, and something broke into clattering fragments. Jimmie partially suppressed a yell and darted down the stairway. Below he paused and listened. He heard howls and curses, groans and shrieks—a confused chorus as if a battle were raging. With it all there was the crash of splintering furniture. The eyes of the urchin glared in his fear that one of them would discover him.

Curious faces appeared in doorways, and whispered

comments passed to and fro. "Ol' Johnson's playin' horse agin."

Jimmie stood until the noises ceased and the other inhabitants of the tenement had all yawned and shut their doors. Then he crawled upstairs with the caution of an invader of a panther's den. Sounds of laboured breathing came through the broken door-panels. He pushed the door open and entered, quaking.

A glow from the fire threw red hues over the bare floor, the cracked and soiled plastering, and the overturned and broken furniture. In the middle of the floor lay his mother asleep. In one corner of the room his father's limp body hung across the seat of a chair.

The urchin stole forward. He began to shiver in dread of awakening his parents. His mother's great chest was heaving painfully. Jimmie paused and looked down at her. Her face was inflamed and swollen from drinking. Her yellow brows shaded eyelids that had grown blue. Her tangled hair tossed in waves over her forehead. Her mouth was set in the same lines of vindictive hatred that it had, perhaps, borne during the fight. Her bare red arms were thrown out above her head in an attitude of exhaustion, something, mayhap, like that of a sated villain.

The urchin bent over his mother. He was fearful lest she should open her eyes, and the dread within him was so strong that he could not forbear to stare, but hung as if fascinated over the woman's grim face. Suddenly her eyes opened. The urchin found himself looking straight into an expression which, it would seem, had the power to change his blood to salt. He howled piercingly and fell backward.

The woman floundered for a moment, tossed her arms about her head as if in combat, and again began to snore. Jimmie crawled back into the shadows and waited. A noise in the next room had followed his cry at the discovery that his mother was awake. He grovelled in the gloom, his eyes riveted upon the intervening door. He heard it creak, and then the sound of a small voice came to him. "Jimmie!

Jimmie! Are yehs dere?" it whispered. The urchin started.
The thin white face of his sister looked at him from the
doorway of the other room. She crept to him across the
floor.

The father had not moved, but lay in the same death-
like sleep. The mother writhed in an uneasy slumber, her
chest wheezing as if she were in the agonies of strangula-
tion. Out at the window a florid moon was peering over
dark roofs, and in the distance the waters of a river glimmered pallidly.

The small frame of the ragged girl was quivering. Her
features were haggard from weeping, and her eyes gleamed
with fear. She grasped the urchin's arm in her little trembling hands and they huddled in a corner. The eyes of
both were drawn, by some force, to stare at the woman's
face, for they thought she need only to awake and all the
fiends would come from below. They crouched until the
ghost mists of dawn appeared at the window, drawing
close to the panes, and looking in at the prostrate, heaving
body of the mother.

IV

The babe, Tommie, died. He went away in an insignificant coffin, his small waxen hand clutching a flower that
the girl, Maggie, had stolen from an Italian.

She and Jimmie lived.

The inexperienced fibres of the boy's eyes were hardened
at an early age. He became a young man of leather. He
lived some red years without labouring. During that time
his sneer became chronic. He studied human nature in the
gutter, and found it no worse than he thought he had
reason to believe it. He never conceived a respect for the
world, because he had begun with no idols that it had
smashed.

He clad his soul in armour by means of happening
hilariously in at a mission church where a man composed
his sermons of "you's." Once a philosopher asked this
man why he did not say "we" instead of "you." The man
replied, "What?" While they got warm at the stove he

told his hearers just where he calculated they stood with
the Lord. Many of the sinners were impatient over the
pictured depths of their degradation. They were waiting
for soup-tickets. A reader of the words of wind-demons
might have been able to see the portions of a dialogue pass
to and fro between the exhorter and his hearers. "You are
damned," said the preacher. And the reader of sounds
might have seen the reply go forth from the ragged people:
"Where's our soup?" Jimmie and a companion sat in a
rear seat and commented upon the things that didn't concern them, with all the freedom of English tourists. When
they grew thirsty and went out, their minds confused the
speaker with Christ.

Momentarily, Jimmie was sullen with thoughts of a
hopeless altitude where grew fruit. His companion said
that if he should ever go to heaven he would ask for a
million dollars and a bottle of beer. Jimmie's occupation
for a long time was to stand at street corners and watch
the world go by, dreaming blood-red dreams at the passing
of pretty women. He menaced mankind at the intersections
of streets. At the corners he was in life and of life. The
world was going on and he was there to perceive it.

He maintained a belligerent attitude toward all well-
dressed men. To him fine raiment was allied to weakness,
and all good coats covered faint hearts. He and his orders
were kings, to a certain extent, over the men of untarnished
clothes, because these latter dreaded, perhaps, to be either
killed or laughed at. Above all things he despised obvious
Christians and ciphers with the chrysanthemums of aristocracy in their buttonholes. He considered himself above
both of these classes. He was afraid of nothing.

When he had a dollar in his pocket his satisfaction with
existence was the greatest thing in the world. So, eventually, he felt obliged to work. His father died, and his
mother's years were divided up into periods of thirty
days.

He became a truck-driver. There was given to him the
charge of a painstaking pair of horses and a large rattling
truck. He invaded the turmoil and tumble of the downtown

streets, and learned to breathe maledictory defiance at the
police, who occasionally used to climb up, drag him from
his perch, and punch him. In the lower part of the city he
daily involved himself in hideous tangles. If he and his
team chanced to be in the rear he preserved a demeanour
of serenity, crossing his legs and bursting forth into yells
when foot passengers took dangerous dives beneath the
noses of his champing horses. He smoked his pipe calmly,
for he knew that his pay was marching on. If his charge
was in the front, and if it became the key-truck of chaos,
he entered terrifically into the quarrel that was raging to
and fro among the drivers on their high seats, and sometimes roared oaths and violently got himself arrested.

After a time his sneer grew so that it turned its glare
upon all things. He became so sharp that he believed in
nothing. To him the police were always actuated by malignant impulses, and the rest of the world was composed,
for the most part, of despicable creatures who were all
trying to take advantage of him, and with whom, in
defence, he was obliged to quarrel on all possible occasions. He himself occupied a downtrodden position, which
had a private but distinct element of grandeur in its
isolation.

The greatest cases of aggravated idiocy were, to his
mind, rampant upon the front platforms of all the street-
cars. At first his tongue strove with these beings, but he
eventually became superior. In him grew a majestic contempt for those strings of street-cars that followed him
like intent bugs. He fell into the habit, when starting on a
long journey, of fixing his eye on a high and distant object,
commanding his horses to start, and then going into a
trance of oblivion. Multitudes of drivers might howl in his
rear, and passengers might load him with opprobrium, but
he would not awaken until some blue policeman turned red
and began frenziedly to seize bridles and beat the soft
noses of the responsible horses.

When he paused to contemplate the attitude of the police
toward himself and his fellows, he believed that they
were the only men in the city who had no rights. When

driving about, he felt that he was held liable by the police for anything that might occur in the streets, and that he was the common prey of all energetic officials. In revenge, he resolved never to move out of the way of anything, until formidable circumstances or a much larger man than himself forced him to it.

Foot passengers were mere pestering flies with an insane disregard for their legs and his convenience. He could not comprehend their desire to cross the streets. Their madness smote him with eternal amazement. He was continually storming at them from his throne. He sat aloft and denounced their frantic leaps, plunges, dives, and straddles. When they would thrust at, or parry, the noses of his champing horses, making them swing their heads and move their feet, and thus disturbing a stolid, dreamy repose, he swore at the men as fools, for he himself could perceive that Providence had caused it to be clearly written that he and his team had the inalienable right to stand in the proper path of the sun-chariot and, if they so minded, to obstruct its mission or take a wheel off. And if the god driver had had a desire to step down, put up his flame-coloured fists, and manfully dispute the right of way, he would have probably been immediately opposed by a scowling mortal with two sets of hard knuckles.

It is possible, perhaps, that this young man would have derided, in an axle-wide alley, the approach of a flying ferryboat. Yet he achieved a respect for a fire-engine. As one charged toward his truck, he would drive fearfully upon a sidewalk, threatening untold people with annihilation. When an engine struck a mass of blocked trucks, splitting it into fragments as a blow annihilates a cake of ice, Jimmie's team could usually be observed high and safe, with whole wheels, on the sidewalk. The fearful coming of the engine could break up the most intricate muddle of heavy vehicles at which the police had been storming for half an hour. A fire-engine was enshrined in his heart as an appalling thing that he loved with a distant, dog-like devotion. It had been known to overturn a street-car. Those leaping horses, striking sparks from the cobbles in their

forward lunge, were creatures to be ineffably admired. The
clang of the gong pierced his breast like a noise of remembered war.

When Jimmie was a little boy he began to be arrested.
Before he reached a great age, he had a fair record. He
developed too great a tendency to climb down from his
truck and fight with other drivers. He had been in quite
a number of miscellaneous fights, and in some general bar-
room rows that had become known to the police. Once he
had been arrested for assaulting a Chinaman. Two women
in different parts of the city, and entirely unknown to each
other, caused him considerable annoyance by breaking
forth, simultaneously, at fateful intervals, into wailings
about marriage and support and infants.

Nevertheless, he had, on a certain star-lit evening, said
wonderingly and quite reverently, "Deh moon looks like
hell, don't it?"

V

The girl, Maggie, blossomed in a mud-puddle. She grew
to be a most rare and wonderful production of a tenement
district, a pretty girl. None of the dirt of Rum Alley
seemed to be in her veins. The philosophers, upstairs,
downstairs, and on the same floor, puzzled over it. When
a child, playing and fighting with gamins in the street, dirt
disgusted her. Attired in tatters and grime, she went unseen.

There came a time, however, when the young men of
the vicinity said, "Dat Johnson goil is a putty good looker."
About this period her brother remarked to her: "Mag, I'll
tell yeh dis! See? Yeh've eeder got t'go on d' toif er go t'
work!" Whereupon she went to work, having the feminine
aversion to the alternative. By a chance, she got a position
in an establishment where they made collars and cuffs. She
received a stool and a machine in a room where sat twenty
girls of various shades of yellow discontent. She perched
on the stool and treadled at her machine all day, turning
out collars with a name which might have been noted for

its irrelevancy to anything connected with collars. At night she returned home to her mother.

Jimmie grew large enough to take the vague position of head of the family. As incumbent of that office, he stumbled upstairs late at night, as his father had done before him. He reeled about the room, swearing at his relations, or went to sleep on the floor.

The mother had gradually risen to such a degree of fame that she could bandy words with her acquaintances among the police justices. Court officials called her by her first name. When she appeared they pursued a course which had been theirs for months. They invariably grinned, and cried out, "Hello, Mary, you here again?" Her grey head wagged in many courts. She always besieged the bench with voluble excuses, explanations, apologies, and prayers. Her flaming face and rolling eyes were a familiar sight on the island. She measured time by means of sprees, and was swollen and dishevelled.

One day the young man Pete, who as a lad had smitten the Devil's Row urchin in the back of the head and put to flight the antagonists of his friend Jimmie, strutted upon the scene. He met Jimmie one day on the street, promised to take him to a boxing match in Williamsburg, and called for him in the evening.

Maggie observed Pete.

He sat on a table in the Johnson home, and dangled his checked legs with an enticing nonchalance. His hair was curled down over his forehead in an oiled bang. His pugged nose seemed to revolt from contact with a bristling moustache of short, wire-like hairs. His blue double-breasted coat, edged with black braid, was buttoned close to a red puff tie, and his patent leather shoes looked like weapons. His mannerisms stamped him as a man who had a correct sense of his personal superiority. There were valour and contempt for circumstances in the glance of his eye. He waved his hands like a man of the world who dismisses religion and philosophy, and says "Rats!" He had certainly seen everything, and with each curl of his lip he declared that it amounted to nothing. Maggie thought he must be a very "elegant" bartender.

He was telling tales to Jimmie. Maggie watched him furtively, with half-closed eyes lit with a vague interest.

"Hully gee! Dey makes me tired," he said. "Mos' e'ry day some farmer comes in an' tries t' run d' shop. See? But d' gits t'rowed right out. I jolt dem right out in d' street before dey knows where dey is. See?"

"Sure," said Jimmie.

"Dere was a mug come in d' place d' odder day wid an idear he was goin' t' own d' place. Hully gee! he was goin' t' own d' place. I see he had a still on, an' I didn' wanna giv 'im no stuff, so I says, 'Git outa here an' don' make no trouble,' I says like dat. See? 'Git outa here an' don' make no trouble'; like dat. 'Git outa here,' I says. See?"

Jimmie nodded understandingly. Over his features played an eager desire to state the amount of his valour in a similar crisis, but the narrator proceeded.

"Well, deh blokie he says: 'T' blazes wid it! I ain' lookin' for no scrap,' he says—see?—'but,' he says, 'I'm 'spectable cit'zen an' I wanna drink, an' quick, too.' See? 'Aw, go ahn!' I says, like dat. 'Aw, go ahn,' I says. See? 'Don' make no trouble,' I says, like dat. 'Don' make no trouble.' See? Den d' mug, he squared off an' said he was fine as silk wid his dukes—see?—an' he wan'ed a drink—quick. Dat's what he said. See?"

"Sure," repeated Jimmie.

Pete continued. "Say, I jes' jumped d' bar, an' d' way I plunked dat blokie was outa sight. See? Dat's right! In d' jaw! See? Hully gee! he t'rowed a spittoon t'rough d' front windee. Say, I t'ought I'd drop dead. But d' boss, he comes in after, an' he says: 'Pete, yehs done jes' right! Yeh've gotta keep order, an' it's all right.' See? 'It's all right,' he says. Dat's what he said."

The two held a technical discussion.

"Dat bloke was a dandy," said Pete in conclusion, "but he hadn' outa made no trouble. Dat's what I says t' dem: 'Don' come in here an' make no trouble,' I says, like dat. 'Don' make no trouble.' See?"

As Jimmie and his friend exchanged tales descriptive of their prowess, Maggie leaned back in the shadow. Her eyes dwelt wonderingly and rather wistfully upon Pete's face. The broken furniture, grimy walls, and general disorder and dirt of her home of a sudden appeared before her and began to take a potential aspect. Pete's aristocratic person looked as if it might soil. She looked keenly at him, occasionally wondering if he was feeling contempt. But Pete seemed to be enveloped in reminiscence.

"Hully gee!" said he, "dose mugs can't feaze me. Dey knows I kin wipe up d' street wid any t'ree of dem."

When he said, "Ah, what d' hell!" his voice was burdened with disdain for the inevitable and contempt for anything that fate might compel him to endure.

Maggie perceived that here was the ideal man. Her dim thoughts were often searching for far-away lands where the little hills sing together in the morning. Under the trees of her dream-gardens there had always walked a lover.

VI

Pete took note of Maggie. "Say, Mag, I'm stuck on yer shape. It's outa sight," he said parenthetically, with an affable grin.

As he became aware that she was listening closely, he grew still more eloquent in his description of various happenings in his career. It appeared that he was invincible in fights. "Why," he said, referring to a man with whom he had had a misunderstanding, "dat mug scrapped like a dago. Dat's right. He was dead easy. See? He t'ought he was a scrapper. But he foun' out diff'ent. Hully gee!"

He walked to and fro in the small room, which seemed then to grow even smaller and unfit to hold his dignity, the attribute of a supreme warrior. That swing of the shoulders which had frozen the timid when he was but a lad had increased with his growth and education in the ratio of ten to one. It, combined with the sneer upon his mouth, told mankind that there was nothing in space which could appal him. Maggie marvelled at him and surrounded him with greatness. She vaguely tried to calculate the altitude of the pinnacle from which he must have looked down upon her.

"I met a chump deh odder day way up in deh city," he said. "I was goin' teh see a frien' of mine. When I was a-crossin' deh street deh chump runned plump inteh me, an' den he turns aroun' an' says, 'Yer insolen' ruffin!' he says, like dat. 'Oh, gee!' I says, 'oh, gee! git off d' eart'!' I says, like dat. See? 'Git off d' eart'!' like dat. Den deh blokie he got wild. He says I was a contempt'ble scoun'el, er somethin' like dat, an' he says I was doom' teh everlastin' pe'dition, er somethin' like dat. 'Gee!' I says, 'gee! Yer joshin' me,' I says. 'Yer joshin' me.' An' den I slugged 'im. See?"

With Jimmie in his company, Pete departed in a sort of blaze of glory from the Johnson home. Maggie, leaning from the window, watched him as he walked down the street. Here was a formidable man who disdained the strength of a world full of fists. Here was one who had contempt for brass-clothed power; one whose knuckles could ring defiantly against the granite of law. He was a knight.

The two men went from under the glimmering street lamp and passed into shadows. Turning, Maggie contemplated the dark, dust-stained walls, and the scant and crude furniture of her home. A clock, in a splintered and battered oblong box of varnished wood, she suddenly regarded as an abomination. She noted that it ticked raspingly. The almost vanished flowers in the carpet pattern, she conceived to be newly hideous. Some faint attempts which she had made with blue ribbon to freshen the appearance of a dingy curtain, she now saw to be piteous.

She wondered what Pete dined on.

She reflected upon the collar-and-cuff factory. It began to appear to her mind as a dreary place of endless grinding. Pete's elegant occupation brought him, no doubt, into contact with people who had money and manners. It was probable that he had a large acquaintance with pretty girls. He must have great sums of money to spend.

To her the earth was composed of hardships and insults. She felt instant admiration for a man who openly defied it. She thought that if the grim angel of death should clutch his heart, Pete would shrug his shoulders and say, "Oh, ev'ryt'ing goes."

She anticipated that he would come again shortly. She spent some of her week's pay in the purchase of flowered cretonne for a lambrequin. She made it with infinite care, and hung it to the slightly careening mantel over the stove in the kitchen. She studied it with painful anxiety from different points in the room. She wanted it to look well on Sunday night when, perhaps, Jimmie's friend would come. On Sunday night, however, Pete did not appear. Afterward the girl looked at it with a sense of humiliation. She was now convinced that Pete was superior to admiration for lambrequins.

A few evenings later Pete entered with fascinating innovations in his apparel. As she had seen him twice and he wore a different suit each time, Maggie had a dim impression that his wardrobe was prodigious.

"Say, Mag," he said, "put on yer bes' duds Friday night an' I'll take yehs t' d' show. See?" He spent a few moments in flourishing his clothes, and then vanished without having glanced at the lambrequin.

Over the eternal collars and cuffs in the factory Maggie spent the most of three days in making imaginary sketches of Pete and his daily environment. She imagined some half-dozen women in love with him, and thought he must lean dangerously toward an indefinite one whom she pictured as endowed with great charms of person, but with an altogether contemptible disposition. She thought he must live in a blare of pleasure. He had friends and people who were afraid of him. She saw the golden glitter of the place where Pete was to take her. It would be an entertainment of many hues and many melodies, where she was afraid she might appear small and mouse-coloured.

Her mother drank whisky all Friday morning. With lurid face and tossing hair she cursed and destroyed furniture all Friday afternoon. When Maggie came home at half-past six her mother lay asleep amid the wreck of chairs and a table. Fragments of various household utensils were scattered about the floor. She had vented some phase of drunken fury upon the lambrequin. It lay in a bedraggled heap in the corner.

"Hah!" she snorted, sitting up suddenly, "where yeh been? Why don' yeh come home earlier? Been loafin' 'round d' streets. Yer gittin' t' be a reg'lar devil."

When Pete arrived, Maggie, in a worn black dress, was waiting for him in the midst of a floor strewn with wreckage. The curtain at the window had been pulled by a heavy hand and hung by one tack, dangling to and fro in the draught through the cracks at the sash. The knots of blue ribbons appeared like violated flowers. The fire in the stove had gone out. The displaced lids and open doors showed heaps of sullen grey ashes. The remnants of a meal, ghastly, lay in a corner. Maggie's mother, stretched on the floor, blasphemed, and gave her daughter a bad name.

VII

An orchestra of yellow silk women and bald-headed men, on an elevated stage near the centre of a great green-hued hall, played a popular waltz. The place was crowded with people grouped about little tables. A battalion of waiters slid among the throng, carrying trays of beer-glasses, and making change from the inexhaustible vaults of their trousers pockets. Little boys, in the costumes of French chefs, paraded up and down the irregular aisles vending fancy cakes. There was a low rumble of conversation and a subdued clinking of glasses. Clouds of tobacco smoke rolled and wavered high in air above the dull gilt of the chandeliers.

The vast crowd had an air throughout of having just quitted labour. Men with calloused hands, and attired in garments that showed the wear of an endless drudging for a living, smoked their pipes contentedly and spent five, ten, or perhaps fifteen cents for beer. There was a mere sprinkling of men who smoked cigars purchased elsewhere. The great body of the crowd was composed of people who showed that all day they strove with their hands. Quiet Germans, with maybe their wives and two or three children, sat listening to the music, with the expressions of happy cows. An occasional party of sailors from a warship, their faces pictures of sturdy health, spent the earlier hours of the evening at the small round tables. Very infrequent tipsy men, swollen with the value of their opinions, engaged their companions in earnest and confidential conversation. In the balcony, and here and there below, shone the impassive faces of women. The nationalities of the Bowery beamed upon the stage from all directions.

Pete walked aggressively up a side aisle and took seats with Maggie at a table beneath the balcony. "Two beehs!" Leaning back, he regarded with eyes of superiority the scene before them. This attitude affected Maggie strongly. A man who could regard such a sight with indifference must be accustomed to very great things. It was obvious that Pete had visited this place many times before, and was very familiar with it. A knowledge of this fact made Maggie feel little and new.

He was extremely gracious and attentive. He displayed the consideration of a cultured gentleman who knew what was due. "Say, what's eatin' yeh? Bring d' lady a big glass! What use is dat pony?"

"Don't be fresh, now," said the waiter, with some warmth, as he departed.

"Ah, git off d' eart'!" said Pete, after the other's retreating form.

Maggie perceived that Pete brought forth all his elegance and all his knowledge of high-class customs for her benefit. Her heart warmed as she reflected upon his condescension.

The orchestra of yellow silk women and bald-headed men gave vent to a few bars of anticipatory music, and a girl, in a pink dress with short skirts, galloped upon the stage. She smiled upon the throng as if in acknowledgment of a warm welcome, and began to walk to and fro, mak-

ing profuse gesticulations, and singing, in brazen soprano
tones, a song the words of which were inaudible. When
she broke into the swift rattling measures of a chorus some
half-tipsy men near the stage joined in the rollicking re-
frain, and glasses were pounded rhythmically upon the
tables. People leaned forward to watch her and to try to
catch the words of the song. When she vanished there were
long rollings of applause. Obedient to more anticipatory
bars, she reappeared among the half-suppressed cheering
of the tipsy men. The orchestra plunged into dance music,
and the laces of the dancer fluttered and flew in the glare
of gas-jets. She divulged the fact that she was attired in
some half-dozen skirts. It was patent that any one of them
would have proved adequate for the purpose for which
skirts are intended. An occasional man bent forward, intent upon the pink stockings. Maggie wondered at the
splendour of the costume and lost herself in calculations
of the cost of the silks and laces.

The dancer's smile of enthusiasm was turned for ten
minutes upon the faces of her audience. In the finale she
fell into some of those grotesque attitudes which were at
the time popular among the dancers in the theatres up-
town, giving to the Bowery public the diversions of the
aristocratic theatre-going public at reduced rates.

"Say, Pete," said Maggie, leaning forward, "dis is great."

"Sure!" said Pete, with proper complacence.

A ventriloquist followed the dancer. He held two fantastic dolls on his knees. He made them sing mournful
ditties and say funny things about geography and Ireland.

"Do dose little men talk?" asked Maggie.

"Naw," said Pete, "it's some big jolly. See?"

Two girls, set down on the bills as sisters, came forth
and sang a duet which is heard occasionally at concerts
given under church auspices. They supplemented it with
a dance, which, of course, can never be seen at concerts
given under church auspices.

After they had retired, a woman of debatable age sang
a negro melody. The chorus necessitated some grotesque

waddlings supposed to be an imitation of a plantation darky, under the influence, probably, of music and the moon. The audience was just enthusiastic enough over it to make her return and sing a sorrowful lay, whose lines told of a mother's love, and a sweetheart who waited, and a young man who was lost at sea under harrowing circumstances. From the faces of a score or so in the crowd the self-contained look faded. Many heads were bent forward with eagerness and sympathy. As the last distressing sentiment of the piece was brought forth, it was greeted by the kind of applause which rings as sincere.

As a final effort, the singer rendered some verses which described a vision of Britain annihilated by America, and Ireland bursting her bonds. A carefully prepared climax was reached in the last line of the last verse, when the singer threw out her arms and cried, "The star-spangled banner." Instantly a great cheer swelled from the throats of this assemblage of the masses, most of them of foreign birth. There was a heavy rumble of booted feet thumping the floor. Eyes gleamed with sudden fire, and calloused hands waved frantically in the air.

After a few moments' rest, the orchestra played noisily, and a small fat man burst out upon the stage. He began to roar a song and to stamp back and forth before the footlights, wildly waving a silk hat and throwing leers broadcast. He made his face into fantastic grimaces until he looked like a devil on a Japanese kite. The crowd laughed gleefully. His short, fat legs were never still a moment. He shouted and roared and bobbed his shock of red wig until the audience broke out in excited applause.

Pete did not pay much attention to the progress of events upon the stage. He was drinking beer and watching Maggie. Her cheeks were blushing with excitement and her eyes were glistening. She drew deep breaths of pleasure. No thoughts of the atmosphere of the collar-and-cuff factory came to her.

With the final crash of the orchestra they jostled their way to the sidewalk in the crowd. Pete took Maggie's arm and pushed a way for her, offering to fight with a man or two. They reached Maggie's home at a late hour and stood for a moment in front of the gruesome doorway.

"Say, Mag," said Pete, "give us a kiss for takin' yeh t d' show, will yer?"

Maggie laughed, as if startled, and drew away from him. "Naw, Pete," she said, "dat wasn't in it."

"Ah, why wasn't it?" urged Pete.

The girl retreated nervously.

"Ah, go ahn!" repeated he.

Maggie darted into the hall and up the stairs. She turned and smiled at him, then disappeared

Pete walked slowly down the street. He had something of an astonished expression upon his features. He paused under a lamp-post and breathed a low breath of surprise. "Gee!" he said, "I wonner if I've been played fer a duffer."

VIII

As thoughts of Pete came to Maggie's mind, she began to have an intense dislike for all of her dresses. "What ails yeh? What makes ye be allus fixin' and fussin'?" her mother would frequently roar at her. She began to note with more interest the well-dressed women she met on the avenues. She envied elegance and soft palms. She craved those adornments of person which she saw every day on the street, conceiving them to be allies of vast importance to women. Studying faces, she thought many of the women and girls she chanced to meet smiled with serenity as though for ever cherished and watched over by those they loved.

The air in the collar-and-cuff establishment strangled her. She knew she was gradually and surely shrivelling in the hot, stuffy room. The begrimed windows rattled incessantly from the passing of elevated trains. The place was filled with a whirl of noises and odours. She became lost in thought as she looked at some of the grizzled women in the room, mere mechanical contrivances sewing seams and grinding out, with heads bent over their work, tales of imagined or real girlhood happiness, or of past drunks, or the baby at home, and unpaid wages. She wondered how long her youth would endure. She began to see the bloom upon her cheeks as something of value. She imagined herself, in an exasperating future, as a scrawny woman with an eternal grievance. She thought Pete to be a very fastidious person concerning the appearance of women.

She felt that she should love to see somebody entangle their fingers in the oily beard of the fat foreigner who owned the establishment. He was a detestable character. He wore white socks with low shoes. He sat all day delivering orations in the depths of a cushioned chair. His pocket-book deprived them of the power of retort. "What do you sink I pie fife dolla a week for? Play? No, py tamn!"

Maggie was anxious for a friend to whom she could talk about Pete. She would have liked to discuss his admirable mannerisms with a reliable mutual friend. At home, she found her mother often drunk and always raving. It seemed that the world had treated this woman very badly, and she took a deep revenge upon such portions of it as came within her reach. She broke furniture as if she were at last getting her rights. She swelled with virtuous indignation as she carried the lighter articles of household use, one by one, under the shadows of the three gilt balls, where Hebrews chained them with chains of interest.

Jimmie came when he was obliged to by circumstances over which he had no control. His well-trained legs brought him staggering home and put him to bed some nights when he would rather have gone elsewhere.

Swaggering Pete loomed like a golden sun to Maggie. He took her to a dime museum, where rows of meek freaks astonished her. She contemplated their deformities with awe, and thought them a sort of chosen tribe. Pete, racking his brains for amusement, discovered the Central Park Menagerie and the Museum of Arts. Sunday afternoons would sometimes find them at these places. Pete did not appear to be particularly interested in what he saw.

He stood around looking heavy, while Maggie giggled in glee.

Once at the menagerie he went into a trance of admiration before the spectacle of a very small monkey threatening to thrash a cageful because one of them had pulled his tail and he had not wheeled about quickly enough to discover who did it. Ever after Pete knew that monkey by sight, and winked at him, trying to induce him to fight with other and larger monkeys.

At the museum, Maggie said, "Dis is outa sight!"

"Aw, rats!" said Pete; "wait till next summer an' I'll take yehs to a picnic."

While the girl wandered in the vaulted rooms, Pete occupied himself in returning, stony stare for stony stare, the appalling scrutiny of the watch-dogs of the treasures. Occasionally he would remark in loud tones, "Dat jay has got glass eyes," and sentences of the sort. When he tired of this amusement he would go to the mummies and moralize over them.

Usually he submitted with silent dignity to all that he had to go through, but at times he was goaded into comment. "Aw!" he demanded once. "Look at all dese little jugs! Hundred jugs in a row! Ten rows in a case, an' 'bout a t'ousand cases! What d' blazes use is dem?"

In the evenings of week days he often took her to see plays in which the dazzling heroine was rescued from the palatial home of her treacherous guardian by the hero with the beautiful sentiments. The latter spent most of his time out at soak in pale-green snow-storms, busy with a nickel-plated revolver rescuing aged strangers from villains. Maggie lost herself in sympathy with the wanderers swooning in snow-storms beneath happy-hued church windows, while a choir within sang "Joy to the World." To Maggie and the rest of the audience this was transcendental realism. Joy always within, and they, like the actor, inevitably without. Viewing it, they hugged themselves in ecstatic pity of their imagined or real condition. The girl thought the arrogance and granite-heartedness of the magnate of the play were very accurately drawn. She echoed the male-dictions that the occupants of the gallery showered on this individual when his lines compelled him to expose his extreme selfishness.

Shady persons in the audience revolted from the pictured villainy of the drama. With untiring zeal they hissed vice and applauded virtue. Unmistakably bad men evinced an apparently sincere admiration for virtue. The loud gallery was overwhelmingly with the unfortunate and the oppressed. They encouraged the struggling hero with cries, and jeered the villain, hooting and calling attention to his whiskers. When anybody died in the pale-green snow-storms, the gallery mourned. They sought out the painted misery and hugged it as akin.

In the hero's erratic march from poverty in the first act to wealth and triumph in the final one, in which he forgives all the enemies that he has left, he was assisted by the gallery, which applauded his generous and noble sentiments and confounded the speeches of his opponents by making irrelevant but very sharp remarks. Those actors who were cursed with the parts of villains were confronted at every turn by the gallery. If one of them rendered lines containing the most subtle distinctions between right and wrong, the gallery was immediately aware that the actor meant wickedness, and denounced him accordingly. The last act was a triumph for the hero, poor and of the masses, the representative of the audience, over the villain and the rich man, his pockets stuffed with bonds, his heart packed with tyrannical purposes, imperturbable amid suffering.

Maggie always departed with raised spirits from these melodramas. She rejoiced at the way in which the poor and virtuous eventually overcame the wealthy and wicked. The theatre made her think. She wondered if the culture and refinement she had seen imitated, perhaps grotesquely, by the heroine on the stage, could be acquired by a girl who lived in a tenement house and worked in a shirt factory.

IX

A group of urchins were intent upon the side door of a saloon. Expectancy gleamed from their eyes. They were twisting their fingers in excitement. "Here she comes!" yelled one of them suddenly. The group of urchins burst instantly asunder and its individual fragments were spread in a wide, respectable half-circle about the point of interest. The saloon door opened with a crash, and the figure of a woman appeared upon the threshold. Her grey hair fell in knotted masses about her shoulders. Her face was crimsoned and wet with perspiration. Her eyes had a rolling glare. "Not a cent more of me money will yehs ever get —not a red! I spent me money here fer t'ree years, an' now yehs tells me yeh'll sell me no more stuff! Go fall on yerself, Johnnie Murckre! 'Disturbance'? Disturbance be blowed! Go fall on yerself, Johnnie—"

The door received a kick of exasperation from within, and the woman lurched heavily out on the sidewalk. The gamins in the half-circle became violently agitated. They began to dance about and hoot and yell and jeer. A wide dirty grin spread over each face.

The woman made a furious dash at a particularly outrageous cluster of little boys. They laughed delightedly, and scampered off a short distance, calling out to her over their shoulders. She stood tottering on the kerb-stone and thundered at them. "Yeh devil's kids!" she howled, shaking her fists. The little boys whooped in glee. As she started up the street they fell in behind and marched uproariously. Occasionally she wheeled about and made charges on them. They ran nimbly out of reach and taunted her.

In the frame of a gruesome doorway she stood for a moment cursing them. Her hair straggled, giving her red features a look of insanity. Her great fists quivered as she shook them madly in the air. The urchins made terrific noises until she turned and disappeared. Then they filed off quietly in the way they had come.

The woman floundered about in the lower hall of the

tenement house, and finally stumbled up the stairs. On an upper hall a door was opened and a collection of heads peered curiously out, watching her. With a wrathful snort the woman confronted the door, but it was slammed hastily in her face and the key was turned.

She stood for a few minutes, delivering a frenzied challenge at the panels. "Come out in deh hall, Mary Murphy, if yehs want a scrap! Come ahn! yeh overgrown terrier, come ahn!" She began to kick the door. She shrilly defied the universe to appear and do battle. Her cursing trebles brought heads from all doors save the one she threatened. Her eyes glared in every direction. The air was full of her tossing fists. "Come ahn! deh hull gang of yehs, come ahn!" she roared at the spectators. An oath or two, cat-calls, jeers, and bits of facetious advice were given in reply. Missiles clattered about her feet.

"What's wrong wi'che?" said a voice in the gathered gloom, and Jimmie came forward. He carried a tin dinner-pail in his hand and under his arm a truckman's brown apron done in a bundle. "What's wrong?" he demanded.

"Come out! all of yehs, come out," his mother was howling. "Come ahn an' I'll stamp yer faces t'rough d' floor."

"Shet yer face, an' come home, yeh old fool!" roared Jimmie at her. She strode up to him and twirled her fingers in his face. Her eyes were darting flames of unreasoning rage, and her frame trembled with eagerness for a fight.

"An' who are youse? I ain't givin' a snap of me fingers fer youse!" she bawled at him. She turned her huge back in tremendous disdain and climbed the stairs to the next floor.

Jimmie followed, and at the top of the flight he seized his mother's arm and started to drag her toward the door of their room. "Come home!" he gritted between his teeth.

"Take yer hands off me! Take yer hands off me!" shrieked his mother. She raised her arm and whirled her great fist at her son's face. Jimmie dodged his head, and the blow struck him in the back of the neck. "Come

home!" he gritted again. He threw out his left hand and
writhed his fingers about her middle arm. The mother and
the son began to sway and struggle like gladiators.

"Whoop!" said the Rum Alley tenement house. The hall
filled with interested spectators. "Hi, ol' lady, dat was a
dandy!" "T'ree t' one on d' red!" "Ah, quit yer scrappin'!"

The door of the Johnson home opened and Maggie
looked out. Jimmie made a supreme cursing effort and
hurled his mother into the room. He quickly followed and
closed the door. The Rum Alley tenement swore disap-
pointedly and retired.

The mother slowly gathered herself up from the floor.
Her eyes glittered menacingly upon her children.

"Here now," said Jimmie, "we've had enough of dis.
Sit down, an' don' make no trouble."

He grasped her arm and, twisting it, forced her into a
creaking chair.

"Keep yer hands off me!" roared his mother again.

"Say, yeh ol' bat! Quit dat!" yelled Jimmie, madly. Maggie shrieked and ran into the other room. To her there
came the sound of a storm of crashes and curses. There
was a great final thump and Jimmie's voice cried: "Dere,
now! Stay still." Maggie opened the door now, and went
warily out. "Oh, Jimmie!"

He was leaning against the wall and swearing. Blood
stood upon bruises on his knotty forearms where they had
scraped against the floor or the walls in the scuffle. The
mother lay screeching on the floor, the tears running down
her furrowed face.

Maggie, standing in the middle of the room, gazed about
her. The usual upheaval of the tables and chairs had taken
place. Crockery was strewn broadcast in fragments. The
stove had been disturbed on its legs, and now leaned idioti-
cally to one side. A pail had been upset and water spread
in all directions.

The door opened and Pete appeared. He shrugged his
shoulders. "Oh, gee!" he observed. He walked over to
Maggie and whispered in her ear: "Ah, what d' hell, Mag?
Come ahn and we'll have a outa-sight time."

The mother in the corner upreared her head and shook her tangled locks. "Aw, yer bote no good, needer of yehs," she said, glowering at her daughter in the gloom. Her eyes seemed to burn balefully. "Yeh've gone t' d' devil, Mag Johnson, yehs knows yehs have gone t' d' devil. Yer a disgrace t' yer people. An' now, git out an' go ahn wid dat doe-faced jude of yours. Go wid him, curse yeh, an' a good riddance. Go, an' see how yeh likes it."

Maggie gazed long at her mother.

"Go now, an' see how yeh likes it. Git out. I won't have sech as youse in me house! Git out, d' yeh hear! Damn yeh, git out!"

The girl began to tremble.

At this instant Pete came forward. "Oh, what d' hell, Mag, see?" whispered he softly in her ear. "Dis all blows over. See? D' ol' woman'll be all right in d' mornin'. Come ahn out wid me! We'll have a outa-sight time."

The woman on the floor cursed. Jimmie was intent upon his bruised forearms. The girl cast a glance about the room filled with a chaotic mass of *débris,* and at the writhing body of her mother.

"Git th' devil outa here."

Maggie went.

X

Jimmie had an idea it wasn't common courtesy for a friend to come to one's home and ruin one's sister. But he was not sure how much Pete knew about the rules of politeness.

The following night he returned home from work at a rather late hour in the evening. In passing through the halls he came upon the gnarled and leathery old woman who possessed the music-box. She was grinning in the dim light that drifted through dust-stained panes. She beckoned to him with a smudged forefinger.

"Ah, Jimmie, what do yehs t'ink I tumbled to, las' night! It was deh funnies' t'ing I ever saw," she cried, coming close to him and leering. She was trembling with eagerness to tell her tale. "I was by me door las' night when

yer sister and her jude feller came in late, oh, very late.
An' she, the dear, she was a-cryin' as if her heart would
break, she was. It was deh funnies' t'ing I ever saw. An'
right out here by me door she asked him did he love her,
did he. An' she was a-crying as if her heart would break,
poor t'ing. An' him, I could see be deh way what he said
it dat she had been askin' orften; he says, 'Oh, gee, yes,'
he says, says he. 'Oh, gee, yes.' "

Storm-clouds swept over Jimmie's face, but he turned
from the leathery old woman and plodded on upstairs.

" 'Oh, gee, yes,' " she called after him. She laughed a
laugh that was like a prophetic croak.

There was no one in at home. The rooms showed that
attempts had been made at tidying them. Parts of the
wreckage of the day before had been repaired by an un-
skilled hand. A chair or two and the table stood uncer-
tainly upon legs. The floor had been newly swept. The
blue ribbons had been restored to the curtains, and the
lambrequin, with its immense sheaves of yellow wheat and
red roses of equal size, had been returned, in a worn and
sorry state, to its place at the mantel. Maggie's jacket and
hat were gone from the nail behind the door.

Jimmie walked to the window and began to look through
the blurred glass. It occurred to him to wonder vaguely,
for an instant, if some of the women of his acquaintance
had brothers.

Suddenly, however, he began to swear. "But he was me
frien'! I brought 'im here! Dat's d' devil of it!" He fumed
about the room, his anger gradually rising to the furious
pitch. "I'll kill deh jay! Dat's what I'll do! I'll kill deh
jay!"

He clutched his hat and sprang toward the door. But it
opened, and his mother's great form blocked the passage.
"What's d' matter wid yeh?" exclaimed she, coming into
the rooms.

Jimmie gave vent to a sardonic curse and then laughed
heavily. "Well, Maggie's gone teh d' devil! Dat's what!
See?"

"Eh?" said his mother.

"Maggie's gone teh d' devil! Are yehs deaf?" roared Jimmie, impatiently.

"Aw, git out!" murmured the mother, astounded.

Jimmie grunted, and then began to stare out the window. His mother sat down in a chair, but a moment later sprang erect and delivered a maddened whirl of oaths. Her son turned to look at her as she reeled and swayed in the middle of the room, her fierce face convulsed with passion, her blotched arms raised high in imprecation.

"May she be cursed for ever!" she shrieked. "May she eat nothin' but stones and deh dirt in deh street. May she sleep in deh gutter an' never see deh sun shine again. D' bloomin'—"

"Here now," said her son. "Go fall on yerself, an' quit dat."

The mother raised lamenting eyes to the ceiling. "She's d' devil's own chil', Jimmie," she whispered. "Ah, who would t'ink such a bad girl could grow up in our fambly, Jimmie, me son. Many d' hour I've spent in talk wid dat girl an' tol' her if she ever went on d' streets I'd see her damned. An' after all her bringin'-up an' what I tol' her and talked wid her, she goes teh d' bad, like a duck teh water."

The tears rolled down her furrowed face. Her hands trembled. "An den when dat Sadie MacMallister next door to us was sent teh d' devil by dat feller what worked in d' soap factory, didn't I tell our Mag dat if she—"

"Ah, dat's anudder story," interrupted the brother. "Of course, dat Sadie was nice an' all dat—but—see?—it ain't dessame as if—well, Maggie was diff'ent—see?—she was diff'ent." He was trying to formulate a theory that he had always unconsciously held, that all sisters excepting his own could, advisedly, be ruined.

He suddenly broke out again. "I'll go t'ump d' mug what done her d' harm. I'll kill 'im! He t'inks he kin scrap, but when he gits me a-chasin' 'im he'll fin' out where he's wrong, d' big stiff! I'll wipe up d' street wid 'im." In a fury he plunged out the doorway.

As he vanished the mother raised her head and lifted

both hands, entreating. "May she be cursed for ever!" she
cried.

In the darkness of the hallway Jimmie discerned a knot
of women talking volubly. When he strode by they paid
no attention to him. "She allus was a bold thing," he heard
one of them cry in an eager voice. "Dere wasn't a feller
come teh deh house but she'd try teh mash 'im. My Annie
says deh shameless t'ing tried teh ketch her feller, her own
feller, what we useter know his fader."

"I could 'a' tol' yehs dis two years ago," said a woman,
in a key of triumph. "Yes, sir, it was over two years ago
dat I says teh my ol' man, I says, 'Dat Johnson girl ain't
straight,' I says. 'Oh, rats!' he says. 'Oh, hell!' 'Dat's all
right,' I says, 'but I know what I knows,' I says, 'an' it'll
come out later. You wait an' see,' I says, 'you see.' "

"Anybody what had eyes could see dat dere was somethin' wrong wid dat girl. I didn't like her actions."

On the street Jimmie met a friend. "What's wrong?"
asked the latter.

Jimmie explained. "An' I'll t'ump 'im till he can't stand."

"Oh, go ahn!" said the friend. "What's deh use! Yeh'll
git pulled in! Everybody'ill be on to it! An' ten plunks!
Gee!"

Jimmie was determined. "He t'inks he kin scrap, but
he'll fin' out diff'ent."

"Gee!" remonstrated the friend, "what's d' use?"

XI

On a corner a glass-fronted building shed a yellow glare
upon the pavements. The open mouth of a saloon called
seductively to passengers to enter and annihilate sorrow
or create rage.

The interior of the place was papered in olive and
bronze tints of imitation leather. A shining bar of coun-
terfeit massiveness extended down the side of the room.
Behind it a great mahogany-imitation sideboard reached
the ceiling. Upon its shelves rested pyramids of shimmering glasses that were never disturbed. Mirrors set in the
face of the sideboard multiplied them. Lemons, oranges,

and paper napkins, arranged with mathematical precision, sat among the glasses. Many-hued decanters of liquor perched at regular intervals on the lower shelves. A nickel-plated cash-register occupied a place in the exact centre of the general effect. The elementary senses of it all seemed to be opulence and geometrical accuracy.

Across from the bar a smaller counter held a collection of plates upon which swarmed frayed fragments of crackers, slices of boiled ham, dishevelled bits of cheese, and pickles swimming in vinegar. An odour of grasping, begrimed hands and munching mouths pervaded all.

Pete, in a white jacket, was behind the bar bending expectantly toward a quiet stranger. "A beeh," said the man. Pete drew a foam-topped glassful, and set it dripping upon the bar.

At this moment the light bamboo doors at the entrance swung open and crashed against the wall. Jimmie and a companion entered. They swaggered unsteadily but belligerently toward the bar, and looked at Pete with bleared and blinking eyes.

"Gin," said Jimmie.

"Gin," said the companion.

Pete slid a bottle and two glasses along the bar. He bent his head sideways as he assiduously polished away with a napkin at the gleaming wood. He wore a look of watchfulness.

Jimmie and his companion kept their eyes upon the bartender and conversed loudly in tones of contempt.

"He's a dandy masher, ain't he?" laughed Jimmie.

"Well, ain't he!" said the companion, sneering. "He's great, he is. Git on to deh mug on deh blokie. Dat's enough to make a feller turn handsprings in 'is sleep."

The quiet stranger moved himself and his glass a trifle farther away and maintained an attitude of obliviousness.

"Gee! ain't he hot stuff?"

"Git on to his shape!"

"Hey!" cried Jimmie, in tones of command. Pete came along slowly, with a sullen dropping of the under lip.

"Well," he growled, "what's eatin' yehs?"

"Gin," said Jimmie.

"Gin," said the companion.

As Pete confronted them with the bottle and the glasses
they laughed in his face. Jimmie's companion, evidently
overcome with merriment, pointed a grimy forefinger in
Pete's direction. "Say, Jimmie," demanded he, "what's dat
behind d' bar?"

"Looks like some chump," replied Jimmie. They laughed
loudly.

Pete put down a bottle with a bang and turned a formidable face toward them. He disclosed his teeth, and his
shoulders heaved restlessly. "You fellers can't guy me," he
said. "Drink yer stuff an' git out an' don' make no
trouble."

Instantly the laughter faded from the faces of the two
men, and expressions of offended dignity immediately
came. "Aw, who has said anyt'ing t' you?" cried they in
the same breath.

The quiet stranger looked at the door calculatingly.

"Ah, come off," said Pete to the two men. "Don't pick
me up fer no jay. Drink yer rum an' git out an' don'
make no trouble."

"Aw, go ahn!" airily cried Jimmie.

"Aw, go ahn!" airily repeated his companion.

"We goes when we git ready! See?" continued Jimmie.

"Well," said Pete in a threatening voice, "don' make no
trouble."

Jimmie suddenly leaned forward with his head on one
side. He snarled like a wild animal. "Well, what if we
does? See?" said he.

Hot blood flushed into Pete's face, and he shot a lurid
glance at Jimmie. "Well, den we'll see who's d' bes' man,
you or me," he said.

The quiet stranger moved modestly toward the door.

Jimmie began to swell with valour. "Don' pick me up
fer no tenderfoot. When yeh tackles me yeh tackles one
of d' bes' men in d' city. See? I'm a scrapper, I am. Ain't
dat right, Billie?"

"Sure, Mike," responded his companion in tones of conviction.

"Aw!" said Pete, easily. "Go fall on yerself."

The two men again began to laugh.

"What is dat talking?" cried the companion.

"Don' ast me," replied Jimmie with exaggerated contempt.

Pete made a furious gesture. "Git outa here now, an' don' make no trouble. See? Youse fellers er lookin' fer a scrap, an' it's like yeh'll fin' one if yeh keeps on shootin' off yer mout's. I know yehs! See? I kin lick better men dan yehs ever saw in yer lifes. Dat's right! See? Don' pick me up fer no stiff, er yeh might be jolted out in d' street before yeh knows where yeh is. When I comes from behind dis bar, I t'rows yehs bote inteh d' street. See?"

"Ah, go ahn!" cried the two men in chorus.

The glare of a panther came into Pete's eyes. "Dat's what I said! Unnerstan'?"

He came through a passage at the end of the bar and swelled down upon the two men. They stepped promptly forward and crowded close to him. They bristled like three roosters. They moved their heads pugnaciously and kept their shoulders braced. The nervous muscles about each mouth twitched with a forced smile of mockery.

"Well, what yer goin' t' do?" gritted Jimmie.

Pete stepped warily back, waving his hands before him to keep the men from coming too near.

"Well, what yer goin' t' do?" repeated Jimmie's ally. They kept close to him, taunting and leering. They strove to make him attempt the initial blow.

"Keep back now! Don' crowd me," said Pete ominously.

Again they chorused in contempt. "Aw, go ahn!"

In a small, tossing group, the three men edged for positions like frigates contemplating battle.

"Well, why don' yeh try t' t'row us out?" cried Jimmie and his ally with copious sneers.

The bravery of bulldogs sat upon the faces of the men. Their clenched fists moved like eager weapons. The allied

two jostled the bartender's elbows, glaring at him with
feverish eyes and forcing him toward the wall.

Suddenly Pete swore furiously. The flash of action
gleamed from his eyes. He threw back his arm and aimed
a tremendous, lightning-like blow at Jimmie's face. His
foot swung a step forward and the weight of his body was
behind his fist. Jimmie ducked his head, Bowery-like, with
the quickness of a cat. The fierce answering blows of
Jimmie and his ally crushed on Pete's bowed head.

The quiet stranger vanished.

The arms of the combatants whirled in the air like
flails. The faces of the men, at first flushed to flame-
coloured anger, now began to fade to the pallor of warriors
in the blood and heat of a battle. Their lips curled back
and stretched tightly over the gums in ghoul-like grins.
Through their white, gripped teeth struggled hoarse whisperings of oaths. Their eyes glittered with murderous fire.

Each head was huddled between its owner's shoulders,
and arms were swinging with marvellous rapidity. Feet
scraped to and fro with a loud scratching sound upon the
sanded floor. Blows left crimson blotches upon the pale
skin. The curses of the first quarter-minute of the fight
died away. The breaths of the fighters came wheezing from
their lips and the three chests were straining and heaving.
Pete at intervals gave vent to low, laboured hisses, that
sounded like a desire to kill. Jimmie's ally gibbered at times
like a wounded maniac. Jimmie was silent, fighting with
the face of a sacrificial priest. The rage of fear shone in
all their eyes, and their blood-coloured fists whirled.

At a critical moment a blow from Pete's hand struck
the ally, and he crashed to the floor. He wriggled instantly
to his feet and, grasping the quiet stranger's beer-glass from
the bar, hurled it at Pete's head.

High on the wall it burst like a bomb, shivering fragments flying in all directions. Then missiles came to every
man's hand. The place had heretofore appeared free of
things to throw, but suddenly glasses and bottles went
singing through the air. They were thrown point-blank at
bobbing heads. The pyramids of shimmering glasses, that

had never been disturbed, changed to cascades as heavy bottles were flung into them. Mirrors splintered to nothing.

The three frothing creatures on the floor buried themselves in a frenzy for blood. There followed in the wake of missiles and fists some unknown prayers, perhaps for death.

The quiet stranger had sprawled very pyrotechnically out on the sidewalk. A laugh ran up and down the avenue for the half of a block. "Dey've t'rowed a bloke inteh deh street."

People heard the sound of breaking glass and shuffling feet within the saloon and came running. A small group, bending down to look under the bamboo doors, and watching the fall of glass and three pairs of violent legs, changed in a moment to a crowd. A policeman came charging down the sidewalk and bounced through the doors into the saloon. The crowd bent and surged in absorbing anxiety to see.

Jimmie caught the first sight of the oncoming interruption. On his feet he had the same regard for a policeman that, when on his truck, he had for a fire-engine. He howled and ran for the side door.

The officer made a terrific advance, club in hand. One comprehensive sweep of the long night-stick threw the ally to the floor and forced Pete to a corner. With his disengaged hand he made a furious effort at Jimmie's coat-tails. Then he regained his balance and paused. "Well, well, you are a pair of pictures. What have ye been up to?"

Jimmie, with his face drenched in blood, escaped up a side street, pursued a short distance by some of the more law-loving or excited individuals of the crowd.

Later, from a safe dark corner, he saw the policeman, the ally, and the bartender emerge from the saloon. Pete locked the doors and then followed up the avenue in the rear of the crowd-encompassed policeman and his charge.

At first Jimmie, with his heart throbbing at battle heat, started to go desperately to the rescue of his friend, but he halted. "Ah, what's d' use?" he demanded of himself.

XII

In a hall of irregular shape sat Pete and Maggie drinking beer. A submissive orchestra dictated to by a spectacled man with frowsy hair and in soiled evening dress, industriously followed the bobs of his head and the waves of his baton. A ballad-singer, in a gown of flaming scarlet, sang in the inevitable voice of brass. When she vanished, men seated at the tables near the front applauded loudly, pounding the polished wood with their beer-glasses. She returned attired in less gown, and sang again. She received another enthusiastic encore. She reappeared in still less gown and danced. The deafening rumble of glasses and clapping of hands that followed her exit indicated an overwhelming desire to have her come on for the fourth time, but the curiosity of the audience was not gratified.

Maggie was pale. From her eyes had been plucked all look of self-reliance. She leaned with a dependent air toward her companion. She was timid, as if fearing his anger or displeasure. She seemed to beseech tenderness of him.

Pete's air of distinguished valour had grown upon him until it threatened to reach stupendous dimensions. He was infinitely gracious to the girl. It was apparent to her that his condescension was a marvel. He could appear to strut even while sitting still, and he showed that he was a lion of lordly characteristics by the air with which he spat.

With Maggie gazing at him wonderingly, he took pride in commanding the waiters, who were, however, indifferent or deaf. "Hi, you, git a russle on yehs! What yehs lookin' at? Two more beehs, d' yeh hear?" He leaned back and critically regarded the person of a girl with a straw-coloured wig who was flinging her heels about upon the stage in somewhat awkward imitation of a well-known *danseuse*.

At times Maggie told Pete long confidential tales of her former home life, dwelling upon the escapades of the other members of the family and the difficulties she had had to combat in order to obtain a degree of comfort. He responded in the accents of philanthropy. He pressed her arm with an air of reassuring proprietorship.

"Dey was cursed jays," he said, denouncing the mother and brother.

The sound of the music which, through the efforts of the frowsy-headed leader, drifted to her ears in the smoke-filled atmosphere, made the girl dream. She thought of her former Rum Alley environment and turned to regard Pete's strong protecting fists. She thought of a collar-and-cuff manufactory and the eternal moan of the proprietor: "What een hale do you sink I pie fife dolla a week for? Play? No, py tamn!" She contemplated Pete's man-subduing eyes and noted that wealth and prosperity were indicated by his clothes. She imagined a future rose-tinted because of its distance from all that she had experienced before.

As to the present she perceived only vague reasons to be miserable. Her life was Pete's, and she considered him worthy of the charge. She would be disturbed by no particular apprehensions so long as Pete adored her as he now said he did. She did not feel like a bad woman. To her knowledge she had never seen any better.

At times men at other tables regarded the girl furtively. Pete, aware of it, nodded at her and grinned. He felt proud. "Mag, yer a bloomin' good looker," he remarked, studying her face through the haze. The men made Maggie fear, but she blushed at Pete's words as it became apparent to her that she was the apple of his eye.

Grey-headed men, wonderfully pathetic in their dissipation, stared at her through clouds. Smooth-cheeked boys, some of them with faces of stone and mouths of sin, not nearly so pathetic as the grey heads, tried to find the girl's eyes in the smoke-wreaths. Maggie considered she was not what they thought her. She confined her glances to Pete and the stage.

The orchestra played negro melodies, and a versatile drummer pounded, whacked, clattered, and scratched on a dozen machines to make noise.

Those glances of the men, shot at Maggie from under

half-closed lids, made her tremble. She thought them all to be worse men than Pete. "Come, let's go," she said.

As they went out Maggie perceived two women seated at a table with some men. They were painted, and their cheeks had lost their roundness. As she passed them the girl, with a shrinking movement, drew back her skirts.

XIII

Jimmie did not return home for a number of days after the fight with Pete in the saloon. When he did, he approached with extreme caution.

He found his mother raving. Maggie had not returned home. The parent continually wondered how her daughter could come to such a pass. She had never considered Maggie as a pearl dropped unstained into Rum Alley from Heaven, but she could not conceive how it was possible for her daughter to fall so low as to bring disgrace upon her family. She was terrific in denunciation of the girl's wickedness.

The fact that the neighbours talked of it maddened her. When women came in, and in the course of their conversation casually asked, "Where's Maggie dese days?" the mother shook her fuzzy head at them and appalled them with curses. Cunning hints inviting confidence she rebuffed with violence.

"An' wid all d' bringin'-up she had, how could she?" moaningly she asked of her son. "Wid all d' talkin' wid her I did an' d' t'ings I tol' her to remember. When a girl is bringed up d' way I bringed up Maggie, how kin she go teh d' devil?"

Jimmie was transfixed by these questions. He could not conceive how, under the circumstances, his mother's daughter and his sister could have been so wicked.

His mother took a drink from a bottle that sat on the table. She continued her lament. "She had a bad heart, dat girl did, Jimmie. She was wicked t' d' heart an' we never knowed it."

Jimmie nodded, admitting the fact.

"We lived in d' same house wid her an' I brought her up, an' we never knowed how bad she was."

Jimmie nodded again.

"Wid a home like dis an' a mudder like me, she went teh d' bad," cried the mother, raising her eyes.

One day Jimmie came home, sat down in a chair, and began to wriggle about with a new and strange nervousness. At last he spoke shamefacedly. "Well, look-a-here, dis t'ing queers us! See? We're queered! An' maybe it 'ud be better if I—well, I t'ink I kin look 'er up an'—maybe it 'ud be better if I fetched her home an'—"

The mother started from her chair and broke forth into a storm of passionate anger. "What! Let 'er come an' sleep under deh same roof wid her mudder agin? Oh, yes, I will, won't I! Sure! Shame on yehs, Jimmie Johnson, fer sayin' such a t'ing teh yer own mudder! Little did I t'ink when yehs was a baby playin' about me feet dat ye'd grow up teh say sech a t'ing teh yer mudder—yer own mudder. I never t'ought—"

Sobs choked her and interrupted her reproaches.

"Dere ain't nottin' teh make sech trouble about," said Jimmie. "I on'y says it 'ud be better if we keep dis t'ing dark, see? It queers us! See?"

His mother laughed a laugh that seemed to ring through the city and be echoed and re-echoed by countless other laughs. "Oh, yes, I will, won't I! Sure!"

"Well, yeh must take me fer a damn fool," said Jimmie, indignant at his mother for mocking him. "I didn't say we'd make 'er inteh a little tin angel, ner nottin', but deh way it is now she can queer us! Don'che see?"

"Ay, she'll git tired of deh life atter a while, an' den she'll wanna be a-comin' home, won' she, deh beast! I'll let 'er in den, won't I?"

"Well, I didn't mean none of dis prod'gal bus'ness anyway," explained Jimmie.

"It wa'n't no prod'gal daughter, yeh fool," said the mother. "It was prod'gal son, anyhow."

"I know dat," said Jimmie.

For a time they sat in silence. The mother's eyes gloated on the scene which her imagination called before her. Her lips were set in a vindictive smile. "Ay, she'll cry, won' she, an' carry on, an' tell how Pete, or some odder feller, beats 'er, an' she'll say she's sorry an' all dat, an' she ain't happy, she ain't, an' she wants to come home agin, she does." With grim humour the mother imitated the possible wailing notes of the daughter's voice. "Den I'll take 'er in, won't I? She kin cry 'er two eyes out on deh stones of deh street before I'll dirty d' place wid her. She abused an' ill-treated her own mudder—her own mudder what loved her, an' she'll never git anodder chance."

Jimmie thought he had a great idea of women's frailty, but he could not understand why any of his kin should be victims. "Curse her!" he said fervidly. Again he wondered vaguely if some of the women of his acquaintance had brothers. Nevertheless, his mind did not for an instant confuse himself with those brothers nor his sister with theirs.

After the mother had, with great difficulty, suppressed the neighbours, she went among them and proclaimed her grief. "May Heaven forgive dat girl," was her continual cry. To attentive ears she recited the whole length and breadth of her woes. "I bringed 'er up deh way a daughter oughta be bringed up, an' dis is how she served me! She went teh deh devil deh first chance she got! May Heaven forgive her."

When arrested for drunkenness she used the story of her daughter's downfall with telling effect upon the police justices. Finally one of them said to her, peering down over his spectacles: "Mary, the records of this and other courts show that you are the mother of forty-two daughters who have been ruined. The case is unparalleled in the annals of this court, and this court thinks—"

The mother went through life shedding large tears of sorrow. Her red face was a picture of agony.

Of course Jimmie publicly damned his sister that he might appear on a higher social plane. But, arguing with himself, stumbling about in ways that he knew not, he,

once, almost came to a conclusion that his sister would
have been more firmly good had she better known how.
However, he felt that he could not hold such a view. He
threw it hastily aside.

XIV

In a hilarious hall there were twenty-eight tables and
twenty-eight women and a crowd of smoking men. Valiant
noise was made on a stage at the end of the hall by an
orchestra composed of men who looked as if they had just
happened in. Soiled waiters ran to and fro, swooping down
like hawks on the unwary in the throng; clattering along
the aisles with trays covered with glasses; stumbling over
women's skirts and charging two prices for everything but
beer, all with a swiftness that blurred the view of the
coconut palms and dusty monstrosities painted upon the
walls of the room. A "bouncer," with an immense load of
business upon his hands, plunged about in the crowd,
dragging bashful strangers to prominent chairs, ordering
waiters here and there, and quarrelling furiously with men
who wanted to sing with the orchestra.

The usual smoke-cloud was present, but so dense that
heads and arms seemed entangled in it. The rumble of
conversation was replaced by a roar. Plenteous oaths
heaved through the air. The room rang with the shrill
voices of women bubbling over with drink-laughter. The
chief element in the music of the orchestra was speed. The
musicians played in intent fury. A woman was singing
and smiling upon the stage, but no one took notice of her.
The rate at which the piano, cornet, and violins were
going seemed to impart wildness to the half-drunken
crowd. Beer-glasses were emptied at a gulp and conversation became a rapid chatter. The smoke eddied and swirled
like a shadowy river hurrying toward some unseen falls.
Pete and Maggie entered the hall and took chairs at a
table near the door. The woman who was seated there
made an attempt to occupy Pete's attention, and, failing,
went away.

Three weeks had passed since the girl had left home. The air of spaniel-like dependence had been magnified and showed its direct effect in the peculiar off-handedness and ease of Pete's ways toward her. She followed Pete's eyes with hers, anticipating with smiles gracious looks from him.

A woman of brilliance and audacity, accompanied by a mere boy, came into the place and took a seat near them. At once Pete sprang to his feet, his face beaming with glad surprise. "Hully gee, dere's Nellie!" he cried. He went over to the table and held out an eager hand to the woman.

"Why, hello, Pete, me boy, how are you?" said she, giving him her fingers.

Maggie took instant note of the woman. She perceived that her black dress fitted her to perfection. Her linen collar and cuffs were spotless. Tan gloves were stretched over her well-shaped hands. A hat of a prevailing fashion perched jauntily upon her dark hair. She wore no jewellery and was painted with no apparent paint. She looked clear-eyed through the stares of the men.

"Sit down, and call your lady friend over," she said to Pete. At his beckoning Maggie came and sat between Pete and the mere boy.

"I t'ought yeh was gone away fer good," began Pete, at once. "When did yeh git back? How did dat Buff'lo business turn out?"

The woman shrugged her shoulders. "Well, he didn't have as many stamps as he tried to make out, so I shook him, that's all."

"Well, I'm glad teh see yehs back in deh city," said Pete, with gallantry. He and the woman entered into a long conversation, exchanging reminiscences of days together. Maggie sat still, unable to formulate an intelligent sentence as her addition to the conversation, and painfully aware of it.

She saw Pete's eyes sparkle as he gazed upon the handsome stranger. He listened smilingly to all she said. The woman was familiar with all his affairs, asked him about mutual friends, and knew the amount of his salary. She paid no attention to Maggie, looking toward her once or twice and apparently seeing the wall beyond.

The mere boy was sulky. In the beginning he had welcomed the additions with acclamations. "Let's all have a drink! What'll you take, Nell? And you, Miss What's-your-name. Have a drink, Mr. —— you, I mean." He had shown a sprightly desire to do the talking for the company and tell all about his family. In a loud voice he declaimed on various topics. He assumed a patronizing air toward Pete. As Maggie was silent, he paid no attention to her. He made a great show of lavishing wealth upon the woman of brilliance and audacity.

"Do keep still, Freddie! You talk like a clock," said the woman to him. She turned away and devoted her attention to Pete. "We'll have many a good time together again, eh?"

"Sure, Mike," said Pete, enthusiastic at once.

"Say," whispered she, leaning forward, "let's go over to Billie's and have a time."

"Well, it's dis way! See?" said Pete. "I got dis lady frien' here."

"Oh, g'way with her," argued the woman.

Pete appeared disturbed.

"All right," said she, nodding her head at him. "All right for you! We'll see the next time you ask me to go any-wheres with you."

Pete squirmed. "Say," he said, beseechingly, "come wid me a minute an' I'll tell yer why."

The woman waved her hand. "Oh, that's all right, you needn't explain, you know. You wouldn't come merely because you wouldn't come, that's all." To Pete's visible distress she turned to the mere boy, bringing him speedily out of a terrific rage. He had been debating whether it would be the part of a man to pick a quarrel with Pete, or would he be justified in striking him savagely with his beer-glass without warning. But he recovered himself when the woman turned to renew her smilings. He beamed upon her with an expression that was somewhat tipsy and inexpressibly tender.

"Say, shake that Bowery jay," requested he, in a loud whisper.

"Freddie, you are so funny," she replied.

Pete reached forward and touched the woman on the arm. "Come out a minute while I tells yeh why I can't go wid yer. Yer doin' me dirt, Nell! I never t'ought ye'd do me dirt, Nell. Come on, will yer?" He spoke in tones of injury.

"Why, I don't see why I should be interested in your explanations," said the woman, with a coldness that seemed to reduce Pete to a pulp.

His eyes pleaded with her. "Come out a minute while I tells yeh. On d' level, now."

The woman nodded slightly at Maggie and the mere boy, saying, " 'Scuse me."

The mere boy interrupted his loving smile and turned a shrivelling glare upon Pete. His boyish countenance flushed and he spoke in a whine to the woman: "Oh, I say, Nellie, this ain't a square deal, you know. You aren't goin' to leave me and go off with that duffer, are you? I should think——"

"Why, you dear boy, of course I'm not," cried the woman, affectionately. She bent over and whispered in his ear. He smiled again and settled in his chair as if resolved to wait patiently.

As the woman walked down between the rows of tables, Pete was at her shoulder talking earnestly, apparently in explanation. The woman waved her hands with studied airs of indifference. The doors swung behind them, leaving Maggie and the mere boy seated at the table.

Maggie was dazed. She could dimly perceive that something stupendous had happened. She wondered why Pete saw fit to remonstrate with the woman, pleading forgiveness with his eyes. She thought she noted an air of submission about her leonine Pete. She was astounded.

The mere boy occupied himself with cocktails and a cigar. He was tranquilly silent for half an hour. Then he bestirred himself and spoke. "Well," he said, sighing, "I knew this was the way it would be. They got cold feet."

There was another stillness. The boy seemed to be musing. "She was pulling m' leg. That's the whole amount of it," he said, suddenly. "It's a bloomin' shame the way that girl does. Why, I've spent over two dollars in drinks to-night. And she goes off with that plug-ugly, who looks as if he had been hit in the face with a coin die. I call it rocky treatment for a fellah like me. Here, waiter, bring me a cocktail, and make it strong."

Maggie made no reply. She was watching the doors.

"It's a mean piece of business," complained the mere boy. He explained to her how amazing it was that anybody should treat him in such a manner. "But I'll get square with her, you bet. She won't get far ahead of yours truly, you know," he added, winking. "I'll tell her plainly that it was bloomin' mean business. And she won't come it over me with any of her 'now-Freddie-dear's.' She thinks my name is Freddie, you know, but of course it ain't. I always tell these people some name like that, because if they got on to your right name they might use it sometime. Understand? Oh, they don't fool me much."

Maggie was paying no attention, being intent upon the doors. The mere boy relapsed into a period of gloom, during which he exterminated a number of cocktails with a determined air, as if replying defiantly to fate. He occasionally broke forth into sentences composed of invectives joined together in a long chain.

The girl was still staring at the doors. After a time the mere boy began to see cobwebs just in front of his nose. He spurred himself into being agreeable and insisted upon her having a Charlotte Russe and a glass of beer.

"They's gone," he remarked, "they's gone." He looked at her through the smoke-wreaths. "Shay, lil' girl, we mightish well make bes' of it. You ain't such bad-lookin' girl, y'know. Not half bad. Can't come up to Nell, though. No, can't do it! Well, I should shay not! Nell fine-lookin' girl! F-i-n-ine. You look bad longsider her, but by y'self ain't so bad. Have to do, anyhow. Nell gone. O'ny you left. Not half bad, though."

Maggie stood up. "I'm going home," she said.

The mere boy started. "Eh? What? Home!" he cried, struck with amazement. "I beg pardon, did hear say home?"

"I'm going home," she repeated.

"Great heavens! what hav' a struck?" demanded the mere boy of himself, stupefied. In a semi-comatose state he conducted her on board an up-town car, ostentatiously paid her fare, leered kindly at her through the rear window, and fell off the steps.

XV

A forlorn woman went along a lighted avenue. The street was filled with people desperately bound on missions. An endless crowd darted at the elevated station stairs, and the horse-cars were thronged with owners of bundles.

The pace of the forlorn woman was slow. She was apparently searching for some one. She loitered near the doors of saloons and watched men emerge from them. She furtively scanned the faces in the rushing stream of pedestrians. Hurrying men, bent on catching some boat or train, jostled her elbows, failing to notice her, their thoughts fixed on distant dinners.

The forlorn woman had a peculiar face. Her smile was no smile. But when in repose her features had a shadowy look that was like a sardonic grin, as if some one had sketched with cruel forefinger indelible lines about her mouth.

Jimmie came strolling up the avenue. The woman encountered him with an aggrieved air. "Oh, Jimmie, I've been lookin' all over for yehs—" she began.

Jimmie made an impatient gesture and quickened his pace. "Ah, don't bodder me!" he said, with the savageness of a man whose life is pestered.

The woman followed him along the sidewalk in somewhat the manner of a suppliant. "But, Jimmie," she said, "yehs told me yehs—"

Jimmie turned upon her fiercely as if resolved to make a last stand for comfort and peace. "Say, Hattie, don' foller me from one end of deh city teh deh odder. Let up, will yehs! Give me a minute's res', can't yehs? Yehs makes me tired, allus taggin' me. See? Ain' yehs got no sense? Do yehs want people teh get on to me? Go chase yerself."

The woman stepped closer and laid her fingers on his arm. "But, look a' here—"

Jimmie snarled. "Oh, go teh blazes!" He darted into the front door of a convenient saloon and a moment later came out into the shadows that surrounded the side door. On the brilliantly lighted avenue he perceived the forlorn woman dodging about like a scout. Jimmie laughed with an air of relief and went away.

When he returned home he found his mother clamouring. Maggie had returned. She stood shivering beneath the torrent of her mother's wrath.

"Well, I'm damned!" said Jimmie in greeting.

His mother, tottering about the room, pointed a quivering forefinger. "Look ut her, Jimmie, look ut her. Dere's yer sister, boy. Dere's yer sister. Look ut her! Look ut her!" She screamed at Maggie with scoffing laughter.

The girl stood in the middle of the room. She edged about as if unable to find a place on the floor to put her feet.

"Ha ha, ha!" bellowed the mother. "Dere she stands! Ain't she purty? Look ut her! Ain' she sweet, deh beast? Look ut her! Ha, ha! look ut her!" She lurched forward and put her red and seamed hands upon her daughter's face. She bent down and peered keenly up into the eyes of the girl. "Oh, she's jes dessame as she ever was, ain' she? She's her mudder's putty darlin' yit, ain' she? Look ut her, Jimmie. Come here and look ut her."

The loud, tremendous railing of the mother brought the denizens of the Rum Alley tenement to their doors. Women came in the hallways. Children scurried to and fro.

"What's up? Dat Johnson party on anudder tear?"

"Naw. Young Mag's come home!"

"Git out!"

Through the open doors curious eyes stared in at Maggie. Children ventured into the room and ogled her as if they formed the front row at a theatre. Women, without, bent toward each other and whispered, nodding their heads with airs of profound philosophy.

A baby, overcome with curiosity concerning this object at which all were looking, sidled forward and touched her dress, cautiously, as if investigating a red-hot stove. Its mother's voice rang out like a warning trumpet. She rushed forward and grabbed her child, casting a terrible look of indignation at the girl.

Maggie's mother paced to and fro, addressing the door-ful of eyes, expounding like a glib showman. Her voice rang through the building. "Dere she stands," she cried, wheeling suddenly and pointing with dramatic finger. "Dere she stands! Look ut her! Ain' she a dandy? An' she was so good as to come home teh her mudder, she was! Ain' she a beaut'? Ain' she a dandy?"

The jeering cries ended in another burst of shrill laughter.

The girl seemed to awaken. "Jimmie—"

He drew hastily back from her. "Well, now, yer a t'ing, ain' yeh?" he said, his lips curling in scorn. Radiant virtue sat upon his brow, and his repelling hands expressed horror of contamination.

Maggie turned and went.

The crowd at the door fell back precipitately. A baby falling down in front of the door wrenched a scream like that of a wounded animal from its mother. Another woman sprang forward and picked it up with a chivalrous air, as if rescuing a human being from an oncoming express train.

As the girl passed down through the hall, she went before open doors framing more eyes strangely microscopic, and sending broad beams of inquisitive light into the darkness of her path. On the second floor she met the gnarled old woman who possessed the music-box.

"So," she cried, " 'ere yehs are back again, are yehs? An' dey've kicked yehs out? Well, come in an' stay wid me t'-night. I ain' got no moral standin'."

From above came an unceasing babble of tongues, over all of which rang the mother's derisive laughter.

XVI

Pete did not consider that he had ruined Maggie. If he had thought that her soul could never smile again, he would have believed the mother and brother, who were pyrotechnic over the affair, to be responsible for it. Besides, in his world, souls did not insist upon being able to smile. "What d' hell?"

He felt a trifle entangled. It distressed him. Revelations and scenes might bring upon him the wrath of the owner of the saloon, who insisted upon respectability of an advanced type. "What do dey wanna raise such a smoke about it fer?" demanded he of himself, disgusted with the attitude of the family. He saw no necessity that people should lose their equilibrium merely because their sister or daughter had stayed away from home. Searching about in his mind for possible reasons for their conduct, he came upon the conclusion that Maggie's motives were correct, but that the two others wished to snare him. He felt pursued.

The woman whom he had met in the hilarious hall showed a disposition to ridicule him. "A little pale thing with no spirit," she said. "Did you note the expression of her eyes? There was something in them about pumpkin pie and virtue. That is a peculiar way the left corner of her mouth has of twitching, isn't it? Dear, dear, Pete, what are you coming to?"

Pete asserted at once that he never was very much interested in the girl. The woman interrupted him, laughing. "Oh, it's not of the slightest consequence to me, my dear young man. You needn't draw maps for my benefit. Why should I be concerned about it?" But Pete continued with his explanations. If he was laughed at for his tastes in women, he felt obliged to say that they were only temporary or indifferent ones.

The morning after Maggie had departed from home

Pete stood behind the bar. He was immaculate in white
jacket and apron, and his hair was plastered over his brow
with infinite correctness. No customers were in the place.
Pete was twisting his napkined fist slowly in a beer-glass,
softly whistling to himself, and occasionally holding the
object of his attention between his eyes and a few weak
beams of sunlight that found their way over the thick
screens and into the shaded rooms.

With lingering thoughts of the woman of brilliance and
audacity, the bartender raised his head and stared through
the varying cracks between the swaying bamboo doors.
Suddenly the whistling pucker faded from his lips. He
saw Maggie walking slowly past. He gave a great start,
fearing for the previously mentioned eminent respectability of the place.

He threw a swift, nervous glance about him, all at once
feeling guilty. No one was in the room. He went hastily
over to the side door. Opening it and looking out, he perceived Maggie standing, as if undecided, at the corner. She
was searching the place with her eyes. As she turned her
face toward him, Pete beckoned to her hurriedly, intent
upon returning with speed to a position behind the bar,
and to the atmosphere of respectability upon which the
proprietor insisted.

Maggie came to him, the anxious look disappearing
from her face and a smile wreathing her lips. "Oh, Pete—"
she began brightly.

The bartender made a violent gesture of impatience.
"Oh, say," cried he vehemently. "What d' yeh wanna hang
aroun' here fer? Do yer wanna git me inteh trouble?" he
demanded with an air of injury.

Astonishment swept over the girl's features. "Why, Pete!
yehs tol' me—"

Pete's glance expressed profound irritation. His countenance reddened with the anger of a man whose respectability is being threatened. "Say, yehs makes me tired! See!
What d' yeh wanna tag aroun' atter me fer? Yeh'll do me
dirt wid' d' ol' man an' dey'll be trouble! If he sees a
woman roun' here he'll go crazy an' I'll lose me job! See?

Ain' yehs got no sense? Don' be allus bodderin' me. See? Yer brudder came in here an' made trouble an' d' ol' man hadda put up fer it! An' now I'm done! See? I'm done."

The girl's eyes stared into his face. "Pete, don' yeh remem—"

"Oh, go ahn!" interrupted Pete, anticipating.

The girl seemed to have a struggle with herself. She was apparently bewildered and could not find speech. Finally she asked in a low voice, "But where kin I go?"

The question exasperated Pete beyond the powers of endurance. It was a direct attempt to give him some responsibility in a matter that did not concern him. In his indignation he volunteered information. "Oh, go to hell!" cried he. He slammed the door furiously and returned, with an air of relief, to his respectability.

Maggie went away. She wandered aimlessly for several blocks. She stopped once and asked aloud a question of herself: "Who?" A man who was passing near her shoulder humorously took the questioning word as intended for him. "Eh! What? Who? Nobody! I didn't say anything," he laughingly said, and continued his way.

Soon the girl discovered that if she walked with such apparent aimlessness, some men looked at her with calculating eyes. She quickened her step, frightened. As a protection, she adopted a demeanour of intentness as if going somewhere.

After a time she left rattling avenues and passed between rows of houses with sternness and stolidity stamped upon their features. She hung her head, for she felt their eyes grimly upon her.

Suddenly she came upon a stout gentleman in a silk hat and a chaste black coat, whose decorous row of buttons reached from his chin to his knees. The girl had heard of the grace of God and she decided to approach this man. His beaming, chubby face was a picture of benevolence and kind-heartedness. His eyes shone good will.

But as the girl timidly accosted him he made a convulsive movement and saved his respectability by a vigorous side-step. He did not risk it to save a soul. For how

was he to know that there was a soul before him that
needed saving?

XVII

Upon a wet evening, several months later, two interminable rows of cars, pulled by slipping horses, jangled along
a prominent side street. A dozen cabs, with coat-
enshrouded drivers, clattered to and fro. Electric lights,
whirring softly, shed a blurred radiance. A flower-dealer,
his feet tapping impatiently, his nose and his wares glistening with raindrops, stood behind an array of roses and
chrysanthemums. Two or three theatres emptied a crowd
upon the stormswept sidewalks. Men pulled their hats
over their eyebrows and raised their collars to their ears.
Women shrugged impatient shoulders in their warm cloaks
and stopped to arrange their skirts for a walk through
the storm. People who had been constrained to comparative silence for two hours burst into a roar of conversation,
their hearts still kindling from the glowings of the stage.

The sidewalks became tossing seas of umbrellas. Men
stepped forth to hail cabs or cars, raising their fingers in
varied forms of polite request or imperative demand. An
endless procession wended toward elevated stations. An
atmosphere of pleasure and prosperity seemed to hang
over the throng, born, perhaps, of good clothes and of two
hours in a place of forgetfulness.

In the mingled light and gloom of an adjacent park, a
handful of wet wanderers, in attitudes of chronic dejection,
were scattered among the benches.

A girl of the painted cohorts of the city went along the
street. She threw changing glances at men who passed her,
giving smiling invitations to those of rural or untaught
pattern and usually seeming sedately unconscious of the
men with a metropolitan seal upon their faces. Crossing
glittering avenues, she went into the throng emerging from
the places of forgetfulness. She hurried forward through
the crowd as if intent upon reaching a distant home, bending forward in her handsome cloak, daintily lifting her

skirts, and picking for her well-shod feet the dryer spots upon the sidewalks.

The restless doors of saloons, clashing to and fro, disclosed animated rows of men before bars and hurrying barkeepers. A concert-hall gave to the street faint sounds of swift, machine-like music, as if a group of phantom musicians were hastening.

A tall young man, smoking a cigarette with a sublime air, strolled near the girl. He had on evening dress, a moustache, a chrysanthemum, and a look of *ennui,* all of which he kept carefully under his eye. Seeing the girl walk on as if such a young man as he was not in existence, he looked back transfixed with interest. He stared glassily for a moment, but gave a slight convulsive start when he discerned that she was neither new, Parisian, nor theatrical. He wheeled about hastily and turned his stare into the air, like a sailor with a searchlight.

A stout gentleman, with pompous and philanthropic whiskers, went stolidly by, the broad of his back sneering at the girl. A belated man in business clothes, and in haste to catch a car, bounced against her shoulder. "Hi, there, Mary, I beg your pardon! Brace up, old girl." He grasped her arm to steady her, and then was away running down the middle of the street.

The girl walked on out of the realm of restaurants and saloons. She passed more glittering avenues and went into darker blocks than those where the crowd travelled.

A young man in light overcoat and Derby hat received a glance shot keenly from the eyes of the girl. He stopped and looked at her, thrusting his hands into his pockets and making a mocking smile curl his lips. "Come, now, old lady," he said, "you don't mean to tell me that you sized me up for a farmer?"

A labouring man marched along with bundles under his arms. To her remarks he replied, "It's a fine evenin', ain't it?"

She smiled squarely into the face of a boy who was hurrying by with his hands buried in his overcoat pockets, his blond locks bobbing on his youthful temples, and a cheery smile of unconcern upon his lips. He turned his head and smiled back at her, waving his hands. "Not this eve—some other eve."

A drunken man, reeling in her pathway, began to roar at her. "I ain' go' no money!" he shouted, in a dismal voice. He lurched on up the street, wailing to himself: "I ain' go' no money. Ba' luck. Ain' go' no more money."

The girl went into gloomy districts near the river, where the tall black factories shut in the street and only occasional broad beams of light fell across the sidewalks from saloons. In front of one of these places, whence came the sound of a violin vigorously scraped, the patter of feet on boards, and the ring of loud laughter, there stood a man with blotched features.

Farther on in the darkness she met a ragged being with shifting, bloodshot eyes and grimy hands.

She went into the blackness of the final block. The shutters of the tall buildings were closed like grim lips. The structures seemed to have eyes that looked over them, beyond them, at other things. Afar off the lights of the avenues glittered as if from an impossible distance. Street-car bells jingled with a sound of merriment.

At the feet of the tall buildings appeared the deathly black hue of the river. Some hidden factory sent up a yellow glare, that lit for a moment the waters lapping oilily against timbers. The varied sounds of life, made joyous by distance and seeming unapproachableness, came faintly and died away to a silence.

XVIII

In a partitioned-off section of a saloon sat a man with a half-dozen women, gleefully laughing, hovering about him. The man had arrived at that stage of drunkenness where affection is felt for the universe. "I'm good f'ler, girls," he said, convincingly. "I'm good f'ler. An'body trea's me right, I allus trea's zem right! See?"

The women nodded their heads approvingly. "To be sure," they cried in hearty chorus. "You're the kind of a man we like, Pete. You're outa sight! What yeh goin' to buy this time, dear?"

"An't'ing yehs wants!" said the man in an abandonment of good will. His countenance shone with the true spirit of benevolence. He was in the proper mood of missionaries. He would have fraternized with obscure Hottentots. And above all he was overwhelmed in tenderness for his friends, who were all illustrious. "An't'ing yehs wants!" repeated he, waving his hands with beneficent recklessness. "I'm good f'ler, girls, an' if an'body trea's me right I— Here," called he through an open door to a waiter, "bring girls drinks. What 'ill yehs have, girls? An't'ing yehs want."

The waiter glanced in with the disgusted look of the man who serves intoxicants for the man who takes too much of them. He nodded his head shortly at the order from each individual, and went.

"W' 're havin' great time," said the man. "I like you girls! Yer right sort! See?" He spoke at length and with feeling concerning the excellences of his assembled friends. "Don' try pull man's leg, but have a good time! Dass right! Dass way teh do! Now, if I s'ought yehs tryin' work me fer drinks, wouldn' buy notting! But yer right sort! Yehs know how ter treat a f'ler, an' I stays by yehs till spen' las' cent! Dass right! I'm good f'ler an' I knows when an'body trea's me right!"

Between the times of the arrival and departure of the waiter, the man discoursed to the women on the tender regard he felt for all living things. He laid stress upon the purity of his motives in all dealings with men in the world, and spoke of the fervour of his friendship for those who were amiable. Tears welled slowly from his eyes. His voice quavered when he spoke to his companions.

Once when the waiter was about to depart with an empty tray, the man drew a coin from his pocket and held it forth. "Here," said he, quite magnificently, "here's quar'."

The waiter kept his hands on his tray. "I don't want yer money," he said.

The other put forth the coin with tearful insistence.

"Here's quar'!" cried he, "take 't! Yer goo' f'ler an' I wan' yehs take 't!"

"Come, come, now," said the waiter, with the sullen air of a man who is forced into giving advice. "Put yer mon in yer pocket! Yer loaded an' yehs on'y makes a fool of yerself."

As the waiter passed out of the door the man turned pathetically to the women. "He don't know I'm goo' f'ler," cried he, dismally.

"Never you mind, Pete, dear," said the woman of brilliance and audacity, laying her hand with great affection upon his arm. "Never you mind, old boy! We'll stay by you, dear!"

"Dass ri'!" cried the man, his face lighting up at the soothing tones of the woman's voice. "Dass ri'; I'm goo' f'ler, an' w'en any one trea's me ri', I trea's zem ri'! Shee?"

"Sure!" cried the women. "And we're not goin' back on you, old man."

The man turned appealing eyes to the woman. He felt that if he could be convicted of a contemptible action he would die. "Shay, Nell, I allus trea's yehs shquare, didn' I? I allus been goo' f'ler wi' yehs, ain't I, Nell?"

"Sure you have, Pete," assented the woman. She delivered an oration to her companions. "Yessir, that's a fact. Pete's a square fellah, he is. He never goes back on a friend. He's the right kind an' we stay by him, don't we, girls?"

"Sure!" they exclaimed. Looking lovingly at him they raised their glasses and drank his health.

"Girlsh," said the man, beseechingly, "I allus trea's yehs ri', didn' I? I'm goo' f'ler, ain' I, girlsh?"

"Sure!" again they chorused.

"Well," said he finally, "le's have nozzer drink, zen."

"That's right," hailed a woman, "that's right. Yer no bloomin' jay! Yer spends yer money like a man. Dat's right."

The man pounded the table with his quivering fists. "Yessir," he cried, with deep earnestness, as if some one disputed him. "I'm goo' f'ler, an' w'en any one trea's me ri',

I allus trea's—le's have nozzer drink." He began to beat the wood with his glass. "Shay!" howled he, growing suddenly impatient. As the waiter did not then come, the man swelled with wrath. "Shay!" howled he again. The waiter appeared at the door. "Bringsh drinksh," said the man.

The waiter disappeared with the orders.

"Zat f'ler fool!" cried the man. "He insul' me! I'm ge'man! Can' stan' be insul'! I'm goin' lick 'im when comes!"

"No, no!" cried the women, crowding about and trying to subdue him. "He's all right! He didn't mean anything! Let it go! He's a good fellah!"

"Di'n' he insul' me?" asked the man earnestly.

"No," said they. "Of course he didn't! He's all right!"

"Sure he didn' insul' me?" demanded the man, with deep anxiety in his voice.

"No, no! We know him! He's a good fellah. He didn't mean anything."

"Well, zen," said the man resolutely, "I'm go' 'pol'gize!"

When the waiter came, the man struggled to the middle of the floor. "Girlsh shed you insul' me! I shay—lie! I 'pol'gize!"

"All right," said the waiter.

The man sat down. He felt a sleepy but strong desire to straighten things out and have a perfect understanding with everybody. "Nell, I allus trea's yeh shquare, di'n' I? Yeh likes me, don' yehs, Nell? I'm goo' f'ler?"

"Sure!" said the woman.

"Yeh knows I'm stuck on yehs, don' yehs, Nell?"

"Sure!" she repeated carelessly.

Overwhelmed by a spasm of drunken adoration, he drew two or three bills from his pocket and, with the trembling fingers of an offering priest, laid them on the table before the woman. "Yehs knows yehs kin have all I got, 'cause I'm stuck on yehs, Nell, I—I'm stuck on yehs, Nell—buy drinksh—we're havin' grea' time—w'en any one trea's me ri'—I—Nell—we're havin' heluva—time."

Presently he went to sleep with his swollen face fallen forward on his chest.

The women drank and laughed, not heeding the slumbering man in the corner. Finally he lurched forward and fell groaning to the floor.

The women screamed in disgust and drew back their skirts.

"Come ahn!" cried one, starting up angrily, "let's get out of here."

The woman of brilliance and audacity stayed behind, taking up the bills and stuffing them into a deep, irregularly shaped pocket. A guttural snore from the recumbent man caused her to turn and look down at him. She laughed. "What a fool!" she said and went.

The smoke from the lamps settled heavily down in the little compartment, obscuring the way out. The smell of oil, stifling in its intensity, pervaded the air. The wine from an overturned glass dripped softly down upon the blotches on the man's neck.

XIX

In a room a woman sat at a table eating like a fat monk in a picture.

A soiled, unshaven man pushed open the door and entered. "Well," said he, "Mag's dead."

"What?" said the woman, her mouth filled with bread.

"Mag's dead," repeated the man.

"Deh blazes she is!" said the woman. She continued her meal.

When she finished her coffee she began to weep. "I kin remember when her two feet was no bigger dan yer t'umb, and she weared worsted boots," moaned she.

"Well, what a' dat?" said the man.

"I kin remember when she weared worsted boots," she cried.

The neighbours began to gather in the hall, staring in at the weeping woman as if watching the contortions of a dying dog. A dozen women entered and lamented with her. Under their busy hands the room took on that appalling appearance of neatness and order with which death is greeted.

Suddenly the door opened and a woman in a black gown rushed in with outstretched arms. "Ah, poor Mary!" she cried, and tenderly embraced the moaning one. "Ah, what ter'ble affliction is dis!" continued she. Her vocabulary was derived from mission churches. "Me poor Mary, how I feel fer yehs! Ah, what a ter'ble affliction is a disobed'ent chile." Her good, motherly face was wet with tears. She trembled in eagerness to express her sympathy.

The mourner sat with bowed head, rocking her body heavily to and fro, and crying out in a high, strained voice that sounded like a dirge on some forlorn pipe. "I kin remember when she weared worsted boots, an' her two feets was no bigger dan yer t'umb, an' she weared worsted boots, Miss Smith," she cried, raising her streaming eyes.

"Ah, me poor Mary!" sobbed the woman in black. With low, coddling cries, she sank on her knees by the mourner's chair, and put her arms about her. The other women began to groan in different keys.

"Yer poor misguided chil' is gone now, Mary, an' let us hope it's fer deh bes'. Yeh'll fergive her now, Mary, won't yehs, dear, all her disobed'ence? All her t'ankless behaviour to her mudder an' all her badness? She's gone where her ter'ble sins will be judged."

The woman in black raised her face and paused. The inevitable sunlight came streaming in at the window and shed a ghastly cheerfulness upon the faded hues of the room. Two or three of the spectators were sniffling, and one was weeping loudly.

The mourner arose and staggered into the other room. In a moment she emerged with a pair of faded baby shoes held in the hollow of her hand. "I kin remember when she used to wear dem!" cried she. The women burst anew into cries as if they had all been stabbed. The mourner turned to the soiled and unshaven man. "Jimmie, boy, go git yer sister! Go git yer sister an' we'll put deh boots on her feets!"

"Dey won't fit her now, yeh fool," said the man.

"Go git yer sister, Jimmie!" shrieked the woman, confronting him fiercely.

The man swore sullenly. He went over to a corner and slowly began to put on his coat. He took his hat and went out, with a dragging, reluctant step.

The woman in black came forward and again besought the mourner. "Yeh'll fergive her, Mary! Yeh'll fergive yer bad, bad chil'! Her life was a curse an' her days were black, an' yeh'll fergive yer bad girl? She's gone where her sins will be judged."

"She's gone where her sins will be judged!" cried the other women, like a choir at a funeral.

"Deh Lord gives and deh Lord takes away," said the woman in black, raising her eyes to the sunbeams.

"Deh Lord gives and deh Lord takes away," responded the others.

"Yeh'll fergive her, Mary?" pleaded the woman in black.

The mourner essayed to speak, but her voice gave way. She shook her great shoulders frantically, in an agony of grief. The tears seemed to scald her face. Finally her voice came and arose in a scream of pain. "Oh, yes, I'll fergive her! I'll fergive her!"

GEORGE'S MOTHER

I

IN THE swirling rain that came at dusk the broad avenue glistened with that deep bluish tint which is so widely condemned when it is put into pictures. There were long rows of shops, whose fronts shone with full, golden light. Here and there, from druggists' windows or from the red street-lamps that indicated the positions of fire-alarm boxes, a flare of uncertain, wavering crimson was thrown upon the wet pavements.

The lights made shadows, in which the buildings loomed with a new and tremendous massiveness, like castles and fortresses. There were endless processions of people, mighty hosts, with umbrellas waving, banner-like, over them. Horse-cars, a-glitter with new paint, rumbled in steady array between the pillars that supported the elevated railroad. The whole street resounded with the tinkle of bells, the roar of iron-shod wheels on the cobbles, the ceaseless trample of the hundreds of feet. Above all, too, could be heard the loud screams of the tiny newsboys who scurried in all directions. Upon the corners, standing in from the dripping eaves, were many loungers, descended from the world that used to prostrate itself before pageantry.

A brown young man went along the avenue. He held a tin lunch-pail under his arm in a manner that was evidently uncomfortable. He was puffing at a corncob pipe. His shoulders had a self-reliant poise, and the hang of his arms and the raised veins of his hands showed him to be a man who worked with his muscles.

As he passed a street-corner a man in old clothes gave a shout of surprise and, rushing impetuously forward, grasped his hand.

"Hello, Kelcey, ol' boy!" cried the man in old clothes. "How's th' boy, anyhow? Where in thunder yeh been fer th' last seventeen years? I'll be hanged if you ain't th' last man I ever expected t' see."

The brown youth put his pail to the ground and grinned. "Well, if it ain't ol' Charley Jones," he said, ecstatically shaking hands. "How are yeh, anyhow? Where yeh been keepin' yerself? I ain't seen yeh fer a year."

"Well, I should say so! Why, th' last time I saw you was up in Handyville!"

"Sure! On Sunday, we—"

"Sure. Out at Bill Sickles's place. Let's go get a drink!"

They made toward a little glass-fronted saloon that sat blinking jovially at the crowds. It engulfed them with a gleeful motion of its two widely smiling lips.

"What'll yeh take, Kelcey?"

"Oh, I guess I'll take a beer."

"Gimme little whisky, John."

The two friends leaned against the bar and looked with enthusiasm upon each other.

"Well, well, I'm thunderin' glad t' see yeh," said Jones.

"Well, I guess," replied Kelcey. "Here's to yeh, ol' man."

"Let 'er go."

They lifted their glasses, glanced fervidly at each other, and drank.

"Yeh ain't changed much, on'y yeh've growed like th' devil," said Jones, reflectively, as he put down his glass. "I'd know yeh anywheres!"

"Certainly yeh would," said Kelcey. "An' I knew you, too, th' minute I saw yeh. Yer changed, though!"

"Yes," admitted Jones with some complacency, "I s'pose I am." He regarded himself in the mirror that multiplied the bottles on the shelf in back of the bar. He should have seen a grinning face with a rather pink nose. His derby was perched carelessly on the back part of his head. Two wisps of hair straggled down over his hollow temples. There was something very worldly and wise about him. Life did not seem to confuse him. Evidently he understood its complications. His hand thrust into his trousers pocket, where he jingled keys, and his hat perched back on his head expressed a young man of vast knowledge. His extensive acquaintance with bartenders aided him materially in this habitual expression of wisdom.

Having finished, he turned to the barkeeper. "John, has any of th' gang been in t'-night yet?"

"No—not yet," said the barkeeper. "Ol' Bleecker was aroun' this afternoon about four. He said if I seen any of th' boys t' tell 'em he'd be up t'-night if he could get away. I saw Connor an' that other fellah goin' down th' avenyeh about an hour ago. I guess they'll be back after a while."

"This is th' hang-out fer a great gang," said Jones, turning to Kelcey. "They're a great crowd, I tell yeh. We own th' place when we get started. Come aroun' some night. Any night, almost. T'-night, b' jiminy. They'll almost all be here, an' I'd like t' interduce yeh. They're a great gang! Gre-e-at!"

"I'd like teh," said Kelcey.

"Well, come ahead, then," cried the other, cordially. "Ye'd like t' know 'em. It's an outa-sight crowd. Come aroun' t'-night!"

"I will if I can."

"Well, yeh ain't got anything t' do, have yeh?" demanded Jones. "Well, come along, then. Yeh might just as well spend yer time with a good crowd a' fellahs. An' it's a great gang. Great! Gre-e-at!"

"Well, I must make fer home now, anyhow," said Kelcey. "It's late as blazes. What'll yeh take this time, ol' man?"

"Gimme little more whisky, John."

"Guess I'll take another beer!"

Jones emptied the whisky into his large mouth and then put the glass upon the bar. "Been in th' city long?" he asked. "Um—well, three years is a good deal fer a slick man. Doin' well? Oh, well, nobody's doin' well these days." He looked down mournfully at his shabby clothes. "Father's dead, ain't 'e? Yeh don't say so? Fell off a scaf-

foldin', didn't 'e? I heard it somewheres. Mother's livin',
of course? I thought she was. Fine ol' lady—fi-i-ne. Well,
you're th' last of her boys. Was five of yeh oncet, wasn't
there? I knew four m'self. Yes, five! I thought so. An'
all gone but you, hey? Well, you'll have t' brace up an'
be a comfort t' th' ol' mother. Well, well, well, who would
'a' thought that on'y you'd be left out a' all that mob a'
towheaded kids? Well, well, well, it's a queer world, ain't
it?"

A contemplation of this thought made him sad. He
sighed, and moodily watched the other sip beer.

"Well, well, it's a queer world—a damn queer world."

"Yes," said Kelcey, "I'm th' on'y one left!" There was
an accent of discomfort in his voice. He did not like this
dwelling upon a sentiment that was connected with himself.

"How is th' ol' lady, anyhow?" continued Jones. "Th'
last time I remember she was as spry as a little ol' cricket,
an' was helpeltin' aroun' th' country lecturin' before
W.C.T.U.'s an' one thing an' another."

"Oh, she's pretty well," said Kelcey.

"An' out a' five boys you're th' on'y one she's got left?
Well, well—have another drink before yeh go."

"Oh, I guess I've had enough."

A wounded expression came into Jones's eyes. "Oh,
come on," he said.

"Well, I'll take another beer!"

"Gimme little more whisky, John!"

When they had concluded this ceremony, Jones went
with his friend to the door of the saloon. "Good-bye, ol'
man," he said genially. His homely features shone with
friendliness. "Come aroun', now, sure. T'-night! See?
They're a great crowd. Gre-e-at!"

II

A man with a red, mottled face put forth his head from
a window and cursed violently. He flung a bottle high
across two back yards at a window of the opposite tenement. It broke against the bricks of the house, and the

fragments fell crackling upon the stones below. The man shook his fist.

A bare-armed woman, making an array of clothes on a line in one of the yards, glanced casually up at the man and listened to his words. Her eyes followed his to the other tenement. From a distant window a youth with a pipe yelled some comments upon the poor aim. Two children, being in the proper yard, picked up the bits of broken glass and began to fondle them as new toys.

From the window at which the man raged came the sound of an old voice, singing. It quavered and trembled out into the air as if a sound-spirit had a broken wing.

> *"Should I be car-reed tew th' skies*
> *O'on flow'ry be-eds of ee-ease,*
> *While others fought tew win th' prize*
> *An' sailed through blood-ee seas?"*

The man in the opposite window was greatly enraged. He continued to swear.

A little old woman was the owner of the voice. In a fourth-storey room of the red-and-black tenement she was trudging on a journey. In her arms she bore pots and pans, and sometimes a broom and dust-pan. She wielded them like weapons. Their weight seemed to have bended her back and crooked her arms until she walked with difficulty. Often she plunged her hands into water at a sink. She splashed about, the dwindled muscles working to and fro under the loose skin of her arms. She came from the sink streaming and bedraggled as if she had crossed a flooded river.

There was the flurry of a battle in this room. Through the clouded dust or steam one could see the thin figure dealing mighty blows. Always her way seemed beset. Her broom was continually poised, lance-wise, at dust demons. There came clashings and clangings as she strove with her tireless foes.

It was a picture of indomitable courage. And as she went on her way her voice was often raised in a long cry, a strange war-chant, a shout of battle and defiance, that

rose and fell in harsh screams, and exasperated the ears of
the man with the red, mottled face.

> *"Should I be car-reed tew th' skies*
> *O'on flow'ry be-eds of ee-ease—"*

Finally she halted for a moment. Going to the window,
she sat down and mopped her face with her apron. It was
a lull, a moment of respite. Still it could be seen that she
even then was planning skirmishes, charges, campaigns.
She gazed thoughtfully about the room and noted the
strength and position of her enemies. She was very alert.

At last she returned to the mantel. "Five o'clock," she
murmured, scrutinizing a little swaggering nickel-plated
clock.

She looked out at chimneys growing thickly on the
roofs. A man at work on one seemed like a bee. In the
intricate yards below, vine-like lines had strange leaves of
cloth. To her ears there came the howl of the man with
the red, mottled face. He was engaged in a furious altercation with the youth who had called attention to his poor
aim. They were like animals in a jungle.

In the distance an enormous brewery towered over the
other buildings. Great gilt letters advertised a brand of
beer. Thick smoke came from funnels and spread near it
like vast and powerful wings. The structure seemed a
great bird, flying. The letters of the sign made a chain of
gold hanging from its neck. The little old woman looked
at the brewery. It vaguely interested her, for a moment,
as a stupendous affair, a machine of mighty strength.

Presently she sprang from her rest and began to buffet
with her shrivelled arms. In a moment the battle was again
in full swing. Terrific blows were given and received. There
arose the clattering uproar of a new fight. The little intent
warrior never hesitated nor faltered. She fought with a
strong and relentless will. Beads and lines of perspiration
stood upon her forehead.

Three blue plates were leaning in a row on the shelf in
back of the stove. The little old woman had seen it done

somewhere. In front of them swaggered the round nickel-plated clock. Her son had stuck many cigarette pictures in the rim of a looking-glass that hung near. Occasional chromos were tacked upon the yellowed walls of the room. There was one in a gilt frame. It was quite an affair, in reds and greens. They all seemed like trophies.

It began to grow dark. A mist came winding. Rain plashed softly upon the window-sill. A lamp had been lighted in the opposite tenement; the strong orange glare revealed the man with a red, mottled face. He was seated by a table, smoking and reflecting.

The little old woman looked at the clock again. "Quarter a' six."

She had paused for a moment, but she now hurled herself fiercely at the stove that lurked in the gloom, red-eyed, like a dragon. It hissed, and there was renewed clangour of blows. The little old woman dashed to and fro.

III

As it grew toward seven o'clock the little old woman became nervous. She often would drop into a chair and sit staring at the little clock.

"I wonder why he don't come," she continually repeated. There was a small, curious note of despair in her voice. As she sat thinking and staring at the clock the expressions of her face changed swiftly. All manner of emotions flickered in her eyes and about her lips. She was evidently perceiving in her imagination the journey of a loved person. She dreamed for him mishaps and obstacles. Something tremendous and irritating was hindering him from coming to her.

She had lighted an oil lamp. It flooded the room with vivid yellow glare. The table, in its oil-cloth covering, had previously appeared like a bit of bare brown desert. It now was a white garden, growing the fruits of her labour.

"Seven o'clock," she murmured, finally. She was aghast.

Then suddenly she heard a step upon the stair. She

sprang up and began to bustle about the room. The little fearful emotions passed at once from her face. She seemed now to be ready to scold.

Young Kelcey entered the room. He gave a sigh of relief, and dropped his pail in a corner. He was evidently greatly wearied by a hard day of toil.

The little old woman hobbled over to him and raised her wrinkled lips. She seemed on the verge of tears and an outburst of reproaches.

"Hello!" he cried, in a voice of cheer. "Been gettin' anxious?"

"Yes," she said, hovering about him. "Where yeh been, George? What made yeh so late? I've been waitin' th' longest while. Don't throw your coat down there. Hang it up behind th' door."

The son put his coat on the proper hook, and then went to splatter water in a tin wash-basin at the sink.

"Well, yeh see, I met Jones—you remember Jones? Ol' Handyville fellah. An' we had t' stop an' talk over ol' times. Jones is quite a boy."

The little old woman's mouth set in a sudden straight line. "Oh, that Jones," she said. "I don't like him."

The youth interrupted a flurry of white towel to give a glance of irritation. "Well, now, what's th' use of talking that way?" he said to her. "What do yeh know 'bout 'im? Ever spoke to 'im in yer life?"

"Well, I don't know as I ever did since he grew up," replied the little old woman. "But I know he ain't th' kind a' man I'd like t' have you go around with. He ain't a good man. I'm sure he ain't. He drinks."

Her son began to laugh. "Th' dickens he does!" He seemed amazed, but not shocked, at this information.

She nodded her head with the air of one who discloses a dreadful thing. "I'm sure of it! Once I saw 'im comin' out a' Simpson's Hotel, up in Handyville, an' he could hardly walk. He drinks! I'm sure he drinks!"

"Holy smoke!" said Kelcey.

They sat down at the table and began to wreck the little

white garden. The youth leaned back in his chair, in the
manner of a man who is paying for things. His mother
bended alertly forward, apparently watching each mouth-
ful. She perched on the edge of her chair, ready to spring
to her feet and run to the closet or the stove for anything
that he might need. She was as anxious as a young mother
with a babe. In the careless and comfortable attitude of
the son there was denoted a great deal of dignity.

"Yeh ain't eatin' much t'-night, George?"

"Well, I ain't very hungry, t' tell th' truth."

"Don't yeh like yer supper, dear? Yeh must eat somethin', chile. Yeh mustn't go without."

"Well, I'm eatin' somethin', ain't I?"

He wandered aimlessly through the meal. She sat over
behind the little blackened coffee-pot and gazed affectionately upon him.

After a time she began to grow agitated. Her worn
fingers were gripped. It could be seen that a great thought
was within her. She was about to venture something. She
had arrived at a supreme moment. "George," she said
suddenly, "come t' prayer-meetin' with me t'-night."

The young man dropped his work. "Say, you must be
crazy," he said, in amazement.

"Yes, dear," she continued, rapidly, in a small pleading
voice, "I'd like t' have yeh go with me oncet in a while.
Yeh never go with me any more, dear, an' I'd like t' have
yeh go. Yeh ain't been anywheres at all with me in th'
longest while."

"Well," he said, "well, but what th' blazes—"

"Ah, come on," said the little old woman. She went to
him and put her arms about his neck. She began to coax
him with caresses.

The young man grinned. "Thunderation!" he said, "what
would I do at a prayer-meetin'?"

The mother considered him to be consenting. She did a
little antique caper.

"Well, yeh can come an' take care a' yer mother," she
cried gleefully. "It's such a long walk every Thursday

night alone, an' don't yeh s'pose that when I have such a big, fine, strappin' boy I want 'im t' beau me aroun' some? Ah, I knew ye'd come!"

He smiled for a moment, indulgent of her humour. But presently his face turned a shade of discomfort. "But," he began, protesting.

"Ah, come on!" she continually repeated.

He began to be vexed. He frowned into the air. A vision came to him of dreary blackness arranged in solemn rows. A mere dream of it was depressing.

"But—" he said again. He was obliged to make great search for an argument. Finally he concluded: "But what th' blazes would I do at prayer-meetin'?"

In his ears was the sound of a hymn, made by people who tilted their heads at a prescribed angle of devotion. It would be too apparent that they were all better than he. When he entered they would turn their heads and regard him with suspicion. This would be an enormous aggravation, since he was certain that he was as good as they.

"Well, now, y' see," he said, quite gently, "I don't wanta go, an' it wouldn't do me no good t' go if I didn't wanta go."

His mother's face swiftly changed. She breathed a huge sigh, the counterpart of ones he had heard upon like occasions. She put a tiny black bonnet on her head, and wrapped her figure in an old shawl. She cast a martyr-like glance upon her son and went mournfully away. She resembled a limited funeral procession.

The young man writhed under it to an extent. He kicked moodily at a table-leg. When the sound of her footfalls died away he felt distinctly relieved.

IV

That night, when Kelcey arrived at the little smiling saloon, he found his friend Jones standing before the bar engaged in a violent argument with a stout man.

"Oh, well," this latter person was saying, "you can make a lot of noise, Charley, for a man that never says anything—let's have a drink!"

Jones was waving his arms and delivering splintering blows upon some distant theories. The stout man chuckled fatly and winked at the bartender.

The orator ceased for a moment to say, "Gimme little whisky, John." At the same time he perceived young Kelcey. He sprang forward with a welcoming cry. "Hello, ol' man! didn't much think ye'd come." He led him to the stout man.

"Mr. Bleecker—my friend Mr. Kelcey!"

"How d' yeh do?"

"Mr. Kelcey, I'm happy to meet you, sir; have a drink."

They drew up in line and waited. The busy hands of the bartender made glasses clink. Mr. Bleecker, in a very polite way, broke the waiting silence.

"Never been here before, I believe, have you, Mr. Kelcey?"

The young man felt around for a high-bred reply. "Er —no—I've never had that—er—pleasure," he said.

After a time the strained and wary courtesy of their manners wore away. It became evident to Bleecker that his importance slightly dazzled the young man. He grew warmer. Obviously, the youth was one whose powers of perception were developed. Directly, then, he launched forth into a tale of bygone days, when the world was better. He had known all the great men of that age. He reproduced his conversations with them. There were traces of pride and of mournfulness in his voice. He rejoiced at the glory of the world of dead spirits. He grieved at the youth and flippancy of the present one. He lived with his head in the clouds of the past, and he seemed obliged to talk of what he saw there.

Jones nudged Kelcey ecstatically in the ribs. "You've got th' ol' man started in great shape," he whispered.

Kelcey was proud that the prominent character of the place talked at him, glancing into his eyes for apprecia-tion of fine points.

Presently they left the bar and, going into a little rear room, took seats about a table. A gas-jet with a coloured globe shed a crimson radiance. The polished wood of walls and furniture gleamed with faint rose-coloured reflections. Upon the floor sawdust was thickly sprinkled.

Two other men presently came. By the time Bleecker had told three tales of the grand past, Kelcey was slightly acquainted with everybody.

He admired Bleecker immensely. He developed a brotherly feeling for the others, who were all gentle-spoken. He began to feel that he was passing the happiest evening of his life. His companions were so jovial and good-natured; and everything they did was marked by such courtesy.

For a time the two men who had come in late did not presume to address him directly. They would say: "Jones, won't your friend have so and so, or so and so?" And Bleecker would begin his orations: "Now, Mr. Kelcey, don't you think—"

Presently he began to believe that he was a most remarkably fine fellow, who had at last found his place in a crowd of most remarkably fine fellows.

Jones occasionally breathed comments into his ear.

"I tell yeh, Bleecker's an ol' timer. He was a husky guy in his day, yeh can bet. He was one a' th' best-known men in N' York oncet. Yeh ought to hear him tell about—"

Kelcey listened intently. He was profoundly interested in these intimate tales of men who had gleamed in the rays of old suns.

"That O'Connor's a damn fine fellah," interjected Jones once, referring to one of the others. "He's one a' th' best fellahs I ever knowed. He's always on th' dead level. An' he's always jest th' same as yeh see him now—good-natured an' grinnin'."

Kelcey nodded. He could well believe it.

When he offered to buy drinks there came a loud volley of protests. "No, no, Mr. Kelcey," cried Bleecker, "no, no. To-night you are our guest. Some other time—"

"Here," said O'Connor, "it's my turn now."

He called and pounded for the bartender. He then sat with a coin in his hand warily eyeing the others. He was ready to frustrate them if they offered to pay.

After a time Jones began to develop qualities of great eloquence and wit. His companions laughed. "It's the whisky talking now," said Bleecker.

He grew earnest and impassioned. He delivered speeches on various subjects. His lectures were to him very imposing. The force of his words thrilled him. Sometimes he was overcome.

The others agreed with him in all things. Bleecker grew almost tender, and considerately placed words here and there for his use. As Jones became fiercely energetic the others became more docile in agreeing. They soothed him with friendly interjections.

His mode changed directly. He began to sing popular airs with enthusiasm. He congratulated his companions upon being in his society. They were excited by his frenzy. They began to fraternize in jovial fashion. It was understood that they were true and tender spirits. They had come away from a grinding world filled with men who were harsh.

When one of them chose to divulge some place where the world had pierced him, there was a chorus of violent sympathy. They rejoiced at their temporary isolation and safety.

Once a man, completely drunk, stumbled along the floor of the saloon. He opened the door of the little room and made a show of entering. The men sprang instantly to their feet. They were ready to throttle any invader of their island. They elbowed each other in rivalry as to who should take upon himself the brunt of an encounter.

"Oh!" said the drunken individual, swaying on his legs and blinking at the party, "oh! thish private room?"

"That's what it is, Willie," said Jones. "An' you git outa here, er we'll throw yeh out."

"That's what we will," said the others.

"Oh," said the drunken man. He blinked at them aggrievedly for an instant and then went away.

They sat down again. Kelcey felt, in a way, that he would have liked to display his fidelity to the others by whipping the intruder.

The bartender came often. "Gee, you fellas er tanks," he said, in a jocular manner, as he gathered empty glasses and polished the table with his little towel.

Through the exertions of Jones the little room began to grow clamorous. The tobacco smoke eddied about the forms of the men in ropes and wreaths. Near the ceiling there was a thick grey cloud.

Each man explained, in his way, that he was totally out of place in the before-mentioned world. They were possessed of various virtues which were unappreciated by those with whom they were commonly obliged to mingle; they were fitted for a tree-shaded land where everything was peace. Now that five of them had congregated it gave them happiness to speak their inmost thoughts without fear of being misunderstood.

As he drank more beer Kelcey felt his breast expand with manly feeling. He knew that he was capable of sublime things. He wished that some day one of his present companions would come to him for relief. His mind pictured a little scene. In it he was magnificent in his friendship.

He looked upon the beaming faces and knew that if at that instant there should come a time for a great sacrifice he would blissfully make it. He would pass tranquilly into the unknown, or into bankruptcy, amid the ejaculations of his companions upon his many virtues.

They had no bickerings during the evening. If one chose to momentarily assert himself, the others instantly submitted.

They exchanged compliments. Once old Bleecker stared at Jones for a few moments. Suddenly he broke out: "Jones, you're one of the finest fellows I ever knew!" A flush of pleasure went over the other's face, and then he made a modest gesture, the protest of a humble man. "Don't flimflam me, ol' boy," he said, with earnestness. But Bleecker roared that he was serious about it. The two men arose and shook hands emotionally. Jones bunted against the table and knocked off a glass.

Afterward a general hand-shaking was inaugurated. Brotherly sentiments flew about the room. There was an uproar of fraternal feeling.

Jones began to sing. He beat time with precision and dignity. He gazed into the eyes of his companions, trying to call music from their souls. O'Connor joined in heartily, but with another tune. Off in a corner old Bleecker was making a speech.

The bartender came to the door. "Gee, you fellahs er making a row. It's time fer me t' shut up th' front th' place, an' you mugs better sit on yerselves. It's one o'clock."

They began to argue with him. Kelcey, however, sprang to his feet. "One o'clock," he said. "Holy smoke, I mus' be flyin'!"

There came protesting howls from Jones. Bleecker ceased his oration. "My dear boy—" he began. Kelcey searched for his hat. "I've gotta go t' work at seven," he said.

The others watched him with discomfort in their eyes. "Well," said O'Connor, "if one goes we might as well all go." They sadly took their hats and filed out.

The cold air of the street filled Kelcey with vague surprise. It made his head feel hot. As for his legs, they were like willow-twigs.

A few yellow lights blinked. In front of an all-night restaurant a huge red electric lamp hung and sputtered. Horse-car bells jingled far down the street. Overhead a train thundered on the elevated road.

On the sidewalk the men took fervid leave. They clutched hands with extraordinary force and proclaimed, for the last time, ardent and admiring friendships.

When he arrived at his home Kelcey proceeded with caution. His mother had left a light burning low. He stumbled once in his voyage across the floor. As he paused to listen he heard the sound of little snores coming from her room.

He lay awake for a few moments and thought of the

evening. He had a pleasurable consciousness that he had
made a good impression upon those fine fellows. He felt
that he had spent the most delightful evening of his life.

V

Kelcey was cross in the morning. His mother had been
obliged to shake him a great deal, and it had seemed to
him a most unjust thing. Also, when he, blinking his eyes,
had entered the kitchen, she had said: "Yeh left th' lamp
burnin' all night last night, George. How many times must
I tell yeh never t' leave th' lamp burnin'?"

He ate the greater part of his breakfast in silence,
moodily stirring his coffee and glaring at a remote corner
of the room with eyes that felt as if they had been baked.
When he moved his eyelids there was a sensation that they
were cracking. In his mouth there was a singular taste.
It seemed to him that he had been sucking the end of a
wooden spoon. Moreover, his temper was rampant within
him. It sought something to devour.

Finally he said savagely: "Damn these early hours!"

His mother jumped as if he had flung a missile at her.
"Why, George—" she began.

Kelcey broke in again. "Oh, I know all that—but this
gettin' up in th' mornin' so early makes me sick. Jest
when a man is gettin' his mornin' nap he's gotta get up.
I—"

"George, dear," said his mother, "yeh know how I
hate yeh t' swear, dear. Now, please don't." She looked
beseechingly at him.

He made a swift gesture. "Well, I ain't swearin', am I?"
he demanded. "I was on'y sayin' that this gettin'-up business gives me a pain, wasn't I?"

"Well, yeh know how swearin' hurts me," protested the
little old woman. She seemed about to sob. She gazed off
retrospectively. She apparently was recalling persons who
had never been profane.

"I don't see where yeh ever caught this way a' swearin'
out at everything," she continued presently. "Fred, ner

John, ner Willie never swore a bit. Ner Tom neither, except when he was real mad."

The son made another gesture. It was directed into the air, as if he saw there a phantom injustice. "Oh, good thunder," he said, with an accent of despair. Thereupon, he relapsed into a mood of silence. He sombrely regarded his plate.

This demeanour speedily reduced his mother to meekness. When she spoke again it was in a conciliatory voice. "George, dear, won't yeh bring some sugar home t'-night?" It could be seen that she was asking for a crown of gold.

Kelcey aroused from his semi-slumber. "Yes, if I kin remember it," he said.

The little old woman arose to stow her son's lunch into the pail. When he had finished his breakfast he stalked for a time about the room in a dignified way. He put on his coat and hat and, taking his lunch-pail, went to the door. There he halted and, without turning his head, stiffly said: "Well, good-bye."

The little old woman saw that she had offended her son. She did not seek an explanation. She was accustomed to these phenomena. She made haste to surrender.

"Ain't yeh goin' t' kiss me good-bye?" she asked in a little woeful voice.

The youth made a pretence of going on, deaf-heartedly. He wore the dignity of an injured monarch.

Then the little old woman called again in forsaken accents: "George—George—ain't yeh goin' t' kiss me good-bye?" When he moved he found that she was hanging to his coat-tails.

He turned eventually with a murmur of a sort of tenderness. "Why, a' course I am," he said. He kissed her. Withal there was an undertone of superiority in his voice, as if he were granting an astonishing suit. She looked at him with reproach and gratitude and affection.

She stood at the head of the stairs and watched his hand sliding along the rail as he went down. Occasionally she could see his arm and part of his shoulder. When he reached the first floor she called to him: "Good-bye!"

The little old woman went back to her work in the kitchen with a frown of perplexity upon her brow. "I wonder what was th' matter with George this mornin'," she mused. "He didn't seem a bit like himself!"

As she trudged to and fro at her labour she began to speculate. She was much worried. She surmised in a vague way that he was a sufferer from a great internal disease. It was something, no doubt, that devoured the kidneys or quietly fed upon the lungs. Later, she imagined a woman, wicked and fair, who had fascinated him and was turning his life into a bitter thing. Her mind created many wondrous influences that were swooping like green dragons at him. They were changing him to a morose man who suffered silently. She longed to discover them, that she might go bravely to the rescue of her heroic son. She knew that he, generous in his pain, would keep it from her. She racked her mind for knowledge.

However, when he came home at night he was extraordinarily blithe. He seemed to be a lad of ten. He capered all about the room. When she was bringing the coffee-pot from the stove to the table he made show of waltzing with her, so that she spilled some of the coffee. She was obliged to scold him.

All through the meal he made jokes. She occasionally was compelled to laugh, despite the fact that she believed that she should not laugh at her own son's jokes. She uttered reproofs at times, but he did not regard them.

"Golly," he said once, "I feel fine as silk. I didn't think I'd get over feelin' bad so quick. It—" He stopped abruptly.

During the evening he sat content. He smoked his pipe and read from an evening paper. She bustled about at her work. She seemed utterly happy with him there, lazily puffing out little clouds of smoke and giving frequent brilliant dissertations upon the news of the day. It seemed to her that she must be a model mother to have such a son, one who came home to her at night and sat contented, in a languor of the muscles after a good day's toil. She pondered upon the science of her management.

The week thereafter, too, she was joyous, for he stayed

at home each night of it, and was sunny-tempered. She became convinced that she was a perfect mother, rearing a perfect son. There came often a love-light into her eyes. The wrinkled, yellow face frequently warmed into a smile of the kind that a maiden bestows upon him who to her is first and perhaps last.

VI

The little old woman habitually discouraged all outbursts of youthful vanity on the part of her son. She feared that he would get to think too much of himself, and she knew that nothing could do more harm. Great self-esteem was always passive, she thought, and if he grew to regard his qualities of mind as forming a dazzling constellation, he would tranquilly sit still and not do those wonders she expected of him. So she was constantly on the alert to suppress even a shadow of such a thing. As for him, he ruminated with the savage, vengeful bitterness of a young man, and decided that she did not comprehend him.

But despite her precautions he often saw that she believed him to be the most marvellous young man on the earth. He had only to look at those two eyes that became lighted with a glow from her heart whenever he did some excessively brilliant thing. On these occasions he could see her glance triumphantly at a neighbour, or whoever happened to be present. He grew to plan for these glances. And then he took a vast satisfaction in detecting and appropriating them.

Nevertheless, he could not understand why, directly after a scene of this kind, his mother was liable to call to him to hang his coat on the hook under the mantel, her voice in a key of despair, as if he were negligent and stupid in what was, after all, the only important thing in life.

"If yeh'll only get in the habit of doin' it, it'll be jest as easy as throwin' it down anywheres," she would say to him. "When ye pitch it down anywheres, somebody's got t' pick it up, an' that'll most likely be your poor ol' mother. Yeh can hang it up yerself, if yeh'll on'y think." This was intolerable. He usually went then and hurled his coat savagely at the hook. The correctness of her position was maddening.

It seemed to him that any one who had a son of his glowing attributes should overlook the fact that he seldom hung up his coat. It was impossible to explain this situation to his mother. She was unutterably narrow. He grew sullen.

There came a time, too, when, even in all his mother's tremendous admiration for him, he did not entirely agree with her. He was delighted that she liked his great wit. He spurred himself to new and flashing effort because of this appreciation. But for the greater part he could see that his mother took pride in him in quite a different way from that in which he took pride in himself. She rejoiced at qualities in him that indicated that he was going to become a white and looming king among men. From these she made pictures in which he appeared as a benign personage, blessed by the filled hands of the poor, one whose brain could hold massive thoughts and awe certain men about whom she had read. She was fêted as the mother of this enormous man. These dreams were her solace. She spoke of them to no one, because she knew that, worded, they would be ridiculous. But she dwelt with them, and they shed a radiance of gold upon her long days, her sorry labour. Upon the dead altars of her life she had builded the little fires of hope for another.

He had a complete sympathy for as much as he understood of these thoughts of his mother. They were so wise that he admired her foresight. As for himself, however, most of his dreams were of a nearer time. He had many of the distant future when he would be a man with a cloak of coldness concealing his gentleness and his faults, of whom the men, and more particularly the women, would think with reverence. He agreed with his mother that at that time he would go through what were obstacles to other men like a flung stone. And then he would have power, and he would enjoy having his bounty and his wrath alike fall swiftly upon those below. They would be awed. And above all he would mystify them.

But then his nearer dreams were a multitude. He had begun to look at the great world revolving near to his nose. He had a vast curiosity concerning this city in whose complexities he was buried. It was an impenetrable mystery, this city. It was a blend of many enticing colours. He longed to comprehend it completely, that he might walk understandingly in its greatest marvels, its mightiest march of life, sin. He dreamed of a comprehension whose pay was the admirable attitude of a man of knowledge. He remembered Jones. He could not but admire a man who knew so many bartenders.

VII

An indefinite woman was in all of Kelcey's dreams. As a matter of fact it was not he whom he pictured as wedding her. It was a vision of himself greater, finer, more terrible. It was himself as he expected to be. In scenes which he took mainly from pictures, this vision conducted a courtship, strutting, posing, and lying through a drama which was magnificent from glow of purple. In it he was icy, self-possessed; but she, the dream-girl, was consumed by wild, torrential passion. He went to the length of having her display it before the people. He saw them wonder at his tranquillity. It amazed them infinitely to see him remain cold before the glory of this peerless woman's love. She was to him as beseeching for affection as a pet animal, but still he controlled appearances, and none knew of his deep abiding love. Some day, at the critical romantic time, he was going to divulge it. In these long dreams there were accessories of castle-like houses, wide lands, servants, horses, clothes.

They began somewhere in his childhood. When he ceased to see himself as a stern general pointing a sword at the nervous and abashed horizon, he became this sublime king of a vague woman's heart. Later, when he had read some books, it all achieved clearer expression. He was told in them that there was a goddess in the world whose business it was to wait until he should exchange a glance with her. It became a creed, subtly powerful. It

saved discomfort for him and for several women who
flitted by him. He used her as a standard.

Often he saw the pathos of her long wait, but his faith
did not falter. The world was obliged to turn gold in time.
His life was to be fine and heroic, else he would not have
been born. He believed that the commonplace lot was the
sentence, the doom, of certain people who did not know
how to feel. His blood was a tender current of life. He
thought that the usual should fall to others whose nerves
were of lead. Occasionally he wondered how fate was
going to begin making an enormous figure of him; but he
had no doubt of the result. A chariot of pink clouds was
coming for him. His faith was his reason for existence.
Meanwhile he could dream of the indefinite woman and
the fragrance of roses that came from her hair.

One day he met Maggie Johnson on the stairs. She had
a pail of beer in one hand and a brown-paper parcel under
her arm. She glanced at him. He discovered that it would
wither his heart to see another man signally successful in
the smiles of her. And the glance that she gave him was
so indifferent and so unresponsive to the sudden vivid admiration in his own eyes that he immediately concluded
that she was magnificent in two ways.

As she came to the landing, the light from a window
passed in a silver gleam over the girlish roundness of her
cheek. It was a thing that he remembered.

He was silent for the most part at supper that night.
He was particularly unkind when he did speak. His mother,
observing him apprehensively, tried in vain to picture the
new terrible catastrophe. She eventually concluded that he
did not like the beef-stew. She put more salt in it.

He saw Maggie quite frequently after the meeting upon
the stairs. He reconstructed his dreams and placed her in
the full glory of that sun. The dream-woman, the goddess, pitched from her pedestal, lay prostrate, unheeded,
save when he brought her forth to call her insipid and
childish in the presence of his new religion.

He was relatively happy sometimes when Maggie's
mother would get drunk and make terrific uproars. He

used then to sit in the dark and make scenes in which he rescued the girl from her hideous environment.

He laid clever plans by which he encountered her in the halls, at the door, on the street. When he succeeded in meeting her he was always overcome by the thought that the whole thing was obvious to her. He could feel the shame of it burn his face and neck. To prove to her that she was mistaken he would turn away his head or regard her with a granite stare.

After a time he became impatient of the distance between them. He saw looming princes who would aim to seize her. Hours of his leisure and certain hours of his labour he spent in contriving. The shade of this girl was with him continually. With her he built his grand dramas so that he trod in clouds, the matters of his daily life obscured and softened by a mist.

He saw that he need only break down the slight conventional barriers and she would soon discover his noble character. Sometimes he could see it all in his mind. It was very skilful. But then his courage flew away at the supreme moment. Perhaps the whole affair was humorous to her. Perhaps she was watching his mental contortions. She might laugh. He felt that he would then die or kill her. He could not approach the dread moment. He sank often from the threshold of knowledge. Directly after these occasions, it was his habit to avoid her to prove that she was a cipher to him.

He reflected that if he could only get a chance to rescue her from something, the whole tragedy would speedily unwind.

He met a young man in the halls one evening who said to him: "Say, me frien', where d' d' Johnson birds live in heh? I can't fin' me feet in dis bloomin' joint. I been battin' around heh fer a half-hour."

"Two flights up," said Kelcey stonily. He had felt a sudden quiver of his heart. The grandeur of the clothes, the fine worldly air, the experience, the self-reliance, the courage that shone in the countenance of this other young man made him suddenly sink to the depths of woe. He stood listening in the hall, flushing and ashamed of it, until he heard them coming downstairs together. He slunk away then. It would have been a horror to him if she had discovered him there. She might have felt sorry for him.

They were going out to a show, perhaps. That pig of the world in his embroidered cloak was going to dazzle her with splendour. He mused upon how unrighteous it was for other men to dazzle women with splendour.

As he appreciated his handicap he swore with savage, vengeful bitterness. In his home his mother raised her voice in a high key of monotonous irritability. "Hang up yer coat, can't yeh, George?" she cried at him. "I can't go round after yeh all th' time. It's jest as easy t' hang it up as it is t' throw it down that way. Don't yeh ever git tired a' hearing me yell at yeh?"

"Yes," he exploded. In this word he put a profundity of sudden anger. He turned toward his mother a face red, seamed, hard with hate and rage. They stared a moment in silence. Then she turned and staggered toward her room. Her hip struck violently against the corner of the table during this blind passage. A moment later the door closed.

Kelcey sank down in a chair with his legs thrust out straight and his hands deep in his trousers pockets. His chin was forward upon his breast, and his eyes stared before him. There swept over him all the self-pity that comes when the soul is turned back from a road.

VIII

During the next few days Kelcey suffered from his first gloomy conviction that the earth was not grateful to him for his presence upon it. When sharp words were said to him, he interpreted them with what seemed to be a lately acquired insight. He could now perceive that the universe hated him. He sank to the most sublime depths of despair.

One evening of this period he met Jones. The latter rushed upon him with enthusiasm. "Why, yer jest th' man I wanted t' see! I was comin' round t' your place t'-night. Lucky I' met yeh! Ol' Bleecker's goin' t' give a blow-out t'-morrah night. Anything yeh want t' drink! All th' boys'll be there, an' everything. He tol' me expressly that he wanted yeh t' be there. Great time! Great! Can yeh come?"

Kelcey grasped the other's hand with fervour. He felt now that there was some solacing friendship in space. "You bet I will, ol' man," he said huskily. "I'd like nothin' better in th' world!"

As he walked home he thought that he was a very grim figure. He was about to taste the delicious revenge of a partial self-destruction. The universe would regret its position when it saw him drunk.

He was a little late in getting to Bleecker's lodging. He was delayed while his mother read aloud a letter from an old uncle, who wrote in one place: "God bless the boy! Bring him up to be the man his father was." Bleecker lived in an old three-storeyed house on a side street. A Jewish tailor lived and worked in the front parlour, and old Bleecker lived in the back parlour. A German, whose family took care of the house, occupied the basement. Another German, with a wife and eight children, rented the dining-room. The two upper floors were inhabited by tailors, dressmakers, a pedlar, and mysterious people who were seldom seen. The door of the little hall bedroom, at the foot of the second flight, was always open, and in there could be seen two bended men who worked at mending opera-glasses. The German woman in the dining-room was not friends with the little dressmaker in the rear room of the third floor, and frequently they yelled the vilest names up and down between the balusters. Each part of the woodwork was scratched and rubbed by the contact of innumerable persons. In one wall there was a long slit with chipped edges, celebrating the time when a man had thrown a hatchet at his wife. In the lower hall there was an eternal woman, with a rag and a pail of suds, who knelt over the worn oil-cloth. Old Bleecker felt that he had quite respectable and high-class apartments. He was glad to invite his friends.

Bleecker met Kelcey in the hall. He wore a collar that was cleaner and higher than his usual one. It changed his appearance greatly. He was now formidably aristocratic. "How are yeh, ol' man?" he shouted. He grasped Kelcey's arm and, babbling jovially, conducted him down the hall and into the ex-parlour.

A group of standing men made vast shadows in the yellow glare of the lamp. They turned their heads as the two entered. "Why, hello, Kelcey, ol' man," Jones exclaimed, coming rapidly forward. "Good fer you! Glad yeh come! Yeh know O'Connor, a' course! An' Schmidt! an' Woods! Then there's Zeusentell! Mr. Zeusentell—my friend Mr. Kelcey! Shake hands—both good fellows, damn-it-all! Then here is—oh, gentlemen, my friend Mr. Kelcey! A good fellow, he is, too. I've known 'im since I was a kid. Come, have a drink!" Everybody was excessively amiable. Kelcey felt that he had social standing. The strangers were cautious and respectful.

"By all means," said old Bleecker, "Mr. Kelcey, have a drink! An' by th' way, gentlemen, while we're about it, let's all have a drink!" There was much laughter. Bleecker was so droll at times.

With mild and polite gesturing they marched up to the table. There were upon it a keg of beer, a long row of whisky-bottles, a little heap of corncob pipes, some bags of tobacco, a box of cigars, and a mighty collection of glasses, cups, and mugs. Old Bleecker had arranged them so deftly that they resembled a primitive bar. There was considerable scuffling for possession of the cracked cups. Jones politely but vehemently insisted upon drinking from the worst of the assortment. He was quietly opposed by others. Everybody showed that they were awed by Bleecker's lavish hospitality. Their demeanours expressed their admiration at the cost of this entertainment.

Kelcey took his second mug of beer away to a corner and sat down with it. He wished to socially reconnoitre. Over in a corner a man was telling a story in which at intervals he grunted like a pig. A half-dozen men were listening. Two or three others sat alone in isolated places. They looked expectantly bright, ready to burst out cordially if any one should address them. The row of bottles made quaint shadows upon the table, and upon a side-wall the keg of beer created a portentous black figure that reared toward the ceiling, hovering over the room and its inmates with spectral stature. Tobacco smoke lay in lazy cloud-banks overhead.

Jones and O'Connor stayed near the table, occasionally being affable in all directions. Kelcey saw old Bleecker go to them and heard him whisper: "Come, we must git th' thing started. Git th' thing started." Kelcey saw that the host was fearing that all were not having a good time. Jones conferred with O'Connor, and then O'Connor went to the man named Zeusentell. O'Connor evidently proposed something. Zeusentell refused at once. O'Connor beseeched. Zeusentell remained implacable. At last O'Connor broke off his argument and, going to the centre of the room, held up his hand. "Gentlemen," he shouted loudly, "we will now have a recitation by Mr. Zeusentell, entitled 'Patrick Clancy's Pig'!" He then glanced triumphantly at Zeusentell and said: "Come on!" Zeusentell had been twisting and making pantomimic appeals. He said, in a reproachful whisper: "You son of a gun."

The men turned their heads to glance at Zeusentell for a moment, and then burst into a sustained clamour. "Hurray! Let 'er go! Come—give it t' us! Spring it! Spring it! Let it come!" As Zeusentell made no advances, they appealed personally. "Come, ol' man, let 'er go! Whatter yeh 'fraid of? Let 'er go! Go ahn! Hurry up!"

Zeusentell was protesting with almost frantic modesty. O'Connor took him by the lapel and tried to drag him; but he leaned back, pulling at his coat and shaking his head. "No, no, I don't know it, I tell yeh! I can't! I don't know it! I tell yeh I don't know it! I've forgotten it, I tell yeh! No—no—no—no. Ah, say, look-a-here, le' go me, can't yeh? What's th' matter with yeh? I tell yeh I don't know it!" The men applauded violently. O'Connor did not relent. A little battle was waged until all of a sudden Zeusentell was seen to grow wondrously solemn. A hush fell upon the men. He was about to begin. He paused in the middle of the floor and nervously adjusted his collar and cravat. The audience became grave. " 'Patrick Clancy's Pig,' " announced Zeusentell in a shrill, dry, unnatural tone. And then he began in rapid sing-song:

> "*Patrick Clancy had a pig*
> *Th' pride uv all th' nation,*
> *The half uv him was half as big*
> *As half uv all creation—*"

When he concluded the others looked at each other to convey their appreciation. They then wildly clapped their hands or tinkled their glasses. As Zeusentell went toward his seat a man leaned over and asked: "Can yeh tell me where I kin git that?" He had made a great success. After an enormous pressure he was induced to recite two more tales. Old Bleecker finally led him forward and pledged him in a large drink. He declared that they were the best things he had ever heard.

The efforts of Zeusentell imparted a gaiety to the company. The men, having laughed together, were better acquainted, and there was now a universal topic. Some of the party, too, began to be quite drunk.

The invaluable O'Connor brought forth a man who could play the mouth-organ. The latter, after wiping his instrument upon his coat-sleeve, played all the popular airs. The men's heads swayed to and fro in the clouded smoke. They grinned and beat time with their feet. A valour, barbaric and wild, began to show in their poses and in their faces, red and glistening from perspiration. The conversation resounded in a hoarse roar. The beer would not run rapidly enough for Jones, so he remained behind to tilt the keg. This caused the black shadow on the wall to retreat and advance, sinking mystically to loom forward again with sudden menace, a huge dark figure controlled as by some unknown emotion. The glasses, mugs, and cups travelled swift and regular, catching orange reflections from the lamp-light. Two or three men were grown so careless that they were continually spilling their drinks. Old Bleecker, cackling with pleasure, seized time to glance triumphantly at Jones. His party was going to be a success.

IX

Of a sudden Kelcey felt the buoyant thought that he was having a good time. He was all at once an enthusiast, as if he were at a festival of a religion. He felt that there was something fine and thrilling in this affair isolated from a stern world, from which the laughter arose like incense. He knew that old sentiment of brotherly regard for those about him. He began to converse tenderly with them. He was not sure of his drift of thought, but he knew that he was immensely sympathetic. He rejoiced at their faces, shining red and wrinkled with smiles. He was capable of heroisms.

His pipe irritated him by going out frequently. He was too busy in amiable conversations to attend to it. When he arose to go for a match he discovered that his legs were a trifle uncertain under him. They bended and did not precisely obey his intent. At the table he lit a match and then, in laughing at a joke made near him, forgot to apply it to the bowl of his pipe. He succeeded with the next match after annoying trouble. He swayed so that the match would appear first on one side of the bowl and then on the other. At last he happily got it directly over the tobacco. He had burned his fingers. He inspected them, laughing vaguely.

Jones came and slapped him on the shoulder. "Well, ol' man, let's take a drink fer ol' Handyville's sake!"

Kelcey was deeply affected. He looked at Jones with moist eyes. "I'll go yeh," he said. With an air of profound melancholy, Jones poured out some whisky. They drank reverently. They exchanged a glistening look of tender recollections and then went over to where Bleecker was telling a humorous story to a circle of giggling listeners. The old man sat like a fat, jolly god. "—And just at that moment th' old woman put her head out of th' window an' said: 'Mike, yez lazy divil, fer phwat do yez be slapin' in me new geranium bid?' An' Mike woke up an' said: 'Domn a washwoman thot do niver wash her own bid-

clues. Here do I be slapin' in nothin' but dhirt an' wades.' "
The men slapped their knees, roaring loudly. They begged
him to tell another. A clamour of comment arose concerning the anecdote, so that when old Bleecker began a
fresh one nobody was heeding.

It occurred to Jones to sing. Suddenly he burst forth
with a ballad that had a rippling waltz movement, and,
seizing Kelcey, made a furious attempt to dance. They
sprawled over a pair of outstretched legs and pitched headlong. Kelcey fell with a yellow crash. Blinding lights
flashed before his vision. But he arose immediately, laughing. He did not feel at all hurt. The pain in his head was
rather pleasant.

Old Bleecker, O'Connor, and Jones, who now limped
and drew breath through his teeth, were about to lead him
with much care and tenderness to the table for another
drink, but he laughingly pushed them away and went un-
assisted. Bleecker told him: "Great Gawd, your head
struck hard enough t' break a trunk."

He laughed again, and with a show of steadiness and
courage he poured out an extravagant portion of whisky.
With cold muscles he put it to his lips and drank it. It
chanced that this addition dazed him like a powerful blow.
A moment later it affected him with blinding and numbing
power. Suddenly unbalanced, he felt the room sway. His
blurred sight could only distinguish a tumbled mass of
shadow through which the beams from the light ran like
swords of flame. The sound of the many voices was to
him like the roar of a distant river. Still, he felt that if
he could only annul the force of these million winding
fingers that gripped his senses, he was capable of most
brilliant and entertaining things.

He was at first of the conviction that his feelings were
only temporary. He waited for them to pass away, but the
mental and physical pause only caused a new reeling and
swinging of the room. Chasms with inclined approaches
were before him; peaks leaned toward him. And withal
he was blind and numb with surprise. He understood

vaguely in his stupefaction that it would disgrace him to fall down a chasm.

At last he perceived a shadow, a form, which he knew to be Jones. The adorable Jones, the supremely wise Jones, was walking in this strange land without fear or care, erect and tranquil. Kelcey murmured in admiration and affection, and fell toward his friend. Jones's voice sounded as from the shores of the unknown. "Come, come, ol' man, this will never do. Brace up." It appeared after all that Jones was not wholly wise. "Oh, I'm—all ri', Jones! I'm all ri'! I wan' shing song! Tha' 's all! I wan' shing song!"

Jones was stupid. "Come, now, sit down an' shut up."

It made Kelcey burn with fury. "Jones, le' me alone, I tell yeh! Le' me alone! I wan' shing song er te' story! G'l'm'n, I lovsh girl live down my shtreet. Thash reason 'm drunk—'tis! She—"

Jones seized him and dragged him toward a chair. He heard him laugh. He could not endure these insults from his friend. He felt a blazing desire to strangle his companion. He threw out his hand violently, but Jones grappled him close and he was no more than a dried leaf. He was amazed to find that Jones possessed the strength of twenty horses. He was forced skilfully to the floor.

As he lay he reflected in great astonishment upon Jones's muscle. It was singular that he had never before discovered it. The whole incident had impressed him immensely. An idea struck him that he might denounce Jones for it. It would be a sage thing. There would be a thrilling and dramatic moment in which he would dazzle all the others. But at this moment he was assailed by a mighty desire to sleep. Sombre and soothing clouds of slumber were heavily upon him. He closed his eyes with a sigh that was yet like that of a babe.

When he awoke there was still the battleful clamour of the revel. He half arose with a plan of participating, when O'Connor came and pushed him down again, throwing out his chin in affectionate remonstrance and saying, "Now, now," as to a child.

The change that had come over these men mystified
Kelcey in a great degree. He had never seen anything so
vastly stupid as their idea of his state. He resolved to prove
to them that they were dealing with one whose mind
was very clear. He kicked and squirmed in O'Connor's
arms, until, with a final wrench, he scrambled to his feet
and stood tottering in the middle of the room. He would
let them see that he had a strangely lucid grasp of events.
"G'l'm'n, I lovsh girl! I ain' drunker'n yeh all are! She—"

He felt them hurl him to a corner of the room and
pile chairs and tables upon him until he was buried beneath a stupendous mountain. Far above, as up a mine's
shaft, there were voices, lights, and vague figures. He was
not hurt physically, but his feelings were unutterably injured. He, the brilliant, the good, the sympathetic, had
been thrust fiendishly from the party. They had had the
comprehension of red lobsters. It was an unspeakable bar-
barism. Tears welled piteously from his eyes. He planned
long diabolical explanations!

X

At first the grey lights of dawn came timidly into the
room, remaining near the windows, afraid to approach certain sinister corners. Finally, mellow streams of sunshine
poured in, undraping the shadows to disclose the putre-
faction, making pitiless revelation. Kelcey awoke with a
groan of undirected misery. He tossed his stiffened arms
about his head for a moment, and then, leaning heavily
upon his elbow, stared blinking at his environment. The
grim truthfulness of the day showed disaster and death.
After the tumults of the previous night the interior of
this room resembled a decaying battlefield. The air hung
heavy and stifling with the odours of tobacco, men's
breaths, and beer half filling forgotten glasses. There was
ruck of broken tumblers, pipes, bottles, spilled tobacco,
cigar-stumps. The chairs and tables were pitched this way
and that way, as after some terrible struggle. In the midst
of it all lay old Bleecker, stretched upon a couch in deep-

est sleep, as abandoned in attitude, as motionless, as ghastly, as if it were a corpse that had been flung there.

A knowledge of the thing came gradually into Kelcey's eyes. He looked about him with an expression of utter woe, regret, and loathing. He was compelled to lie down again. A pain above his eyebrows was like that from an iron clamp.

As he lay pondering, his bodily condition created for him a bitter philosophy, and he perceived all the futility of a red existence. He saw his life problems confronting him like granite giants, and he was no longer erect to meet them. He had made a calamitous retrogression in his war. Spectres were to him now as large as clouds.

Inspired by the pitiless ache in his head, he was prepared to reform and live a white life. His stomach informed him that a good man was the only being who was wise. But his perception of his future was hopeless. He was aghast at the prospect of the old routine. It was impossible. He trembled before its exactions.

Turning toward the other way, he saw that the gold portals of vice no longer enticed him. He could not hear the strains of alluring music. The beckoning sirens of drink had been killed by this pain in his head. The desires of his life suddenly lay dead like mullein-stalks. Upon reflection, he saw, therefore, that he was perfectly willing to be virtuous if somebody would come and make it easy for him.

When he stared over at old Bleecker, he felt a sudden contempt and dislike for him. He considered him to be a tottering old beast. It was disgusting to perceive aged men so weak in sin. He dreaded to see him awaken, lest he should be required to be somewhat civil to him.

Kelcey wished for a drink of water. For some time he had dreamed of the liquid, deliciously cool. It was an abstract, uncontained thing that poured upon him and tumbled him, taking away his pain like a kind of surgery. He arose and staggered slowly toward a little sink in a corner of the room. He understood that any rapid movement might cause his head to split.

The little sink was filled with a chaos of broken glass and spilled liquids. A sight of it filled him with horror, but he rinsed a glass with scrupulous care and, filling it, took an enormous drink. The water was an intolerable disappointment. It was insipid and weak to his scorched throat, and not at all cool. He put down the glass with a gesture of despair. His face became fixed in the stony and sullen expression of a man who waits for the recuperative power of morrows.

Old Bleecker awakened. He rolled over and groaned loudly. For a while he thrashed about in a fury of displeasure at his bodily stiffness and pain. Kelcey watched him as he would have watched a death agony. "Good Gawd!" said the old man, "beer an' whisky make th' devil of a mix! Did yeh see th' fight?"

"No," said Kelcey stolidly.

"Why, Zeusentell an' O'Connor had a great old mill. They were scrappin' all over th' place. I thought we were all goin' t' get pulled. Thompson, that fellah over in th' corner, though, he sat down on th' whole business. He was a dandy! He had t' poke Zeusentell! He was a bird! Lord, I wish I had a Manhattan!"

Kelcey remained in bitter silence while old Bleecker dressed. "Come an' get a cocktail," said the latter briskly. This was part of his aristocracy. He was the only man of them who knew much about cocktails. He perpetually referred to them. "It'll brace yeh right up! Come along! Say, you get full too soon. You oughter wait until later, me boy! You're too speedy!" Kelcey wondered vaguely where his companion had lost his zeal for polished sentences, his iridescent mannerisms.

"Come along," said Bleecker.

Kelcey made a movement of disdain for cocktails, but he followed the other to the street. At the corner they separated. Kelcey attempted a friendly parting smile and then went on up the street. He had to reflect to know that he was erect and using his own muscles in walking. He felt like a man of paper, blown by the winds. Withal, the dust of the avenue was galling to his throat, eyes, and nostrils, and the roar of traffic cracked his head. He was glad, however, to be alone, to be rid of old Bleecker. The sight of him had been as the contemplation of a disease.

His mother was not at home. In his little room he mechanically undressed and bathed his head, arms, and shoulders. When he crawled between the two white sheets he felt a first lifting of his misery. His pillow was soothingly soft. There was an effect that was like the music of tender voices.

When he awoke again his mother was bending over him giving vent to alternate cries of grief and joy. Her hands trembled so that they were useless to her. "Oh, George, George, where have yeh been? What has happened t' yeh? Oh, George, I've been so worried! I didn't sleep a wink all night!"

Kelcey was instantly wide awake. With a moan of suffering he turned his face to the wall before he spoke. "Never mind, mother, I'm all right. Don't fret now! I was knocked down by a truck last night in th' street, and they took me t' th' hospital; but it's all right now. I got out jest a little while ago. They told me I'd better go home an' rest up."

His mother screamed in pity, horror, joy, and self-reproach for something unknown. She frenziedly demanded the details. He sighed with unutterable weariness. "Oh—wait—wait—wait," he said, shutting his eyes as from the merciless monotony of a pain. "Wait—wait—please wait. I can't talk now. I want t' rest."

His mother condemned herself with a little cry. She adjusted his pillow, her hands shaking with love and tenderness. "There, there, don't mind, dearie! But yeh can't think how worried I was—an' crazy. I was near frantic. I went down t' th' shop, an' they said they hadn't seen anything a' yeh there. The foreman was awful good t' me. He said he'd come up this afternoon t' see if yeh had come home yet. He tol' me not t' worry. Are yeh sure yer all right? Ain't there anythin' I kin git fer yeh? What did th' doctor say?"

Kelcey's patience was worn. He gestured, and then spoke querulously. "Now—now—mother, it's all right, I tell yeh!

All I need is a little rest, an' I'll be as well as ever. But it makes it all th' worse if yeh stand there an' ask me questions an' make me think. Jest leave me alone fer a little while, an' I'll be as well as ever. Can't yeh do that?"

The little old woman puckered her lips funnily. "My, what an old bear th' boy is!" She kissed him blithely. Presently she went out, upon her face a bright and glad smile that must have been a reminiscence of some charming girlhood.

XI

At one time Kelcey had a friend who was struck in the head by the pole of a truck and knocked senseless. He was taken to the hospital, from which he emerged in the morning an astonished man, with rather a dim recollection of the accident. He used to hold an old brier-wood pipe in his teeth in a manner peculiar to himself, and, with a brown derby hat tilted back on his head, recount his strange sensations. Kelcey had always remembered it as a bit of curious history. When his mother cross-examined him in regard to the accident, he told this story with barely a variation. Its truthfulness was incontestable.

At the shop he was welcomed on the following day with considerable enthusiasm. The foreman had told the story, and there were already jokes created concerning it. Mike O'Donnell, whose wit was famous, had planned a humorous campaign, in which he made charges against Kelcey which were, as a matter of fact, almost the exact truth. Upon hearing it, Kelcey looked at him suddenly from the corners of his eyes, but otherwise remained imperturbable. O'Donnell eventually despaired. "Yez can't goiy that kid! He takes ut all loike mate an' dhrink." Kelcey often told the story, his pipe held in his teeth peculiarly, and his derby tilted back on his head.

He remained at home for several evenings, content to read the papers and talk with his mother. She began to look around for the tremendous reason for it. She suspected that his nearness to death in the recent accident had sobered his senses and made him think of high things.

She mused upon it continually. When he sat moodily pondering she watched him. She said to herself that she saw the light breaking in upon his spirit. She felt that it was a very critical period of his existence. She resolved to use all her power and skill to turn his eyes toward the lights in the sky. Accordingly, she addressed him one evening. "Come, go t' prayer-meetin' t'-night with me, will yeh, George?" It sounded more blunt than she intended.

He glanced at her in sudden surprise. "Huh?"

As she repeated her request, her voice quavered. She felt that it was a supreme moment. "Come, go t' prayer-meetin' t'-night, won't yeh?"

He seemed amazed. "Oh, I don't know," he began. He was fumbling in his mind for a reason for refusing. "I don't wanta go. I'm tired as the dickens!" His obedient shoulders sank down languidly. His head mildly drooped.

The little old woman, with a quick perception of her helplessness, felt a motherly rage at her son. It was intolerable that she could not impart motion to him in a chosen direction. The waves of her desires were puny against the rocks of his indolence. She had a great wish to beat him. "I don't know what I'm ever goin' t' do with yeh," she told him, in a choking voice. "Yeh won't do anything I ask yeh to. Yeh never pay th' least bit a' attention t' what I say. Yeh don't mind me any more than yeh would a fly. Whatever am I goin' t' do with yeh?" She faced him in a battleful way, her eyes blazing with a sombre light of despairing rage.

He looked up at her ironically. "I don't know," he said, with calmness. "What are yeh?" He had traced her emotions and seen her fear of his rebellion. He thrust out his legs in the easy scorn of a rapier-bravo. "What are yeh?"

The little old woman began to weep. They were tears without a shame of grief. She allowed them to run unheeded down her cheeks. As she stared into space her son saw her regarding there the powers and influences that she had held in her younger life. She was in some way acknowledging to fate that she was now but withered grass, with no power but the power to feel the winds. He was

smitten with a sudden shame. Besides, in the last few days
he had gained quite a character for amiability. He saw
something grand in relenting at this point. "Well," he said,
trying to remove a sulky quality from his voice, "well, if
yer bound t' have me go, I s'pose I'll have t' go."

His mother, with strange, immobile face, went to him
and kissed him on the brow. "All right, George!" There
was in her wet eyes an emotion which he could not fathom.

She put on her bonnet and shawl, and they went out
together. She was unusually silent, and made him wonder
why she did not appear gleeful at his coming. He was
resentful because she did not display more appreciation
of his sacrifice. Several times he thought of halting and
refusing to go farther, to see if that would not wring from
her some acknowledgment.

In a dark street the little chapel sat humbly between
two towering apartment-houses. A red street-lamp stood in
front. It threw a marvellous reflection upon the wet pavements. It was like the death-stain of a spirit. Farther up, the
brilliant lights of an avenue made a span of gold across
the black street. A roar of wheels and a clangour of bells
came from this point, interwoven into a sound emblematic
of the life of the city. It seemed somehow to affront this
solemn and austere little edifice. It suggested an approaching barbaric invasion. The little church, pierced, would die
with a fine illimitable scorn for its slayers.

When Kelcey entered with his mother he felt a sudden
quaking. His knees shook. It was an awesome place to him.
There was a menace in the red padded carpet and the
leather doors, studded with little brass tacks that penetrated
his soul with their pitiless glances. As for his mother, she
had acquired such a new air that he would have been
afraid to address her. He felt completely alone and isolated
at this formidable time.

There was a man in the vestibule who looked at them
blandly. From within came the sound of singing. To Kelcey
there was a million voices. He dreaded the terrible moment
when the doors should swing back. He wished to recoil,
but at that instant the bland man pushed the doors aside,

and he followed his mother up the centre aisle of the little chapel. To him there was a riot of lights that made him transparent. The multitudinous pairs of eyes that turned toward him were implacable in their cool valuations.

They had just ceased singing. He who conducted the meeting motioned that the service should wait until the newcomers found seats. The little old woman went slowly on toward the first rows. Occasionally she paused to scrutinize vacant places, but they did not seem to meet her requirements. Kelcey was in agony. He thought the moment of her decision would never come. In his unspeakable haste he walked a little faster than his mother. Once she paused to glance in her calculating way at some seats, and he forged ahead. He halted abruptly and returned, but by that time she had resumed her thoughtful march up the aisle. He could have assassinated her. He felt that everybody must have seen his torture, during which his hands were to him like monstrous swollen hides. He was wild with a rage in which his lips turned slightly livid. He was capable of doing some furious, unholy thing.

When the little old woman at last took a seat, her son sat down beside her slowly and stiffly. He was opposing his strong desire to drop.

When from the mists of his shame and humiliation the scene came before his vision, he was surprised to find that all eyes were not fastened upon his face. The leader of the meeting seemed to be the only one who saw him. He stared gravely, solemnly, regretfully. He was a pale-faced but plump young man in a black coat that buttoned to his chin. It was evident to Kelcey that his mother had spoken of him to the young clergyman, and that the latter was now impressing upon him the sorrow caused by the contemplation of his sin. Kelcey hated the man.

A man seated alone over in a corner began to sing. He closed his eyes and threw back his head. Others, scattered sparsely throughout the innumerable light-wood chairs, joined him as they caught the air. Kelcey heard his mother's frail, squeaking soprano. The chandelier in the centre was the only one lighted, and far at the end of the room one could discern the pulpit swathed in gloom, solemn and mystic as a bier. It was surrounded by vague shapes of darkness on which at times was the glint of brass, or of glass that shone like steel, until one could feel there the presence of the army of the unknown, possessors of the great eternal truths, and silent listeners at this ceremony. High up, the stained-glass windows loomed in leaden array like dull-hued banners, merely catching occasional splashes of dark wine-colour from the lights. Kelcey fell to brooding concerning this indefinable presence which he felt in a church.

One by one people arose and told little tales of their religious faith. Some were tearful, and others calm, emotionless, and convincing. Kelcey listened closely for a time. These people filled him with a great curiosity. He was not familiar with their types.

At last the young clergyman spoke at some length. Kelcy was amazed, because, from the young man's appearance, he would not have suspected him of being so glib; but the speech had no effect on Kelcey, excepting to prove to him again that he was damned.

XII

Kelcey sometimes wondered whether he liked beer. He had been obliged to cultivate a talent for imbibing it. He was born with an abhorrence which he had steadily battled until it had come to pass that he could drink from ten to twenty glasses of beer without the act of swallowing causing him to shiver. He understood that drink was an essential to joy, to the coveted position of a man of the world and of the streets. The saloons contained the mystery of a street for him. When he knew its saloons he comprehended the street. Drink and its surroundings were the eyes of a superb green dragon to him. He followed a fascinating glitter, and the glitter required no explanation.

Directly after old Bleecker's party he almost reformed. He was tired and worn from the tumult of it, and he saw it as one might see a skeleton emerged from a crimson cloak. He wished then to turn his face away. Gradually, however, he recovered his mental balance. Then he admitted again by his point of view that the thing was not so terrible. His headache had caused him to exaggerate. A drunk was not the blight which he had once remorsefully named it. On the contrary, it was a mere unpleasant incident. He resolved, however, to be more cautious.

When prayer-meeting night came again his mother approached him hopefully. She smiled like one whose request is already granted. "Well, will yeh go t' prayer-meetin' with me t'-night again?"

He turned toward her with eloquent suddenness, and then riveted his eyes upon a corner of the floor. "Well, I guess not," he said.

His mother tearfully tried to comprehend his state of mind. "What has come over yeh?" she said tremblingly. "Yeh never used t' be this way, George. Yeh never used t' be so cross an' mean t' me—"

"Oh, I ain't cross an' mean t' yeh," he interpolated, exasperated and violent.

"Yes, yeh are, too! I ain't hardly had a decent word from yeh in ever so long. Yer as cross an' as mean as yeh can be. I don't know what t' make of it. It can't be"—there came a look in her eyes that told that she was going to shock and alarm him with her heaviest sentence—"it can't be that yeh've got t' drinkin'."

Kelcey grunted with disgust at the ridiculous thing. "Why, what an old goose yer gettin' t' be!"

She was compelled to laugh a little, as a child laughs between tears at a hurt. She had not been serious. She was only trying to display to him how she regarded his horrifying mental state. "Oh, of course, I didn't mean that, but I think yeh act jest as bad as if yeh did drink. I wish yeh would do better, George!"

She had grown so much less frigid and stern in her censure that Kelcey seized the opportunity to try to make a joke of it. He laughed at her, but she shook her head and continued: "I do wish yeh would do better. I don't know what's t' become of yeh, George. Yeh don't mind what I say no more 'n if I was th' wind in th' chimbly. Yeh don't care about nothin' 'cept goin' out nights. I can't ever get yeh t' prayer-meetin' ner church; yeh never go out with me anywheres unless yeh can't get out of it; yeh swear an' take on sometimes like everything; yeh never—"

He gestured wrathfully in interruption. "Say, look-a here, can't yeh think a' something I do?"

She ended her oration then in the old way. "An' I don't know what's goin' t' become a' yeh."

She put on her bonnet and shawl and then came and stood near him, expectantly. She imparted to her attitude a subtle threat of unchangeableness. He pretended to be engrossed in his newspaper. The little swaggering clock on the mantel became suddenly evident, ticking with loud monotony. Presently she said, firmly: "Well, are yeh comin'?"

He was reading. "Well, are yeh comin'?"

He threw his paper down, angrily. "Oh, why don't yeh go on an' leave me alone?" he demanded in supreme impatience. "What do yeh wanta pester me fer? Ye'd think there was robbers. Why can't yeh go alone or else stay home? You wanta go, an' I don't wanta go, an' yeh keep all time tryin' t' drag me. Yeh know I don't wanta go." He concluded in a last defiant wounding of her. "What do I care 'bout those ol' bags-a'-wind, anyhow? They gimme a pain!"

His mother turned her face and went from him. He sat staring with a mechanical frown. Presently he went and picked up his newspaper.

Jones told him that night that everybody had had such a good time at old Bleecker's party that they were going to form a club. They waited at the little smiling saloon, and then amid much enthusiasm all signed a membership-roll. Old Bleecker, late that night, was violently elected president. He made speeches of thanks and gratification during the remainder of the meeting. Kelcey went home rejoicing. He felt that at any rate he could have true friends. The dues were a dollar for each week.

He was deeply interested. For a number of evenings he fairly gobbled his supper in order that he might be off to the little smiling saloon to discuss the new organization. All the men were wildly enthusiastic. One night the saloon-keeper announced that he would donate half the rent of quite a large room over his saloon. It was an occasion for great cheering. Kelcey's legs were like whalebone when he tried to go upstairs upon his return home, and the edge of each step was moved curiously forward.

His mother's questions made him snarl. "Oh, nowheres!" At other times he would tell her: "Oh, t' see some friends a' mine! Where d' yeh s'pose?"

Finally, some of the women of the tenement concluded that the little old mother had a wild son. They came to condole with her. They sat in the kitchen for hours. She told them of his wit, his cleverness, his kind heart.

XIII

At a certain time Kelcey discovered that some young men who stood in the cinders between a brick wall and the pavement, and near the side-door of a corner saloon, knew more about life than other people. They used to lean there smoking and chewing, and comment upon events and persons. They knew the neighbourhood extremely well. They debated upon small typical things that transpired before them, until they had extracted all the information that existence contained. They sometimes inaugurated little fights with foreigners or well-dressed men. It was here that Sapristi Glielmi, the pedlar, stabbed Pete Brady to death, for which he got a life-sentence. Each patron of the saloon was closely scrutinized as he entered the place. Sometimes they used to throng upon the heels of a man and in at the bar assert that he had asked them in to drink. When he objected, they would claim with one voice that it was too deep an insult and gather about to thrash him. When they had caught chance customers and absolute strangers, the barkeeper had remained in stolid neutrality, ready to serve one or seven, but two or three times they had encountered the wrong men. Finally, the proprietor had come out one morning and told them, in the fearless way of his class, that their pastime must cease. "It's quits right here!

See? Right here! Th' nex' time yeh try t' work it, I come with th' bung-starter, an' th' mugs I miss with it git pulled. See? It quits!" Infrequently, however, men did ask them in to drink.

The policeman of that beat grew dignified and shrewd whenever he approached this corner. Sometimes he stood with his hands behind his back and cautiously conversed with them. It was understood on both sides that it was a good thing to be civil.

In winter this band, a trifle diminished in numbers, huddled in their old coats and stamped little flat places in the snow, their faces turned always toward the changing life in the streets. In the summer they became more lively. Sometimes, then, they walked out to the kerb to look up and down the street. Over in a trampled vacant lot, surrounded by high tenement-houses, there was a sort of den among some boulders. An old truck was made to form a shelter. The small hoodlums of that vicinity all avoided the spot. So many of them had been thrashed upon being caught near it. It was the summer-time lounging place of the band from the corner.

They were all too clever to work. Some of them had worked, but these used their experiences as stores from which to draw tales. They were like veterans with their wars. One lad in particular used to recount how he whipped his employer, the proprietor of a large grain and feed establishment. He described his victim's features and form and clothes with minute exactness. He bragged of his wealth and social position. It had been a proud moment of the lad's life. He was like a savage who had killed a great chief.

Their feeling for contemporaneous life was one of contempt. Their philosophy taught that in a large part the whole thing was idle and a great bore. With fine scorn they sneered at the futility of it. Work was done by men who had not the courage to stand still and let the skies clap together if they willed.

The vast machinery of the popular law indicated to them that there were people in the world who wished to remain quiet. They awaited the moment when they could prove to them that a riotous upheaval, a cloudburst of destruction, would be a delicious thing. They thought of their fingers buried in the lives of these people. They longed dimly for a time when they could run through decorous streets with crash and roar of war, an army of revenge for pleasures long possessed by others, a wild sweeping compensation for their years without crystal and gilt, women and wine. This thought slumbered in them, as the image of Rome might have lain small in the hearts of the barbarians.

Kelcey respected these youths so much that he ordinarily used the other side of the street. He could not go near to them, because if a passer-by minded his own business he was a disdainful prig and had insulted them; if he showed that he was aware of them they were likely to resent his not minding his own business and prod him into a fight if the opportunity were good. Kelcey longed for their acquaintance and friendship, for with it came social safety and ease; they were respected so universally.

Once in another street Fidsey Corcoran was whipped by a short, heavy man. Fidsey picked himself up, and in the fury of defeat hurled pieces of brick at his opponent. The short man dodged with skill, and then pursued Fidsey for over a block. Sometimes he got near enough to punch him. Fidsey raved in maniacal fury. The moment the short man would attempt to resume his own affairs, Fidsey would turn upon him again, tears and blood upon his face, with the lashed rage of a vanquished animal. The short man used to turn about, swear madly, and make little dashes. Fidsey always ran, and then returned as pursuit ceased. The short man apparently wondered if this maniac was ever going to allow him to finish whipping him. He looked helplessly up and down the street. People were there who knew Fidsey, and they remonstrated with him; but he continued to confront the short man, gibbering like a wounded ape, using all the eloquence of the street in his wild oaths.

Finally, the short man was exasperated to black fury. He decided to end the fight. With low snarls, ominous as death, he plunged at Fidsey.

Kelcey happened there then. He grasped the short man's shoulder. He cried out in the peculiar whine of the man who interferes. "Oh, hol' on! Yeh don't wanta hit 'im any more! Yeh've done enough to 'im now! Leave 'im be!"

The short man wrenched and tugged. He turned his face until his teeth were almost at Kelcey's cheek. "Le' go me! Le' go me, you—" The rest of his sentence was screamed curses.

Kelcey's face grew livid from fear, but he somehow managed to keep his grip. Fidsey, with but an instant's pause, plunged into the new fray.

They beat the short man. They forced him against a high board fence, where for a few seconds their blows sounded upon his head in swift thuds. A moment later Fidsey descried a running policeman. He made off, fleet as a shadow. Kelcey noted his going. He ran after him.

Three or four blocks away they halted. Fidsey said: "I'd 'a' licked dat big stiff in 'bout a minute more," and wiped the blood from his eyes.

At the gang's corner, they asked: "Who soaked yeh, Fidsey?" His description was burning. Everybody laughed. "Where is 'e now?" Later they began to question Kelcey. He recited a tale in which he allowed himself to appear prominent and redoubtable. They looked at him then as if they thought he might be quite a man.

Once when the little old woman was going out to buy something for her son's supper, she discovered him standing at the side-door of the saloon engaged intimately with Fidsey and the others. She slunk away, for she understood that it would be a terrible thing to confront him and his pride there with youths who were superior to mothers.

When he arrived home he threw down his hat with a weary sigh, as if he had worked long hours, but she attacked him before he had time to complete the falsehood. He listened to her harangue with a curled lip. In defence he merely made a gesture of supreme exasperation. She never understood the advanced things in life. He felt the hopelessness of ever making her comprehend. His mother was not modern.

XIV

The little old woman arose early and bustled in the preparation of breakfast. At times she looked anxiously at the
clock. An hour before her son should leave for work she
went to his room and called him in the usual tone of sharp-
ness. "George! George!"

A sleepy growl came to her.

"Come, come, it's time t' git up," she continued. "Come,
now, git right up!"

Later she went again to the door. "George, are yeh gittin'
up?"

"Huh?"

"Are yeh gittin' up?"

"Yes, I'll git right up!" He had introduced a valour into
his voice which she detected to be false. She went to his
bedside and took him by the shoulder. "George—George
—git up!"

From the mist-lands of sleep he began to protest incoher-
ently. "Oh, le' me be, won' yeh? 'm sleepy!"

She continued to shake him. "Well, it's time t' git up.
Come—come—come on, now."

Her voice, shrill with annoyance, pierced his ears in a
slender, piping thread of sound. He turned over on the
pillow to bury his head in his arms. When he expostulated,
his tones came half smothered. "Oh, le' me be, can't yeh?
There's plenty a' time! Jest fer ten minutes! 'm sleepy!"

She was implacable. "No, yeh must git up now! Yeh
ain't got more'n time enough t' eat yer breakfast an' git
t' work."

Eventually he arose, sullen and grumbling. Later he
came to his breakfast, blinking his dry eyelids, his stiffened
features set in a mechanical scowl.

Each morning his mother went to his room, and fought
a battle to arouse him. She was like a soldier. Despite his
pleadings, his threats, she remained at her post, imperturbable and unyielding. These affairs assumed large proportions in his life. Sometimes he grew beside himself with a
bland, unformulated wrath. The whole thing was a consum-

mate imposition. He felt that he was being cheated of his
sleep. It was an injustice to compel him to arise morning
after morning with bitter regularity, before the sleep-gods
had at all loosened their grasp. He hated that unknown
force which directed his life.

One morning he swore a tangled mass of oaths, aimed
into the air, as if the injustice poised there. His mother
flinched at first; then her mouth set in the little straight
line. She saw that the momentous occasion had come. It
was the time of the critical battle. She turned upon him
valorously. "Stop your swearin', George Kelcey. I won't
have yeh talk so before me! I won't have it! Stop this
minute! Not another word! Do yeh think I'll allow yeh t'
swear b'fore me like that? Not another word! I won't have
it! I declare I won't have it another minute!"

At first her projected words had slid from his mind as
if striking against ice, but at last he heeded her. His face
grew sour with passion and misery. He spoke in tones
dark with dislike. "Th' 'ell yeh won't! Whatter yeh goin' t'
do 'bout it?" Then, as if he considered that he had not been
sufficiently impressive, he arose and slowly walked over to
her. Having arrived at point-blank range he spoke again.
"Whatter yeh goin' t' do 'bout it?" He regarded her then
with an unaltering scowl, albeit his mien was as dark and
cowering as that of a condemned criminal.

She threw out her hands in the gesture of an impotent
one. He was acknowledged victor. He took his hat and
slowly left her.

For three days they lived in silence. He brooded upon
his mother's agony and felt a singular joy in it. As opportunity offered, he did little despicable things. He was going
to make her abject. He was now uncontrolled, ungov-
erned; he wished to be an emperor. Her suffering was all
a sort of compensation for his own dire pains.

She went about with a grey, impassive face. It was as if
she had survived a massacre in which all that she loved had
been torn from her by the brutality of savages.

One evening at six he entered and stood looking at his

mother as she peeled potatoes. She had hearkened to his coming listlessly, without emotion, and at his entrance she did not raise her eyes.

"Well, I'm fired," he said suddenly.

It seemed to be the final blow. Her body gave a convulsive movement in the chair. When she finally lifted her eyes, horror possessed her face. Her under jaw had fallen. "Fired? Outa work? Why—George?" He went over to the window and stood with his back to her. He could feel her grey stare upon him.

"Yep! Fired!"

At last she said: "Well, whatter yeh goin' t' do?"

He tapped the pane with his fingernail. He answered in a tone made hoarse and unnatural by an assumption of gay carelessness: "Oh, nothin'!"

She began, then, her first weeping. "Oh—George— George—George—"

He looked at her scowling. "Ah, whatter yeh givin' us? Is this all I git when I come home f'm bein' fired? Anybody 'ud think it was my fault. I couldn't help it."

She continued to sob in a dull, shaking way. In the pose of her head there was an expression of her conviction that comprehension of her pain was impossible to the universe. He paused for a moment, and then, with his usual tactics, went out, slamming the door. A pale flood of sunlight, imperturbable at its vocation, streamed upon the little old woman, bowed with pain, forlorn in her chair.

XV

Kelcey was standing on the corner next day when three little boys came running. Two halted some distance away, and the other came forward. He halted before Kelcey, and spoke importantly.

"Hey, your ol' woman's sick."

"What?"

"Your ol' woman's sick."

"Git out!"

"She is, too!"

"Who tol' yeh?"

"Mis' Callahan. She said fer me t' run an' tell yeh. Dey want yeh."

A swift dread struck Kelcey. Like flashes of light little scenes from the past shot through his brain. He had thoughts of a vengeance from the clouds. As he glanced about him the familiar view assumed a meaning that was ominous and dark. There was prophecy of disaster in the street, the buildings, the sky, the people. Something tragic and terrible in the air was known to his nervous, quivering nostrils. He spoke to the little boy in a tone that quavered. "All right!"

Behind him he felt the sudden contemplative pause of his companions of the gang. They were watching him. As he went rapidly up the street he knew that they had come out to the middle of the walk and were staring after him. He was glad that they could not see his face, his trembling lips, his eyes wavering in fear. He stopped at the door of his home and stared at the panel as if he saw written thereon a word. A moment later he entered. His eyes comprehended the room in a frightened glance.

His mother sat gazing out at the opposite walls and windows. She was leaning her head upon the back of the chair. Her face was overspread with a singular pallor, but the glance of her eyes was strong, and the set of her lips was tranquil.

He felt an unspeakable thrill of thanksgiving at seeing her seated there calmly. "Why, mother, they said yeh was sick," he cried, going toward her impetuously. "What's th' matter?"

She smiled at him. "Oh, it ain't nothin'! I on'y got kinda dizzy, that's all." Her voice was sober and had the ring of vitality in it.

He noted her commonplace air. There was no alarm or pain in her tones, but the misgivings of the street, the prophetic twinges of his nerves, made him still hesitate. "Well—are you sure it ain't? They scared me 'bout t' death."

"No, it ain't anything, on'y some sorta dizzy feelin'. I

fell down b'hind th' stove. Missis Callahan, she came an'
picked me up. I must 'a' laid there fer quite a while. Th'
doctor said he guessed I'd be all right in a couple a' hours.
I don't feel nothin'!"

Kelcey heaved a great sigh of relief. "Lord, I was
scared!" He began to beam joyously, since he was escaped
from his fright. "Why, I couldn't think what had happened," he told her.

"Well, it ain't nothin'," she said.

He stood about awkwardly, keeping his eyes fastened
upon her in a sort of surprise, as if he had expected to
discover that she had vanished. The reaction from his
panic was a thrill of delicious contentment. He took a
chair and sat down near her, but presently he jumped up
to ask: "There ain't nothin' I can git fer yeh, is ther?"
He looked at her eagerly. In his eyes shone love and joy.
If it were not for the shame of it, he would have called
her endearing names.

"No, ther ain't nothin'," she answered. Presently she
continued, in a conversational way: "Yeh ain't found no
work yit, have yeh?"

The shadow of his past fell upon him then, and he became suddenly morose. At last he spoke in a sentence that
was a vow, a declaration of change. "No, I ain't, but I'm
goin' t' hunt fer it hard, you bet."

She understood from his tone that he was making peace
with her. She smiled at him gladly. "Yer a good boy,
George!" A radiance from the stars lit her face.

Presently she asked: "D' yeh think yer old boss would
take yeh on ag'in if I went t' see him?"

"No," said Kelcey at once. "It wouldn't do no good!
They got all th' men they want. There ain't no room there.
It wouldn't do no good." He ceased to beam for a moment as he thought of certain disclosures. "I'm goin' t'
try to git work everywheres. I'm goin' t' make a wild
break t' git a job, an' if there's one anywheres I'll git it."

She smiled at him again. "That's right, George!"

When it came supper-time he dragged her in her chair
over to the table and then scurried to and fro to prepare

a meal for her. She laughed gleefully at him. He was awkward and densely ignorant. He exaggerated his helplessness sometimes until she was obliged to lean back in her
chair to laugh. Afterward they sat by the window. Her
hand rested upon his hair.

XVI

When Kelcey went to borrow money from old Bleecker,
Jones, and the others, he discovered that he was below
them in social position. Old Bleecker said gloomily that
he did not see how he could loan money at that time.
When Jones asked him to have a drink, his tone was
careless. O'Connor recited at length some bewildering
financial troubles of his own. In them all he saw that
something had been reversed. They remained silent upon
many occasions when they might have grunted in sympathy for him.

As he passed along the street near his home he perceived
Fidsey Corcoran and another of the gang. They made
eloquent signs. "Are yeh wid us?"

He stopped and looked at them. "What's wrong with
yeh?"

"Are yeh wid us er not?" demanded Fidsey. "New bar-
keep'! Big can! We got it over in d' lot. Big can, I tell
yeh." He drew a picture in the air, so to speak, with his
enthusiastic fingers.

Kelcey turned dejectedly homeward. "Oh, I guess not,
this roun'."

"What's d' matter wi'che?" said Fidsey. "Yer gittin' t'
be a reg'lar Willie! Come ahn, I tell yeh! Youse gits one
smoke at d' can b'cause yeh b'longs t' d' gang, an' yeh
don't wanta give it up widout er scrap! See? Some udder
john'll git yer smoke. Come ahn!"

When they arrived at the place among the boulders in
the vacant lot, one of the band had a huge and battered
tin pail tilted afar up. His throat worked convulsively.
He was watched keenly and anxiously by five or six
others. Their eyes followed carefully each fraction of distance that the pail was lifted. They were very silent.

Fidsey burst out violently as he perceived what was in progress. "Heh, Tim, yeh big sojer, le' go d' can! Whatta yeh t'ink? Wees er in dis! Le' go dat!"

He who was drinking made several angry protesting contortions of his throat. Then he put down the pail and swore. "Who's a big sojer? I ain't gittin' more'n me own smoke! Yer too bloomin' swift! Ye'd t'ink yeh was d' on'y mug what owned dis can! Close yer face while I gits me smoke!"

He took breath for a moment and then returned the pail to its tilted position. Fidsey went to him and worried and clamoured. He interfered so seriously with the action of drinking that the other was obliged to release the pail again for fear of choking.

Fidsey grabbed it and glanced swiftly at the contents. "Dere! Dat's what I was hollerin' at! Look-ut d' beer! Not 'nough t' wet yer t'roat! Yehs can't have nottin' on d' level wid youse damn' tanks! Youse was a reg'lar rese'voiy, Tim Connigan! Look what yeh lef' us! Ah, say, youse was a dandy! Whatta yeh t'ink we ah? Willies? Don' we want no smoke? Say, look-ut dat can! It's drier'n hell! Whatta yeh t'ink?"

Tim glanced in at the beer. Then he said: "Well, d' mug what come b'fore me, he on'y lef' me dat much. Blue Billie, he done d' swallerin'! I on'y had a tas'e!"

Blue Billie, from his seat near, called out in wrathful protest: "Yeh lie, Tim. I never had more'n a mouf-ful!" An inspiration evidently came to him then, for his countenance suddenly brightened, and, arising, he went toward the pail. "I ain't had me reg'lar smoke yit! Guess I come in ahead a' Fidsey, don't I?"

Fidsey, with a sardonic smile, swung the pail behind him. "I guess nit! Not dis minnet! Youse hadger smoke. If yeh ain't, yeh don't git none. See?"

Blue Billie confronted Fidsey determinedly. "D' 'ell I don't!"

"Nit," said Fidsey.

Billie sat down again.

Fidsey drank his portion. Then he manœuvred skilfully

before the crowd until Kelcey and the other youth took
their shares. "Youse er a mob a' tanks," he told the gang.
"Nobody 'ud git nottin' if dey wasn't on t' yehs!"

Blue Billie's soul had been smouldering in hate against
Fidsey. "Ah, shut up! Youse ain't gotta take care a' dose
two mugs, dough. Youse hadger smoke, ain't yeh? Den
yer t'rough. G' home!"

"Well, I hate t' see er bloke use 'imself fer a tank," said
Fidsey. "But youse don't wanta go jollyin' 'round 'bout d'
can, Blue, er youse'll git done."

"Who'll do me?" demanded Blue Billie, casting his eye
about him.

"Kel will," said Fidsey bravely.

"D' 'ell he will!"

"Dat's what he will!"

Blue Billie made the gesture of a warrior. "He never
saw d' day a' his life dat he could do me little finger. If
'e says much t' me, I'll push 'is face all over d' lot."

Fidsey called to Kelcey. "Say, Kel, hear what dis mug
is chewin'?"

Kelcey was apparently deep in other matters. His back
was half turned.

Blue Billie spoke to Fidsey in a battleful voice. "Did 'e
ever say 'e could do me?"

Fidsey said: "Soitenly 'e did. Youse is dead easy, 'e
says. He says he kin punch holes in you, Blue!"

"When did 'e say it?"

"Oh—any time. Youse is a cinch, Kel says."

Blue Billie walked over to Kelcey. The others of the
band followed him, exchanging joyful glances.

"Did youse say yeh could do me?"

Kelcey slowly turned, but he kept his eyes upon the
ground. He heard Fidsey darting among the others, telling
of his prowess, preparing them for the downfall of Blue
Billie. He stood heavily on one foot and moved his hands
nervously. Finally he said, in a low growl: "Well, what
if I did?"

The sentence sent a happy thrill through the band. It
was the formidable question. Blue Billie braced himself.

Upon him came the responsibility of the next step. The gang fell back a little upon all sides. They looked expectantly at Blue Billie.

He walked forward with a deliberate step until his face was close to Kelcey.

"Well, if you did," he said, with a snarl between his teeth, "I'm goin' t' t'ump d' life outa yeh right heh!"

A little boy, wild of eye and puffing, came down the slope as from an explosion. He burst out in a rapid treble: "Is dat Kelcey feller here? Say, yeh ol' woman's sick again. Dey want yeh! Yehs better run! She's awful sick!"

The gang turned with loud growls. "Ah, git outa here!" Fidsey threw a stone at the little boy and chased him a short distance, but he continued to clamour: "Youse better come, Kelcey feller! She's awful sick! She was hollerin'! Dey been lookin' fer yeh over 'an hour!" In his eagerness he returned part way, regardless of Fidsey.

Kelcey had moved away from Blue Billie. He said: "I guess I'd better go." They howled at him. "Well," he continued, "I can't—I don't wanta—I don't wanta leave me mother be—she—"

His words were drowned in the chorus of their derision. "Well, look-a-here," he would begin, and at each time their cries and screams ascended. They dragged at Blue Billie. "Go fer 'im, Blue! Slug 'im! Go ahn!"

Kelcey went slowly away while they were urging Blue Billie to do a decisive thing. Billie stood fuming and blustering and explaining himself. When Kelcey had achieved a considerable distance from him, he stepped forward a few paces and hurled a terrible oath. Kelcey looked back darkly.

XVII

When he entered the chamber of death, he was brooding over the recent encounter and devising extravagant revenges upon Blue Billie and the others.

The little old woman was stretched upon her bed. Her face and hands were of the hue of the blankets. Her hair, seemingly of a new and wondrous greyness, hung over her temples in whips and tangles. She was sickeningly motionless, save for her eyes, which rolled and swayed in maniacal glances.

A young doctor had just been administering medicine. "There," he said, with a great satisfaction, "I guess that'll do her good!" As he went briskly toward the door he met Kelcey. "Oh," he said. "Son?"

Kelcey had that in his throat which was like fur. When he forced his voice, the words came first low and then high, as if they had broken through something. "Will she —will she—"

The doctor glanced back at the bed. She was watching them as she would have watched ghouls, and muttering.

"Can't tell," he said. "She's a wonderful woman! Got more vitality than you and I together! Can't tell! May— may not! Good-day! Back in two hours."

In the kitchen Mrs. Callahan was feverishly dusting the furniture, polishing this and that. She arranged everything in decorous rows. She was preparing for the coming of death. She looked at the floor as if she longed to scrub it.

The doctor paused to speak in an undertone to her, glancing at the bed. When he departed she laboured with a renewed speed.

Kelcey approached his mother. From a little distance he called to her. "Mother—mother—" He proceeded with caution lest this mystic being upon the bed should clutch at him.

"Mother—mother—don't yeh know me?" He put forth apprehensive, shaking fingers and touched her hand.

There were two brilliant steel-coloured points upon her eyeballs. She was staring off at something sinister.

Suddenly she turned to her son in a wild babbling appeal. "Help me! Help me! Oh, help me! I see them coming."

Kelcey called to her as to a distant place. "Mother! Mother!" She looked at him, and then there began within her a struggle to reach him with her mind. She fought with some implacable power whose fingers were in her

brain. She called to Kelcey in stammering, incoherent cries
for help.

Then she again looked away. "Ah, there they come!
There they come! Ah, look—look—loo—" She arose to a
sitting posture without the use of her arms.

Kelcey felt himself being choked. When her voice
pealed forth in a scream he saw crimson curtains moving
before his eyes. "Mother—oh, mother—there's nothin'—
there's nothin'—"

She was at a kitchen door with a dish-cloth in her
hand. Within there had just been a clatter of crockery.
Down through the trees of the orchard she could see a
man in a field ploughing. "Bill—o-o-oh, Bill—have yeh
seen Georgie? Is he out there with you? Georgie! Georgie!
Come right here this minnet! Right—this—minnet!"

She began to talk to some people in the room. "I want
t' know what yeh want here! I want yeh t' git out! I don't
want yeh here! I don't feel good t'-day, an' I don't want
yeh here! I don't feel good t'-day! I want yeh t' git out!"
Her voice became peevish. "Go away! Go away! Go
away!"

Kelcey lay in a chair. His nerveless arms allowed his
fingers to sweep the floor. He became so that he could
not hear the chatter from the bed, but he was always conscious of the ticking of the little clock out on the kitchen
shelf.

When he aroused, the pale-faced but plump young clergyman was before him.

"My poor lad!" began this latter.

The little old woman lay still with her eyes closed. On
the table at the head of the bed was a glass containing a
water-like medicine. The reflected lights made a silver star
on its side. The two men sat side by side, waiting. Out in
the kitchen Mrs. Callahan had taken a chair by the stove
and was waiting.

Kelcey began to stare at the wall-paper. The pattern
was clusters of brown roses. He felt them like hideous
crabs crawling upon his brain.

Through the doorway he saw the oil-cloth covering of

the table catching a glimmer from the warm afternoon sun. The window disclosed a fair, soft sky, like blue enamel, and a fringe of chimneys and roofs, resplendent here and there. An endless roar, the eternal trample of the marching city, came mingled with vague cries. At intervals the woman out by the stove moved restlessly and coughed.

Over the transom from the hallway came two voices.

"Johnnie!"

"Wot!"

"You come right here t' me! I want yehs t' go t' d' store fer me!"

"Ah, ma, send Sally!"

"No, I will not! You come right here!"

"All right, in a minnet!"

"Johnnie!"

"In a minnet, I tell yeh!"

"Johnnie—" There was the sound of a heavy tread, and later a boy squealed. Suddenly the clergyman started to his feet. He rushed forward and peered. The little old woman was dead.

HOWELLS FEARS REALISTS MUST WAIT [1]

❋ ❋ ❋

Fears Realists Must Wait

AN INTERESTING TALK WITH
WILLIAM DEAN HOWELLS

The Eminent Novelist Still Holds a Firm
Faith in Realism, but Confesses a Doubt if Its Day
Has Yet Come—He Has Observed a Change in the
Literary Pulse of the Country Within the Last Few
Months—A Reactionary Wave.

William Dean Howells leaned his cheek upon the two
outstretched fingers of his right hand and gazed thoughtfully at the window—the panes black from the night without, although studded once or twice with little electric stars
far up on the west side of the Park. He was looking at
something which his memory had just brought to him.

"I have a little scheme," he at last said, slowly. "I saw
a young girl out in a little Ohio town once—she was the
daughter of the carpetwoman there—that is to say, her
mother made ragcarpets and rugs for the villagers. And
this girl had the most wonderful instinct in manner and
dress. Her people were of the lowest of the low in a way
and yet this girl was a lady. It used to completely amaze
me—to think how this girl could grow there in that
squalor. She was as chic as chic could be, and yet the
money spent and the education was nothing—nothing at

---

[1] Reprinted verbatim from the *New York Times*, Sunday, October 28, 1894.

all. Where she procured her fine taste you could not imagine. It was deeply interesting to me—it overturned so many of my rooted social dogmas. It was the impossible, appearing suddenly. And then there was another in Cambridge—a wonderful type. I have come upon them occasionally here and there. I intend to write something of the kind if I can. I have thought of a good title, too, I think—a name of a flower—'The Ragged Lady.' "

"I suppose this is a long way off," said the other man reflectively. "I am anxious to hear what you say in 'The Story of a Play.' Do you raise your voice toward reforming the abuses that are popularly supposed to hide in the manager's office for use upon the struggling artistic playwright and others? Do you recite the manager's divine misapprehension of art?"

"No, I do not," said Mr. Howells.

"Why?" said the other man.

"Well, in the first place, the manager is a man of business. He preserves himself. I suppose he judges not against art, but between art and act. He looks at art through the crowds."

"I don't like reformatory novels anyhow," said the other man.

"And in the second place," continued Mr. Howells, "it does no good to go at things hammer and tongs in this obvious way. I believe that every novel should have an intention. A man should mean something when he writes. Ah, this writing merely to amuse people—why, it seems to me altogether vulgar. A man may as well blacken his face and go out and dance on the street for pennies. The author is a sort of trained bear, if you accept certain standards. If literary men are to be the public fools, let us at any rate have it clearly understood, so that those of us who feel differently can take measures. But, on the other hand, a novel should never preach and berate and storm. It does no good. As a matter of fact, a book of that kind is ineffably tiresome. People don't like to have their lives half cudgeled out in that manner, especially in these days, when a man, likely enough, only reaches for a book when he wishes to be fanned, so to speak, after the heat of the daily struggle. When a writer desires to preach in an obvious way he should announce his intention—let him cry out then that he is in the pulpit. But it is the business of the novel—"

"Ah!" said the other man.

"It is the business of the novel to picture the daily life in the most exact terms possible, with an absolute and clear sense of proportion. That is the important matter—the proportion. As a usual thing, I think, people have absolutely no sense of proportion. Their noses are tight against life, you see. They perceive mountains where there are no mountains, but frequently a great peak appears no larger than a rat trap. An artist sees a dog down the street—well, his eye instantly relates the dog to its surroundings. The dog is proportioned to the buildings and the trees. Whereas, many people can conceive of that dog's tail resting upon a hill top."

"You have often said that the novel is a perspective," observed the other man.

"A perspective, certainly. It is a perspective made for the benefit of people who have no true use of their eyes. The novel, in its real meaning, adjusts the proportions. It preserves the balances. It is in this way that lessons are to be taught and reforms to be won. When people are introduced to each other they will see the resemblances, and won't want to fight so badly."

"I suppose that when a man tries to write 'what the people want'—when he tries to reflect the popular desire, it is a bad quarter of an hour for the laws of proportion."

"Do you recall any of the hosts of stories that began in love and ended a little further on. Those stories used to represent life to the people, and I believe they do now to a large class. Life began when the hero saw a certain girl, and it ended abruptly when he married her. Love and courtship was not an incident, a part of life—it was the whole of it. All else was of no value. Men of that religion must have felt very stupid when they were engaged at anything but courtship. Do you see the false proportion?

Do you see the dog with his tail upon the hilltop? Somebody touched the universal heart with the fascinating theme —the relation of man to maid—and, for many years, it was as if no other relation could be recognized in fiction. Here and there an author raised his voice, but not loudly. I like to see the novelists treating some of the other important things of life—the relation of mother and son, of husband and wife, in fact all those things that we live in continually. The other can be but fragmentary."

"I suppose there must be two or three new literary people just back of the horizon somewhere," said the other man. "Books upon these lines that you speak of are what might be called unpopular. Do you think them to be a profitable investment?"

"From my point of view it is the right—it is sure to be a profitable investment. After that it is a question of perseverance, courage. A writer of skill cannot be defeated because he remains true to his conscience. It is a long, serious conflict sometimes, but he must win, if he does not falter. Lowell said to me one time: 'After all, the barriers are very thin. They are paper. If a man has his conscience and one or two friends who can help him, it becomes very simple at last.' "

"Mr. Howells," said the other man, suddenly, "have you observed a change in the literary pulse of the country within the last four months? Last Winter, for instance, it seemed that realism was about to capture things, but then recently I have thought that I saw coming a sort of counter wave, a flood of the other—a reaction, in fact. Trivial, temporary, perhaps, but a reaction, certainly."

Mr. Howells dropped his hand in a gesture of emphatic assent. "What you say is true. I have seen it coming. . . . I suppose we shall have to wait."

STEPHEN CRANE.[2]

---

[2] Discovered by George Arms, this article was reprinted in *Americana* for April 1943.

ON THE NEW JERSEY COAST [1]

❋ ❋ ❋

Guests Continue to Arrive in Large Numbers.

Parades and Entertainments—Well-Known
People Who are Registered at the Various Hotels.

Asbury Park, N. J., Aug. 20 (Special).—The parade
of the Junior Order of United American Mechanics here
on Wednesday afternoon was a deeply impressive one to
some persons. There were hundreds of the members of
the order, and they wound through the streets to the music
of enough brass bands to make furious discords. It probably was the most awkward, ungainly, uncut and uncarved
procession that ever raised clouds of dust on sun-beaten
streets. Nevertheless, the spectacle of an Asbury Park
crowd confronting such an aggregation was an interesting
sight to a few people.

Asbury Park creates nothing. It does not make; it
merely amuses. There is a factory where nightshirts are
manufactured, but it is some miles from town. This is a
resort of wealth and leisure, of women and considerable
wine. The throng along the line of march was composed
of summer gowns, lace parasols, tennis trousers, straw hats
and indifferent smiles. The procession was composed of
men, bronzed, slope-shouldered, uncouth and begrimed

[1] Reprinted from the *New York Tribune*, August 21, 1892. Crane's
article was attacked in the *Asbury Park Journal* and in the *Daily Spray*,
where it was reprinted in full. It is reprinted in Melvin Schoberlin's
Introduction to *The Sullivan County Sketches of Stephen Crane* (1949)
and discussed there in detail. Its first book appearance was in *The
Public Papers of a Bibliomaniac*, by Charles Honce (Golden Eagle
Press, 1942). Beer's account is corrected by Willis Fletcher Johnson in
Literary Digest International Book Review, 4 (April 1926), 290. See
also Victor Elconin in *American Literature*, 20 (November 1948),
275–90.

with dust. Their clothes fitted them illy, for the most part, and they had no ideas of marching. They merely plodded along, not seeming quite to understand, stolid, unconcerned and, in a certain sense, dignified—a pace and a bearing emblematic of their lives. They smiled occasionally and from time to time greeted friends in the crowd on the sidewalk. Such an assemblage of the spraddle-legged men of the middle class, whose hands were bent and shoulders stooped from delving and constructing, had never appeared to an Asbury Park summer crowd, and the latter was vaguely amused.

The bona fide Asbury Parker is a man to whom a dollar, when held close to his eye, often shuts out any impression he may have had that other people possess rights. He is apt to consider that men and women, especially city men and women, were created to be mulcted by him. Hence the tan-colored, sun-beaten honesty in the faces of the members of the Junior Order of United American Mechanics is expected to have a very staggering effect upon them. The visitors were men who possessed principles. . . .

PART II

War Tales

INTRODUCTION

HERE are the three best war tales Crane wrote: *A Mystery of Heroism, The Upturned Face,* and *An Episode of War.* All three are inventions, like *The Red Badge.* For their conception and for their photographic resemblance to reality, as one contemporary review put it, "the author might have stayed for the one as for the other in his own armchair, and never have gone at all to the wars" (the *Academy,* October 6, 1900). Two of these imaginary pieces are staged in the Civil War; the third—*The Upturned Face*—belongs to no actual war or time or place. The scene is Rostina, the army is the "Spitzbergen army," and Timothy Lean belongs to the legendary "Twelfth Regiment of the Line."

This "Kicking Twelfth" Regiment is dealt with in four related pieces, two of them no more than fragments. In the first of this group, *Kim Up, the Kickers,* we meet the same Timothy Lean. The second one is good only in its title: *The Shrapnel of their Friends.* The third, *The End of the Battle,* is sentimental, the theme or meaning evoked being in excess of the motivating situation. Two soldiers pilfer an orchard and get reprimanded by the sergeant: "You're the kind of soldiers a man wants to choose for a dangerous outpost duty, ain't you?" Apparently, his men are not fit to belong to the Twelfth Regiment, but they die heroes—these culprits. One of the enemy, surprised to find the dead men so few in number, says: "God, I should have estimated them at least a hundred strong." It is a limp ending for a drama of such force, and it comes all too neat and pat. The beginning situation predicts too much, especially for a story whose theme is the unpredictableness of human nature.

Crane is always dealing with the paradox of man. That defines what his stories are really all about. Paradox patterns all his best stories; it defines their kinship one to another. The reading of fear as the "theme" of everything he wrote ignores about as many of his stories as, superficially, it accounts for. The soldiers in *The End of the Battle* are as fearless as the sheriff in *The Bride Comes to Yellow Sky. Maggie* and *George's Mother* have nothing to do with fear, and there is no trace of panic in *An Episode of War.*

On February 15, 1896 Crane, writing to the editor of the *Critic* from his brother's home at Hartwood, said: "I am now finishing a little novelette for S. S. McClure called *The Little Regiment* which represents my work at its best I think and is positively my last thing dealing with battle." But Crane did not keep to this intention. He published a second collection of war sketches in 1900, *Wounds in the Rain;* a downright bad war novel in 1899, *Active Service;* and among the last things he wrote was *Great Battles of the World,* potboiler Grub Street stuff published just before he died in 1900. War figures, too, in the title of his last book of poems, *War is Kind* (1899). By no stretch of terms can *The Little Regiment* (1896) be said to be a "little novelette": the six stories bear no relationship to each other except in subject; nor can that book be said to represent "my work at its best." *A Mystery of Heroism* is the only story in that volume having designed significance.

A Mystery of Heroism was written before Crane had occasion to witness actual warfare; *An Episode of War* likewise portrays a war he never saw; and *The Upturned Face* deals with a war that never existed. But no matter; what counts is the created illusion of reality, and in any work of art fact cannot be divided from fiction. *A Mys-*

tery of Heroism was probably written in Mexico during the summer of 1895 when Crane was out west looking for material to supply the Bacheller syndicate. It appeared first on August 1–2 in the *Philadelphia Press,* the newspaper that had serialized *The Red Badge* the year before (December 3–8, 1894), and so in point of publication made its appearance before the novel—*The Red Badge* being published in September 1895. The other two stories, written much later, were not published in America until 1921 (in *Men, Women and Boats*), though they had English publication in 1902 in the posthumous *Last Words. The Upturned Face* came out in *Ainslee's Magazine* in March 1900, just two months before Crane died. *A Mystery of Heroism, The Upturned Face,* and *An Episode of War* have never before been brought together.

The Upturned Face, though wholly imaginary, was inspired by the Spanish-American War. Timothy Lean and the adjutant must bury their comrade amidst riflefire, and they are puzzled about how to perform this delicate task. The story opens and ends with a question. " 'What do we do now?' said the adjutant, troubled and excited. 'Bury him,' said Timothy Lean." That opening question evokes the mood of hesitation and doubt, and Lean's answer— "bury him"—intensifies the question and does not answer it. It is the question of how to come to terms with the real thing. Even after burying him they are still in doubt. It is as though their coming to terms with the actuality has exploded their theory about it. " 'Perhaps we have been wrong,' said the adjutant. His glance wavered *stupidly.* 'It might have been better if we hadn't buried him *just at this time.*' 'Damn you,' said Lean, 'shut your mouth!' He was not the senior officer." In cursing the adjutant, Lean was breaking code, and this has its parallel in the abstract code or ritual of burial, which is shattered by its impingement upon a point in time. The final question in the story is, as it were, the unspoken query of the corpse, "which from its chalkblue face looked keenly out from the grave."

The one moment *before* the first shovel-load of earth is

emptied upon the corpse pinpoints the whole story. It is the moment *while* the shovel is "held poised above the corpse," fixed "for *a moment of inexplicable hesitation*. . . ." Keenly, "in curious *abstraction* they looked at the body." They cannot bring themselves to face up to the real thing—"Both were particular that their fingers should not feel the corpse." But the abstract code becomes far more terrifyingly real to them than the bullets spitting overhead, and, in a sense, more real than the corpse. Louder than any riflefire is the sound of the earth landing upon the upturned face—"plop!" How poignant the reality of life, all its values realized in that impact! It is this burden that fills the grave. (In Bierce's *An Occurrence at Owl Creek Bridge* the same theme is evoked, and the same structural conception underlies the story: illusion shattered by realities.) "And from Thy superb heights," says Lean, reading the burial service. But he can remember only two lines of it. All that is now remaining of this ritual is but a fragment. " 'Oh, well,' he cried suddenly, 'let us—let us say something—while he can hear us.' " It is as though he were denying the fact; it is as though the dead man were *alive*. Then the first shovel is emptied "on —on the feet. Timothy Lean felt as if tons had been swiftly lifted from off his forehead." It is as though the living man had been thus *exhumed*. But the key paradox is that in honoring their beloved comrade they dishonor him and honor themselves. Their consecration is a desecration: the ritual consecrates him, but the act of the ritual desecrates him. "Always the earth made that sound —plop!" So all relationships, like this one, involve that shock of reality by which intentions are contradicted by the act.

The story is a parable and, like *An Episode of War,* it is built on a paradox. The wounded lieutenant in *An Episode of War* sees life with new insight because, being wounded, he is removed from the flux of things and can observe life instead of merely experiencing it.

In *War Memories* Crane wrote: " 'But to get at the real

thing!' cried Vernall, the war-correspondent. 'It seems impossible! It is because war is neither magnificent nor squalid; it is simply life, and an expression of life can always evade us. We can never tell life, one to another, although sometimes we think we can." Life evades us when we try to recapture it, as Crane attempted in *War Memories* to recapture his experiences. More real is the unreal, the imagined experience.

An Episode of War is about the withdrawal of the wounded lieutenant from the real world into an imaginary world. Wounded, he was puzzled what to do with his unsheathed sword: "this weapon had of a sudden become a strange thing to him. He looked at it in a kind of stupefaction, as if he had been endowed with a trident, a sceptre, or a spade." He has become another person, a king or mythical figure, and his wounded arm seems fabulous— "made of very brittle glass." The wound is the symbol of his change of vision, enabling him now "to see many things which as a participant in the fight were unknown to him." The wounded, "no longer having part in the battle, knew more of it than others." "A wound gives strange dignity to him who bears it. Well men shy from this new and terrible majesty." The real world seen from the point of view of the wounded spectator now seems unreal, more like something in "a historical painting," and the men who belong to it seem immobilized as they gaze "statue-like and silent." *An Episode* thus bears comparison with *The Upturned Face* and, in its theme of a change of vision, it links with *A Mystery of Heroism* and *The Red Badge of Courage*. In structure *An Episode* is exactly like *The Red Badge*. It is formed of alternations of moods: perspectives of motion and change shifting into picture-postcard impressions where everything is felt as fixed and static. Henry Fleming is duped by realities; Collins is likewise disillusioned; and the lieutenant is deceived. "I won't amputate it," says the surgeon when asked about the wounded arm. "Come along. Don't be a baby." Like *The Red Badge*, *A Mystery of Heroism* is an analysis of disillusionment. The mood of disillusionment is evoked in the final symbol of the story: "The bucket lay on the ground, empty."

Crane's best stories are all of a piece, similar in theme and design. What Carl Van Doren said about *A Mystery of Heroism*—"pure, concentrated Crane"—applies equally to *An Episode* and *The Upturned Face*. The germinal situations of these two stories reappear in *The Price of the Harness,* a story of the Spanish-American War published in 1898 and probably written before them. *The Upturned Face* is a reworking, apparently, of this episode:

—Cover his face—said Grierson, in a low and husky voice afterwards.
    —What'll I cover it with?—said Watkins.
    They looked at themselves. They stood in their shirts, trousers, leggings, shoes; they had nothing.
    Oh—said Grierson—here's his hat—He brought it and laid it on the face of the dead man. They stood for a time. It was apparent that they thought it essential and decent to say or do something.

And *An Episode of War* has its parallel in this episode in *The Price of the Harness:*

. . . —I'm hit, sir—he said.
    The lieutenant was very busy. —All right, all right—he said, just heeding the man enough to learn where he was wounded. —Go over that way. You ought to see a dressing-station under those trees.—
    Martin found himself dizzy and sick. The sensation in his arm was distinctly galvanic. The feeling was so strange that he could wonder at times if a wound was really what ailed him.

As *The Price of the Harness* repeats several episodes and images from *The Red Badge,* so *An Episode of War* harks back to the novel too, to the incident of the wounded lieutenant there (chapter iv). More important are the external kinships between Crane's stories—*A Mystery* and *An Episode*—and Hemingway's novels of the wounded hero or outcast. In *The Sun Also Rises* Hemingway employs the same symbolism of wound as Crane in *An Episode* and in *The Red Badge.* Hemingway's social outcasts stand in

line of descent as much from Crane's mental outcasts—
Henry Fleming and, in *A Mystery*, Collins—as from
Twain's Huck Finn. Crane's heroes experience a change
of vision or a change of heart, and so does the wounded
hero of *Farewell to Arms*. Frederic Henry is saved *because*
he is wounded.

A MYSTERY OF HEROISM

THE DARK uniforms of the men were so coated with dust from the incessant wrestling of the two armies that the regiment almost seemed a part of the clay bank which shielded them from the shells. On the top of the hill a battery was arguing in tremendous roars with some other guns, and to the eye of the infantry the artillerymen, the guns, the caissons, the horses, were distinctly outlined upon the blue sky. When a piece was fired, a red streak as round as a log flashed low in the heavens, like a monstrous bolt of lightning. The men of the battery wore white duck trousers, which somehow emphasized their legs; and when they ran and crowded in little groups at the bidding of the shouting officers, it was more impressive than usual to the infantry.

Fred Collins, of A Company, was saying: "Thunder! I wisht I had a drink. Ain't there any water round here?" Then somebody yelled: "There goes th' bugler!"

As the eyes of half the regiment swept in one machine-like movement, there was an instant's picture of a horse in a great convulsive leap of a death-wound and a rider leaning back with a crooked arm and spread fingers before his face. On the ground was the crimson terror of an exploding shell, with fibres of flame that seemed like lances. A glittering bugle swung clear of the rider's back as fell headlong the horse and the man. In the air was an odour as from a conflagration.

Sometimes they of the infantry looked down at a fair little meadow which spread at their feet. Its long green grass was rippling gently in a breeze. Beyond it was the grey form of a house half torn to pieces by shells and by the busy axes of soldiers who had pursued firewood. The line of an old fence was now dimly marked by long weeds and by an occasional post. A shell had blown the well-house to fragments. Little lines of grey smoke ribboning upward from some embers indicated the place where had stood the barn.

From beyond a curtain of green woods there came the sound of some stupendous scuffle, as if two animals of the size of islands were fighting. At a distance there were occasional appearances of swift-moving men, horses, batteries, flags, and with the crashing of infantry volleys were heard, often, wild and frenzied cheers. In the midst of it all Smith and Ferguson, two privates of A Company, were engaged in a heated discussion which involved the greatest questions of the national existence.

The battery on the hill presently engaged in a frightful duel. The white legs of the gunners scampered this way and that way, and the officers redoubled their shouts. The guns, with their demeanours of stolidity and courage, were typical of something infinitely self-possessed in this clamour of death that swirled around the hill.

One of a "swing" team was suddenly smitten quivering to the ground, and his maddened brethren dragged his torn body in their struggle to escape from this turmoil and danger. A young soldier astride one of the leaders swore and fumed in his saddle and furiously jerked at the bridle. An officer screamed out an order so violently that his voice broke and ended the sentence in a falsetto shriek.

The leading company of the infantry regiment was somewhat exposed, and the colonel ordered it moved more fully under the shelter of the hill. There was the clank of steel against steel.

A lieutenant of the battery rode down and passed them, holding his right arm carefully in his left hand. And it was as if this arm was not at all a part of him, but belonged to another man. His sober and reflective charger went slowly. The officer's face was grimy and perspiring, and his uniform was tousled as if he had been in direct grapple with an enemy. He smiled grimly when the men stared at him. He turned his horse toward the meadow.

Collins, of A Company, said: "I wisht I had a drink. I bet there's water in that there ol' well yonder!"

"Yes; but how you goin' to git it?"

For the little meadow which intervened was now suffering a terrible onslaught of shells. Its green and beautiful calm had vanished utterly. Brown earth was being flung in monstrous handfuls. And there was a massacre of the young blades of grass. They were being torn, burned, obliterated. Some curious fortune of the battle had made this gentle little meadow the object of the red hate of the shells, and each one as it exploded seemed like an imprecation in the face of a maiden.

The wounded officer who was riding across this expanse said to himself: "Why, they couldn't shoot any harder if the whole army was massed here!"

A shell struck the grey ruins of the house, and as, after the roar, the shattered wall fell in fragments, there was a noise which resembled the flapping of shutters during a wild gale of winter. Indeed, the infantry paused in the shelter of the bank appeared as men standing upon a shore contemplating a madness of the sea. The angel of calamity had under its glance the battery upon the hill. Fewer white-legged men laboured about the guns. A shell had smitten one of the pieces, and after the flare, the smoke, the dust, the wrath of this blow were gone, it was possible to see white legs stretched horizontally upon the ground. And at the interval to the rear where it is the business of battery horses to stand with their noses to the fight, awaiting the command to drag their guns out of the destruction, or into it, or wheresoever these incomprehensible humans demanded with whip and spur—in this line of passive and dumb spectators, whose fluttering hearts yet would not let them forget the iron laws of man's control of them—in this rank of brute-soldiers there had been relentless and hideous carnage. From the ruck of bleeding and prostrate horses, the men of the infantry could see one animal raising its stricken body with its forelegs and turning its nose with mystic and profound eloquence toward the sky.

Some comrades joked Collins about his thirst. "Well, if yeh want a drink so bad, why don't yeh go git it?"

"Well, I will in a minnet, if yeh don't shut up!"

A lieutenant of artillery floundered his horse straight down the hill with as little concern as if it were level ground. As he galloped past the colonel of the infantry, he threw up his hand in swift salute. "We've got to get out of that," he roared angrily. He was a black-bearded officer, and his eyes, which resembled beads, sparkled like those of an insane man. His jumping horse sped along the column of infantry.

The fat major, standing carelessly with his sword held horizontally behind him and with his legs far apart, looked after the receding horseman and laughed. "He wants to get back with orders pretty quick, or there'll be no batt'ry left," he observed.

The wise young captain of the second company hazarded to the lieutenant-colonel that the enemy's infantry would probably soon attack the hill, and the lieutenant-colonel snubbed him.

A private in one of the rear companies looked out over the meadow, and then turned to a companion and said, "Look there, Jim!" It was the wounded officer from the battery, who some time before had started to ride across the meadow, supporting his right arm carefully with his left hand. This man had encountered a shell, apparently, at a time when no one perceived him, and he could now be seen lying face downward with a stirruped foot stretched across the body of his dead horse. A leg of the charger extended slantingly upward, precisely as stiff as a stake. Around this motionless pair the shells still howled.

There was a quarrel in A Company. Collins was shaking his fist in the faces of some laughing comrades. "Dern yeh! I ain't afraid t' go. If yeh say much, I will go!"

"Of course, yeh will! You'll run through that there medder, won't yeh?"

Collins said, in a terrible voice: "You see now!"

At this ominous threat his comrades broke into renewed jeers.

Collins gave them a dark scowl, and went to find his captain. The latter was conversing with the colonel of the regiment.

"Captain," said Collins, saluting and standing at attention—in those days all trousers bagged at the knees— "Captain, I want t' get permission to go git some water from that there well over yonder!"

The colonel and the captain swung about simultaneously and stared across the meadow. The captain laughed. "You must be pretty thirsty, Collins?"

"Yes, sir, I am."

"Well—ah," said the captain. After a moment, he asked, "Can't you wait?"

"No, sir."

The colonel was watching Collins's face. "Look here, my lad," he said, in a pious sort of voice—"Look here, my lad"—Collins was not a lad—"don't you think that's taking pretty big risks for a little drink of water?"

"I dunno," said Collins uncomfortably. Some of the resentment toward his companions, which perhaps had forced him into this affair, was beginning to fade. "I dunno w'ether 'tis."

The colonel and the captain contemplated him for a time.

"Well," said the captain finally.

"Well," said the colonel, "if you want to go, why, go."

Collins saluted. "Much obliged t' yeh."

As he moved away the colonel called after him. "Take some of the other boys' canteens with you, an' hurry back, now."

"Yes, sir, I will."

The colonel and the captain looked at each other then, for it had suddenly occurred that they could not for the life of them tell whether Collins wanted to go or whether he did not.

They turned to regard Collins, and as they perceived

him surrounded by gesticulating comrades, the colonel
said: "Well, by thunder! I guess he's going."

Collins appeared as a man dreaming. In the midst of
the questions, the advice, the warnings, all the excited talk
of his company mates, he maintained a curious silence.

They were very busy in preparing him for his ordeal.
When they inspected him carefully, it was somewhat like
the examination that grooms give a horse before a race;
and they were amazed, staggered, by the whole affair. Their
astonishment found vent in strange repetitions.

"Are yeh sure a-goin'?" they demanded again and again.

"Certainly I am," cried Collins at last, furiously.

He strode sullenly away from them. He was swinging
five or six canteens by their cords. It seemed that his cap
would not remain firmly on his head, and often he reached
and pulled it down over his brow.

There was a general movement in the compact column.
The long animal-like thing moved slightly. Its four hundred eyes were turned upon the figure of Collins.

"Well, sir, if that ain't th' derndest thing! I never
thought Fred Collins had the blood in him for that kind
of business."

"What's he goin' to do, anyhow?"

"He's goin' to that well there after water."

"We ain't dyin' of thirst, are we? That's foolishness."

"Well, somebody put him up to it, an' he's doin' it."

"Say, he must be a desperate cuss."

When Collins faced the meadow and walked away from
the regiment, he was vaguely conscious that a chasm, the
deep valley of all prides, was suddenly between him and
his comrades. It was provisional, but the provision was
that he return as a victor. He had blindly been led by
quaint emotions, and laid himself under an obligation to
walk squarely up to the face of death.

But he was not sure that he wished to make a retrac-
tion, even if he could do so without shame. As a matter
of truth, he was sure of very little. He was mainly surprised.

It seemed to him supernaturally strange that he had

allowed his mind to manœuvre his body into such a situation. He understood that it might be called dramatically great.

However, he had no full appreciation of anything, excepting that he was actually conscious of being dazed. He could feel his dulled mind groping after the form and colour of this incident. He wondered why he did not feel some keen agony of fear cutting his sense like a knife. He wondered at this, because human expression had said loudly for centuries that men should feel afraid of certain things, and that all men who did not feel this fear were phenomena—heroes.

He was, then, a hero. He suffered that disappointment which we would all have if we discovered that we were ourselves capable of those deeds which we most admire in history and legend. This, then, was a hero. After all, heroes were not much.

No, it could not be true. He was not a hero. Heroes had no shames in their lives, and, as for him, he remembered borrowing fifteen dollars from a friend and promising to pay it back the next day, and then avoiding that friend for ten months. When, at home, his mother had aroused him for the early labour of his life on the farm, it had often been his fashion to be irritable, childish, diabolical; and his mother had died since he had come to the war.

He saw that, in this matter of the well, the canteens, the shells, he was an intruder in the land of fine deeds.

He was now about thirty paces from his comrades. The regiment had just turned its many faces toward him.

From the forest of terrific noises there suddenly emerged a little uneven line of men. They fired fiercely and rapidly at distant foliage on which appeared little puffs of white smoke. The spatter of skirmish firing was added to the thunder of the guns on the hill. The little line of men ran forward. A colour-sergeant fell flat with his flag as if he had slipped on ice. There was hoarse cheering from this distant field.

Collins suddenly felt that two demon fingers were pressed into his ears. He could see nothing but flying arrows, flaming red. He lurched from the shock of this explosion, but he made a mad rush for the house, which he viewed as a man submerged to the neck in a boiling surf might view the shore. In the air little pieces of shell howled, and the earthquake explosions drove him insane with the menace of their roar. As he ran the canteens knocked together with a rhythmical tinkling.

As he neared the house, each detail of the scene became vivid to him. He was aware of some bricks of the vanished chimney lying on the sod. There was a door which hung by one hinge.

Rifle bullets called forth by the insistent skirmishers came from the far-off bank of foliage. They mingled with the shells and the pieces of shells until the air was torn in all directions by hootings, yells, howls. The sky was full of fiends who directed all their wild rage at his head.

When he came to the well, he flung himself face downward and peered into its darkness. There were furtive silver glintings some feet from the surface. He grabbed one of the canteens and, unfastening its cap, swung it down by the cord. The water flowed slowly in with an indolent gurgle.

And now, as he lay with his face turned away, he was suddenly smitten with the terror. It came upon his heart like the grasp of claws. All the power faded from his muscles. For an instant he was no more than a dead man.

The canteen filled with a maddening slowness, in the manner of all bottles. Presently he recovered his strength and addressed a screaming oath to it. He leaned over until it seemed as if he intended to try to push water into it with his hands. His eyes as he gazed down into the well shone like two pieces of metal, and in their expression was a great appeal and a great curse. The stupid water derided him.

There was the blaring thunder of a shell. Crimson light shone through the swift-boiling smoke and made a pink reflection on part of the wall of the well. Collins jerked out his arm and canteen with the same motion that a man would use in withdrawing his head from a furnace.

He scrambled erect and glared and hesitated. On the ground near him lay the old well bucket, with a length of rusty chain. He lowered it swiftly into the well. The bucket struck the water and then, turning lazily over, sank. When, with hand reaching tremblingly over hand, he hauled it out, it knocked often against the walls of the well and spilled some of its contents.

In running with a filled bucket, a man can adopt but one kind of gait. So, through this terrible field over which screamed practical angels of death, Collins ran in the manner of a farmer chased out of a dairy by a bull.

His face went staring white with anticipation—anticipation of a blow that would whirl him around and down. He would fall as he had seen other men fall, the life knocked out of them so suddenly that their knees were no more quick to touch the ground than their heads. He saw the long blue line of the regiment, but his comrades were standing looking at him from the edge of an impossible star. He was aware of some deep wheel-ruts and hoofprints in the sod beneath his feet.

The artillery officer who had fallen in this meadow had been making groans in the teeth of the tempest of sound. These futile cries, wrenched from him by his agony, were heard only by shells, bullets. When wild-eyed Collins came running, this officer raised himself. His face contorted and blanched from pain, he was about to utter some great beseeching cry. But suddenly his face straightened, and he called: "Say, young man, give me a drink of water, will you?"

Collins had no room amid his emotions for surprise. He was mad from the threats of destruction.

"I can't!" he screamed, and in his reply was a full description of his quaking apprehension. His cap was gone and his hair was riotous. His clothes made it appear that he had been dragged over the ground by the heels. He ran on.

The officer's head sank down, and one elbow crooked. His foot in its brass-bound stirrup still stretched over the body of his horse, and the other leg was under the steed.

But Collins turned. He came dashing back. His face had now turned grey, and in his eyes was all terror. "Here it is! Here it is!"

The officer was as a man gone in drink. His arm bent like a twig. His head drooped as if his neck were of willow. He was sinking to the ground, to lie face downward.

Collins grabbed him by the shoulder. "Here it is. Here's your drink. Turn over. Turn over, man, for God's sake!"

With Collins hauling at his shoulder, the officer twisted his body and fell with his face turned toward that region where lived the unspeakable noises of the swirling missiles. There was the faintest shadow of a smile on his lips as he looked at Collins. He gave a sigh, a little primitive breath like that from a child.

Collins tried to hold the bucket steadily, but his shaking hands caused the water to splash all over the face of the dying man. Then he jerked it away and ran on.

The regiment gave him a welcoming roar. The grimed faces were wrinkled in laughter.

His captain waved the bucket away. "Give it to the men!"

The two genial, skylarking young lieutenants were the first to gain possession of it. They played over it in their fashion.

When one tried to drink, the other teasingly knocked his elbow. "Don't Billie! You'll make me spill it," said the one. The other laughed.

Suddenly there was an oath, the thud of wood on the ground, and a swift murmur of astonishment among the ranks. The two lieutenants glared at each other. The bucket lay on the ground, empty.

THE UPTURNED FACE

"WHAT will we do now?" said the adjutant, troubled and excited.

"Bury him," said Timothy Lean.

The two officers looked down close to their toes where lay the body of their comrade. The face was chalk-blue; gleaming eyes stared at the sky. Over the two upright figures was a windy sound of bullets, and on the top of the hill Lean's prostrate company of Spitzbergen infantry was firing measured volleys.

"Don't you think it would be better—" began the adjutant. "We might leave him until to-morrow."

"No," said Lean. "I can't hold that post an hour longer. I've got to fall back, and we've got to bury old Bill."

"Of course," said the adjutant, at once. "Your men got entrenching tools?"

Lean shouted back to his little line, and two men came slowly, one with a pick, one with a shovel. They started in the direction of the Rostina sharpshooters. Bullets cracked near their ears. "Dig here," said Lean gruffly. The men, thus caused to lower their glances to the turf, became hurried and frightened, merely because they could not look to see whence the bullets came. The dull beat of the pick striking the earth sounded amid the swift snap of close bullets. Presently the other private began to shovel.

"I suppose," said the adjutant, slowly, "we'd better search his clothes for—things."

Lean nodded. Together in curious abstraction they looked at the body. Then Lean stirred his shoulders suddenly, arousing himself.

"Yes," he said, "we'd better see what he's got." He dropped to his knees, and his hands approached the body of the dead officer. But his hands wavered over the buttons of the tunic. The first button was brick-red with drying blood, and he did not seem to dare touch it.

"Go on," said the adjutant, hoarsely.

Lean stretched his wooden hand, and his fingers fumbled the bloodstained buttons. At last he rose with ghastly face. He had gathered a watch, a whistle, a pipe, a tobacco-pouch, a handkerchief, a little case of cards and papers. He looked at the adjutant. There was a silence. The adjutant was feeling that he had been a coward to make Lean do all the grisly business.

"Well," said Lean, "that's all, I think. You have his sword and revolver?"

"Yes," said the adjutant, his face working, and then he burst out in a sudden strange fury at the two privates. "Why don't you hurry up with that grave? What are you doing, anyhow? Hurry, do you hear? I never saw such stupid—"

Even as he cried out in his passion the two men were labouring for their lives. Ever overhead the bullets were spitting.

The grave was finished. It was not a masterpiece—a poor little shallow thing. Lean and the adjutant again looked at each other in a curious silent communication.

Suddenly the adjutant croaked out a weird laugh. It was a terrible laugh, which had its origin in that part of the mind which is first moved by the singing of the nerves. "Well," he said humorously to Lean, "I suppose we had best tumble him in."

"Yes," said Lean. The two privates stood waiting, bent over their implements. "I suppose," said Lean, "it would be better if we laid him in ourselves."

"Yes," said the adjutant. Then, apparently remembering that he had made Lean search the body, he stooped with great fortitude and took hold of the dead officer's clothing. Lean joined him. Both were particular that their fingers should not feel the corpse. They tugged away; the corpse lifted, heaved, toppled, flopped into the grave, and the two officers, straightening, looked again at each other

—they were always looking at each other. They sighed with relief.

The adjutant said, "I suppose we should—we should say something. Do you know the service, Tim?"

"They don't read the service until the grave is filled in," said Lean, pressing his lips to an academic expression.

"Don't they?" said the adjutant, shocked that he had made the mistake. "Oh, well," he cried, suddenly, "let us— let us say something—while he can hear us."

"All right," said Lean. "Do you know the service?"

"I can't remember a line of it," said the adjutant.

Lean was extremely dubious. "I can repeat two lines, but—"

"Well, do it," said the adjutant. "Go as far as you can. That's better than nothing. And the beasts have got our range exactly."

Lean looked at his two men. "Attention," he barked. The privates came to attention with a click, looking much aggrieved. The adjutant lowered his helmet to his knee. Lean, bareheaded, stood over the grave. The Rostina sharpshooters fired briskly.

"O Father, our friend has sunk in the deep waters of death, but his spirit has leaped toward Thee as the bubble arises from the lips of the drowning. Perceive, we beseech, O Father, the little flying bubble, and—"

Lean, although husky and ashamed, had suffered no hesitation up to this point, but he stopped with a hopeless feeling and looked at the corpse.

The adjutant moved uneasily. "And from Thy superb heights—" he began, and then he too came to an end.

"And from Thy superb heights," said Lean.

The adjutant suddenly remembered a phrase in the back of the Spitzbergen burial service, and he exploited it with the triumphant manner of a man who has recalled everything, and can go on.

"O God, have mercy—"

"O God, have mercy—" said Lean.

"Mercy," repeated the adjutant, in quick failure.

"Mercy," said Lean. And then he was moved by some

violence of feeling, for he turned upon his two men and tigerishly said, "Throw the dirt in."

The fire of the Rostina sharpshooters was accurate and continuous.

One of the aggrieved privates came forward with his shovel. He lifted his first shovel-load of earth, and for a moment of inexplicable hesitation it was held poised above this corpse, which from its chalk-blue face looked keenly out from the grave. Then the soldier emptied his shovel on—on the feet.

Timothy Lean felt as if tons had been swiftly lifted from off his forehead. He had felt that perhaps the private might empty the shovel on—on the face. It had been emptied on the feet. There was a great point gained there —ha, ha!—the first shovelful had been emptied on the feet. How satisfactory!

The adjutant began to babble. "Well, of course—a man we've messed with all these years—impossible—you can't, you know, leave your intimate friends rotting on the field. Go on, for God's sake, and shovel, you."

The man with the shovel suddenly ducked, grabbed his left arm with his right hand, and looked at his officer for orders. Lean picked the shovel from the ground. "Go to the rear," he said to the wounded man. He also addressed the other private. "You get under cover, too; I'll finish this business."

The wounded man scrambled hard still for the top of the ridge without devoting any glances to the direction from whence the bullets came, and the other man followed at an equal pace; but he was different, in that he looked back anxiously three times.

This is merely the way—often—of the hit and unhit.

Timothy Lean filled the shovel, hesitated, and then, in a movement which was like a gesture of abhorrence, he flung the dirt into the grave, and as it landed it made a sound—plop. Lean suddenly stopped and mopped his brow —a tired labourer.

"Perhaps we have been wrong," said the adjutant. His

glance wavered stupidly. "It might have been better if we hadn't buried him just at this time. Of course, if we advance to-morrow the body would have been—"

"Damn you," said Lean, "shut your mouth." He was not the senior officer.

He again filled the shovel and flung the earth. Always the earth made that sound—plop. For a space Lean worked frantically, like a man digging himself out of danger.

Soon there was nothing to be seen but the chalk-blue face. Lean filled the shovel. "Good God," he cried to the adjutant. "Why didn't you turn him somehow when you put him in? This—" Then Lean began to stutter.

The adjutant understood. He was pale to the lips. "Go on, man," he cried, beseechingly, almost in a shout.

Lean swung back the shovel. It went forward in a pendulum curve. When the earth landed it made a sound —plop.

AN EPISODE OF WAR

THE LIEUTENANT's rubber blanket lay on the ground, and upon it he had poured the company's supply of coffee. Corporals and other representatives of the grimy and hot-throated men who lined the breast-work had come for each squad's portion.

The lieutenant was frowning and serious at this task of division. His lips pursed as he drew with his sword various crevices in the heap, until brown squares of coffee, astoundingly equal in size, appeared on the blanket. He was on the verge of a great triumph in mathematics, and the corporals were thronging forward, each to reap a little square, when suddenly the lieutenant cried out and looked quickly at a man near him as if he suspected it was a case of personal assault. The others cried out also when they saw blood upon the lieutenant's sleeve.

He had winced like a man stung, swayed dangerously, and then straightened. The sound of his hoarse breathing was plainly audible. He looked sadly, mystically, over the breast-work at the green face of a wood, where now were many little puffs of white smoke. During this moment the men about him gazed statue-like and silent, astonished and awed by this catastrophe which happened when catastrophes were not expected—when they had leisure to observe it.

As the lieutenant stared at the wood, they too swung their heads, so that for another instant all hands, still silent, contemplated the distant forest as if their minds were fixed upon the mystery of a bullet's journey.

The officer had, of course, been compelled to take his sword into his left hand. He did not hold it by the hilt. He gripped it at the middle of the blade, awkwardly. Turning his eyes from the hostile wood, he looked at the sword as he held it there, and seemed puzzled as to what to do with it, where to put it. In short, this weapon had of a sudden become a strange thing to him. He looked at it in a kind of stupefaction, as if he had been endowed with a trident, a sceptre, or a spade.

Finally he tried to sheathe it. To sheathe a sword held by the left hand, at the middle of the blade, in a scabbard hung at the left hip, is a feat worthy of a sawdust ring. This wounded officer engaged in a desperate struggle with the sword and the wobbling scabbard, and during the time of it he breathed like a wrestler.

But at this instant the men, the spectators, awoke from their stone-like poses and crowded forward sympathetically. The orderly-sergeant took the sword and tenderly placed it in the scabbard. At the time, he leaned nervously backward, and did not allow even his finger to brush the body of the lieutenant. A wound gives strange dignity to him who bears it. Well men shy from this new and terrible majesty. It is as if the wounded man's hand is upon the curtain which hangs before the revelations of all existence—the meaning of ants, potentates, wars, cities, sunshine, snow, a feather dropped from a bird's wing; and the power of it sheds radiance upon a bloody form, and makes the other men understand sometimes that they are little. His comrades look at him with large eyes thoughtfully. Moreover, they fear vaguely that the weight of a finger upon him might send him headlong, precipitate the tragedy, hurl him at once into the dim, grey unknown. And so the orderly-sergeant, while sheathing the sword, leaned nervously backward.

There were others who proffered assistance. One timidly presented his shoulder and asked the lieutenant if he cared to lean upon it, but the latter waved him away mournfully. He wore the look of one who knows he is the victim of a terrible disease and understands his helplessness. He again stared over the breast-work at the forest, and then, turning, went slowly rearward. He held his right wrist tenderly in his left hand as if the wounded arm was made of very brittle glass.

And the men in silence stared at the wood, then at the departing lieutenant; then at the wood, then at the lieutenant.

As the wounded officer passed from the line of battle, he was enabled to see many things which as a participant in the fight were unknown to him. He saw a general on a black horse gazing over the lines of blue infantry at the green woods which veiled his problems. An aide galloped furiously, dragged his horse suddenly to a halt, saluted, and presented a paper. It was, for a wonder, precisely like a historical painting.

To the rear of the general and his staff a group, composed of a bugler, two or three orderlies, and the bearer of the corps standard, all upon maniacal horses, were working like slaves to hold their ground, preserve their respectful interval, while the shells boomed in the air about them, and caused their chargers to make furious quivering leaps.

A battery, a tumultuous and shining mass, was swirling toward the right. The wild thud of hoofs, the cries of the riders shouting blame and praise, menace and encouragement, and, last, the roar of the wheels, the slant of the glistening guns, brought the lieutenant to an intent pause. The battery swept in curves that stirred the heart; it made halts as dramatic as the crash of a wave on the rocks, and when it fled onward this aggregation of wheels, levers, motors had a beautiful unity, as if it were a missile. The sound of it was a war-chorus that reached into the depths of man's emotion.

The lieutenant, still holding his arm as if it were of glass, stood watching this battery until all detail of it was lost, save the figures of the riders, which rose and fell and waved lashes over the black mass.

Later, he turned his eyes toward the battle, where the shooting sometimes crackled like bush-fires, sometimes sputtered with exasperating irregularity, and sometimes reverberated like the thunder. He saw the smoke rolling upward and saw crowds of men who ran and cheered, or stood and blazed away at the inscrutable distance.

He came upon some stragglers, and they told him how
to find the field hospital. They described its exact location.
In fact, these men, no longer having part in the battle,
knew more of it than others. They told the performance
of every corps, every division, the opinion of every general. The lieutenant, carrying his wounded arm rearward,
looked upon them with wonder.

At the roadside a brigade was making coffee and buzz-
ing with talk like a girls' boarding-school. Several officers
came out to him and inquired concerning things of which
he knew nothing. One, seeing his arm, began to scold.
"Why, man, that's no way to do. You want to fix that
thing." He appropriated the lieutenant and the lieutenant's
wound. He cut the sleeve and laid bare the arm, every
nerve of which softly fluttered under his touch. He bound
his handkerchief over the wound, scolding away in the
meantime. His tone allowed one to think that he was in
the habit of being wounded every day. The lieutenant
hung his head, feeling, in this presence, that he did not
know how to be correctly wounded.

The low white tents of the hospital were grouped around
an old schoolhouse. There was here a singular commo-
tion. In the foreground two ambulances interlocked wheels
in the deep mud. The drivers were tossing the blame of it
back and forth, gesticulating and berating, while from the
ambulances, both crammed with wounded, there came an
occasional groan. An interminable crowd of bandaged men
were coming and going. Great numbers sat under the trees
nursing heads or arms or legs. There was a dispute of
some kind raging on the steps of the schoolhouse. Sitting
with his back against a tree a man with a face as grey as a
new army blanket was serenely smoking a corncob pipe.
The lieutenant wished to rush forward and inform him that
he was dying.

A busy surgeon was passing near the lieutenant. "Good-
morning," he said, with a friendly smile. Then he caught
sight of the lieutenant's arm, and his face at once changed.
"Well, let's have a look at it." He seemed possessed suddenly of a great contempt for the lieutenant. This wound

evidently placed the latter on a very low social plane. The doctor cried out impatiently: "What mutton-head had tied it up that way anyhow?" The lieutenant answered, "Oh, a man."

When the wound was disclosed the doctor fingered it disdainfully. "Humph," he said. "You come along with me and I'll 'tend to you." His voice contained the same scorn as if he were saying: "You will have to go to jail."

The lieutenant had been very meek, but now his face flushed, and he looked into the doctor's eyes. "I guess I won't have it amputated," he said.

"Nonsense, man! Nonsense! Nonsense!" cried the doctor. "Come along, now. I won't amputate it. Come along. Don't be a baby."

"Let go of me," said the lieutenant, holding back wrathfully, his glance fixed upon the door of the old schoolhouse, as sinister to him as the portals of death.

And this is the story of how the lieutenant lost his arm. When he reached home, his sisters, his mother, his wife, sobbed for a long time at the sight of the flat sleeve. "Oh, well," he said, standing shamefaced amid these tears, "I don't suppose it matters so much as all that."

STEPHEN CRANE'S VIVID STORY OF THE BATTLE OF SAN JUAN [1]

❖ ❖ ❖

Victory Gained Not by the Officers, but by the Audacious Bravery of the Men

---

"GRAND POPULAR MOVEMENT"

With or Without Orders, They Marched Doggedly Forward in the Face of Death

---

DESPERATE VALOR AT EL CANEY

Cuban Soldiers Demoralized, Lazy, Worthless and Heartily Despised by the American Troops

IN FRONT OF SANTIAGO, July 4, via Old Point Comfort, Va., July 13.—The action at San Juan on July 1 was, particularly speaking, a soldiers' battle. It was like Inkerman, where the English fought half leaderless all day in a fog. Only the Cuban forest was worse than any fog.

No doubt when history begins to grind out her story we will find that many a thundering, fine, grand order was given for that day's work: but after all there will be no harm in contending that the fighting line, the men and their regimental officers, took the hill chiefly because they knew they could take it, some having no orders and others disobeying whatever orders they had.

In civil life the newspapers would have called it a grand, popular movement. It will never be forgotten as long as America has a military history.

[1] Reprinted verbatim from the *World*, New York, Thursday, July 14, 1898, p. 3.

A line of intrenched hills held by men armed with a weapon like the Mauser is not to be taken by a front attack of infantry unless the trenches have first been heavily shaken by artillery fire. Any theorist will say that it is impossible, and prove it to be impossible. But it was done, and we owe the success to the splendid gallantry of the American private soldier.

As near as one can learn, headquarters expected little or no fighting on the 1st. Lawton's division was to go by the Caney road, chase the Spaniards out of that interesting village, and then, wheeling half to the left, march down to join the other divisions in some kind of attack on San Juan at daybreak on the 2d.

MISINFORMED AS TO SPANISH STRENGTH

But somebody had been entirely misinformed as to the strength and disposition of the Spanish forces at Caney, and instead of taking Lawton six minutes to capture the town it took him nearly all day, as well it might.

The other divisions lying under fire, waiting for Lawton, grew annoyed at a delay which was, of course, not explained to them, and suddenly arose and took the formidable hills of San Juan. It was impatience suddenly exalted to one of the sublime passions.

Lawton was well out toward Caney soon after daybreak, and by 7 o'clock we could hear the boom of Capron's guns in support of the infantry. The remaining divisions—Kent's and Wheeler's—were trudging slowly along the muddy trail through the forest.

When the first gun was fired a grim murmur passed along the lean column. "They're off!" somebody said.

The marching was of necessity very slow, and even then the narrow road was often blocked. The men, weighted with their packs, cartridge belts and rifles, forded many streams, climbed hills, slid down banks and forced their way through thickets.

Suddenly there was a roar of guns just ahead and a little to the left. This was Grimes's battery going into action on the hill which is called El Paso. Then, all in a moment, the quiet column moving forward was opposed by men carrying terrible burdens. Wounded Cubans were being carried to the rear. Most of them were horribly mangled.

The second brigade of dismounted American cavalry had been in support of the battery, its position being directly to the rear. Some Cubans had joined there. The Spanish shrapnel fired at the battery was often cut too long, and, passing over, burst amid the supports and the Cubans.

SHORT LULL IN THE BATTLE

The loss of the battery, the cavalry and the Cubans from this fire was forty men in killed and wounded, the First regular cavalry probably suffering most grievously. Presently there was a lull in the artillery fire, and down through spaces in the trees we could see the infantry still plodding with its packs steadily toward the front.

The artillerymen were greatly excited. Some showed with glee fragments of Spanish shells which had come dangerously near their heads. They had gone through their ordeal and were talking over it lightly.

In the mean time Lawton's division, some three miles away, was making plenty of noise. Caney is just at the base of a high willow-green, crinkled mountain, and Lawton was making his way over little knolls which might be termed foothills. We could see the great white clouds of smoke from Capron's guns and hear their roar punctuating the incessant drumming of the infantry. It was plain even then that Lawton was having considerably more of a fete than anybody had supposed previously.

At about 2,500 yards in front of Grimes's position on El Paso arose the gentle green hills of San Juan, dotted not too plentifully with trees—hills that resembled the sloping orchards of Orange County in summer. Here and there were houses built, evidently as summer villas, but now loopholed and barricaded. They had heavy roofs of red tiles and were shaped much like Japanese, or, better, Javanese, houses. Here and there, too, along the crests of these curving hillocks were ashen streaks, the rifle-pits of the Spaniards.

At the principal position of the enemy were a flag, a redoubt, a block-house and some sort of pagoda, in the shade of which Spanish officers were wont to promenade during lulls and negligently gossip about the battle. There was one man in a summer-resort straw hat. He did a deal of sauntering in the coolest manner possible, walking out in the clear sunshine and gazing languidly in our direction. He seemed to be carrying a little cane.

GRIMES SMASHED THEM

At 11.25 our artillery reopened on the central block-house and intrenchments. The Spanish fire had been remarkably fine, but it was our turn now. Grimes had his ranges to a nicety. After the great "shout of the gun" came the broad, windy, diminishing noise of the flung shell: then a fainter boom and a cloud of red debris out of the block-house or up from the ground near the trenches.

The Spanish infantry in the trenches fired a little volley immediately after every one of the American shells. It puzzled many to decide at what they could be firing, but it was finally resolved that they were firing just to show us that they were still there and were not afraid.

It must have been about 2 o'clock when the enemy's battery again retorted.

The cruel thing about this artillery duel was that our battery had nothing but old-fashioned powder, and its position was always as clearly defined as if it had been the Chicago fire. There is no secrecy about a battery that uses that kind of powder. The great billowy white smoke can be seen for miles. On the other hand, the Spaniards were using the best smokeless. There is no use groaning over what was to be, but!—

However, fate elected that the Spanish shooting should be very bad. Only two-thirds of their shells exploded in this second affair. They all whistled high, and those that exploded raked the ground long since evacuated by the supports and the timbers. No one was hurt.

A MISPLACED BALLOON

From El Paso to San Juan there is a broad expanse of dense forest, spotted infrequently with vividly green fields. It is traversed by a single narrow road which leads straight between the two positions, fording two little streams. Along this road had gone our infantry and also the military balloon. Why it was ever taken to such a position nobody knows, but there it was—huge, fat, yellow, quivering—being dragged straight into a zone of fire that would surely ruin it.

There were two officers in the car for the greater part of the way, and there surely were never two men who valued their lives less. But they both escaped unhurt, while the balloon sank down, torn to death by the bullets that were volleyed at it by the nervous Spaniards, who suspected dynamite. It was never brought out of the woods where it recklessly met its fate.

In these woods, unknown to some, including the Spaniards, was fulminated the gorgeous plan of taking an impregnable position.

One saw a thin line of black figures moving across a field. They disappeared in the forest. The enemy was keeping up a terrific fire. Then suddenly somebody yelled, "By God, there go our boys up the hill!"

There is many a good American who would give an arm to get the thrill of patriotic insanity that coursed through us when we heard that yell.

Yes, they were going up the hill, up the hill. It was the best moment of anybody's life. An officer said to me afterward: "If we had been in that position and the Spaniards had come at us, we would have piled them up so high the last man couldn't have climbed over." But up went the regiments with no music save that ceaseless, fierce crashing of rifles.

FOREIGN ATTACHES SAID "IMPOSSIBLE"

The foreign attaches were shocked. "It is very gallant, but very foolish," said one sternly.

"Why, they can't take it, you know. Never in the world," cried another, much agitated. "It is slaughter, absolute slaughter."

The little Japanese shrugged his shoulders. He was one who said nothing.

The road from El Paso to San Juan was now a terrible road. It should have a tragic fame like the sunken road at Waterloo. Why we did not later hang some of the gentry who contributed from the trees to the terror of this road is not known.

The wounded were stringing back from the front, hundreds of them. Some walked unaided, an arm or a shoulder having been dressed at a field station. They stopped often enough to answer the universal hail "How is it going?" Others hobbled or clung to a friend's shoulders. Their slit trousers exposed red bandages. A few were shot horribly in the face and were led, bleeding and blind, by their mates.

And then there were the slow pacing stretcher-bearers with the dying or the insensible, the badly wounded, still figures with blood often drying brick color on their hot bandages.

Prostrate at the roadside were many, others who had made their way thus far and were waiting for strength. Everywhere moved the sure-handed, invaluable Red Cross men.

Over this scene was a sort of haze of bullets. They were of two kinds. First, the Spanish lines were firing just a trifle high. Their bullets swept over our firing lines and poured into this devoted roadway, the single exit, even as it had been the single approach. The second fire was from guerillas concealed in the trees and in the thickets along the trail. They had come in under the very wings of our strong advance, taken good positions on either side of the road and were peppering our line of communication whenever they got a good target, no matter, apparently, what the target might be.

Red Cross men, wounded men, sick men, correspondents and attaches were all one to the guerilla. The move of sending an irregular force around the flanks of the enemy as he is making his front attack is so legitimate that some of us could not believe at first that the men hidden in the forest were really blazing away at the non-combatants or the wounded. Viewed simply as a bit of tactics, the scheme was admirable. But there is no doubt now that they intentionally fired at anybody they thought they could kill.

You can't mistake an ambulance driver when he is driving his ambulance. You can't mistake a wounded man when he is lying down and being bandaged. And when you see a field hospital you don't mistake it for a squadron of cavalry or a brigade of infantry.

PROFOUND PATIENCE OF THE WOUNDED

As we went along the road we suddenly heard a cry behind us. "Oh, come quick! Come quick!" We turned and saw a young soldier spinning around frantically and grabbing at his leg. Evidently he had been going to the stream to fill his canteen, but a guerilla had barred him from that drink. Two Red Cross men rushed for him.

At the last ford, and in the shelter of the muddy bank, lay a dismal band, forty men on their backs with doctors working at them and bullets singing in flocks over their heads. They rolled their eyes quietly at us. There was no groaning. They exhibited that profound patience which has been the marvel of every one.

After the ford was passed the woods cleared. The road passed through lines of barbed wire. There were, in fact, barbed wire fences running in almost every direction.

The mule train, galloping like a troop of cavalry, dashed up with a reinforcement of ammunition, every mule on the jump, the cowboys swinging their whips. They were under a fairly strong fire, but up they went.

One does not expect gallantry in a pack train, but incidentally it may be said that this charge, led by the bell mare, was one of the sights of the day.

BURROWE'S DYNAMITE GUN

At a place where the road cut through the crest of the ridge Burrowe and some of his men were working over his dynamite gun. After the fifth discharge something had got jammed. There was never such devotion to an inanimate thing as these men give to their dynamite gun. They will quarrel for her, starve for her, lose sleep for her and fight for her to the last ditch.

In the army there have always been two opinions of the dynamite gun. Some have said it was a most terrific engine of destruction, while others have called it a toy. With the bullets winging their long flights not very high overhead, Burrowe and his crowd, at sight of us, began their little hymn of praise, the chief note of which was one of almost pathetic insistence. If they ever get that gun into action again, they will make her hum.

The discomfited Spaniards, recovering from their panic, opened from their second line a most furious fire. It was first directed against one part of our line and then against another, as if they were feeling for our weakest point, fumbling around after the throat of the army.

Somebody on the left caught it for a time, and then suddenly the enemy apparently devoted their entire attention to the position occupied by the Rough Riders. Some shrapnel, with fuses cut too long, passed over and burst from 100 to 200 yards to the rear. They acted precisely like things with strings to them. When the string was jerked, bang! went the hurtling explosive. But the infantry fire was very heavy, albeit high.

The American reply was in measured volleys. Part of a regiment would remain on the firing line while the other companies rested near by under the brow of the hill. Parties were sent after the packs. The commands knew with what other organizations they were in touch on the two flanks. Otherwise they knew nothing, save that they were going to hold their ground. They said so.

From our line could be seen a long, gray, Spanish intrenchment, from 400 to 1,000 yards away, according to what part of our line one measured from. From it floated no smoke and no men appeared there, but it was making a noise like a million champagne corks.

Back of their entrenchments, perhaps another thousand

yards, was a long building of masonry tinted pink. It flew many Red Cross flags and near it were other smaller structures also flying Red Cross flags. In fact, the enemy's third line of defense seemed to be composed of hospitals.

The city itself slanted down toward the bay, just a glimpse of silver. In the clear, white sunshine the houses of the suburbs, the hospitals and the long gray trenches were so vivid that they seemed far closer than they were.

To the rear, over the ground that the army had taken, a breeze was gently stirring the long grass and ruffling the surface of a pool that lay in a sort of meadow. The army took its glory calmly. Having nothing else to do, the army sat down and looked tranquilly at the scenery. There was not that exuberance of enthusiasm which surrounds the vicinity of a candidate for the Assembly.

The army was dusty, dishevelled, its hair matted to its forehead with sweat, its shirts glued to its back with the same, and indescribably dirty, thirsty, hungry, and a-weary from its bundles and its marches and its fights. It sat down on the conquered crest and felt satisfied.

"Well, hell! here we are."

LAWTON'S HEAVY LOSSES

News began to pass along the line. Lawton had taken Caney after a long fight and had lost heavily. The siege pieces were being unloaded at Siboney. Pando had succeeded in reinforcing Santiago that very morning with 8,400 men, 6,000 men, 4,500 men. Pando had not succeeded. And so on.

At dusk a comparative stillness settled upon the ridge. The shooting subsided to little nervous outbursts. In the trenches taken by our troops lay dead Spaniards.

The road to the rear increased its terrors in the darkness. The wounded men, stumbling along in the mud, a miasmic mist from the swampish ground filling their nostrils, heard often in the air the whiplash sound of a bullet that was meant for them by the lurking guerillas. A mile, two miles, two miles and a half to the rear, great populous hospitals had been formed.

CAMPING ON THE GROUND THEY WON

The long lines of the hill began to intrench under cover of night, each regiment for itself, still, however, keeping in touch on the flanks. Each regiment dug in the ground that it had taken by its own valor. Some commands had two or three shovels, an axe or two, maybe a pick. Other regiments dug with their bayonets and shovelled out the dirt with their meat ration cans.

Darkness swallowed Santiago and the new intrenchments. The large tropic stars illumined the sky. On the safe side of the ridge our men had built some little red fires, no larger than hats, at which they cooked what food they possessed. There was no sound save to the rear, where throughout the night our pickets could be faintly heard exchanging shots with the guerillas.

On the very moment, it seemed, of the break of day, bang! the fight was on again. The firing broke out from one end of the prodigious V-shaped formation to the other. Our artillery took new advanced positions, but they were driven away by the swirling Mauser fire.

When the day was in full bloom Lawton's division, having marched all night, appeared in the road. The long, long column wound around the base of the ridge and disappeared among the woods and knolls on the right of Wheeler's line. The army was now concentrated in a splendid position.

CUBANS HELD IN CONTEMPT

It becomes necessary to speak of the men's opinion of the Cubans. To put it shortly, both officers and privates have the most lively contempt for the Cubans. They despise them. They came down here expecting to fight side by side with an ally, but this ally has done little but stay in the rear and eat army rations, manifesting an indifference to the cause of Cuban liberty which could not be exceeded by some one who had never heard of it.

In the great charge up the hills of San Juan the American soldiers who, for their part, sprinkled a thousand bodies in the grass, were not able to see a single Cuban assisting in what might easily turn out to be the decisive battle for Cuban freedom.

At Caney a company of Cubans came into action on the left flank of one of the American regiments just before the place was taken. Later they engaged a block-house at 2,000 yards and fired away all their ammunition. They sent back to the American commander for more, but they got only a snort of indignation.

As a matter of fact, the Cuban soldier, ignorant as only such isolation as has been his can make him, does not appreciate the ethics of the situation.

This great American army he views is furious, too, because the Cubans apparently consider themselves under no obligation to take part in an engagement; because the Cubans will stay at the rear and collect haversacks, blankets, coats and shelter tents dropped by our troops.

The average Cuban here will not speak to an American unless to beg. He forgets his morning, afternoon or evening salutation unless he is reminded. If he takes a dislike to you he talks about you before your face, using a derisive undertone.

DEMORALIZED BY AID

The truth probably is that the food, raiment and security furnished by the Americans have completely demoralized the insurgents. When the force under Gomez came to Guantanamo to assist the marines they were a most efficient body of men. They guided the marines to the enemy and fought with them shoulder to shoulder, not very skilfully in the matter of shooting, but still with courage and determination.

After this action there ensued at Guantanamo a long peace. The Cubans built themselves a permanent camp and they began to eat, eat much, and to sleep long, day and night, until now, behold, there is no more useless body of men anywhere! A trifle less than half of them are on Dr. Edgar's sick list, and the others are practically insubordinate. So much food seems to act upon them like a drug.

Here with the army the demoralization has occurred on a big scale. It is dangerous, too, for the Cuban. If he stupidly, drowsily remains out of these fights, what weight is his voice to have later in the final adjustments? The officers and men of the army, if their feeling remains the same, will not be happy to see him have any at all. The situation needs a Gomez. It is more serious than these be-starred machete bearers know how to appreciate, and it is the worst thing for the cause of an independent Cuba that could possibly exist.

THE BATTLE OF JULY 2

At San Juan the 2d of July was a smaller edition of the 1st. The men deepened their intrenchments, shot, slept and ate. On the 1st every man had been put into the fighting line. There was not a reserve as big as your hat. If the enemy broke through any part of the line there was nothing to stop them short of Siboney. On the 2d, however, some time after the arrival of Lawton, the Ninth Massachusetts and the Thirty-fourth Michigan came up.

Along the road from El Paso they had to pass some pretty grim sights. And there were some pretty grim odors, but the men were steady enough. "How far are they off?" they asked of a passing regular. "Oh, not far; but it's all right. We think they may run out of ammunition in the course of a week or ten days."

The volunteers laughed. But the pitiful thing about this advance was to see in the hands of the boys those terrible old rifles that smoke like brush fires and give the regimental line away to the enemy as plainly as an illuminated sign.

I remember that on the first day men of the Seventy-first who had lost their command would try to join one of the regular regiments, but the regulars would have none of them. "Get out of here with that —— gun!" the regulars would say. During the battle just one shot from a Springfield would call a volley, for the Spaniards then knew just where to shoot. It was very hard on the Seventy-first New York and the Second Massachusetts.

At Caney about two hundred prisoners were taken. Two big squads of them were soldiers of the regular Spanish infantry in the usual blue-and-white pajamas. The others were the rummiest-looking set of men one could possibly imagine. They were native-born Cubans, reconcentrados, traitors, guerillas of the kind that bushwacked us so unmercifully. Some were doddering old men, shaking with the palsy of their many years. Some were slim, dirty, bad-eyed boys. They were all of a lower class than one could find in any United States jail.

At first they had all expected to be butchered. In fact, to encourage them to fight, their officers had told them that if they gave in they need expect no mercy from the dreadful Americans.

Our great, good, motherly old country has nothing in her heart but mercy, and nothing in her pockets but beef, hardtack and coffee for all of them—lemon-colored refugee from Santiago, wild-eyed prisoner from the trenches, Spanish guerilla from out the thickets, half-naked insurgent from the mountains—all of them.

STEPHEN CRANE

PART III

A Tale of the Sea

INTRODUCTION

IN THE winter of 1892–3 Crane roomed with some young painters and newspaper illustrators at the Art Students' League on Twenty-third Street, and he used to visit the near-by studio of one of these artist friends, Corwin Linson.

Sitting on my couch, rings of gray smoke circling about him, a pad on his knee, he would turn out a complete story in a half-hour. Sometimes it was a fragment that would be laid by for future use. Several sparkling sketches were invented and written in that atmosphere of melancholy, while I sat at my easel dabbling at a drawing and wondering how a new illustrator could get in his "wedge." [1]

One morning when Linson called at Crane's room he discovered him "feverishly writing. He waved me to a seat, and soon handed me the first pages of a story. 'Been at it most of the night, and it's nearly finished.'" Short stories, Crane told another friend, "are the easiest things to write."

Three years later, when Crane was living at Hartwood "very quietly and alone mostly," he looked back on the array of writings he had published and remarked in a letter to his former schoolmate C. L. Peaslee: "it appears that I have worked, but as a matter of truth I am very lazy, hating work and only taking up a pen when circumstances drive me." [2] Two of his major books were finished and his

[1] "Little Stories of 'Steve' Crane," *Saturday Evening Post*, April 11, 1903, p. 19.
[2] This letter appears in "The College Days of Stephen Crane," *Monthly Illustrator*, 13 (1896), 27.

third was under way in that wonderful year 1893, and he did a lot of other pieces. One of these, written that spring, was *The Reluctant Voyagers*—his first attempt at a sea-story. It is a kind of *New Yorker* sketch about two men who are carried out to sea on a derelict raft, rescued by a coast schooner, and deposited at New York harbor in their bathing suits. Corwin Linson drew illustrations for it, using Crane to pose for "the tall man." But the sketch did not pay off. No magazine would take *The Reluctant Voyagers,* and it never reached print until 1902, in the posthumous *Last Words.* It is fifth-rate Crane. The plot drifts like the raft itself, breaking loose from what looked like a good beginning.

Crane did not have to invent any plot for *The Open Boat:* he transcribed the whole from his own experience. Yet it is as much an invention as *The Reluctant Voyagers.* Crane always was concerned to get facts down with scrupulous fidelity to the truth of experience, and he went to extraordinary pains to be certain that the facts in *The Open Boat* squared with what actually happened. To find out whether he had them right, he checked them with the captain of the *Commodore.* Their conversation was over-heard by Ralph Paine and recorded in his *Roads of Adventure* (1922):

—Listen, Ed, I want to have this *right,* from your point of view. How does it sound so far?—
—You've got it, Steve—said the other man.—That is just how it happened, and how we felt. Read me some more of it.—

Accounts of the wreck in dispatches to the *New York Press* and the *Florida Times-Union* (here abridged and collected for the first time, pages 242–54), together with Crane's own report, furnished a history of the tragedy. Crane did not alter the facts or their sequence, yet the difference between what happened and what Crane reconstructed from his experience is immense. It is the difference that distinguishes life from art. In *The Open Boat* the whole event is charged with significance. Every fact has been charged with meaning and patterned into a scheme of relationships. Realistic details have been converted into symbols, and their sequence forms a designed whole possessing a life of its own.

By what methods has Crane brought about this symbolic conversion? Let us examine some of his symbols and see how symbols are created.

Symbols are created by establishing correlations between the plight of the characters and their environment (for example, battlefield, forest, or sea). The mental state, feeling, or mood is transposed and objectified in things, in natural objects or in other persons whose plight parallels the central situation or stands in contrast to it. Thus in *The Red Badge* Henry's mental state is objectified in a single recurrent object, the flag, and the meaning of the whole book gradually accretes around this dominant or focal symbol. In *The Open Boat* the confused mental state of the men is identified with the confused and "broken sea," and it is obversely objectified in the contradictory gulls that hover "comfortably" over them, gruesome and ominous birds utterly indifferent to the plight of the men. The bird's "black eyes were *wistfully* fixed upon the captain's head." The unconcern of the universe is symbolized by the wind-tower as it appears to them when they head for the beach:

This tower was a giant, standing with its back to the plight of the ants. It represented in a degree, to the correspondent, the serenity of nature amid the struggles of the individual— nature in the wind, and nature in the vision of the men. She did not seem cruel to him then, nor beneficent, nor treacherous, nor wise. But she was indifferent, flatly indifferent.

Symbols are generated by parallelisms and repetitions. A symbolic detail at the very beginning of *The Open Boat* prepares for the final incident, the death of the oiler. He is represented by the oar he steers: "It was a thin little oar and it seemed often ready to snap." In *The Red Badge* the chattering fear of a frightened squirrel, fleeing when Henry Fleming throws a pine cone at him (Chapter vii), parallels the plight of the hero under shellfire.

Symbols are at their most effective when they radiate

multiple correspondences or different contents—at different times or at the same time. Colors, used *only* as decorative pattern in *Maggie* and *An Experiment in Misery,* are symbolically employed in *The Red Badge.* Here the symbolic value of any given color varies according to its location in a specific context. Symbolic patterns of life and death are established, for example, by the *same* color. The one is signified by the *yellow* of the sun and the other by the *yellow* of uniforms on dead soldiers.

The Open Boat and *The Red Badge* are identical in form, in theme, and even in their patterns of leitmotivs and imagery. In *The Open Boat* the despair-hope mood of the men is established (and the point of view prepared for) in the opening sentence: "None of them knew the colour of the sky"; and the final scene repeats the same contrast mood. At the end, when the men are tossed upon "the lonely and indifferent shore," the once barbarously abrupt waves now pace "to and fro in the moonlight." As the sea changes, so the men change. They experience a change of heart. Their serenity, we are made to feel, is signified by the seemingly quieted waves. But the serenity of the waves is deceptive, for the violent sea actually remains unabated. Their victory over nature has cost them one of their brotherhood—the oiler lies face-downward in the shallows.

The death of Higgins symbolizes nature's injustice, her treachery and indifference, but it is *through* his death that this truth is revealed to the others. It is his death that changes their vision. (Similarly, in *The Red Badge,* it is the death of Jim Conklin that changes Henry Fleming's vision.) At the end, when the men hear "the great sea's voice," they understand what it says, what life means, because they have suffered the worst that the sea can exact from them—"they felt that they could *then* be interpreters." Life—represented by the ritual of comfort bestowed on the saved men by the people on the beach—life now becomes "sacred to their minds."

This theme of insight through suffering is prepared for by the very first image of the story: "None of them knew the colour of the sky." It is foreshadowed and epitomized in the song that the correspondent recites to himself: "A soldier of the Legion lay dying in Algiers." The correspondent had known this verse when a child, but *then* he had not regarded the death of that soldier as important or meaningful. He had never felt any sympathy for the soldier's plight because he himself had not yet experienced it. "It was less to him than the breaking of a pencil's point." The soldier's plight parallels and foremirrors the oiler's plight. The image of the delicate pencil point correlates with the image of the thin oar of the oiler that "seemed often ready to snap." The whole meaning of *The Open Boat* is focused in the death of the oiler.

The Open Boat was sold by Irvin Bacheller to *Scribner's Magazine* for three hundred and fifty dollars. It appeared there in June 1897 and in *The Open Boat and Other Stories* the next year, with Crane's dedication to "the late William Higgins and to Captain Edward Murphy and Steward C. B. Montgomery. . . ." *The Open Boat,* said H. G. Wells, is "beyond all question, the crown of all his work." Conrad deeply admired it: "the deep and simple humanity of its presentation seems somehow to illustrate the essentials of life itself, like a symbolic tale."

Both Conrad and Crane showed themselves very early in their career to be symbolic artists—Conrad in his very first story, *The Lagoon,* and Crane in one of his earliest, *The Men in the Storm.* The greater number of Crane's stories, however, are non-symbolic. When he does attempt symbolism, the potential symbols all too often collapse. The beginning of *The Reluctant Voyagers* is wasted by what follows, and the pathetic episode of *An Auction,* while intending a symbolism, remains merely pathetic. Crane's technique is best studied in *The Red Badge* and *The Open Boat.* The device of a double vision, for instance, was first introduced in *The Open Boat.* Things viewed by the men at sea are viewed *as though* they were men on land. In *An Episode of War,* similarly, we get the point of view of the wounded simultaneously with the point of view of the unwounded. It is this technical trick that Joyce employed so expertly in *The Dead.* In *The Open Boat* this double vision manifests the two-part contrast of Crane's theme: sea and land symbolizing two opposite ways of life.

Of all Crane's works *The Open Boat* is the most direct manifestation of his belief that no man can interpret life without first experiencing it. The key to the whole work of Crane is that he passionately believed in this theme and that as artist he put his belief into practice. And that is the paradox of his whole career: *The Red Badge* is the product of his *imaginative* belief in the same theme. What is important to the artist is not that he experience his theme but that he believe in it.

I have said that *The Open Boat* and *The Red Badge* embody the same theme. In change lies salvation. This theme of immersion and regeneration is exploited in *King Lear;* it is uttered by Heyst in Conrad's *Victory;* and it is expressed as the credo of Stein in *Lord Jim.* The way is to immerse oneself in the destructive element. In *The Red Badge* the destructive element is the battle; in *The Open Boat* it is the sea. The rescue of the men from the sea has cost them "a terrible grace"—the oiler lies face-downward in the shallows. To the correspondent the man on the shore seemed like a savior. He had a halo "about his head, and he shone like a saint."

THE OPEN BOAT

A Tale Intended to be after the Fact:
Being the Experience of Four Men
from the Sunk Steamer Commodore

I

NONE of them knew the colour of the sky. Their eyes glanced level, and were fastened upon the waves that swept toward them. These waves were of the hue of slate, save for the tops, which were of foaming white, and all of the men knew the colours of the sea. The horizon narrowed and widened, and dipped and rose, and at all times its edge was jagged with waves that seemed thrust up in points like rocks.

Many a man ought to have a bathtub larger than the boat which here rode upon the sea. These waves were most wrongfully and barbarously abrupt and tall, and each froth-top was a problem in small-boat navigation.

The cook squatted in the bottom, and looked with both eyes at the six inches of gunwale which separated him from the ocean. His sleeves were rolled over his fat forearms, and the two flaps of his unbuttoned vest dangled as he bent to bail out the boat. Often he said, "Gawd! that was a narrow clip." As he remarked it he invariably gazed eastward over the broken sea.

The oiler, steering with one of the two oars in the boat, sometimes raised himself suddenly to keep clear of water that swirled in over the stern. It was a thin little oar, and it seemed often ready to snap.

The correspondent, pulling at the other oar, watched the waves and wondered why he was there.

The injured captain, lying in the bow, was at this time buried in that profound dejection and indifference which comes, temporarily at least, to even the bravest and most enduring when, willy-nilly, the firm fails, the army loses, the ship goes down. The mind of the master of a vessel is rooted deep in the timbers of her, though he command for a day or a decade; and this captain had on him the stern impression of a scene in the greys of dawn of seven turned faces, and later a stump of a topmast with a white ball on it, that slashed to and fro at the waves, went low and lower, and down. Thereafter there was something strange in his voice. Although steady, it was deep with mourning, and of a quality beyond oration or tears.

"Keep 'er a little more south, Billie," said he.

"A little more south, sir," said the oiler in the stern.

A seat in his boat was not unlike a seat upon a bucking broncho, and by the same token a broncho is not much smaller. The craft pranced and reared and plunged like an animal. As each wave came, and she rose for it, she seemed like a horse making at a fence outrageously high. The manner of her scramble over these walls of water is a mystic thing, and, moreover, at the top of them were ordinarily these problems in white water, the foam racing down from the summit of each wave requiring a new leap, and a leap from the air. Then, after scornfully bumping a crest, she would slide and race and splash down a long incline, and arrive bobbing and nodding in front of the next menace.

A singular disadvantage of the sea lies in the fact that after successfully surmounting one wave you discover that there is another behind it just as important and just as nervously anxious to do something effective in the way of swamping boats. In a ten-foot dinghy one can get an idea of the resources of the sea in the line of waves that is not probable to the average experience which is never at sea in a dinghy. As each slaty wall of water approached, it shut all else from the view of the men in the boat, and it was not difficult to imagine that this particular wave was the final outburst of the ocean, the last effort of the grim water. There was a terrible grace in the move of the waves, and they came in silence, save for the snarling of the crests.

In the wan light the faces of the men must have been

grey. Their eyes must have glinted in strange ways as they gazed steadily astern. Viewed from a balcony, the whole thing would doubtless have been weirdly picturesque. But the men in the boat had no time to see it, and if they had had leisure, there were other things to occupy their minds. The sun swung steadily up the sky, and they knew it was broad day because the colour of the sea changed from slate to emerald green streaked with amber lights, and the foam was like tumbling snow. The process of the breaking day was unknown to them. They were aware only of this effect upon the colour of the waves that rolled toward them.

In disjointed sentences the cook and the correspondent argued as to the difference between a life-saving station and a house of refuge. The cook had said: "There's a house of refuge just north of the Mosquito Inlet Light, and as soon as they see us they'll come off in their boat and pick us up."

"As soon as who see us?" said the correspondent.

"The crew," said the cook.

"Houses of refuge don't have crews," said the correspondent. "As I understand them, they are only places where clothes and grub are stored for the benefit of shipwrecked people. They don't carry crews."

"Oh, yes, they do," said the cook.

"No, they don't," said the correspondent.

"Well, we're not there yet, anyhow," said the oiler, in the stern.

"Well," said the cook, "perhaps it's not a house of refuge that I'm thinking of as being near Mosquito Inlet Light; perhaps it's a life-saving station."

"We're not there yet," said the oiler in the stern.

II

As the boat bounced from the top of each wave the wind tore through the hair of the hatless men, and as the craft plopped her stern down again the spray slashed past them. The crest of each of these waves was a hill, from the top of which the men surveyed for a moment a broad tumultuous expanse, shining and wind-riven. It was probably splendid, it was probably glorious, this play of the free sea, wild with lights of emerald and white and amber.

"Bully good thing it's an on-shore wind," said the cook. "If not, where would we be? Wouldn't have a show."

"That's right," said the correspondent.

The busy oiler nodded his assent.

Then the captain, in the bow, chuckled in a way that expressed humour, contempt, tragedy, all in one. "Do you think we've got much of a show now, boys?" said he.

Whereupon the three were silent, save for a trifle of hemming and hawing. To express any particular optimism at this time they felt to be childish and stupid, but they all doubtless possessed this sense of the situation in their minds. A young man thinks doggedly at such times. On the other hand, the ethics of their condition was decidedly against any open suggestion of hopelessness. So they were silent.

"Oh, well," said the captain, soothing his children, "we'll get ashore all right."

But there was that in his tone which made them think; so the oiler quoth, "Yes! if this wind holds."

The cook was bailing. "Yes! if we don't catch hell in the surf."

Canton-flannel gulls flew near and far. Sometimes they sat down on the sea, near patches of brown seaweed that rolled over the waves with a movement like carpets on a line in a gale. The birds sat comfortably in groups, and they were envied by some in the dinghy, for the wrath of the sea was no more to them than it was to a covey of prairie chickens a thousand miles inland. Often they came very close and stared at the men with black bead-like eyes. At these times they were uncanny and sinister in their unblinking scrutiny, and the men hooted angrily at them, telling them to be gone. One came, and evidently decided to alight on the top of the captain's head. The bird flew parallel to the boat and did not circle, but made short sidelong jumps in the air in chicken-fashion. His black eyes were wistfully fixed upon the captain's head. "Ugly brute," said the oiler to the bird. "You look as if you were made with a jackknife." The cook and the correspondent swore darkly at the creature. The captain naturally wished to knock it away with the end of the heavy painter, but he did not dare do it, because anything resembling an emphatic gesture would have capsized this freighted boat; and so, with his open hand, the captain gently and carefully waved the gull away. After it had been discouraged from the pursuit the captain breathed easier on account of his hair, and others breathed easier because the bird struck their minds at this time as being somehow gruesome and ominous.

In the meantime the oiler and the correspondent rowed. And also they rowed. They sat together in the same seat, and each rowed an oar. Then the oiler took both oars; then the correspondent took both oars; then the oiler; then the correspondent. They rowed and they rowed. The very ticklish part of the business was when the time came for the reclining one in the stern to take his turn at the oars. By the very last star of truth, it is easier to steal eggs from under a hen than it was to change seats in the dinghy. First the man in the stern slid his hand along the thwart and moved with care, as if he were of Sèvres. Then the man in the rowing-seat slid his hand along the other thwart. It was all done with the most extraordinary care. As the two sidled past each other, the whole party kept watchful eyes on the coming wave, and the captain cried: "Look out, now! Steady, there!"

The brown mats of seaweed that appeared from time to time were like islands, bits of earth. They were travelling, apparently, neither one way nor the other. They were, to all intents, stationary. They informed the men in the boat that it was making progress slowly toward the land.

The captain, rearing cautiously in the bow after the dinghy soared on a great swell, said that he had seen the lighthouse at Mosquito Inlet. Presently the cook remarked that he had seen it. The correspondent was at the oars then, and for some reason he too wished to look at the lighthouse; but his back was toward the far shore, and the waves were important, and for some time he could not seize an opportunity to turn his head. But at last there came a wave more gentle than the others, and when at the crest of it he swiftly scoured the western horizon.

"See it?" said the captain.

"No," said the correspondent, slowly; "I didn't see anything."

"Look again," said the captain. He pointed. "It's exactly in that direction."

At the top of another wave the correspondent did as he was bid, and this time his eyes chanced on a small, still thing on the edge of the swaying horizon. It was precisely like the point of a pin. It took an anxious eye to find a lighthouse so tiny.

"Think we'll make it, Captain?"

"If this wind holds and the boat don't swamp, we can't do much else," said the captain.

The little boat, lifted by each towering sea and splashed viciously by the crests, made progress that in the absence of seaweed was not apparent to those in her. She seemed just a wee thing wallowing, miraculously top up, at the mercy of five oceans. Occasionally a great spread of water, like white flames, swarmed into her.

"Bail her, cook," said the captain, serenely.

"All right, Captain," said the cheerful cook.

III

It would be difficult to describe the subtle brotherhood of men that was here established on the seas. No one said that it was so. No one mentioned it. But it dwelt in the boat, and each man felt it warm him. They were a captain, an oiler, a cook, and a correspondent, and they were friends—friends in a more curiously iron-bound degree than may be common. The hurt captain, lying against the water-jar in the bow, spoke always in a low voice and calmly; but he could never command a more ready and swiftly obedient crew than the motley three of the dinghy. It was more than a mere recognition of what was best for the common safety. There was surely in it a quality that was personal and heart-felt. And after this devotion to the commander of the boat, there was this comradeship, that the correspondent, for instance, who had been taught to be cynical of men, knew even at the time was the best experience of his life. But no one said that it was so. No one mentioned it.

"I wish we had a sail," remarked the captain. "We might try my overcoat on the end of an oar, and give you two boys a chance to rest." So the cook and the correspondent held the mast and spread wide the overcoat; the oiler steered; and the little boat made good way with her new rig. Sometimes the oiler had to scull sharply to keep a sea from breaking into the boat, but otherwise sailing was a success.

Meanwhile the lighthouse had been growing slowly larger. It had now almost assumed colour, and appeared like a little grey shadow on the sky. The man at the oars could not be prevented from turning his head rather often to try for a glimpse of this little grey shadow.

At last, from the top of each wave, the men in the tossing boat could see land. Even as the lighthouse was an upright shadow on the sky, this land seemed but a long black shadow on the sea. It certainly was thinner than paper. "We must be about opposite New Smyrna," said the cook, who had coasted this shore often in schooners. "Captain, by the way, I believe they abandoned that life-saving station there about a year ago."

"Did they?" said the captain.

The wind slowly died away. The cook and the correspondent were not now obliged to slave in order to hold high the oar. But the waves continued their old impetuous swooping at the dinghy, and the little craft, no longer under way, struggled woundily over them. The oiler or the correspondent took the oars again.

Shipwrecks are apropos of nothing. If men could only train for them and have them occur when the men had reached pink condition, there would be less drowning at sea. Of the four in the dinghy none had slept any time worth mentioning for two days and two nights previous to embarking in the dinghy, and in the excitement of clambering about the deck of a foundering ship they had also forgotten to eat heartily.

For these reasons, and for others, neither the oiler nor the correspondent was fond of rowing at this time. The correspondent wondered ingenuously how in the name of all that was sane could there be people who thought it amusing to row a boat. It was not an amusement; it was a diabolical punishment, and even a genius of mental aberrations could never conclude that it was anything but a horror to the muscles and a crime against the back. He mentioned to the boat in general how the amusement of rowing struck him, and the weary-faced oiler smiled in full sympathy. Previously to the foundering, by the way, the oiler had worked a double watch in the engine-room of the ship.

"Take her easy now, boys," said the captain. "Don't spend yourselves. If we have to run a surf you'll need all your strength, because we'll sure have to swim for it. Take your time."

Slowly the land arose from the sea. From a black line it became a line of black and a line of white—trees and sand. Finally the captain said that he could make out a house on the shore. "That's the house of refuge, sure," said the cook. "They'll see us before long, and come out after us."

The distant lighthouse reared high. "The keeper ought to be able to make us out now, if he's looking through a glass," said the captain. "He'll notify the life-saving people."

"None of those other boats could have got ashore to give word of this wreck," said the oiler, in a low voice, "else the life-boat would be out hunting us."

Slowly and beautifully the land loomed out of the sea. The wind came again. It had veered from the north-east to the south-east. Finally a new sound struck the ears of the men in the boat. It was the low thunder of the surf on the shore. "We'll never be able to make the lighthouse now," said the captain. "Swing her head a little more north, Billie."

"A little more north, sir," said the oiler.

Whereupon the little boat turned her nose once more down the wind, and all but the oarsman watched the shore grow. Under the influence of this expansion doubt and direful apprehension were leaving the minds of the men. The management of the boat was still most absorbing, but it could not prevent a quiet cheerfulness. In an hour, perhaps, they would be ashore.

Their backbones had become thoroughly used to balancing in the boat, and they now rode this wild colt of a dinghy like circus men. The correspondent thought that he had been drenched to the skin, but happening to feel in the top pocket of his coat, he found therein eight cigars. Four of them were soaked with sea-water; four were perfectly scatheless. After a search, somebody produced three dry matches; and thereupon the four waifs rode impudently in their little boat and, with an assurance of an impending rescue shining in their eyes, puffed at the big cigars, and judged well and ill of all men. Everybody took a drink of water.

IV

"Cook," remarked the captain, "there don't seem to be any signs of life about your house of refuge."

"No," replied the cook. "Funny they don't see us!"

A broad stretch of lowly coast lay before the eyes of the men. It was of low dunes topped with dark vegetation. The roar of the surf was plain, and sometimes they could see the white lip of a wave as it spun up the beach. A tiny house was blocked out black upon the sky. Southward, the slim lighthouse lifted its little grey length.

Tide, wind, and waves were swinging the dinghy northward. "Funny they don't see us," said the men.

The surf's roar was here dulled, but its tone was nevertheless thunderous and mighty. As the boat swam over the great rollers the men sat listening to this roar. "We'll swamp sure," said everybody.

It is fair to say here that there was not a life-saving station within twenty miles in eitheı direction; but the men did not know this fact, and in consequence they made dark and opprobrious remarks concerning the eyesight of the nation's life-savers. Four scowling men sat in the dinghy and surpassed records in the invention of epithets.

"Funny they don't see us."

The light-heartedness of a former time had completely faded. To their sharpened minds it was easy to conjure pictures of all kinds of incompetency and blindness and, indeed, cowardice. There was the shore of the populous land, and it was bitter and bitter to them that from it came no sign.

"Well," said the captain, ultimately, "I suppose we'll have to make a try for ourselves. If we stay out here too long, we'll none of us have strength left to swim after the boat swamps."

And so the oiler, who was at the oars, turned the boat straight for the shore. There was a sudden tightening of muscles. There was some thinking.

"If we don't all get ashore," said the captain—"if we don't all get ashore, I suppose you fellows know where to send news of my finish?"

They then briefly exchanged some addresses and admonitions. As for the reflections of the men, there was a great deal of rage in them. Perchance they might be formulated thus: "If I am going to be drowned—if I am going to be drowned—if I am going to be drowned, why, in the name of the seven mad gods who rule the sea, was I allowed to come thus far and contemplate sand and trees? Was I brought here merely to have my nose dragged away as I was about to nibble the sacred cheese of life? It is preposterous. If this old ninny-woman, Fate, cannot do better than this, she should be deprived of the management of men's fortunes. She is an old hen who knows not her intention. If she has decided to drown me, why did she not do it in the beginning and save me all this trouble? The whole affair is absurd.—But no; she cannot mean to drown me. She dare not drown me. She cannot drown me. Not after all this work." Afterward the man might have had an impulse to shake his fist at the clouds. "Just you drown me, now, and then hear what I call you!"

The billows that came at this time were more formidable. They seemed always just about to break and roll over the little boat in a turmoil of foam. There was a preparatory and long growl in the speech of them. No mind unused to the sea would have concluded that the dinghy could ascend these sheer heights in time. The shore was still afar. The oiler was a wily surfman. "Boys," he said swiftly, "she won't live three minutes more, and we're too far out to swim. Shall I take her to sea again, Captain?"

"Yes; go ahead!" said the captain.

This oiler, by a series of quick miracles and fast and steady oarsmanship, turned the boat in the middle of the surf and took her safely to sea again.

There was a considerable silence as the boat bumped over the furrowed sea to deeper water. Then somebody in gloom spoke: "Well, anyhow, they must have seen us from the shore by now."

The gulls went in slanting flight up the wind toward the grey, desolate east. A squall, marked by dingy clouds and clouds brick-red like smoke from a burning building, appeared from the south-east.

"What do you think of those life-saving people? Ain't they peaches?"

"Funny they haven't seen us."

"Maybe they think we're out here for sport! Maybe they think we're fishin'. Maybe they think we're damned fools."

It was a long afternoon. A changed tide tried to force them southward, but wind and wave said northward. Far ahead, where coast-line, sea, and sky formed their mighty angle, there were little dots which seemed to indicate a city on the shore.

"St. Augustine?"

The captain shook his head. "Too near Mosquito Inlet."

And the oiler rowed, and then the correspondent rowed; then the oiler rowed. It was a weary business. The human back can become the seat of more aches and pains than are registered in books for the composite anatomy of a regiment. It is a limited area, but it can become the theatre of innumerable muscular conflicts, tangles, wrenches, knots, and other comforts.

"Did you ever like to row, Billie?" asked the correspondent.

"No," said the oiler; "hang it!"

When one exchanged the rowing-seat for a place in the bottom of the boat, he suffered a bodily depression that caused him to be careless of everything save an obligation to wiggle one finger. There was cold sea-water swashing to and fro in the boat, and he lay in it. His head, pillowed on a thwart, was within an inch of the swirl of a wave-crest, and sometimes a particularly obstreperous sea came inboard and drenched him once more. But these matters did not annoy him. It is almost certain that if the boat had capsized he would have tumbled comfortably out upon the ocean as if he felt sure that it was a great soft mattress.

"Look! There's a man on the shore!"

"Where?"

"There! See 'im? See 'im?"

"Yes, sure! He's walking along."

"Now he's stopped. Look! He's facing us!"

"He's waving at us!"

"So he is! By thunder!"

"Ah, now we're all right! Now we're all right! There'll be a boat out here for us in half an hour."

"He's going on. He's running. He's going up to that house there."

The remote beach seemed lower than the sea, and it required a searching glance to discern the little black figure. The captain saw a floating stick, and they rowed to it. A bath towel was by some weird chance in the boat, and, tying this on the stick, the captain waved it. The oarsman did not dare turn his head, so he was obliged to ask questions.

"What's he doing now?"

"He's standing still again. He's looking, I think.—There he goes again—toward the house.—Now he's stopped again."

"Is he waving at us?"

"No, not now; he was, though."

"Look! There comes another man!"

"He's running."

"Look at him go, would you!"

"Why, he's on a bicycle. Now he's met the other man. They're both waving at us. Look!"

"There comes something up the beach."

"What the devil is that thing?"

"Why, it looks like a boat."

"Why, certainly, it's a boat."

"No; it's on wheels."

"Yes, so it is. Well, that must be the life-boat. They drag them along shore on a wagon."

"That's the life-boat, sure."

"No, by God, it's—it's an omnibus."

"I tell you it's a life-boat."

"It is not! It's an omnibus. I can see it plain. See? One of these big hotel omnibuses."

"By thunder, you're right. It's an omnibus, sure as fate. What do you suppose they are doing with an omnibus? Maybe they are going around collecting the life-crew, hey?"

"That's it, likely. Look! There's a fellow waving a little black flag. He's standing on the steps of the omnibus. There come those other two fellows. Now they're all talking together. Look at the fellow with the flag. Maybe he ain't waving it!"

"That ain't a flag, is it? That's his coat. Why, certainly, that's his coat."

"So it is; it's his coat. He's taken it off and is waving it around his head. But would you look at him swing it!"

"Oh, say, there isn't any life-saving station there. That's

just a winter-resort hotel omnibus that has brought over some of the boarders to see us drown."

"What's that idiot with the coat mean? What's he signalling, anyhow?"

"It looks as if he were trying to tell us to go north. There must be a life-saving station up there."

"No; he thinks we're fishing. Just giving us a merry hand. See? Ah, there, Willie!"

"Well, I wish I could make something out of those signals. What do you suppose he means?"

"He don't mean anything; he's just playing."

"Well, if he'd just signal us to try the surf again, or to go to sea and wait, or go north, or go south, or go to hell, there would be some reason in it. But look at him! He just stands there and keeps his coat revolving like a wheel. The ass!"

"There come more people."

"Now there's quite a mob. Look! Isn't that a boat?"

"Where? Oh, I see where you mean. No, that's no boat."

"That fellow is still waving his coat."

"He must think we like to see him do that. Why don't he quit it? It don't mean anything."

"I don't know. I think he is trying to make us go north. It must be that there's a life-saving station there somewhere."

"Say, he ain't tired yet. Look at 'im wave!"

"Wonder how long he can keep that up. He's been revolving his coat ever since he caught sight of us. He's an idiot. Why aren't they getting men to bring a boat out? A fishing-boat—one of those big yawls—could come out here all right. Why don't he do something?"

"Oh, it's all right now."

"They'll have a boat out here for us in less than no time, now that they've seen us."

A faint yellow tone came into the sky over the low land. The shadows on the sea slowly deepened. The wind bore coldness with it, and the men began to shiver.

"Holy smoke!" said one, allowing his voice to express

his impious mood, "if we keep on monkeying out here! If we've got to flounder out here all night!"

"Oh, we'll never have to stay here all night! Don't you worry. They've seen us now, and it won't be long before they'll come chasing out after us."

The shore grew dusky. The man waving a coat blended gradually into this gloom, and it swallowed in the same manner the omnibus and the group of people. The spray, when it dashed uproariously over the side, made the voyagers shrink and swear like men who were being branded.

"I'd like to catch the chump who waved the coat. I feel like socking him one, just for luck."

"Why? What did he do?"

"Oh, nothing, but then he seemed so damned cheerful."

In the meantime the oiler rowed, and then the correspondent rowed, and then the oiler rowed. Grey-faced and bowed forward, they mechanically, turn by turn, plied the leaden oars. The form of the lighthouse had vanished from the southern horizon, but finally a pale star appeared, just lifting from the sea. The streaked saffron in the west passed before the all-merging darkness, and the sea to the east was black. The land had vanished, and was expressed only by the low and drear thunder of the surf.

"If I am going to be drowned—if I am going to be drowned—if I am going to be drowned, why, in the name of the seven mad gods who rule the sea, was I allowed to come thus far and contemplate sand and trees? Was I brought here merely to have my nose dragged away as I was about to nibble the sacred cheese of life?"

The patient captain, drooped over the water-jar, was sometimes obliged to speak to the oarsman.

"Keep her head up! Keep her head up!"

"Keep her head up, sir." The voices were weary and low.

This was surely a quiet evening. All save the oarsman lay heavily and listlessly in the boat's bottom. As for him, his eyes were just capable of noting the tall black waves that swept forward in a most sinister silence, save for an occasional subdued growl of a crest.

The cook's head was on a thwart, and he looked without interest at the water under his nose. He was deep in other scenes. Finally he spoke. "Billie," he murmured, dreamfully, "what kind of pie do you like best?"

V

"Pie!" said the oiler and the correspondent, agitatedly. "Don't talk about those things, blast you!"

"Well," said the cook, "I was just thinking about ham sandwiches and—"

A night on the sea in an open boat is a long night. As darkness settled finally, the shine of the light, lifting from the sea in the south, changed to full gold. On the northern horizon a new light appeared, a small bluish gleam on the edge of the waters. These two lights were the furniture of the world. Otherwise there was nothing but waves.

Two men huddled in the stern, and distances were so magnificent in the dinghy that the rower was enabled to keep his feet partly warm by thrusting them under his companions. Their legs indeed extended far under the rowing-seat until they touched the feet of the captain forward. Sometimes, despite the efforts of the tired oarsman, a wave came piling into the boat, an icy wave of the night, and the chilling water soaked them anew. They would twist their bodies for a moment and groan, and sleep the dead sleep once more, while the water in the boat gurgled about them as the craft rocked.

The plan of the oiler and the correspondent was for one to row until he lost the ability, and then arouse the other from his sea-water couch in the bottom of the boat.

The oiler plied the oars until his head drooped forward and the overpowering sleep blinded him; and he rowed yet afterward. Then he touched a man in the bottom of the boat, and called his name. "Will you spell me for a little while?" he said, meekly.

"Sure, Billie," said the correspondent, awaking and dragging himself to a sitting position. They exchanged places carefully, and the oiler, cuddling down in the sea-water at the cook's side, seemed to go to sleep instantly.

The particular violence of the sea had ceased. The waves came without snarling. The obligation of the man at the oars was to keep the boat headed so that the tilt of the rollers would not capsize her, and to preserve her from filling when the crests rushed past. The black waves were silent and hard to be seen in the darkness. Often one was almost upon the boat before the oarsman was aware.

In a low voice the correspondent addressed the captain. He was not sure that the captain was awake, although this iron man seemed to be always awake. "Captain, shall I keep her making for that light north, sir?"

The same steady voice answered him. "Yes. Keep it about two points off the port bow."

The cook had tied a life-belt around himself in order to get even the warmth which this clumsy cork contrivance could donate, and he seemed almost stove-like when a rower, whose teeth invariably chattered wildly as soon as he ceased his labour, dropped down to sleep.

The correspondent, as he rowed, looked down at the two men sleeping underfoot. The cook's arm was around the oiler's shoulders, and, with their fragmentary clothing and haggard faces, they were the babes of the sea—a grotesque rendering of the old babes in the wood.

Later he must have grown stupid at his work, for suddenly there was a growling of water, and a crest came with a roar and a swash into the boat, and it was a wonder that it did not set the cook afloat in his life-belt. The cook continued to sleep, but the oiler sat up, blinking his eyes and shaking with the new cold.

"Oh, I'm awful sorry, Billie," said the correspondent, contritely.

"That's all right, old boy," said the oiler, and lay down again and was asleep.

Presently it seemed that even the captain dozed, and the correspondent thought that he was the one man afloat on all the oceans. The wind had a voice as it came over the waves, and it was sadder than the end.

There was a long, loud swishing astern of the boat, and a gleaming trail of phosphorescence, like blue flame, was furrowed on the black waters. It might have been made by a monstrous knife.

Then there came a stillness, while the correspondent breathed with open mouth and looked at the sea.

Suddenly there was another swish and another long flash of bluish light, and this time it was alongside the boat, and might almost been reached with an oar. The correspondent saw an enormous fin speed like a shadow through the water, hurling the crystalline spray and leaving the long glowing trail.

The correspondent looked over his shoulder at the captain. His face was hidden, and he seemed to be asleep. He looked at the babes of the sea. They certainly were asleep. So, being bereft of sympathy, he leaned a little way to one side and swore softly into the sea.

But the thing did not then leave the vicinity of the boat. Ahead or astern, on one side or the other, at intervals long or short, fled the long sparkling streak, and there was to be heard the *whirroo* of the dark fin. The speed and power of the thing was greatly to be admired. It cut the water like a gigantic and keen projectile.

The presence of this biding thing did not affect the man with the same horror that it would if he had been a picnicker. He simply looked at the sea dully and swore in an undertone.

Nevertheless, it is true that he did not wish to be alone with the thing. He wished one of his companions to awake by chance and keep him company with it. But the captain hung motionless over the water-jar, and the oiler and the cook in the bottom of the boat were plunged in slumber.

VI

"If I am going to be drowned—if I am going to be drowned—if I am going to be drowned, why, in the name of the seven mad gods who rule the sea, was I allowed to come thus far and contemplate sand and trees?"

During this dismal night, it may be remarked that a man would conclude that it was really the intention of the seven mad gods to drown him, despite the abominable injustice of it. For it was certainly an abominable injustice to drown a man who had worked so hard, so hard. The man felt it would be a crime most unnatural. Other people had drowned at sea since galleys swarmed with painted sails, but still—

When it occurs to a man that nature does not regard him as important, and that she feels she would not maim the universe by disposing of him, he at first wishes to throw bricks at the temple, and he hates deeply the fact that there are no bricks and no temples. Any visible expression of nature would surely be pelleted with his jeers.

Then, if there be no tangible thing to hoot, he feels, perhaps, the desire to confront a personification and indulge in pleas, bowed to one knee, and with hands supplicant, saying, "Yes, but I love myself."

A high cold star on a winter's night is the word he feels that she says to him. Thereafter he knows the pathos of his situation.

The men in the dinghy had not discussed these matters, but each had, no doubt, reflected upon them in silence and according to his mind. There was seldom any expression upon their faces save the general one of complete weariness. Speech was devoted to the business of the boat.

To chime the notes of his emotion, a verse mysteriously entered the correspondent's head. He had even forgotten that he had forgotten this verse, but it suddenly was in his mind.

A soldier of the Legion lay dying in Algiers;
There was lack of woman's nursing, there was dearth of
*   woman's tears;*
But a comrade stood beside him, and he took that comrade's
*   hand,*
And he said, "I never more shall see my own, my native land."

In his childhood the correspondent had been made acquainted with the fact that a soldier of the Legion lay dying in Algiers, but he had never regarded the fact as important. Myriads of his school-fellows had informed him of the soldier's plight, but the dinning had naturally ended by making him perfectly indifferent. He had never con-

sidered it his affair that a soldier of the Legion lay dying
in Algiers, nor had it appeared to him as a matter for
sorrow. It was less to him than the breaking of a pencil's
point.

Now, however, it quaintly came to him as a human, living thing. It was no longer merely a picture of a few
throes in the breast of a poet, meanwhile drinking tea and
warming his feet at the grate; it was an actuality—stern,
mournful, and fine.

The correspondent plainly saw the soldier. He lay on
the sand with his feet out straight and still. While his pale
left hand was upon his chest in an attempt to thwart the
going of his life, the blood came between his fingers. In
the far Algerian distance, a city of low square forms was
set against a sky that was faint with the last sunset hues.
The correspondent, plying the oars and dreaming of the
slow and slower movements of the lips of the soldier, was
moved by a profound and perfectly impersonal comprehension. He was sorry for the soldier of the Legion who
lay dying in Algiers.

The thing which had followed the boat and waited had
evidently grown bored at the delay. There was no longer
to be heard the slash of the cutwater, and there was no
longer the flame of the long trail. The light in the north
still glimmered, but it was apparently no nearer to the
boat. Sometimes the boom of the surf rang in the correspondent's ears, and he turned the craft seaward then and
rowed harder. Southward, some one had evidently built a
watch-fire on the beach. It was too low and too far to be
seen, but it made a shimmering, roseate reflection upon
the bluff in back of it, and this could be discerned from
the boat. The wind came stronger, and sometimes a wave
suddenly raged out like a mountain cat, and there was to
be seen the sheen and sparkle of a broken crest.

The captain, in the bow, moved on his water-jar and
sat erect. "Pretty long night," he observed to the correspondent. He looked at the shore. "Those life-saving people take their time."

"Did you see that shark playing around?"

"Yes, I saw him. He was a big fellow, all right."

"Wish I had known you were awake."

Later the correspondent spoke into the bottom of the boat. "Billie!" There was a slow and gradual disentanglement. "Billie, will you spell me?"

"Sure," said the oiler.

As soon as the correspondent touched the cold, comfortable sea-water in the bottom of the boat and had huddled close to the cook's life-belt he was deep in sleep, despite the fact that his teeth played all the popular airs. This sleep was so good to him that it was but a moment before he heard a voice call his name in a tone that demonstrated the last stages of exhaustion. "Will you spell me?"

"Sure, Billie."

The light in the north had mysteriously vanished, but the correspondent took his course from the wide-awake captain.

Later in the night they took the boat farther out to sea, and the captain directed the cook to take one oar at the stern and keep the boat facing the seas. He was to call out if he should hear the thunder of the surf. This plan enabled the oiler and the correspondent to get respite together. "We'll give those boys a chance to get into shape again," said the captain. They curled down and, after a few preliminary chatterings and trembles, slept once more the dead sleep. Neither knew they had bequeathed to the cook the company of another shark, or perhaps the same shark.

As the boat caroused on the waves, spray occasionally bumped over the side and gave them a fresh soaking, but this had no power to break their repose. The ominous slash of the wind and the water affected them as it would have affected mummies.

"Boys," said the cook, with the notes of every reluctance in his voice, "she's drifted in pretty close. I guess one of you had better take her to sea again." The correspondent, aroused, heard the crash of the toppled crests.

As he was rowing, the captain gave him some whisky-and-water, and this steadied the chills out of him. "If I ever get ashore and anybody shows me even a photograph of an oar—"

At last there was a short conversation.

"Billie!—Billie, will you spell me?"

"Sure," said the oiler.

VII

When the correspondent again opened his eyes, the sea and the sky were each of the grey hue of the dawning. Later, carmine and gold was painted upon the waters. The morning appeared finally, in its splendour, with a sky of pure blue, and the sunlight flamed on the tips of the waves.

On the distant dunes were set many little black cottages, and a tall white windmill reared above them. No man, nor dog, nor bicycle appeared on the beach. The cottages might have formed a deserted village.

The voyagers scanned the shore. A conference was held in the boat. "Well," said the captain, "if no help is coming, we might better try a run through the surf right away. If we stay out here much longer we will be too weak to do anything for ourselves at all." The others silently acquiesced in this reasoning. The boat was headed for the beach. The correspondent wondered if none ever ascended the tall wind-tower, and if then they never looked seaward. This tower was a giant, standing with its back to the plight of the ants. It represented in a degree, to the correspondent, the serenity of nature amid the struggles of the individual—nature in the wind, and nature in the vision of men. She did not seem cruel to him then, nor beneficent, nor treacherous, nor wise. But she was indifferent, flatly indifferent. It is, perhaps, plausible that a man in this situation, impressed with the unconcern of the universe, should see the innumerable flaws of his life, and have them taste wickedly in his mind, and wish for another chance. A distinction between right and wrong seems absurdly clear to him, then, in this new ignorance of the grave-edge, and he understands that if he were given another opportunity he would mend his conduct and his words, and be better and brighter during an introduction or at a tea.

"Now, boys," said the captain, "she is going to swamp sure. All we can do is to work her in as far as possible, and then when she swamps, pile out and scramble for the beach. Keep cool now, and don't jump until she swamps sure."

The oiler took the oars. Over his shoulders he scanned the surf. "Captain," he said, "I think I'd better bring her about and keep her head-on to the seas and back her in."

"All right, Billie," said the captain. "Back her in." The oiler swung the boat then, and, seated in the stern, the cook and the correspondent were obliged to look over their shoulders to contemplate the lonely and indifferent shore.

The monstrous inshore rollers heaved the boat high until the men were again enabled to see the white sheets of water scudding up the slanted beach. "We won't get in very close," said the captain. Each time a man could wrest his attention from the rollers, he turned his glance toward the shore, and in the expression of the eyes during this contemplation there was a singular quality. The correspondent, observing the others, knew that they were not afraid, but the full meaning of their glances was shrouded.

As for himself, he was too tired to grapple fundamentally with the fact. He tried to coerce his mind into thinking of it, but the mind was dominated at this time by the muscles, and the muscles said they did not care. It merely occurred to him that if he should drown it would be a shame.

There were no hurried words, no pallor, no plain agitation. The men simply looked at the shore. "Now, remember to get well clear of the boat when you jump," said the captain.

Seaward the crest of a roller suddenly fell with a thunderous crash, and the long white comber came roaring down upon the boat.

"Steady now," said the captain. The men were silent.

They turned their eyes from the shore to the comber and waited. The boat slid up the incline, leaped at the furious top, bounced over it, and swung down the long back of the wave. Some water had been shipped, and the cook bailed it out.

But the next crest crashed also. The tumbling, boiling flood of white water caught the boat and whirled it almost perpendicular. Water swarmed in from all sides. The correspondent had his hands on the gunwale at this time, and when the water entered at that place he swiftly withdrew his fingers, as if he objected to wetting them.

The little boat, drunken with this weight of water, reeled and snuggled deeper into the sea.

"Bail her out, cook! Bail her out!" said the captain.

"All right, Captain," said the cook.

"Now, boys, the next one will do for us sure," said the oiler. "Mind to jump clear of the boat."

The third wave moved forward, huge, furious, implacable. It fairly swallowed the dinghy, and almost simultaneously the men tumbled into the sea. A piece of life-belt had lain in the bottom of the boat, and as the correspondent went overboard he held this to his chest with his left hand.

The January water was icy, and he reflected immediately that it was colder than he had expected to find it off the coast of Florida. This appeared to his dazed mind as a fact important enough to be noted at the time. The coldness of the water was sad; it was tragic. This fact was somehow mixed and confused with his opinion of his own situation, so that it seemed almost a proper reason for tears. The water was cold.

When he came to the surface he was conscious of little but the noisy water. Afterward he saw his companions in the sea. The oiler was ahead in the race. He was swimming strongly and rapidly. Off to the correspondent's left, the cook's great white and corked back bulged out of the water; and in the rear the captain was hanging with his one good hand to the keel of the overturned dinghy.

There is a certain immovable quality to a shore, and

the correspondent wondered at it amid the confusion of the sea.

It seemed also very attractive; but the correspondent knew that it was a long journey, and he paddled leisurely. The piece of life-preserver lay under him, and sometimes he whirled down the incline of a wave as if he were on a hand-sled.

But finally he arrived at a place in the sea where travel was beset with difficulty. He did not pause swimming to inquire what manner of current had caught him, but there his progress ceased. The shore was set before him like a bit of scenery on a stage, and he looked at it and understood with his eyes each detail of it.

As the cook passed, much farther to the left, the captain was calling to him, "Turn over on your back, cook! Turn over on your back and use the oar."

"All right, sir." The cook turned on his back, and, paddling with an oar, went ahead as if he were a canoe.

Presently the boat also passed to the left of the correspondent, with the captain clinging with one hand to the keel. He would have appeared like a man raising himself to look over a board fence if it were not for the extraordinary gymnastics of the boat. The correspondent marvelled that the captain could still hold to it.

They passed on nearer to shore—the oiler, the cook, the captain—and following them went the water-jar, bouncing gaily over the seas.

The correspondent remained in the grip of this strange new enemy—a current. The shore, with its white slope of sand and its green bluff topped with little silent cottages, was spread like a picture before him. It was very near to him then, but he was impressed as one who, in a gallery, looks at a scene from Brittany or Algiers.

He thought: "I am going to drown? Can it be possible? Can it be possible? Can it be possible?" Perhaps an individual must consider his own death to be the final phenomenon of nature.

But later a wave perhaps whirled him out of this small deadly current, for he found suddenly that he could again

make progress toward the shore. Later still he was aware
that the captain, clinging with one hand to the keel of
the dinghy, had his face turned away from the shore and
toward him, and was calling his name. "Come to the boat!
Come to the boat!"

In his struggle to reach the captain and the boat, he
reflected that when one gets properly wearied drowning
must really be a comfortable arrangement—a cessation of
hostilities accompanied by a large degree of relief; and he
was glad of it, for the main thing in his mind for some
moments had been horror of the temporary agony. He did
not wish to be hurt.

Presently he saw a man running along the shore. He
was undressing with most remarkable speed. Coat, trousers,
shirt, everything flew magically off him.

"Come to the boat!" called the captain.

"All right, Captain." As the correspondent paddled, he
saw the captain let himself down to bottom and leave the
boat. Then the correspondent performed his one little
marvel of the voyage. A large wave caught him and flung
him with ease and supreme speed completely over the boat
and far beyond it. It struck him even then as an event in
gymnastics and a true miracle of the sea. An overturned
boat in the surf is not a plaything to a swimming man.

The correspondent arrived in water that reached only
to his waist, but his condition did not enable him to stand
for more than a moment. Each wave knocked him into a
heap, and the undertow pulled at him.

Then he saw the man who had been running and undressing, and undressing and running, come bounding into
the water. He dragged ashore the cook, and then waded
toward the captain; but the captain waved him away and
sent him to the correspondent. He was naked—naked as
a tree in winter; but a halo was about his head, and he
shone like a saint. He gave a strong pull, and a long drag,
and a bully heave at the correspondent's hand. The correspondent, schooled in the minor formulæ, said, "Thanks,
old man." But suddenly the man cried, "What's that?" He
pointed a swift finger. The correspondent said, "Go."

In the shallows, face downward, lay the oiler. His forehead touched sand that was periodically, between each wave, clear of the sea.

The correspondent did not know all that transpired afterward. When he achieved safe ground he fell, striking the sand with each particular part of his body. It was as if he had dropped from a roof, but the thud was grateful to him.

It seemed that instantly the beach was populated with men with blankets, clothes, and flasks, and women with coffee-pots and all the remedies sacred to their minds. The welcome of the land to the men from the sea was warm and generous; but a still and dripping shape was carried slowly up the beach, and the land's welcome for it could only be the different and sinister hospitality of the grave.

When it came night, the white waves paced to and fro in the moonlight, and the wind brought the sound of the great sea's voice to the men on the shore, and they felt that they could then be interpreters.

A TALE OF THE SEA

THE WRECK OF THE *COMMODORE*

❋   ❋   ❋

I

THE COMMODORE SINKS AT SEA [1]

The Little Vessel Lost with Her Cargo of Arms and
Ammunition

Her Numerous Company Reach Land in Safety

They are Compelled to Take to the Boats and Abandon
the Sinking Vessel

AN OVERLOAD OF COAL THE PROBABLE CAUSE

It is Thought That When the Vessel Went Ashore in
the St. Johns River, Her Heavy Shock Caused Her
Seams to Open—Cubans in Jacksonville Much Distressed Over the Serious Loss—An Unfounded Rumor
of Treachery

THE STEAMER COMMODORE, which left here Thursday night with an expedition for the Cuban insurgents, is
now resting on the bottom of the sea, twenty fathoms below the surface, about eighteen miles northeast of Mosquito Inlet.

All of the men on the vessel, twenty-eight in number,
reached the shore in safety, and twelve of them arrived in
Jacksonville last night over the Florida East Coast railway.

---

[1] *Florida Times-Union*, Sunday, January 3, 1897, p. 1. These
accounts from the *Florida Times-Union* and the *New York Press* are
reproduced here for the first time.

The other sixteen are still down the coast, but are expected to arrive here on a special train this morning. . . .

DETAILS OF THE ACCIDENT

From the accounts given by the different ones in the party, the following details of the accident were learned: The Commodore crossed the St. Johns bar at 2 o'clock Friday afternoon while the sea was running very high. As she was crossing the bar she got in the trough of the sea and came very near being swamped.

About 12 o'clock Friday night it was discovered that the boat was leaking badly. The swash of the water in the hold as the vessel rolled from side to side soon alarmed everyone on board. A panic ensued, but Captain Murphy, Stephen Crane, R. A. Delgado and one or two others soon quieted the excitement and put everybody to work on the pumps and with buckets. The steam pump was started and for two hours the water was poured over the sides in streams. The men worked with a will and in the meantime the steamer's bow had been turned to the westward, and she was making good time toward the shore, which was estimated to be at least forty miles away, for the steamer had headed due east after leaving the bar, as she wished to keep out of the way of the cruiser Newark.

At 2:30 a.m., it was seen that the water was steadily gaining, and it was then decided to abandon the vessel.

IN THE BOATS

Paul Rojo, R. A. Delgado, Franco Blanco, the old Cuban pilot, and nine other men took one of the boats and left the steamer. Captain Murphy, the first and second mate, the engineer and assistant, Stephen Crane and ten men took the large yawl boat, and at 3 o'clock they left the Commodore to her fate. The night was dark and they could not see what became of her, but as she was rapidly filling with water, they are all confident that she is now resting on the bottom, and old Neptune has been supplied with enough arms and ammunition to blow up the island of Cuba. . . .

II

MORE OF THE FILIBUSTERS SAFE [2]

Commodore's Wrecked Seamen Struggle for Life in a Heavy Surf

STEPHEN CRANE, NOVELIST, SWIMS ASHORE

Young New York Writer Astonishes the Sea Dogs by His Courage in the Face of Death

CUBANS ASSERT A TRAITOR SUNK THE VESSEL

Federal Authorities Order Out the Three Friends to Aid in the Work of Rescue

JACKSONVILLE, FLA., Jan. 3.—Seventeen men accounted for out of the twenty-eight on the Cuban filibuster Commodore is the record here to-night, with a slight chance of seven more yet alive. Five men came ashore at Daytona this noon—Captain Murphy, Stephen Crane, the novelist, the cook and two sailors. One of the latter, William Higgins of Rhode Island, died soon after reaching land from the effects of severe wounds received while landing through the high surf. His family live in Boston. One of the survivors gives the following graphic details:

STORY OF A SURVIVOR

"The tug sank at 7 o'clock Saturday morning, twenty miles off New Smyrna, and the Americans on board remained till the last moment. A traitor in Spanish pay was the cause of the leak. Should he be found he will be dealt with severely. The leak was discovered at about 3 a.m.

[2] *New York Press*, Monday, January 4, 1897, pp. 1–2.

The pumps would not work long, though they did good service for awhile.

"Finding that the water gained on us, the captain called all hands and at 3 the vessel was turned shoreward. As she still continued to sink, two boat loads of Cubans, twelve men in all, were first sent off. One boat containing six men was capsized, and I am afraid that the men were lost. The Americans all remained on the tug till she sank. One of the lifeboats containing nine men was swamped and a hastily constructed raft was made up from materials thrown to them, and they then disappeared from our sight. Captain Murphy, Stephen Crane, the novelist and correspondent; Higgins, myself and one other sailor took to the ten-foot dingy at the last moment. We tried to save the men in the water around us, but the heavy seas and blinding wind swept them from us. The spray was so thick that we could see only a few rods. Their cries were heartrending, but we could do nothing, it requiring all our efforts to keep our small boat right side up.

THROWN INTO THE BREAKERS

"For twenty-four hours we battled with the heavy seas, constantly bailing, and at last land was sighted. As we attempted to land the wind drove us into the breakers and in an instant the boat was overturned and we were struggling for life. For an hour almost we battled for life, and then managed to crawl out on the sands, almost dead. Captain Murphy saved Mr. Crane by helping him when a cramp caught him. Higgins was struck on the head by floating timbers and he died soon after landing. He was a good sailor and a brave man. He worked to save his comrades." . . .

PRAISE FOR CRANE

DAYTONA, FLA., Jan. 3.—"That newspaper feller was a nervy man," said the cook of the ill-fated Commodore to-night in reference to Stephen Crane, the novelist, who is after material for stories. "He didn't seem to know what fear was. He was down on the ship's papers as an able seaman at $20 a month. When we started out he insisted upon doing a seaman's work, and he did it well, too. When aroused Saturday morning he never quailed when he came on deck and saw the foaming and raging billows and knew that the vessel was sinking and that it was only a question of time when we would be at the mercy of the terrible sea in a small ten-foot dingy.

"He stood on the bridge with glasses in hand, sweeping the horizon in an effort to get a glimpse of land. He had one of the sailor lads above him on the short mast, and once he mounted the rigging to get a better view. I thought sure that he would be swept off as the vessel rolled from side to side, her yards almost touching the water as she rolled down. One of the Cubans got rattled and tried to run out one of the boats before time, and Crane let him have it right from the shoulder, and the man rolled down the leeway, stunned for the moment.

"When the boats were launched he was the last one, except Captain Murphy, to get in, and his nerve greatly encouraged all hands. In the small dingy he rowed as well as the others, notwithstanding he was so worn out that he could hardly hold his oar straight in the terrific seas. At the last moment he rose on his seat, and, seeing the big wave coming that overthrew us, cried out, 'Look out, boys, there's trouble for us. Jump, captain!'

SAVES A DROWNING MAN

"Both he and Captain Murphy were thrown out on the same side. Crane was partially thrown under the over-turned boat and but for Captain Murphy's readiness in catching him by the collar he would have gone under. We all battled there in the water for hours, it seemed to us. Crane was a good swimmer, and he really saved one of the sailors, as the man could not swim a stroke, and Crane had to keep him up by the aid of an oar. These newspaper fellers have got spunk, if they do tell such awful woppers at times," concluded the cook, as he took another big swig of the "life preservative" provided by the good people here. . . .

III

STEPHEN CRANE AND HIS WORK [3]

How He Came to Be on the Unlucky Commodore

TO WRITE FOR THE PRESS

Brilliant Author Not of the Sort to Give Up His
Cuban Letters Because of Shipwreck

STEPHEN CRANE, the writer, is safe and readers of The Press may expect in a short time a treat from his versatile pen. . . .

Mr. Crane was on the way to Cuba to write about the war there. He will get to Cuba as soon as he can. He is not of the sort who are frightened by an experience in a lifeboat. His letters will appear in The Press as soon as they arrive.

Mr. Crane has not intimated just what he is going to write; probably he does not know himself. But that his letters will be intensely interesting and true to life readers of his stories, "The Red Badge of Courage," "The Third Violet," "George's Mother" and "Maggie, a Girl of the Streets," feel assured.

EXPERIENCE AS A REPORTER

Stephen Crane has been talked about more in New York than any writer of recent years. He was a New York reporter at the age of 16. In his newspaper work he early showed remarkable command of the English language, but his nature revolted at the slavish devotion to facts which

[3] *New York Press*, Monday, January 4, 1897, p. 2.

makes a successful reporter. So he took to writing stories.

The Tenderloin was gayer then than now. Its lights and shadows attracted his artistic genius. There he found the whole gamut of human emotions. He listened and studied. His stories had as their background the slums oftener than the palaces. They were intensely realistic. His training as a reporter accounts in part for that, and his English flowed simple and pure.

HIS GENIUS RECOGNIZED

Though but a boy in years, his work became the subject of gossip in literary circles. The critics recognized the merit of his stories. The old novelists read with wonder. They found his war scenes so vivid that they could scarcely believe they were painted by one who never had smelled gunpowder except at a shooting match. . . .

IV

TWELVE MEN LOST THROUGH TREACHERY [4]

Sinking of the Commodore Caused by a Traitor, Says Montgomery

STEAM PUMPS TAMPERED WITH, IS THE SUSPICION

Eight Men Are Now at Sea on a Raft, and Four Others are Still Missing

STOKER KILLED WHILE LANDING IN THE SURF

Captain Murphy, Stephen Crane and C. M. Montgomery Now at Daytona—Three Friends Delayed Thirty Hours from Going to the Rescue Through Red Tape of Treasury Department Officials—The Newark's Searchlight to be Used

[4] *Florida Times-Union,* Tuesday, January 5, 1897, p. 1.

. . . . . .

THE RAFT LOST

"THE mate's boat, containing nine Americans, was smashed and the mate, two engineers, six firemen and sailors were lashed to a raft which Captain Murphy attempted to tow ashore twenty miles away, but the terrible sea and northeast gale swept them away.

"The dingy, occupied by the captain and companions, was twenty-seven hours at sea, Montgomery and Crane holding Captain Murphy's overcoat as a sail until the beach was sighted. High seas were breaking a half mile from shore. Montgomery, Crane and Murphy were washed onto the beach where citizens provided them with medical attendance. Higgins was killed at the overturning of the boat which made ten American and six Cubans lost. . . ."

V

CAPTAIN MURPHY'S SHIPWRECKED CREW [5]

Twenty Men Are Now Safe in Jacksonville With Friends

BUT EIGHT OTHERS MAY BE AT THE BOTTOM

Story of the Wreck of the Commodore Told by the Commander of the Ill-Fated Vessel

THERE IS STILL SOME TALK OF TREACHERY

Three Men Were Drowned as the Steamer Sunk—One Died on the Beach and Five Are at Sea on a Raft—The Newark and Three Friends Are Still Looking for Them, but There Is Little or No Hope That Any More Will be Saved

[5] *Florida Times-Union*, Tuesday, January 5, 1897, p. 6.

.   .   .   .   .   .

CAPTAIN MURPHY'S story is as follows:

"The engineer reported to me, about midnight, that the vessel was gaining water in her hold and that he was unable to get the pumps to work. They had tried to get the water out, but the pumps would not heave the water. The pipe was evidently choked or the suction gone. It is customary to keep the water clear of the hold. All necessary was to run the steam pumps now and then. If the water is allowed to get up into the coal, the coal is washed down and chokes the pumps. All the water that entered the ship was in the engine room."

"Was it treachery, do you think?" asked the Times-Union reporter.

"No, I don't think so. It was neglect, more than anything else.

"I gave the order to use the buckets: also an order to pile into the furnace wood, oil and alcohol, hoping to get up sufficient steam to run into Mosquito Inlet, about eighteen miles almost due west of us. The men used the buckets with a will. None stood back, but to our chagrin the water gained upon us slowly and surely, and we had not proceeded three miles when the fires were quenched. There was no hope then of saving the ship. I let go the anchor to get her head to the sea and told the men to quietly proceed to man the boats. We got two of the boats off. They contained all the Cubans.

"One boat was in command of Julio Rodriguez Baz, and those with him were Manuel Gonzalez, Luis Sierra Mederos and Jesus Alvarez.

"The other, in command of Paul F. Rojo, contained Ricardo Delgado, Felix de los Rios, Emelio Marquez, Ventura Linares, Romeo Hernandez, J. Francisco Blanco, Jose Hernandez, T. Bencenor, Lino Soldera, Gabriel Martinez and Santiago Diaz. Senor Baz's boat stood by for a considerable time to render us assistance, but finally, as we had boats sufficient for the rescue of all those left aboard, we told them to go ahead. Later on we launched the ship's boat, with seven men, in charge of Mate Grane. I told all those to go who desired to do so. All went except Mr. Crane, a brave little gentleman, Steward Montgomery and William Higgins. I intended to stand by the ship and then put ashore in the dingy. Later on we also embarked. We had proceeded but a few yards when we heard a cry from the ship:

ONE BOAT STOVE IN

" 'The big boat is stove!' They were also flying a distress flag.

"I don't know how this happened unless the mate returned and attempted to get some article that he had forgotten. We immediately put back in the dingy, and I told the men to construct a raft. They made three and got on these. Meanwhile, our little boat was remaining distant about 200 yards.

"Finally, they begged us to take them in tow. We put back against the waves and wind and made a towline fast. The first sea nearly filled our boat, and we were compelled to let go and bail our own craft dry. We went back again and once more made fast, but the first sea parted the rafts and broke over our towline. The rafts all parted and were scattered. I told them to return to the vessel and make another raft while I bailed out. When fifty yards away, the vessel went down broadside. Three men went down with her, like heroes with no cry of despair, not a murmur. I remained by the rafts twenty minutes longer, but as the 'boat was being filled by almost every sea, and as the wind was constantly increasing in force, we allowed our boat to go whither the elements carried her.

HOW THEY LANDED

"Saturday afternoon at 4 o'clock, we came in sight of the coast north of Mosquito inlet. We saw people on shore and I flew a flag of distress, and repeatedly fired my pistol to attract their attention. I do not see how they could have failed to see us and appreciate our perilous position, for we were only a half mile from shore. Feeling certain that we had been seen, and thinking that they would send to us a staunch surf boat, we waited at the spot, pulling like Trojans against the heavy sea and wind all that afternoon and all that night. I do not see now, looking back upon it, how human strength could have successfully contended against the fierce odds of nature. We had a little store of brandy and this stood us in good stead. The next morning we found ourselves off the beach opposite Daytona, and seeing no one, resolved to make one last desperate effort with our little remaining strength to reach shore through the breakers. I gave one life belt to the steward and one to Mr. Crane. (The captain does not say that he, with a badly injured arm and shoulder, took none himself.) The sea upset the boat and washed us all away. I grabbed it and got on the bottom, but she was rolled over again. Higgins tried to swim, but sank. I tried to encourage him, and he made another attempt. The boat went over again, and I saw no more of him until his corpse came up on the beach.

DEATH OF HIGGINS

"John Getchell, one of nature's noblemen, who lives upon the beach, saw our dreadful predicament. He stripped to the skin and plunged into the surf and helped the steward and Mr. Crane in. I was safe in shallow water. I then saw Higgins' body on the wet sand. We rolled him and made every effort to bring him to life, but unfortunately failed. Poor fellow, he was brave and did his duty faithfully.

"We had not been on the beach long before the good women of the town came to us with hot coffee and all kinds of restoratives. Their attentions warmed a man's heart to the appreciation of human charity. Not one of these women came to us without some present of food, clothing, and all with offers of shelter. The people of Daytona burried poor Higgins at their own expense." . . .

VI

COMMODORE SAID TO BE OVERLADEN [6]

Many Think That Fact, and Not Treachery, Sunk Her

FOUR MORE MEN RESCUED

Half-Famished Filibusters Land at Port Orange—
Captain Murphy Compliments Crane

.   .   .   .

CAPTAIN MURPHY TALKS

. . . Captain Murphy had his arm in a sling, but otherwise seemed all right. All of them looked tired and worn out.

The captain paid a marked compliment to his men for their orderly conduct. He said that Higgins was a game man, and fought hard for his life and to aid his shipmates. Higgins was buried at Daytona yesterday.

Captain Murphy, in response to a direct question, answered evasively as to the report of the treachery, and stated that the leaks were not there early Friday evening, but were there at midnight.

Cubans here feel much dispirited over the sad affair, and the terrible ending of the expedition from which so much was expected.

CRANE'S SPLENDID GRIT

"That man Crane is the spunkiest fellow out," said Captain Murphy to-night to The Press correspondent, in speaking of the wreck and incidents pertaining to it. "The sea was so rough that even old sailors got seasick when we struck the open sea after leaving the bar, but Crane be-

---

[6] *New York Press*, Tuesday, January 5, 1897, p. 1.

haved like a born sailor. He and I were about the only ones
not affected by the big seas which tossed us about. As we
went south he sat in the pilot house with me, smoking and
telling yarns. When the leak was discovered he was the
first man to volunteer aid.

JOKES AMID DANGER

"His shoes, new ones, were slippery on the deck, and
he took them off and tossed them overboard, saying, with
a laugh: 'Well, captain, I guess I won't need them if we
have to swim.' He stood on the deck by me all the while,
smoking his cigarette, and aided me greatly while the boats
were getting off. When in the dingey he suggested putting
up the overcoat for a sail, and he took his turn at the oars
or holding up the oar mast.

TRIES TO SAVE HIGGINS

"When we went over I called to him to see that his
life preserver was on all right and he replied in his usual
tones, saying that he would obey orders. He was under the
boat once, but got out in some way. He held up Higgins
when the latter got so terribly tired and endeavored to
bring him in, but the sailor was so far gone that he could
hardly help himself. When we were thrown up by the
waves, Crane was the first man to stagger up the beach
looking for houses. He's a thoroughbred," concluded the
captain, "and a brave man, too, with plenty of grit."

VII

STEPHEN CRANE'S OWN STORY

He Tells How the Commodore Was Wrecked and How He Escaped

FEAR-CRAZED NEGRO NEARLY SWAMPS BOAT

Young Writer Compelled to Work in Stifling Atmosphere of the Fire Room

BRAVERY OF CAPTAIN MURPHY AND HIGGINS

Tried to Tow Their Companions Who Were on the Raft— Last Dash for the Shore Through the Surf

JACKSONVILLE, FLA., Jan. 6.—It was the afternoon of New Year's. The Commodore lay at her dock in Jacksonville and negro stevedores processioned steadily toward her with box after box of ammunition and bundle after bundle of rifles. Her hatch, like the mouth of a monster, engulfed them. It might have been the feeding time of some legendary creature of the sea. It was in broad daylight and the crowd of gleeful Cubans on the pier did not forbear to sing the strange patriotic ballads of their island.

Everything was perfectly open. The Commodore was cleared with a cargo of arms and munition for Cuba. There was none of that extreme modesty about the proceeding which had marked previous departures of the famous tug. She loaded up as placidly as if she were going to carry oranges to New York, instead of Remingtons to Cuba. Down the river, furthermore, the revenue cutter Boutwell, the old isosceles triangle that protects United States interests in the St. John's, lay at anchor, with no sign of excitement aboard her.

EXCHANGING FAREWELLS

On the decks of the Commodore there were exchanges of farewells in two languages. Many of the men who were to sail upon her had many intimates in the old Southern town, and we who had left our friends in the remote North received our first touch of melancholy on witnessing these strenuous and earnest goodbys.

It seems, however, that there was more difficulty at the custom house. The officers of the ship and the Cuban leaders were detained there until a mournful twilight settled upon the St. John's, and through a heavy fog the lights of Jacksonville blinked dimly. Then at last the Commodore swung clear of the dock, amid a tumult of goodbys. As she turned her bow toward the distant sea the Cubans ashore cheered and cheered. In response the Commodore gave three long blasts of her whistle, which even to this time impressed me with their sadness. Somehow, they sounded as wails.

Then at last we began to feel like filibusters. I don't suppose that the most stolid brain could contrive to believe that there is not a mere trifle of danger in filibustering, and so as we watched the lights of Jacksonville swing past us and heard the regular thump, thump, thump of the engines we did considerable reflecting.

But I am sure that there were no hifalutin emotions visible upon any of the faces which fronted the speeding shore. In fact, from cook's boy to captain, we were all enveloped in a gentle satisfaction and cheerfulness. But less than two miles from Jacksonville, this atrocious fog caused the pilot to ram the bow of the Commodore hard upon the mud and in this ignominious position we were compelled to stay until daybreak.

HELP FROM THE BOUTWELL

It was to all of us more than a physical calamity. We were now no longer filibusters. We were men on a ship stuck in the mud. A certain mental somersault was made once more necessary.

But word had been sent to Jacksonville to the captain of the revenue cutter Boutwell, and Captain Kilgore turned out promptly and generously fired up his old triangle, and came at full speed to our assistance. She dragged us out of the mud, and again we headed for the mouth of the river. The revenue cutter pounded along a half mile astern of us, to make sure that we did not take on board at some place along the river men for the Cuban army.

This was the early morning of New Year's Day, and the fine golden southern sunlight fell full upon the river. It flashed over the ancient Boutwell, until her white sides gleamed like pearl, and her rigging was spun into little threads of gold.

Cheers greeted the old Commodore from passing ship and from the shore. It was a cheerful, almost merry, beginning to our voyage. At Mayport, however, we changed our river pilot for a man who could take her to open sea, and again the Commodore was beached. The Boutwell was fussing around us in her venerable way, and, upon seeing our predicament, she came again to assist us, but this time, with engines reversed, the Commodore dragged herself away from the grip of the sand and again headed for the open sea.

The captain of the revenue cutter grew curious. He hailed the Commodore: "Are you fellows going to sea to-day?"

Captain Murphy of the Commodore called back: "Yes, sir."

And then as the whistle of the Commodore saluted him, Captain Kilgore doffed his cap and said: "Well, gentlemen, I hope you have a pleasant cruise," and this was our last word from shore.

When the Commodore came to enormous rollers that flee over the bar a certain light-heartedness departed from the ship's company.

SLEEP IMPOSSIBLE

As darkness came upon the waters, the Commodore was a broad, flaming path of blue and silver phosphorescence, and as her stout bow lunged at the great black waves she threw flashing, roaring cascades to either side. And all that was to be heard was the rhythmical and mighty pounding of the engines. Being an inexperienced filibuster, the writer had undergone considerable mental excitement since the starting of the ship, and in consequence he had not yet been to sleep and so I went to the first mate's bunk to indulge myself in all the physical delights of holding one's-self in bed. Every time the ship lurched I expected to be fired through a bulkhead, and it was neither amusing nor instructive to see in the dim light a certain accursed valise aiming itself at the top of my stomach with every lurch of the vessel.

THE COOK IS HOPEFUL

The cook was asleep on a bench in the galley. He is of a portly and noble exterior, and by means of a checker board he had himself wedged on this bench in such a manner the motion of the ship would be unable to dislodge him. He woke as I entered the galley and delivered himself of some dolorous sentiments: "God," he said in the course of his observations, "I don't feel right about this ship, somehow. It strikes me that something is going to happen to us. I don't know what it is, but the old ship is going to get it in the neck, I think."

"Well, how about the men on board of her?" said I. "Are any of us going to get out, prophet?"

"Yes," said the cook. "Sometimes I have these damned feelings come over me, and they are always right, and it seems to me, somehow, that you and I will both get and meet again somewhere, down at Coney Island, perhaps, or some place like that."

ONE MAN HAS ENOUGH

Finding it impossible to sleep, I went back to the pilot house. An old seaman, Tom Smith, from Charleston, was then at the wheel. In the darkness I could not see Tom's face, except at those times when he leaned forward to scan the compass and the dim light from the box came upon his weatherbeaten features.

"Well, Tom," said I, "how do you like filibustering?"

He said "I think I am about through with it. I've been in a number of these expeditions and the pay is good, but I think if I ever get back safe this time I will cut it."

I sat down in the corner of the pilot house and almost went to sleep. In the meantime the captain came on duty and he was standing near me when the chief engineer rushed up the stairs and cried hurriedly to the captain that there was something wrong in the engine room. He and the captain departed swiftly.

I was drowsing there in my corner when the captain returned, and, going to the door of the little room directly back of the pilothouse, he cried to the Cuban leader:

"Say, can't you get those fellows to work. I can't talk their language and I can't get them started. Come on and get them going."

HELPS IN THE FIREROOM

The Cuban leader turned to me and said: "Go help in the fireroom. They are going to bail with buckets."

The engine room, by the way, represented a scene at this time taken from the middle kitchen of hades. In the first place, it was insufferably warm, and the lights burned faintly in a way to cause mystic and grewsome shadows. There was a quantity of soapish sea water swirling and sweeping and swishing among machinery that roared and banged and clattered and steamed, and, in the second place, it was a devil of a ways down below.

Here I first came to know a certain young oiler named Billy Higgins. He was sloshing around this inferno filling buckets with water and passing them to a chain of men that extended up the ship's side. Afterward we got orders to change our point of attack on water and to operate through a little door on the windward side of the ship that led into the engine room.

NO PANIC ON BOARD

During this time there was much talk of pumps out of order and many other statements of a mechanical kind, which I did not altogether comprehend but understood to mean that there was a general and sudden ruin in the engine room.

There was no particular agitation at this time, and even later there was never a panic on board the Commodore. The party of men who worked with Higgins and me at this time were all Cubans, and we were under the direction of the Cuban leaders. Presently we were ordered again to the afterhold, and there was some hesitation about going into the abominable fireroom again, but Higgins dashed down the companionway with a bucket.

LOWERING BOATS

The heat and hard work in the fireroom affected me and I was obliged to come on deck again. Going forward, I heard as I went talk of lowering the boats. Near the corner of the galley the mate was talking with a man.

"Why don't you send up a rocket?" said this unknown man. And the mate replied: "What the hell do we want to send up a rocket for? The ship is all right."

Returning with a little rubber and cloth overcoat, I saw the first boat about to be lowered. A certain man was the first person in this first boat, and they were handing him in a valise about as large as a hotel. I had not entirely recovered from astonishment and pleasure in witnessing this noble deed when I saw another valise go to him.

HUMAN HOG APPEARS

This valise was not perhaps so large as a hotel, but it was a big valise anyhow. Afterward there went to him something which looked to me like an overcoat.

Seeing the chief engineer leaning out of his little window, I remarked to him:

"What do you think of that blank, blank, blank?"

"Oh, he's a bird," said the old chief.

It was now that was heard the order to get away the lifeboat, which was stowed on top of the deckhouse. The deckhouse was a mighty slippery place, and with each roll of the ship, the men there thought themselves likely to take headers into the deadly black sea.

Higgins was on top of the deckhouse, and, with the first mate and two colored stokers, we wrestled with that boat, which, I am willing to swear, weighed as much as a Broadway cable car. She might have been spiked to the deck. We could have pushed a little brick schoolhouse along a corduroy road as easily as we could have moved this boat. But the first mate got a tackle to her from a leeward davit, and on the deck below the captain corralled enough men to make an impression upon the boat.

We were ordered to cease hauling then, and in this lull the cook of the ship came to me and said: "What are you going to do?"

I told him my plans, and he said:

"Well, my God, that's what I am going to do."

A WHISTLE OF DESPAIR

Now the whistle of the Commodore had been turned loose, and if there ever was a voice of despair and death, it was in the voice of this whistle. It had gained a new tone. It was as if its throat was already choked by the water, and this cry on the sea at night, with a wind blowing the spray over the ship, and the waves roaring over the bow, and swirling white along the decks, was to each of us probably a song of man's end.

It was now that the first mate showed a sign of losing his grip. To us who were trying in all stages of competence and experience to launch the lifeboat he raged in all terms of fiery satire and hammerlike abuse. But the boat moved at last and swung down toward the water.

Afterward, when I went aft, I saw the captain standing, with his arm in a sling, holding on to a stay with his one good hand and directing the launching of the boat. He gave me a five-gallon jug of water to hold, and asked me what I was going to do. I told him what I thought was

about the proper thing, and he told me then that the cook
had the same idea, and ordered me to go forward and be
ready to launch the ten-foot dingy.

IN THE TEN-FOOT DINGY

I remember well that he turned then to swear at a
colored stoker who was prowling around, done up in life
preservers until he looked like a feather bed. I went forward with my five-gallon jug of water, and when the captain came we launched the dingy, and they put me over
the side to fend her off from the ship with an oar.

They handed me down the water jug, and then the cook
came into the boat, and we sat there in the darkness, wondering why, by all our hopes of future happiness, the
captain was so long in coming over to the side and ordering
us away from the doomed ship.

The captain was waiting for the other boat to go. Finally
he hailed in the darkness: "Are you all right, Mr.
Graines?"

The first mate answered: "All right, sir."

"Shove off, then," cried the captain.

The captain was just about to swing over the rail when
a dark form came forward and a voice said: "Captain, I
go with you."

The captain answered: "Yes, Billy; get in."

HIGGINS LAST TO LEAVE SHIP

It was Billy Higgins, the oiler. Billy dropped into the
boat and a moment later the captain followed, bringing
with him an end of about forty yards of lead line. The
other end was attached to the rail of the ship.

As we swung back to leeward the captain said: "Boys,
we will stay right near the ship till she goes down."

This cheerful information, of course, filled us all with
glee. The line kept us headed properly into the wind, and
as we rode over the monstrous waves we saw upon each
rise the swaying lights of the dying Commodore.

When came the gray shade of dawn, the form of the

Commodore grew slowly clear to us as our little ten-foot boat rose over each swell. She was floating with such an air of buoyancy that we laughed when we had time, and said "What a gag it would be on those other fellows if she didn't sink at all."

But later we saw men aboard of her, and later still they began to hail us.

HELPING THEIR MATES

I had forgot to mention that previously we had loosened the end of the lead line and dropped much further to leeward. The men on board were a mystery to us, of course, as we had seen all the boats leave the ship. We rowed back to the ship, but did not approach too near, because we were four men in a ten-foot boat, and we knew that the touch of a hand on our gunwale would assuredly swamp us.

The first mate cried out from the ship that the third boat had foundered alongside. He cried that they had made rafts, and wished us to tow them.

The captain said, "All right."

Their rafts were floating astern. "Jump in!" cried the captain, but there was a singular and most harrowing hesitation. There were five white men and two negroes. This scene in the gray light of morning impressed one as would a view into some place where ghosts move slowly. These seven men on the stern of the sinking Commodore were silent. Save the words of the mate to the captain there was no talk. Here was death, but here also was a most singular and indefinable kind of fortitude.

Four men, I remember, clambered over the railing and stood there watching the cold, steely sheen of the sweeping waves.

"Jump," cried the captain again.

The old chief engineer first obeyed the order. He landed on the outside raft and the captain told him how to grip the raft and he obeyed as promptly and as docilely as a scholar in riding school.

THE MATE'S MAD PLUNGE

A stoker followed him, and then the first mate threw his hands over his head and plunged into the sea. He had no life belt and for my part, even when he did this horrible thing, I somehow felt that I could see in the expression of his hands, and in the very toss of his head, as he leaped thus to death, that it was rage, rage, rage unspeakable that was in his heart at the time.

And then I saw Tom Smith, the man who was going to quit filibustering after this expedition, jump to a raft and turn his face toward us. On board the Commodore three men strode, still in silence and with their faces turned toward us. One man had his arms folded and was leaning against the deckhouse. His feet were crossed, so that the toe of his left foot pointed downward. There they stood gazing at us, and neither from the deck nor from the rafts was a voice raised. Still was there this silence.

TRIED TO TOW THE RAFTS

The colored stoker on the first raft threw us a line and we began to tow. Of course, we perfectly understood the absolute impossibility of any such thing; our dingy was within six inches of the water's edge, there was an enormous sea running, and I knew that under the circumstances a tugboat would have no light task in moving these rafts.

But we tried it, and would have continued to try it indefinitely, but that something critical came to pass. I was at an oar and so faced the rafts. The cook controlled the line. Suddenly the boat began to go backward and then we saw this negro on the first raft pulling on the line hand over hand and drawing us to him.

He had turned into a demon. He was wild—wild as a tiger. He was crouched on this raft and ready to spring. Every muscle of him seemed to be turned into an elastic spring. His eyes were almost white. His face was the face of a lost man reaching upward, and we knew that the weight of his hand on our gunwale doomed us.

THE COMMODORE SINKS

The cook let go of the line. We rowed around to see if we could not get a line from the chief engineer, and all this time, mind you, there were no shrieks, no groans, but silence, silence and silence, and then the Commodore sank.

She lurched to windward, then swung afar back, righted and dove into the sea, and the rafts were suddenly swallowed by this frightful maw of the ocean. And then by the men on the ten-foot dingy were words said that were still not words—something far beyond words.

The lighthouse of Mosquito Inlet stuck up above the horizon like the point of a pin. We turned our dingy toward the shore.

The history of life in an open boat for thirty hours would no doubt be instructive for the young, but none is to be told here and now. For my part I would prefer to tell the story at once, because from it would shine the splendid manhood of Captain Edward Murphy and of William Higgins, the oiler, but let it suffice at this time to say that when we were swamped in the surf and making the best of our way toward the shore the captain gave orders amid the wildness of the breakers as clearly as if he had been on the quarter deck of a battleship.

John Kitchell [7] of Daytona came running down the beach, and as he ran the air was filled with clothes. If he had pulled a single lever and undressed, even as the fire horses harness, he could not seem to me to have stripped with more speed. He dashed into the water and dragged the cook. Then he went after the captain, but the captain sent him to me, and then it was that he saw Billy Higgins lying with his forehead on sand that was clear of the water, and he was dead.

STEPHEN CRANE [8]

[7] Getchell, according to the Captain's account.
[8] Reprinted from the *New York Press*, January 7, 1897, p. 1.

PART IV

Western Tales

INTRODUCTION

The Bride Comes to Yellow Sky is the best short story Crane wrote beyond his major achievements: *Maggie, The Red Badge,* and *The Open Boat.* It is the single perfect bead on his string of Western tales. Crane spent most of his twenty-third year out in the Far West and in Mexico. Frederic Remington's pictures and Mark Twain's *Huckleberry Finn* and *Life on the Mississippi* inspired him to want to see cowboys and the big river, but his main purpose in going west was to collect short-story and sketch material. Writing, he said, is a business like any other. One trained one's mind to observe and a man should be able to say something "worth while" about any event (quoted from Beer, page 252). "When I was 23, I devoted most of my time to travelling for the Bacheller and Johnson syndicate and in writing short stories for English magazines." When he was out west he wrote a war tale— *A Mystery of Heroism*—and only one Western piece. The only Western story he wrote this year (1895) was *Horses —One Dash!* He wrote the first draft of this story in Philadelphia (see letter to Hawkins for September 18, 1895). And of his six Western sketches or stories,[1] only

---

[1] In order of publication the Western tales are *Horses—One Dash!* (Philadelphia *Press,* January 1896), *A Man and Some Others* (Century, February 1897), *The Bride Comes to Yellow Sky* (*McClure's Magazine,* February 1898), *Five White Mice* (New York *World,* April 1898), *The Blue Hotel* (*Collier's Weekly,* November 26, 1898), and *Twelve O'Clock* (*Pall Mall Gazette,* December 1899). Four of these appeared in *The Open Boat and Other Stories* (1898). The

one was published in an English magazine, and this one
—*Twelve O'Clock*—did not appear until December 1899.
So he did not write his Westerns in the West; they were
written the next year and some of them much later: That
is, after *The Open Boat* (1897). The style of *The Bride
Comes to Yellow Sky* is different from the style of *The
Open Boat. The Open Boat* was written first. He wrote
The Bride in England and sent it to his American agent,
Paul Reynolds, with a note that *The Bride* "is a daisy and
don't let them talk funny about it."

Out West Crane wrote such journalistic pieces as *Mexican Sights and Street Scenes,* published in the *Philadelphia
Press,* May 19. *Horses—One Dash!* is a direct transcript
of personal experience, but none of the other Western
stories draws upon his own adventures. *The Blue Hotel*
and *A Man and Some Others* make use of the persons he
met, an incident he witnessed, the scenery, and his knowledge of the frontier code, but the dramatic situation in
both stories was invented. *A Man and Some Others* had
its beginning in a story told him by a Bowery fellow whom
Crane met in a Mexican lodging-house. Some Mexicans
tried to run this sheep-herder off his land, and he shot
them down. Crane recast even this germinal part. In the
story it is Bill, the former Bowery saloon-keeper, who is
shot down by the Mexicans. Conrad wrote: "But my great
excitement was reading your stories. Garnett's right. *A
Man and Some Others* is immense. . . . I admire it without reserve. It is an amazing bit of biography." But there's
nothing "immense" about it except its length—the whole
thing is very badly put together, with a false middle and a
melodramatic end. I can't conceive what Conrad saw in
this piece to say: "I am envious of you—horribly." His
reason for envy should have been *The Bride* and the opening part of *The Blue Hotel.*

As in *The Red Badge,* so in all the Mexican and Texan
sketches, as Beer says, there appears "a vision of man's
identity faced by its end, by incomprehensible death." In

Blue Hotel received first book publication in *The Monster* (1899 and
1901), and *Twelve O'Clock* in *The Monster* (1901).

Horses—One Dash! the Mexican José and Richardson, whose experience mirrors Crane's own, are forced to ride for their lives to escape a Mexican band of cutthroats out to murder them for the possession of a pair of boots. This experience, supposedly, terrified Crane; no other occasion in all his life instilled in him such fear. And so, according to this critic, "from Richardson's emotions we learn something of the author's" (*Stephen Crane*, 1950, p. 104). Perhaps so, but I think that in so far as Crane's stories attain to perfection this question of the personal equation never arises. What do you learn about Shakespeare's emotions from *Macbeth*? Criticism constantly confuses these two kinds of literary discussion, the one having to do with the creative process by which the work came into being and the other with the work as a thing in itself. The critical point to make about *Horses—One Dash!* is that it has not a dash of significance. No significance emerges from the story of Richardson; it is his plight not mine. And like many other Crane pieces, this story is not in Crane's own idiom and could have been written by some other author. Although it is an autobiographical sketch, it might very well have come from the pen of Cunninghame Graham. It has been doubted whether anyone has ever rendered better than Crane the exotic spirit and color of Latin America. But it is Cunninghame Graham, that romantic adventurer and most picturesque personality of the nineties, who captures it with photographic fidelity. Crane, as comparison with Graham's sensory kodaking shows, was no realist. But he was the superior artist, using in his best works only so much realistic detail as his design required.

The Blue Hotel was written in early 1898 and finished in February at Brede Place in England three years after Crane visited a desolate junction town in Nebraska (in February 1895) and saw there a hotel that was painted a light blue. Crane begged Paul Reynolds: "Try to sell it as soon as possible. I must have some money by the first of April." Reynolds sold it to *Collier's* for three hundred dollars, but before it was accepted there it had been turned down by *Scribner's* in March and by the *Atlantic Monthly*

in April (1898). Crane said: "to my mind, it is a daisy."
But he said the same about *The Bride,* and in a letter to
William (October 29, 1897) he wrote: "My next short
thing after the novelette (The Monster) was The Bride
Comes to Yellow Sky. All my friends come here [*sic*] say
it is my very best thing." Crane was not sure which one
was his best, and his critics have not yet decided for him.
The Blue Hotel happens to be Hemingway's favorite, and
one or another Crane critic has rated it "one of the most
vivid short stories ever written by an American." This
story, said Mencken in 1927, "is superlative among short
stories." Howells, however, thought *The Monster* "the
greatest short story ever written by an American." John
Berryman claims that *The Blue Hotel* forms with *The Open
Boat* Crane's "masterwork." And *The Monster* is *The
Blue Hotel* "in more terrible form." So one critic applauds
the story because its values are to him social and political,
and another because he too finds in it what he is looking
for—psychological source-material. It is Crane's mind, not
Crane's story, that concerns him. *The Blue Hotel* localizes
Crane's own "thrust toward suicide." The Swede in the
blizzard is Crane in the blizzard "hearing the *bugles* of the
tempest; and he *likes* this weather, 'I like it. It suits me.'
Crane was going to war again." By my reading of the
story, however, the Swede is Crane's diametric opposite.
The man who wrote *Maggie* believed that our environment shapes our life; yet he himself did nothing to shape
his own. He shared with Conrad a fatalistic resignation to
what happens. The Swede in *The Blue Hotel* distrusts life
and runs to meet and shape his destiny.

But consider the story *critically,* and you see at once
that Crane has here violated his own artistic canon. He
intrudes to preach a deliberate moral. The story ends with
the grotesque image of the murdered Swede whose eyes
stare "upon a dreadful legend that dwelt atop of the cash-
machine: 'This registers the amount of your purchase.' "
This point marks the legitimate end of the story. Crane
spoiled the whole thing by tacking on a moralizing ap-
pendix. The off-key tone is at odds with the tone of the

preceding part, and the theme that his beginning prepared
for stands at odds with the trumped-up theme announced
in the totally irrelevant and non-ironic conclusion. In *The
Upturned Face,* a slight thing but a perfection, Crane's
grotesquerie is integral to his theme. In *The Blue Hotel* it
is there on the page and it is misspent.

Ford Madox Ford said that *The Bride Comes to Yellow
Sky* was the story that had "influenced" him "more than
anything else I ever read." But then, elsewhere, he also
said that it was Crane's *Five White Mice.* Ford was given
to distortion of facts, misquotation, and faulty memory.
Of some dozen portraits he has sketched of Crane, this one,
exaggerated but in substance likely enough, puts us in
mind of *The Bride,* which Crane wrote about this time.
Ford says that Crane "in those days, and for my benefit,
was in the habit of posing as an almost fabulous Billy the
Kid." This Stephen Crane looks more like Scratchy Wilson
himself:

I can see him sitting in the singularly ugly drawing room of
the singularly hideous villa he lived in for a time at Oxted.
Then he wore—I dare say to shock me—cowboy breeches and
no coat, and all the time he was talking he wagged in his
hand an immense thing that he called a gun and that we
should call a revolver. From time to time he would attempt
to slay with the bead-sight of this Colt such flies as settled on
the table, and a good deal of his conversation would be taken
up with fantastic boasts about what can be done with these
lethal instruments. I don't know that he celebrated his own
prowess, but he boasted about what heroes in the Far West
were capable of. I did not much believe him then and I believe him still less now. *I don't believe any one is capable of
anything with a revolver.*[2]

But neither did Crane believe that; Ford has lifted his
belief from Crane's story of Jack Potter. Scratchy Wilson
"is a wonder with a gun—a perfect wonder," but the point
of the story is that no man "is capable of anything with
a revolver."

The whole story turns on a single ironic moment. The
sheriff, whose business is gunfire, carries no gun; and Wil-

son, who always shoots, is disarmed by no gun at all. Potter's weapon is a spiritual one.

—I ain't got a gun because I've just come from San Anton' with my wife. I'm married—said Potter. . . .
—Married?—said Scratchy. Seemingly for the first time, he saw the drooping, drowning woman at the other man's side.—No!—he said. He was like a creature allowed a glimpse of another world.

Potter has married, as it were, a vision, and it is this dream —"all the glory of the marriage, the environment of the new estate"—that buoys him up through the crisis. He is a new man now, and his new world saves him. It is Wilson's getting a glimpse of it that saves him, too. When the shock of recognition comes he feels ashamed. His abasement is symbolized thus: "His feet made *funnel-shaped* tracks in the *heavy* sand." The only code he has ever known to live by, the frontier code that Potter no longer lives by, seems for once to have failed him. Potter and Wilson represent two opposite worlds or points of view: the idealistic world of spiritual values whose force lies in its innocence, and the non-imaginative world of crass realities. *This same conflict, the conflict between ideals and realities, ruled Crane's struggle as artist and gave his life and his art all their bitter ironies.*

The Bride is built on a paradoxical reversal of situation. Structurally it has close affinities, therefore, with Crane's *Mystery of Heroism, The Upturned Face,* and *An Episode of War.* In all four stories, that which is predictable—a code, a theory, or an ideal—is discovered to be unpredictable when faced by the realities. Wilson's "theory" about the sheriff collapses; the trapped man is Wilson himself. It is the same with Henry Fleming. The trapped or "baited" man is the characteristic ingredient of a Crane tale. The corollary is an ironic turnabout, a reversal of situation. Crane's fiction at its best combines these two ironic ingredients. No reversal occurs in *The Blue Hotel,* and there the baited character has set his own trap. Potter, unlike the Swede, accepts his moment of destiny. It has been shaped for him by a man who (allegorically speaking) is not "married." In that crucial moment of impending death Potter attains spiritual triumph. *The Bride Comes to Yellow Sky* thus anticipates in both its theme and its structure Hemingway's *Short Happy Life of Francis Macomber*.

THE BRIDE COMES TO YELLOW SKY

I

THE great Pullman was whirling onward with such dignity of motion that a glance from the window seemed simply to prove that the plains of Texas were pouring eastward. Vast flats of green grass, dull-hued spaces of mesquit and cactus, little groups of frame houses, woods of light and tender trees, all were sweeping into the east, sweeping over the horizon, a precipice.

A newly married pair had boarded this coach at San Antonio. The man's face was reddened from many days in the wind and sun, and a direct result of his new black clothes was that his brick-coloured hands were constantly performing in a most conscious fashion. From time to time he looked down respectfully at his attire. He sat with a hand on each knee, like a man waiting in a barber's shop. The glances he devoted to other passengers were furtive and shy.

The bride was not pretty, nor was she very young. She wore a dress of blue cashmere, with small reservations of velvet here and there, and with steel buttons abounding. She continually twisted her head to regard her puff sleeves, very stiff, straight, and high. They embarrassed her. It was quite apparent that she had cooked, and that she expected to cook, dutifully. The blushes caused by the careless scrutiny of some passengers as she had entered the car were strange to see upon this plain, under-class countenance, which was drawn in placid, almost emotionless lines.

They were evidently very happy. "Ever been in a parlour-car before?" he asked, smiling with delight.

"No," she answered; "I never was. It's fine, ain't it?"

"Great! And then after a while we'll go forward to the diner, and get a big lay-out. Finest meal in the world. Charge a dollar."

"Oh, do they?" cried the bride. "Charge a dollar? Why, that's too much—for us—ain't it, Jack?"

"Not this trip, anyhow," he answered bravely. "We're going to go the whole thing."

Later he explained to her about the trains. "You see, it's a thousand miles from one end of Texas to the other; and this train runs right across it, and never stops but four times." He had the pride of an owner. He pointed out to her the dazzling fittings of the coach; and in truth her eyes opened wider as she contemplated the sea-green figured velvet, the shining brass, silver, and glass, the wood that gleamed as darkly brilliant as the surface of a pool of oil. At one end a bronze figure sturdily held a support for a separated chamber, and at convenient places on the ceiling were frescos in olive and silver.

To the minds of the pair, their surroundings reflected the glory of their marriage that morning in San Antonio; this was the environment of their new estate; and the man's face in particular beamed with an elation that made him appear ridiculous to the negro porter. This individual at times surveyed them from afar with an amused and superior grin. On other occasions he bullied them with skill in ways that did not make it exactly plain to them that they were being bullied. He subtly used all the manners of the most unconquerable kind of snobbery. He oppressed them; but of this oppression they had small knowledge, and they speedily forgot that infrequently a number of travellers covered them with stares of derisive enjoyment. Historically there was supposed to be something infinitely humorous in their situation.

"We are due in Yellow Sky at 3:42," he said, looking tenderly into her eyes.

"Oh, are we?" she said, as if she had not been aware of it. To evince surprise at her husband's statement was part of her wifely amiability. She took from a pocket a

little silver watch; and as she held it before her, and stared
at it with a frown of attention, the new husband's face
shone.

"I bought it in San Anton' from a friend ɔf mine," he
told her gleefully.

"It's seventeen minutes past twelve," she said, looking
up at him with a kind of shy and clumsy coquetry. A passenger, noting this play, grew excessively sardonic, and
winked at himself in one of the numerous mirrors.

At last they went to the dining-car. Two rows of negro
waiters, in glowing white suits, surveyed their entrance
with the interest, and also the equanimity, of men who had
been forewarned. The pair fell to the lot of a waiter who
happened to feel pleasure in steering them through their
meal. He viewed them with the manner of a fatherly pilot,
his countenance radiant with benevolence. The patronage,
entwined with the ordinary deference, was not plain to
them. And yet, as they returned to their coach, they
showed in their faces a sense of escape.

To the left, miles down a long purple slope, was a
little ribbon of mist where moved the keening Rio Grande.
The train was approaching it at an angle, and the apex
was Yellow Sky. Presently it was apparent that, as the
distance from Yellow Sky grew shorter, the husband became commensurately restless. His brick-red hands were
more insistent in their prominence. Occasionally he was
even rather absent-minded and far-away when the bride
leaned forward and addressed him.

As a matter of truth, Jack Potter was beginning to find
the shadow of a deed weigh upon him like a leaden slab.
He, the town marshal of Yellow Sky, a man known, liked,
and feared in his corner, a prominent person, had gone to
San Antonio to meet a girl he believed he loved, and there,
after the usual prayers, had actually induced her to marry
him, without consulting Yellow Sky for any part of the
transaction. He was now bringing his bride before an innocent and unsuspecting community.

Of course people in Yellow Sky married as it pleased

them, in accordance with a general custom; but such was Potter's thought of his duty to his friends, or of their idea of his duty, or of an unspoken form which does not control men in these matters, that he felt he was heinous. He had committed an extraordinary crime. Face to face with this girl in San Antonio, and spurred by his sharp impulse, he had gone headlong over all the social hedges. At San Antonio he was like a man hidden in the dark. A knife to sever any friendly duty, any form, was easy to his hand in that remote city. But the hour of Yellow Sky —the hour of daylight—was approaching.

He knew full well that his marriage was an important thing to his town. It could only be exceeded by the burning of the new hotel. His friends could not forgive him. Frequently he had reflected on the advisability of telling them by telegraph, but a new cowardice had been upon him. He feared to do it. And now the train was hurrying him toward a scene of amazement, glee, and reproach. He glanced out of the window at the line of haze swinging slowly in toward the train.

Yellow Sky had a kind of brass band, which played painfully, to the delight of the populace. He laughed without heart as he thought of it. If the citizens could dream of his prospective arrival with his bride, they would parade the band at the station and escort them, amid cheers and laughing congratulations, to his adobe home.

He resolved that he would use all the devices of speed and plainscraft in making the journey from the station to his house. Once within that safe citadel, he could issue some sort of vocal bulletin, and then not go among the citizens until they had time to wear off a little of their enthusiasm.

The bride looked anxiously at him. "What's worrying you, Jack?"

He laughed again. "I'm not worrying, girl; I'm only thinking of Yellow Sky."

She flushed in comprehension.

A sense of mutual guilt invaded their minds and developed a finer tenderness. They looked at each other with eyes softly aglow. But Potter often laughed the same nervous laugh; the flush upon the bride's face seemed quite permanent.

The traitor to the feelings of Yellow Sky narrowly watched the speeding landscape. "We're nearly there," he said.

Presently the porter came and announced the proximity of Potter's home. He held a brush in his hand, and, with all his airy superiority gone, he brushed Potter's new clothes as the latter slowly turned this way and that way. Potter fumbled out a coin and gave it to the porter, as he had seen others do. It was a heavy and muscle-bound business, as that of a man shoeing his first horse.

The porter took their bag, and as the train began to slow they moved forward to the hooded platform of the car. Presently the two engines and their long string of coaches rushed into the station of Yellow Sky.

"They have to take water here," said Potter, from a constricted throat and in mournful cadence, as one announcing death. Before the train stopped his eye had swept the length of the platform, and he was glad and astonished to see there was none upon it but the station-agent, who, with a slightly hurried and anxious air, was walking toward the water-tanks. When the train had halted, the porter alighted first, and placed in position a little temporary step.

"Come on, girl," said Potter, hoarsely. As he helped her down they each laughed on a false note. He took the bag from the negro, and bade his wife cling to his arm. As they slunk rapidly away, his hang-dog glance perceived that they were unloading the two trunks, and also that the station-agent, far ahead near the baggage-car, had turned and was running toward him, making gestures. He laughed, and groaned as he laughed, when he noted the first effect of his marital bliss upon Yellow Sky. He gripped his wife's arm firmly to his side, and they fled. Behind them the porter stood, chuckling fatuously.

II

The California express on the Southern Railway was due
at Yellow Sky in twenty-one minutes. There were six men
at the bar of the Weary Gentleman saloon. One was a
drummer who talked a great deal and rapidly; three were
Texans who did not care to talk at that time; and two were
Mexican sheep-herders, who did not talk as a general practice in the Weary Gentleman saloon. The barkeeper's dog
lay on the board walk that crossed in front of the door.
His head was on his paws, and he glanced drowsily here
and there with the constant vigilance of a dog that is
kicked on occasion. Across the sandy street were some
vivid green grass-plots, so wonderful in appearance, amid
the sands that burned near them in a blazing sun, that
they caused a doubt in the mind. They exactly resembled
the grass mats used to represent lawns on the stage. At
the cooler end of the railway station, a man without a
coat sat in a tilted chair and smoked his pipe. The fresh-
cut bank of the Rio Grande circled near the town, and
there could be seen beyond it a great plum-coloured plain
of mesquit.

Save for the busy drummer and his companions in the
saloon, Yellow Sky was dozing. The new-comer leaned
gracefully upon the bar, and recited many tales with the
confidence of a bard who has come upon a new field.

"—and at the moment that the old man fell downstairs
with the bureau in his arms, the old woman was coming
up with two scuttles of coal, and of course—"

The drummer's tale was interrupted by a young man
who suddenly appeared in the open door. He cried:
"Scratchy Wilson's drunk, and has turned loose with both
hands." The two Mexicans at once set down their glasses
and faded out of the rear entrance of the saloon.

The drummer, innocent and jocular, answered: "All
right, old man. S'pose he has? Come in and have a drink,
anyhow."

But the information had made such an obvious cleft in
every skull in the room that the drummer was obliged to

see its importance. All had become instantly solemn. "Say," said he, mystified, "what is this?" His three companions made the introductory gesture of eloquent speech; but the young man at the door forestalled them.

"It means, my friend," he answered, as he came into the saloon, "that for the next two hours this town won't be a health resort."

The barkeeper went to the door, and locked and barred it; reaching out of the window, he pulled in heavy wooden shutters, and barred them. Immediately a solemn, chapel-like gloom was upon the place. The drummer was looking from one to another.

"But say," he cried, "what is this, anyhow? You don't mean there is going to be a gun-fight?"

"Don't know whether there'll be a fight or not," answered one man, grimly; "but there'll be some shootin'—some good shootin'."

The young man who had warned them waved his hand. "Oh, there'll be a fight fast enough, if any one wants it. Anybody can get a fight out there in the street. There's a fight just waiting."

The drummer seemed to be swayed between the interest of a foreigner and a perception of personal danger.

"What did you say his name was?" he asked.

"Scratchy Wilson," they answered in chorus.

"And will he kill anybody? What are you going to do? Does this happen often? Does he rampage around like this once a week or so? Can he break in that door?"

"No; he can't break down that door," replied the barkeeper. "He's tried it three times. But when he comes you'd better lay down on the floor, stranger. He's dead sure to shoot at it, and a bullet may come through."

Thereafter the drummer kept a strict eye upon the door. The time had not yet been called for him to hug the floor, but, as a minor precaution, he sidled near to the wall. "Will he kill anybody?" he said again.

The men laughed low and scornfully at the question.

"He's out to shoot, and he's out for trouble. Don't see any good in experimentin' with him."

"But what do you do in a case like this? What do you do?"

A man responded: "Why, he and Jack Potter—"

"But," in chorus the other men interrupted, "Jack Potter's in San Anton'."

"Well, who is he? What's he got to do with it?"

"Oh, he's the town marshal. He goes out and fights Scratchy when he gets on one of these tears."

"Wow!" said the drummer, mopping his brow. "Nice job he's got."

The voices had toned away to mere whisperings. The drummer wished to ask further questions, which were born of an increasing anxiety and bewilderment; but when he attempted them, the men merely looked at him in irritation and motioned him to remain silent. A tense waiting hush was upon them. In the deep shadows of the room their eyes shone as they listened for sounds from the street. One man made three gestures at the barkeeper; and the latter, moving like a ghost, handed him a glass and a bottle. The man poured a full glass of whisky, and set down the bottle noiselessly. He gulped the whisky in a swallow, and turned again toward the door in immovable silence. The drummer saw that the barkeeper, without a sound, had taken a Winchester from beneath the bar. Later he saw this individual beckoning to him, so he tiptoed across the room.

"You better come with me back of the bar."

"No, thanks," said the drummer, perspiring; "I'd rather be where I can make a break for the back door."

Whereupon the man of bottles made a kindly but peremptory gesture. The drummer obeyed it, and, finding himself seated on a box with his head below the level of the bar, balm was laid upon his soul at sight of various zinc and copper fittings that bore a resemblance to armour-plate. The barkeeper took a seat comfortably upon an adjacent box.

"You see," he whispered, "this here Scratchy Wilson is a wonder with a gun—a perfect wonder; and when he goes on the war-trail, we hunt our holes—naturally. He's about the last one of the old gang that used to hang out along the river here. He's a terror when he's drunk. When he's sober he's all right—kind of simple—wouldn't hurt a fly—nicest fellow in town. But when he's drunk—whoo!"

There were periods of stillness. "I wish Jack Potter was back from San Anton'," said the barkeeper. "He shot Wilson up once—in the leg—and he would sail in and pull out the kinks in this thing."

Presently they heard from a distance the sound of a shot, followed by three wild yowls. It instantly removed a bond from the men in the darkened saloon. There was a shuffling of feet. They looked at each other. "Here he comes," they said.

III

A man in a maroon-coloured flannel shirt, which had been purchased for purposes of decoration, and made principally by some Jewish women on the East Side of New York, rounded a corner and walked into the middle of the main street of Yellow Sky. In either hand the man held a long, heavy, blue-black revolver. Often he yelled, and these cries rang through a semblance of a deserted village, shrilly flying over the roofs in a volume that seemed to have no relation to the ordinary vocal strength of a man. It was as if the surrounding stillness formed the arch of a tomb over him. These cries of ferocious challenge rang against walls of silence. And his boots had red tops with gilded imprints, of the kind beloved in winter by little sledding boys on the hillsides of New England.

The man's face flamed in a rage begot of whisky. His eyes, rolling, and yet keen for ambush, hunted the still doorways and windows. He walked with the creeping movement of the midnight cat. As it occurred to him, he roared menacing information. The long revolvers in his hands were as easy as straws; they were moved with an electric swiftness. The little fingers of each hand played sometimes in a musician's way. Plain from the low collar of the shirt, the cords of his neck straightened and sank, straightened and sank, as passion moved him. The only

sounds were his terrible invitations. The calm adobes preserved their demeanour at the passing of this small thing
in the middle of the street.

There was no offer of fight—no offer of fight. The man
called to the sky. There were no attractions. He bellowed
and fumed and swayed his revolvers here and everywhere.

The dog of the barkeeper of the Weary Gentleman
saloon had not appreciated the advance of events. He yet
lay dozing in front of his master's door. At sight of the
dog, the man paused and raised his revolver humorously.
At sight of the man, the dog sprang up and walked diago-
nally away, with a sullen head, and growling. The man
yelled, and the dog broke into a gallop. As it was about
to enter an alley, there was a loud noise, a whistling, and
something spat the ground directly before it. The dog
screamed, and, wheeling in terror, galloped headlong in a
new direction. Again there was a noise, a whistling, and
sand was kicked viciously before it. Fear-stricken, the dog
turned and flurried like an animal in a pen. The man stood
laughing, his weapons at his hips.

Ultimately the man was attracted by the closed door of
the Weary Gentleman saloon. He went to it and, hammering with a revolver, demanded drink.

The door remaining imperturbable, he picked a bit of
paper from the walk, and nailed it to the framework with
a knife. He then turned his back contemptuously upon
this popular resort and, walking to the opposite side of
the street and spinning there on his heel quickly and
lithely, fired at the bit of paper. He missed it by a half-
inch. He swore at himself, and went away. Later he comfortably fusilladed the windows of his most intimate friend.
The man was playing with this town; it was a toy for him.

But still there was no offer of fight. The name of Jack
Potter, his ancient antagonist, entered his mind, and he
concluded that it would be a glad thing if he should go to
Potter's house, and by bombardment induce him to come
out and fight. He moved in the direction of his desire,
chanting Apache scalp-music.

When he arrived at it, Potter's house presented the same

still front as had the other adobes. Taking up a strategic
position, the man howled a challenge. But this house regarded him as might a great stone god. It gave no sign.
After a decent wait, the man howled further challenges,
mingling with them wonderful epithets.

Presently there came the spectacle of a man churning
himself into deepest rage over the immobility of a house.
He fumed at it as the winter wind attacks a prairie cabin
in the North. To the distance there should have gone the
sound of a tumult like the fighting of two hundred Mexicans. As necessity bade him, he paused for breath or to
reload his revolvers.

IV

Potter and his bride walked sheepishly and with speed.
Sometimes they laughed together shamefacedly and low.

"Next corner, dear," he said finally.

They put forth the efforts of a pair walking bowed
against a strong wind. Potter was about to raise a finger
to point the first appearance of the new home when, as
they circled the corner, they came face to face with a
man in a maroon-coloured shirt, who was feverishly pushing cartridges into a large revolver. Upon the instant the
man dropped his revolver to the ground and, like lightning, whipped another from its holster. The second weapon
was aimed at the bridegroom's chest.

There was a silence. Potter's mouth seemed to be merely
a grave for his tongue. He exhibited an instinct to at once
loosen his arm from the woman's grip, and he dropped
the bag to the sand. As for the bride, her face had gone
as yellow as old cloth. She was a slave to hideous rites,
gazing at the apparitional snake.

The two men faced each other at a distance of three
paces. He of the revolver smiled with a new and quiet
ferocity.

"Tried to sneak up on me," he said. "Tried to sneak up
on me!" His eyes grew more baleful. As Potter made a
slight movement, the man thrust his revolver venomously
forward. "No; don't you do it, Jack Potter. Don't you

move a finger toward a gun just yet. Don't you move an
eyelash. The time has come for me to settle with you,
and I'm goin' to do it my own way, and loaf along with
no interferin'. So if you don't want a gun bent on you,
just mind what I tell you."

Potter looked at his enemy. "I ain't got a gun on me
Scratchy," he said. "Honest, I ain't." He was stiffening and
steadying, but yet somewhere at the back of his mind a
vision of the Pullman floated: the sea-green figured velvet,
the shining brass, silver, and glass, the wood that gleamed
as darkly brilliant as the surface of a pool of oil—all the
glory of the marriage, the environment of the new estate.
"You know I fight when it comes to fighting, Scratchy
Wilson; but I ain't got a gun on me. You'll have to do all
the shootin' yourself."

His enemy's face went livid. He stepped forward, and
lashed his weapon to and fro before Potter's chest. "Don't
you tell me you ain't got no gun on you, you whelp. Don't
tell me no lie like that. There ain't a man in Texas ever
seen you without no gun. Don't take me for no kid." His
eyes blazed with light, and his throat worked like a pump.

"I ain't takin' you for no kid," answered Potter. His
heels had not moved an inch backward. "I'm takin' you
for a damn fool. I tell you I ain't got a gun, and I ain't.
If you're goin' to shoot me up, you better begin now;
you'll never get a chance like this again."

So much enforced reasoning had told on Wilson's rage;
he was calmer. "If you ain't got a gun, why ain't you got
a gun?" he sneered. "Been to Sunday-school?"

"I ain't got a gun because I've just come from San
Anton' with my wife. I'm married," said Potter. "And if
I'd thought there was going to be any galoots like you
prowling around when I brought my wife home, I'd had
a gun, and don't you forget it."

"Married!" said Scratchy, not at all comprehending.

"Yes, married. I'm married," said Potter, distinctly.

"Married?" said Scratchy. Seemingly for the first time,
he saw the drooping, drowning woman at the other man's
side. "No!" he said. He was like a creature allowed a

glimpse of another world. He moved a pace backward, and his arm, with the revolver, dropped to his side. "Is this the lady?" he asked.

"Yes; this is the lady," answered Potter.

There was another period of silence.

"Well," said Wilson at last, slowly, "I s'pose it's all off now."

"It's all off if you say so, Scratchy. You know I didn't make the trouble." Potter lifted his valise.

"Well, I 'low it's off, Jack," said Wilson. He was looking at the ground. "Married!" He was not a student of chivalry; it was merely that in the presence of this foreign condition he was a simple child of the earlier plains. He picked up his starboard revolver, and, placing both weapons in their holsters, he went away. His feet made funnel-shaped tracks in the heavy sand.

THE BLUE HOTEL

I

THE Palace Hotel at Fort Romper was painted a light
blue, a shade that is on the legs of a kind of heron, causing the bird to declare its position against any background.
The Palace Hotel, then, was always screaming and howling in a way that made the dazzling winter landscape of
Nebraska seem only a grey swampish hush. It stood alone
on the prairie, and when the snow was falling the town
two hundred yards away was not visible. But when the
traveller alighted at the railway station he was obliged to
pass the Palace Hotel before he could come upon the
company of low clapboard houses which composed Fort
Romper, and it was not to be thought that any traveller
could pass the Palace Hotel without looking at it. Pat
Scully, the proprietor, had proved himself a master of
strategy when he chose his paints. It is true that on clear
days, when the great transcontinental expresses, long lines
of swaying Pullmans, swept through Fort Romper, passengers were overcome at the sight, and the cult that knows
the brown-reds and the subdivisions of the dark greens
of the East expressed shame, pity, horror, in a laugh. But
to the citizens of this prairie town and to the people who
would naturally stop there, Pat Scully had performed a
feat. With this opulence and splendour, these creeds,
classes, egotisms, that streamed through Romper on the
rails day after day, they had no colour in common.

As if the displayed delights of such a blue hotel were
not sufficiently enticing, it was Scully's habit to go every
morning and evening to meet the leisurely trains that
stopped at Romper and work his seductions upon any man
that he might see wavering, gripsack in hand.

One morning, when a snow-crusted engine dragged its

long string of freight cars and its one passenger coach to the station, Scully performed the marvel of catching three men. One was a shaky and quick-eyed Swede, with a great shining cheap valise; one was a tall bronzed cowboy, who was on his way to a ranch near the Dakota line; one was a little silent man from the East, who didn't look it, and didn't announce it. Scully practically made them prisoners. He was so nimble and merry and kindly that each probably felt it would be the height of brutality to try to escape. They trudged off over the creaking board sidewalks in the wake of the eager little Irishman. He wore a heavy fur cap squeezed tightly down on his head. It caused his two red ears to stick out stiffly, as if they were made of tin.

At last, Scully, elaborately, with boisterous hospitality, conducted them through the portals of the blue hotel. The room which they entered was small. It seemed to be merely a proper temple for an enormous stove, which, in the centre, was humming with godlike violence. At various points on its surface the iron had become luminous and glowed yellow from the heat. Beside the stove Scully's son Johnnie was playing High-Five with an old farmer who had whiskers both grey and sandy. They were quarrelling. Frequently the old farmer turned his face toward a box of sawdust—coloured brown from tobacco juice—that was behind the stove, and spat with an air of great impatience and irritation. With a loud flourish of words Scully destroyed the game of cards, and bustled his son upstairs with part of the baggage of the new guests. He himself conducted them to three basins of the coldest water in the world. The cowboy and the Easterner burnished themselves fiery red with this water, until it seemed to be some kind of metal-polish. The Swede, however, merely dipped his fingers gingerly and with trepidation. It was notable that throughout this series of small ceremonies the three travellers were made to feel that Scully was very benevolent. He was conferring great favours upon them. He handed the towel from one to another with an air of philanthropic impulse.

Afterward they went to the first room, and, sitting about the stove, listened to Scully's officious clamour at his daughters, who were preparing the midday meal. They reflected in the silence of experienced men who tread carefully amid new people. Nevertheless, the old farmer, stationary, invincible in his chair near the warmest part of the stove, turned his face from the sawdust-box frequently and addressed a glowing commonplace to the strangers. Usually he was answered in short but adequate sentences by either the cowboy or the Easterner. The Swede said nothing. He seemed to be occupied in making furtive estimates of each man in the room. One might have thought that he had the sense of silly suspicion which comes to guilt. He resembled a badly frightened man.

Later, at dinner, he spoke a little, addressing his conversation entirely to Scully. He volunteered that he had come from New York, where for ten years he had worked as a tailor. These facts seemed to strike Scully as fascinating, and afterward he volunteered that he had lived at Romper for fourteen years. The Swede asked about the crops and the price of labour. He seemed barely to listen to Scully's extended replies. His eyes continued to rove from man to man.

Finally, with a laugh and a wink, he said that some of these Western communities were very dangerous; and after his statement he straightened his legs under the table, tilted his head, and laughed again, loudly. It was plain that the demonstration had no meaning to the others. They looked at him wondering and in silence.

II

As the men trooped heavily back into the front room, the two little windows presented views of a turmoiling sea of snow. The huge arms of the wind were making attempts —mighty, circular, futile—to embrace the flakes as they sped. A gate-post like a still man with a blanched face stood aghast amid this profligate fury. In a hearty voice Scully announced the presence of a blizzard. The guests of the blue hotel, lighting their pipes, assented with grunts of lazy masculine contentment. No island of the sea could be exempt in the degree of this little room with its humming stove. Johnnie, son of Scully, in a tone which defined his opinion of his ability as a card-player, challenged the old farmer of both grey and sandy whiskers to a game of High-Five. The farmer agreed with a contemptuous and bitter scoff. They sat close to the stove, and squared their knees under a wide board. The cowboy and the Easterner watched the game with interest. The Swede remained near the window, aloof, but with a countenance that showed signs of an inexplicable excitement.

The play of Johnnie and the grey-beard was suddenly ended by another quarrel. The old man arose while casting a look of heated scorn at his adversary. He slowly buttoned his coat, and then stalked with fabulous dignity from the room. In the discreet silence of all the other men the Swede laughed. His laughter rang somehow childish. Men by this time had begun to look at him askance, as if they wished to inquire what ailed him.

A new game was formed jocosely. The cowboy volunteered to become the partner of Johnnie, and they all then turned to ask the Swede to throw in his lot with the little Easterner. He asked some questions about the game, and, learning that it wore many names, and that he had played it when it was under an alias, he accepted the invitation. He strode toward the men nervously, as if he expected to be assaulted. Finally, seated, he gazed from face to face and laughed shrilly. This laugh was so strange that the Easterner looked up quickly, the cowboy sat intent and with his mouth open, and Johnnie paused, holding the cards with still fingers.

Afterward there was a short silence. Then Johnnie said, "Well, let's get at it. Come on now!" They pulled their chairs forward until their knees were bunched under the board. They began to play, and their interest in the game caused the others to forget the manner of the Swede.

The cowboy was a board-whacker. Each time that he held superior cards he whanged them, one by one, with exceeding force, down upon the improvised table, and took the tricks with a glowing air of prowess and pride that sent thrills of indignation into the hearts of his opponents. A game with a board-whacker in it is sure to become intense. The countenances of the Easterner and the Swede were miserable whenever the cowboy thundered down his aces and kings, while Johnnie, his eyes gleaming with joy, chuckled and chuckled.

Because of the absorbing play none considered the strange ways of the Swede. They paid strict heed to the game. Finally, during a lull caused by a new deal, the Swede suddenly addressed Johnnie: "I suppose there have been a good many men killed in this room." The jaws of the others dropped and they looked at him.

"What in hell are you talking about?" said Johnnie.

The Swede laughed again his blatant laugh, full of a kind of false courage and defiance. "Oh, you know what I mean all right," he answered.

"I'm a liar if I do!" Johnnie protested. The card was halted, and the men stared at the Swede. Johnnie evidently felt that as the son of the proprietor he should make a direct inquiry. "Now, what might you be drivin' at, mister?" he asked. The Swede winked at him. It was a wink full of cunning. His fingers shook on the edge of the board. "Oh, maybe you think I have been to nowheres. Maybe you think I'm a tenderfoot?"

"I don't know nothin' about you," answered Johnnie, "and I don't give a damn where you've been. All I got to say is that I don't know what you're driving at. There hain't never been nobody killed in this room."

The cowboy, who had been steadily gazing at the Swede, then spoke: "What's wrong with you, mister?"

Apparently it seemed to the Swede that he was formidably menaced. He shivered and turned white near the corners of his mouth. He sent an appealing glance in the direction of the little Easterner. During these moments he did not forget to wear his air of advanced pot-valour. "They say they don't know what I mean," he remarked mockingly to the Easterner.

The latter answered after prolonged and cautious reflection. "I don't understand you," he said, impassively.

The Swede made a movement then which announced that he thought he had encountered treachery from the only quarter where he had expected sympathy, if not help. "Oh, I see you are all against me. I see—"

The cowboy was in a state of deep stupefaction. "Say," he cried, as he tumbled the deck violently down upon the board, "say, what are you gittin' at, hey?"

The Swede sprang up with the celerity of a man escaping from a snake on the floor. "I don't want to fight!" he shouted. "I don't want to fight!"

The cowboy stretched his long legs indolently and deliberately. His hands were in his pockets. He spat into the sawdust-box. "Well, who the hell thought you did?" he inquired.

The Swede backed rapidly toward a corner of the room. His hands were out protectingly in front of his chest, but he was making an obvious struggle to control his fright. "Gentlemen," he quavered, "I suppose I am going to be killed before I can leave this house! I suppose I am going to be killed before I can leave this house!" In his eyes was the dying-swan look. Through the windows could be seen the snow turning blue in the shadow of dusk. The wind tore at the house, and some loose thing beat regularly against the clapboards like a spirit tapping.

A door opened, and Scully himself entered. He paused in surprise as he noted the tragic attitude of the Swede. Then he said, "What's the matter here?"

The Swede answered him swiftly and eagerly: "These men are going to kill me."

"Kill you!" ejaculated Scully. "Kill you! What are you talkin'?"

The Swede made the gesture of a martyr.

Scully wheeled sternly upon his son. "What is this, Johnnie?"

The lad had grown sullen. "Damned if I know," he answered. "I can't make no sense to it." He began to

shuffle the cards, fluttering them together with an angry
snap. "He says a good many men have been killed in this
room, or something like that. And he says he's goin' to be
killed here too. I don't know what ails him. He's crazy, I
shouldn't wonder."

Scully then looked for explanation to the cowboy, but
the cowboy simply shrugged his shoulders.

"Kill you?" said Scully again to the Swede. "Kill you?
Man, you're off your nut."

"Oh, I know," burst out the Swede. "I know what will
happen. Yes, I'm crazy—yes. Yes, of course, I'm crazy—
yes. But I know one thing—" There was a sort of sweat
of misery and terror upon his face. "I know I won't get
out of here alive."

The cowboy drew a deep breath, as if his mind was
passing into the last stages of dissolution. "Well, I'm dog-
goned," he whispered to himself.

Scully wheeled suddenly and faced his son. "You've
been troublin' this man!"

Johnnie's voice was loud with its burden of grievance.
"Why, good Gawd, I ain't done nothin' to 'im."

The Swede broke in. "Gentlemen, do not disturb yourselves. I will leave this house. I will go away, because"—
he accused them dramatically with his glance—"because
I do not want to be killed."

Scully was furious with his son. "Will you tell me what
is the matter, you young divil? What's the matter, anyhow? Speak out!"

"Blame it!" cried Johnnie in despair, "don't I tell you
I don't know? He—he says we want to kill him, and that's
all I know. I can't tell what ails him."

The Swede continued to repeat: "Never mind, Mr.
Scully; never mind. I will leave this house. I will go away,
because I do not wish to be killed. Yes, of course, I am
crazy—yes. But I know one thing! I will go away. I will
leave this house. Never mind, Mr. Scully; never mind.
I will go away."

"You will not go 'way," said Scully. "You will not go

'way until I hear the reason of this business. If anybody has troubled you I will take care of him. This is my house. You are under my roof, and I will not allow any peaceable man to be troubled here." He cast a terrible eye upon Johnnie, the cowboy, and the Easterner.

"Never mind, Mr. Scully; never mind. I will go away. I do not wish to be killed." The Swede moved toward the door which opened upon the stairs. It was evidently his intention to go at once for his baggage.

"No, no," shouted Scully peremptorily; but the white-faced man slid by him and disappeared. "Now," said Scully severely, "what does this mane?"

Johnnie and the cowboy cried together: "Why, we didn't do nothin' to 'im!"

Scully's eyes were cold. "No," he said, "you didn't?"

Johnnie swore a deep oath. "Why, this is the wildest loon I ever see. We didn't do nothin' at all. We were jest sittin' here playin' cards, and he—"

The father suddenly spoke to the Easterner. "Mr. Blanc," he asked, "what has these boys been doin'?"

The Easterner reflected again. "I didn't see anything wrong at all," he said at last, slowly.

Scully began to howl. "But what does it mane?" He stared ferociously at his son. "I have a mind to lather you for this, me boy."

Johnnie was frantic. "Well, what have I done?" he bawled at his father.

III

"I think you are tongue-tied," said Scully finally to his son, the cowboy, and the Easterner; and at the end of this scornful sentence he left the room.

Upstairs the Swede was swiftly fastening the straps of his great valise. Once his back happened to be half turned toward the door, and, hearing a noise there, he wheeled and sprang up, uttering a loud cry. Scully's wrinkled visage showed grimly in the light of the small lamp he carried. This yellow effulgence, streaming upward, coloured only his prominent features, and left his eyes, for instance, in mysterious shadow. He resembled a murderer.

"Man! man!" he exclaimed, "have you gone daffy?"

"Oh, no! Oh, no!" rejoined the other. "There are people in this world who know pretty nearly as much as you do —understand?"

For a moment they stood gazing at each other. Upon the Swede's deathly pale cheeks were two spots brightly crimson and sharply edged, as if they had been carefully painted. Scully placed the light on the table and sat himself on the edge of the bed. He spoke ruminatively. "By cracky, I never heard of such a thing in my life. It's a complete muddle. I can't, for the soul of me, think how you ever got this idea into your head." Presently he lifted his eyes and asked: "And did you sure think they were going to kill you?"

The Swede scanned the old man as if he wished to see into his mind. "I did," he said at last. He obviously suspected that this answer might precipitate an outbreak. As he pulled on a strap his whole arm shook, the elbow wavering like a bit of paper.

Scully banged his hand impressively on the footboard of the bed. "Why, man, we're goin' to have a line of ilictric street-cars in this town next spring."

" 'A line of electric street-cars,' " repeated the Swede, stupidly.

"And," said Scully, "there's a new railroad goin' to be built down from Broken Arm to here. Not to mintion the four churches and the smashin' big brick school-house. Then there's the big factory, too. Why, in two years Romper'll be a met-tro-*pol*-is."

Having finished the preparation of his baggage, the Swede straightened himself. "Mr. Scully," he said, with sudden hardihood, "how much do I owe you?"

"You don't owe me anythin'," said the old man, angrily.

"Yes, I do," retorted the Swede. He took seventy-five cents from his pocket and tendered it to Scully; but the latter snapped his fingers in disdainful refusal. However, it happened that they both stood gazing in a strange fashion at three silver pieces on the Swede's open palm.

"I'll not take your money," said Scully at last. "Not after what's been goin' on here." Then a plan seemed to strike him. "Here," he cried, picking up his lamp and moving toward the door. "Here! Come with me a minute."

"No," said the Swede, in overwhelming alarm.

"Yes," urged the old man. "Come on! I want you to come and see a picter—just across the hall—in my room."

The Swede must have concluded that his hour was come. His jaw dropped and his teeth showed like a dead man's. He ultimately followed Scully across the corridor, but he had the step of one hung in chains.

Scully flashed the light high on the wall of his own chamber. There was revealed a ridiculous photograph of a little girl. She was leaning against a balustrade of gorgeous decoration, and the formidable bang to her hair was prominent. The figure was as graceful as an upright sled-stake, and, withal, it was of the hue of lead. "There," said Scully, tenderly, "that's the picter of my little girl that died. Her name was Carrie. She had the purtiest hair you ever saw! I was that fond of her, she—"

Turning then, he saw that the Swede was not contemplating the picture at all, but, instead, was keeping keen watch on the gloom in the rear.

"Look, man!" cried Scully, heartily. "That's the picter of my little gal that died. Her name was Carrie. And then here's the picter of my oldest boy, Michael. He's a lawyer in Lincoln, an' doin' well. I gave that boy a grand eddication, and I'm glad for it now. He's a fine boy. Look at 'im now. Ain't he bold as blazes, him there in Lincoln, an honoured an' respicted gintleman! An honoured and respicted gintleman," concluded Scully with a flourish. And, so saying, he smote the Swede jovially on the back.

The Swede faintly smiled.

"Now," said the old man, "there's only one more thing." He dropped suddenly to the floor and thrust his head beneath the bed. The Swede could hear his muffled voice. "I'd keep it under me piller if it wasn't for that boy

Johnnie. Then there's the old woman— Where is it now?
I never put it twice in the same place. Ah, now come out
with you!"

Presently he backed clumsily from under the bed, dragging with him an old coat rolled into a bundle. "I've
fetched him," he muttered. Kneeling on the floor, he un-
rolled the coat and extracted from its heart a large yellow-
brown whisky-bottle.

His first manœuvre was to hold the bottle up to the light.
Reassured, apparently, that nobody had been tampering
with it, he thrust it with a generous movement toward the
Swede.

The weak-kneed Swede was about to eagerly clutch this
element of strength, but he suddenly jerked his hand away
and cast a look of horror upon Scully.

"Drink," said the old man affectionately. He had risen
to his feet, and now stood facing the Swede.

There was a silence. Then again Scully said: "Drink!"

The Swede laughed wildly. He grabbed the bottle, put
it to his mouth; and as his lips curled absurdly around
the opening and his throat worked, he kept his glance,
burning with hatred, upon the old man's face.

IV

After the departure of Scully the three men, with the card-
board still upon their knees, preserved for a long time an
astounded silence. Then Johnnie said: "That's the dod-
dangedest Swede I ever see."

"He ain't no Swede," said the cowboy, scornfully.

"Well, what is he then?" cried Johnnie. "What is he
then?"

"It's my opinion," replied the cowboy deliberately, "he's
some kind of a Dutchman." It was a venerable custom of
the country to entitle as Swedes all light-haired men who
spoke with a heavy tongue. In consequence the idea of
the cowboy was not without its daring. "Yes, sir," he repeated. "It's my opinion this feller is some kind of a
Dutchman."

"Well, he says he's a Swede, anyhow," muttered Johnnie, sulkily. He turned to the Easterner: "What do you think, Mr. Blanc?"

"Oh, I don't know," replied the Easterner.

"Well, what do you think makes him act that way?" asked the cowboy.

"Why, he's frightened." The Easterner knocked his pipe against a rim of the stove. "He's clear frightened out of his boots."

"What at?" cried Johnnie and the cowboy together.

The Easterner reflected over his answer.

"What at?" cried the others again.

"Oh, I don't know, but it seems to me this man has been reading dime novels, and he thinks he's right out in the middle of it—the shootin' and stabbin' and all."

"But," said the cowboy, deeply scandalized, "this ain't Wyoming, ner none of them places. This is Nebrasker."

"Yes," added Johnnie, "an' why don't he wait till he gits *out West?*"

The travelled Easterner laughed. "It isn't different there even—not in these days. But he thinks he's right in the middle of hell."

Johnnie and the cowboy mused long.

"It's awful funny," remarked Johnnie at last.

"Yes," said the cowboy. "This is a queer game. I hope we don't git snowed in, because then we'd have to stand this here man bein' around with us all the time. That wouldn't be no good."

"I wish pop would throw him out," said Johnnie.

Presently they heard a loud stamping on the stairs, accompanied by ringing jokes in the voice of old Scully, and laughter, evidently from the Swede. The men around the stove stared vacantly at each other. "Gosh!" said the cowboy. The door flew open, and old Scully, flushed and anecdotal, came into the room. He was jabbering at the Swede, who followed him, laughing bravely. It was the entry of two roisterers from a banquet hall.

"Come now," said Scully sharply to the three seated men, "move up and give us a chance at the stove." The cowboy and the Easterner obediently sidled their chairs

to make room for the new-comers. Johnnie, however, simply arranged himself in a more indolent attitude, and then
remained motionless.

"Come! Git over, there," said Scully.

"Plenty of room on the other side of the stove," said
Johnnie.

"Do you think we want to sit in the draught?" roared
the father.

But the Swede here interposed with a grandeur of confidence. "No, no. Let the boy sit where he likes," he cried
in a bullying voice to the father.

"All right! All right!" said Scully, deferentially. The
cowboy and the Easterner exchanged glances of wonder.

The five chairs were formed in a crescent about one
side of the stove. The Swede began to talk; he talked ar-
rogantly, profanely, angrily. Johnnie, the cowboy, and the
Easterner maintained a morose silence, while old Scully
appeared to be receptive and eager, breaking in constantly
with sympathetic ejaculations.

Finally the Swede announced that he was thirsty. He
moved in his chair, and said that he would go for a drink
of water.

"I'll git it for you," cried Scully at once.

"No," said the Swede, contemptuously. "I'll get it for
myself." He arose and stalked with the air of an owner off
into the executive parts of the hotel.

As soon as the Swede was out of hearing Scully sprang
to his feet and whispered intensely to the others: "Upstairs he thought I was tryin' to poison 'im."

"Say," said Johnnie, "this makes me sick. Why don't
you throw 'im out in the snow?"

"Why, he's all right now," declared Scully. "It was only
that he was from the East, and he thought this was a
tough place. That's all. He's all right now."

The cowboy looked with admiration upon the Easterner.
"You were straight," he said. "You were on to that there
Dutchman."

"Well," said Johnnie to his father, "he may be all right

now, but I don't see it. Other time he was scared, but now he's too fresh."

Scully's speech was always a combination of Irish brogue and idiom, Western twang and idiom, and scraps of curiously formal diction taken from the story-books and newspapers. He now hurled a strange mass of language at the head of his son. "What do I keep? What do I keep? What do I keep?" he demanded, in a voice of thunder. He slapped his knee impressively, to indicate that he himself was going to make reply, and that all should heed. "I keep a hotel," he shouted. "A hotel, do you mind? A guest under my roof has sacred privileges. He is to be intimidated by none. Not one word shall he hear that would prijudice him in favour of goin' away. I'll not have it. There's no place in this here town where they can say they iver took in a guest of mine because he was afraid to stay here." He wheeled suddenly upon the cowboy and the Easterner. "Am I right?"

"Yes, Mr. Scully," said the cowboy, "I think you're right."

"Yes, Mr. Scully," said the Easterner, "I think you're right."

V

At six-o'clock supper, the Swede fizzed like a fire-wheel. He sometimes seemed on the point of bursting into riotous song, and in all his madness he was encouraged by old Scully. The Easterner was encased in reserve; the cowboy sat in wide-mouthed amazement, forgetting to eat, while Johnnie wrathily demolished great plates of food. The daughters of the house, when they were obliged to replenish the biscuits, approached as warily as Indians, and, having succeeded in their purpose, fled with ill-concealed trepidation. The Swede domineered the whole feast, and he gave it the appearance of a cruel bacchanal. He seemed to have grown suddenly taller; he gazed, brutally disdainful, into every face. His voice rang through the room. Once when he jabbed out harpoon-fashion with

his fork to pinion a biscuit, the weapon nearly impaled
the hand of the Easterner, which had been stretched quietly
out for the same biscuit.

After supper, as the men filed toward the other room,
the Swede smote Scully ruthlessly on the shoulder. "Well,
old boy, that was a good, square meal." Johnnie looked
hopefully at his father; he knew that shoulder was tender
from an old fall; and, indeed, it appeared for a moment
as if Scully was going to flame out over the matter, but
in the end he smiled a sickly smile and remained silent.
The others understood from his manner that he was admitting his responsibility for the Swede's new view-point.

Johnnie, however, addressed his parent in an aside.
"Why don't you license somebody to kick you downstairs?" Scully scowled darkly by way of reply.

When they were gathered about the stove, the Swede
insisted on another game of High-Five. Scully gently depre-
cated the plan at first, but the Swede turned a wolfish glare
upon him. The old man subsided, and the Swede can-
vassed the others. In his tone there was always a great
threat. The cowboy and the Easterner both remarked indifferently that they would play. Scully said that he would
presently have to go to meet the 6.58 train, and so the
Swede turned menacingly upon Johnnie. For a moment
their glances crossed like blades, and then Johnnie smiled
and said, "Yes, I'll play."

They formed a square, with the little board on their
knees. The Easterner and the Swede were again partners.
As the play went on, it was noticeable that the cowboy
was not board-whacking as usual. Meanwhile, Scully, near
the lamp, had put on his spectacles and, with an appearance curiously like an old priest, was reading a newspaper.
In time he went out to meet the 6.58 train, and, despite
his precautions, a gust of polar wind whirled into the room
as he opened the door. Besides scattering the cards, it
chilled the players to the marrow. The Swede cursed fright-
fully. When Scully returned, his entrance disturbed a cosy
and friendly scene. The Swede again cursed. But presently
they were once more intent, their heads bent forward and

their hands moving swiftly. The Swede had adopted the fashion of board-whacking.

Scully took up his paper and for a long time remained immersed in matters which were extraordinarily remote from him. The lamp burned badly, and once he stopped to adjust the wick. The newspaper, as he turned from page to page, rustled with a slow and comfortable sound. Then suddenly he heard three terrible words: "You are cheatin'!"

Such scenes often prove that there can be little of dramatic import in environment. Any room can present a tragic front; any room can be comic. This little den was now hideous as a torture-chamber. The new faces of the men themselves had changed it upon the instant. The Swede held a huge fist in front of Johnnie's face, while the latter looked steadily over it into the blazing orbs of his accuser. The Easterner had grown pallid; the cowboy's jaw had dropped in that expression of bovine amazement which was one of his important mannerisms. After the three words, the first sound in the room was made by Scully's paper as it floated forgotten to his feet. His spectacles had also fallen from his nose, but by a clutch he had saved them in air. His hand, grasping the spectacles, now remained poised awkwardly and near his shoulder. He stared at the card-players.

Probably the silence was while a second elapsed. Then, if the floor had been suddenly twitched out from under the men they could not have moved quicker. The five had projected themselves headlong toward a common point. It happened that Johnnie, in rising to hurl himself upon the Swede, had stumbled slightly because of his curiously instinctive care for the cards and the board. The loss of the moment allowed time for the arrival of Scully, and also allowed the cowboy time to give the Swede a great push which sent him staggering back. The men found tongue together, and hoarse shouts of rage, appeal, or fear burst from every throat. The cowboy pushed and jostled feverishly at the Swede, and the Easterner and Scully clung wildly to Johnnie; but through the smoky air, above the swaying bodies of the peace-compellers, the eyes of the two warriors ever sought each other in glances of challenge that were at once hot and steely.

Of course the board had been overturned, and now the whole company of cards was scattered over the floor, where the boots of the men trampled the fat and painted kings and queens as they gazed with their silly eyes at the war that was waging above them.

Scully's voice was dominating the yells. "Stop now! Stop, I say! Stop, now—"

Johnnie, as he struggled to burst through the rank formed by Scully and the Easterner, was crying, "Well, he says I cheated! He says I cheated! I won't allow no man to say I cheated! If he says I cheated, he's a —— ——!"

The cowboy was telling the Swede, "Quit, now! Quit, d'ye hear—"

The screams of the Swede never ceased: "He did cheat! I saw him! I saw him—"

As for the Easterner, he was importuning in a voice that was not heeded: "Wait a moment, can't you? Oh, wait a moment. What's the good of a fight over a game of cards? Wait a moment—"

In this tumult no complete sentences were clear. "Cheat"—"Quit"—"He says"—these fragments pierced the uproar and rang out sharply. It was remarkable that, whereas Scully undoubtedly made the most noise, he was the least heard of any of the riotous band.

Then suddenly there was a great cessation. It was as if each man had paused for breath; and although the room was still lighted with the anger of men, it could be seen that there was no danger of immediate conflict, and at once Johnnie, shouldering his way forward, almost succeeded in confronting the Swede. "What did you say I cheated for? What did you say I cheated for? I don't cheat, and I won't let no man say I do!"

The Swede said, "I saw you! I saw you!"

"Well," cried Johnnie, "I'll fight any man what says I cheat!"

"No, you won't," said the cowboy. "Not here."

"Ah, be still, can't you?" said Scully, coming between them.

The quiet was sufficient to allow the Easterner's voice to be heard. He was repeating, "Oh, wait a moment, can't you? What's the good of a fight over a game of cards? Wait a moment!"

Johnnie, his red face appearing above his father's shoulder, hailed the Swede again. "Did you say I cheated?"

The Swede showed his teeth. "Yes."

"Then," said Johnnie, "we must fight."

"Yes, fight," roared the Swede. He was like a demoniac. "Yes, fight! I'll show you what kind of a man I am! I'll show you who you want to fight! Maybe you think I can't fight! Maybe you think I can't! I'll show you, you skin, you card-sharp! Yes, you cheated! You cheated! You cheated!"

"Well, let's go at it, then, mister," said Johnnie, coolly.

The cowboy's brow was beaded with sweat from his efforts in intercepting all sorts of raids. He turned in despair to Scully. "What are you goin' to do now?"

A change had come over the Celtic visage of the old man. He now seemed all eagerness; his eyes glowed.

"We'll let them fight," he answered, stalwartly. "I can't put up with it any longer. I've stood this damned Swede till I'm sick. We'll let them fight."

VI

The men prepared to go out of doors. The Easterner was so nervous that he had great difficulty in getting his arms into the sleeves of his new leather coat. As the cowboy drew his fur cap down over his ears his hands trembled. In fact, Johnnie and old Scully were the only ones who displayed no agitation. These preliminaries were conducted without words.

Scully threw open the door. "Well, come on," he said. Instantly a terrific wind caused the flame of the lamp to struggle at its wick, while a puff of black smoke sprang from the chimney-top. The stove was in mid-current of the blast, and its voice swelled to equal the roar of the storm.

Some of the scarred and bedabbled cards were caught up from the floor and dashed helplessly against the farther wall. The men lowered their heads and plunged into the tempest as into a sea.

No snow was falling, but great whirls and clouds of flakes, swept up from the ground by the frantic winds, were streaming southward with the speed of bullets. The covered land was blue with the sheen of an unearthly satin, and there was no other hue save where, at the low, black railway station—which seemed incredibly distant—one light gleamed like a tiny jewel. As the men floundered into a thigh-deep drift, it was known that the Swede was bawling out something. Scully went to him, put a hand on his shoulder, and projected an ear. "What's that you say?" he shouted.

"I say," bawled the Swede again, "I won't stand much show against this gang. I know you'll all pitch on me."

Scully smote him reproachfully on the arm. "Tut, man!" he yelled. The wind tore the words from Scully's lips and scattered them far alee.

"You are all a gang of—" boomed the Swede, but the storm also seized the remainder of this sentence.

Immediately turning their backs upon the wind, the men had swung around a corner to the sheltered side of the hotel. It was the function of the little house to preserve here, amid this great devastation of snow, an irregular V-shape of heavily encrusted grass, which crackled beneath the feet. One could imagine the great drifts piled against the windward side. When the party reached the comparative peace of this spot it was found that the Swede was still bellowing.

"Oh, I know what kind of a thing this is! I know you'll all pitch on me. I can't lick you all!"

Scully turned upon him panther-fashion. "You'll not have to whip all of us. You'll have to whip my son Johnnie. An' the man what troubles you durin' that time will have me to dale with."

The arrangements were swiftly made. The two men

faced each other, obedient to the harsh commands of Scully, whose face, in the subtly luminous gloom, could be seen set in the austere impersonal lines that are pictured on the countenances of the Roman veterans. The Easterner's teeth were chattering, and he was hopping up and down like a mechanical toy. The cowboy stood rock-like.

The contestants had not stripped off any clothing. Each was in his ordinary attire. Their fists were up, and they eyed each other in a calm that had the elements of leonine cruelty in it.

During this pause, the Easterner's mind, like a film, took lasting impressions of three men—the iron-nerved master of the ceremony; the Swede, pale, motionless, terrible; and Johnnie, serene yet ferocious, brutish yet heroic. The entire prelude had in it a tragedy greater than the tragedy of action, and this aspect was accentuated by the long, mellow cry of the blizzard, as it sped the tumbling and wailing flakes into the black abyss of the south.

"Now!" said Scully.

The two combatants leaped forward and crashed together like bullocks. There was heard the cushioned sound of blows, and of a curse squeezing out from between the tight teeth of one.

As for the spectators, the Easterner's pent-up breath exploded from him with a pop of relief, absolute relief from the tension of the preliminaries. The cowboy bounded into the air with a yowl. Scully was immovable as from supreme amazement and fear at the fury of the fight which he himself had permitted and arranged.

For a time the encounter in the darkness was such a perplexity of flying arms that it presented no more detail than would a swiftly revolving wheel. Occasionally a face, as if illumined by a flash of light, would shine out, ghastly and marked with pink spots. A moment later, the men might have been known as shadows, if it were not for the involuntary utterance of oaths that came from them in whispers.

Suddenly a holocaust of warlike desire caught the cowboy, and he bolted forward with the speed of a broncho. "Go it, Johnnie! go it! Kill him! Kill him!"

Scully confronted him. "Kape back," he said; and by his glance the cowboy could tell that this man was Johnnie's father.

To the Easterner there was a monotony of unchangeable fighting that was an abomination. This confused mingling was eternal to his sense, which was concentrated in a longing for the end, the priceless end. Once the fighters lurched near him, and as he scrambled hastily backward he heard them breathe like men on the rack.

"Kill him, Johnnie! Kill him! Kill him! Kill him!" The cowboy's face was contorted like one of those agony masks in museums.

"Keep still," said Scully, icily.

Then there was a sudden loud grunt, incomplete, cut short, and Johnnie's body swung away from the Swede and fell with sickening heaviness to the grass. The cowboy was barely in time to prevent the mad Swede from flinging himself upon his prone adversary. "No, you don't," said the cowboy, interposing an arm. "Wait a second."

Scully was at his son's side. "Johnnie! Johnnie, me boy!" His voice had a quality of melancholy tenderness. "Johnnie! Can you go on with it?" He looked anxiously down into the bloody, pulpy face of his son.

There was a moment of silence, and then Johnnie answered in his ordinary voice, "Yes, I—it—yes."

Assisted by his father he struggled to his feet. "Wait a bit now till you git your wind," said the old man.

A few paces away the cowboy was lecturing the Swede. "No, you don't! Wait a second!"

The Easterner was plucking at Scully's sleeve. "Oh, this is enough," he pleaded. "This is enough! Let it go as it stands. This is enough!"

"Bill," said Scully, "git out of the road." The cowboy stepped aside. "Now." The combatants were actuated by a new caution as they advanced toward collision. They glared at each other, and then the Swede aimed a lightning blow that carried with it his entire weight. Johnnie was evidently half stupid from weakness, but he miraculously dodged, and his fist sent the overbalanced Swede sprawling.

The cowboy, Scully, and the Easterner burst into a cheer that was like a chorus of triumphant soldiery, but before its conclusion the Swede had scuffled agilely to his feet and come in berserk abandon at his foe. There was another perplexity of flying arms, and Johnnie's body again swung away and fell, even as a bundle might fall from a roof. The Swede instantly staggered to a little wind-waved tree and leaned upon it, breathing like an engine, while his savage and flame-lit eyes roamed from face to face as the men bent over Johnnie. There was a splendour of isolation in his situation at this time which the Easterner felt once when, lifting his eyes from the man on the ground, he beheld that mysterious and lonely figure, waiting.

"Are you any good yet, Johnnie?" asked Scully in a broken voice.

The son gasped and opened his eyes languidly. After a moment he answered, "No—I ain't—any good—any—more." Then, from shame and bodily ill, he began to weep, the tears furrowing down through the blood-stains on his face. "He was too—too—too heavy for me."

Scully straightened and addressed the waiting figure. "Stranger," he said, evenly, "it's all up with our side." Then his voice changed into that vibrant huskiness which is commonly the tone of the most simple and deadly announcements. "Johnnie is whipped."

Without replying, the victor moved off on the route to the front door of the hotel.

The cowboy was formulating new and unspellable blasphemies. The Easterner was startled to find that they were out in a wind that seemed to come direct from the shadowed arctic floes. He heard again the wail of the snow as it was flung to its grave in the south. He knew now that all this time the cold had been sinking into him deeper and deeper, and he wondered that he had not perished. He felt indifferent to the condition of the vanquished man.

"Johnnie, can you walk?" asked Scully.

"Did I hurt—hurt him any?" asked the son.

"Can you walk, boy? Can you walk?"

Johnnie's voice was suddenly strong. There was a robust impatience in it. "I asked you whether I hurt him any!"

"Yes, yes, Johnnie," answered the cowboy, consolingly; "he's hurt a good deal."

They raised him from the ground, and as soon as he was on his feet he went tottering off, rebuffing all attempts at assistance. When the party rounded the corner they were fairly blinded by the pelting of the snow. It burned their faces like fire. The cowboy carried Johnnie through the drift to the door. As they entered, some cards again rose from the floor and beat against the wall.

The Easterner rushed to the stove. He was so profoundly chilled that he almost dared to embrace the glowing iron. The Swede was not in the room. Johnnie sank into a chair and, folding his arms on his knees, buried his face in them. Scully, warming one foot and then the other at a rim of the stove, muttered to himself with Celtic mournfulness. The cowboy had removed his fur cap, and with a dazed and rueful air he was running one hand through his tousled locks. From overhead they could hear the creaking of boards, as the Swede tramped here and there in his room.

The sad quiet was broken by the sudden flinging open of a door that led toward the kitchen. It was instantly followed by an inrush of women. They precipitated themselves upon Johnnie amid a chorus of lamentation. Before they carried their prey off to the kitchen, there to be bathed and harangued with that mixture of sympathy and abuse which is a feat of their sex, the mother straightened herself and fixed old Scully with an eye of stern reproach. "Shame be upon you, Patrick Scully!" she cried. "Your own son, too. Shame be upon you!"

"There, now! Be quiet, now!" said the old man, weakly.

"Shame be upon you, Patrick Scully!" The girls, rallying to this slogan, sniffed disdainfully in the direction of those trembling accomplices, the cowboy and the Easterner. Presently they bore Johnnie away, and left the three men to dismal reflection.

VII

"I'd like to fight this here Dutchman myself," said the cowboy, breaking a long silence.

Scully wagged his head sadly. "No, that wouldn't do. It wouldn't be right. It wouldn't be right."

"Well, why wouldn't it?" argued the cowboy. "I don't see no harm in it."

"No," answered Scully, with mournful heroism. "It wouldn't be right. It was Johnnie's fight, and now we mustn't whip the man just because he whipped Johnnie."

"Yes, that's true enough," said the cowboy; "but—he better not get fresh with me, because I couldn't stand no more of it."

"You'll not say a word to him," commanded Scully, and even then they heard the tread of the Swede on the stairs. His entrance was made theatric. He swept the door back with a bang and swaggered to the middle of the room. No one looked at him. "Well," he cried, insolently, at Scully, "I s'pose you'll tell me now how much I owe you?"

The old man remained stolid. "You don't owe me nothin'."

"Huh!" said the Swede, "huh! Don't owe 'im nothin'."

The cowboy addressed the Swede. "Stranger, I don't see how you come to be so gay around here."

Old Scully was instantly alert. "Stop!" he shouted, holding his hand forth, fingers upward. "Bill, you shut up!"

The cowboy spat carelessly into the sawdust-box. "I didn't say a word, did I?" he asked.

"Mr. Scully," called the Swede, "how much do I owe you?" It was seen that he was attired for departure, and that he had his valise in his hand.

"You don't owe me nothin'," repeated Scully in the same imperturbable way.

"Huh!" said the Swede. "I guess you're right. I guess if it was any way at all, you'd owe me somethin'. That's what I guess." He turned to the cowboy. " 'Kill him! Kill him! Kill him!' " he mimicked, and then guffawed victori-

ously. " 'Kill him!' " He was convulsed with ironical humour.

But he might have been jeering the dead. The three men
were immovable and silent, staring with glassy eyes at the
stove.

The Swede opened the door and passed into the storm,
giving one derisive glance backward at the still group.

As soon as the door was closed, Scully and the cowboy
leaped to their feet and began to curse. They trampled to
and fro, waving their arms and smashing into the air with
their fists. "Oh, but that was a hard minute!" wailed Scully.
"That was a hard minute! Him there leerin' and scoffin'!
One bang at his nose was worth forty dollars to me that
minute! How did you stand it, Bill?"

"How did I stand it?" cried the cowboy in a quivering
voice. "How did I stand it? Oh!"

The old man burst into sudden brogue. "I'd loike to take
that Swade," he wailed, "and hould 'im down on a shtone
flure and bate 'im to a jelly wid a shtick!"

The cowboy groaned in sympathy. "I'd like to git him
by the neck and ha-ammer him"—he brought his hand down
on a chair with a noise like a pistol-shot—"hammer that
there Dutchman until he couldn't tell himself from a dead
coyote!"

"I'd bate 'im until he—"

"I'd show *him* some things—"

And then together they raised a yearning, fanatic cry—
"Oh-o-oh! if we only could—"

"Yes!"

"Yes!"

"And then I'd—"

"O-o-oh!"

VIII

The Swede, tightly gripping his valise, tacked across the
face of the storm as if he carried sails. He was following
a line of little naked, grasping trees which, he knew, must
mark the way of the road. His face, fresh from the pounding of Johnnie's fists, felt more pleasure than pain in the

wind and the driving snow. A number of square shapes loomed upon him finally, and he knew them as the houses of the main body of the town. He found a street and made travel along it, leaning heavily upon the wind whenever, at a corner, a terrific blast caught him.

He might have been in a deserted village. We picture the world as thick with conquering and elate humanity, but here, with the bugles of the tempest pealing, it was hard to imagine a peopled earth. One viewed the existence of man then as a marvel, and conceded a glamour of wonder to these lice which were caused to cling to a whirling, fire-smitten, ice-locked, disease-stricken, space-lost bulb. The conceit of man was explained by this storm to be the very engine of life. One was a coxcomb not to die in it. However, the Swede found a saloon.

In front of it an indomitable red light was burning, and the snowflakes were made blood-colour as they flew through the circumscribed territory of the lamp's shining. The Swede pushed open the door of the saloon and entered. A sanded expanse was before him, and at the end of it four men sat about a table drinking. Down one side of the room extended a radiant bar, and its guardian was leaning upon his elbows listening to the talk of the men at the table. The Swede dropped his valise upon the floor and, smiling fraternally upon the barkeeper, said, "Gimme some whisky, will you?" The man placed a bottle, a whisky-glass, and a glass of ice-thick water upon the bar. The Swede poured himself an abnormal portion of whisky and drank it in three gulps. "Pretty bad night," remarked the bartender, indifferently. He was making the pretension of blindness which is usually a distinction of his class; but it could have been seen that he was furtively studying the half-erased blood-stains on the face of the Swede. "Bad night," he said again.

"Oh, it's good enough for me," replied the Swede, hardily, as he poured himself some more whisky. The barkeeper took his coin and manœuvred it through its reception by the highly nickelled cash-machine. A bell rang; a card labelled "20 cts." had appeared.

"No," continued the Swede, "this isn't too bad weather. It's good enough for me."

"So?" murmured the barkeeper, languidly.

The copious drams made the Swede's eyes swim, and he breathed a trifle heavier. "Yes, I like this weather. I like it. It suits me." It was apparently his design to impart a deep significance to these words.

"So?" murmured the bartender again. He turned to gaze dreamily at the scroll-like birds and bird-like scrolls which had been drawn with soap upon the mirrors in back of the bar.

"Well, I guess I'll take another drink," said the Swede, presently. "Have something?"

"No, thanks; I'm not drinkin'," answered the bartender. Afterward he asked, "How did you hurt your face?"

The Swede immediately began to boast loudly. "Why, in a fight. I thumped the soul out of a man down here at Scully's hotel."

The interest of the four men at the table was at last aroused.

"Who was it?" said one.

"Johnnie Scully," blustered the Swede. "Son of the man what runs it. He will be pretty near dead for some weeks, I can tell you. I made a nice thing of him, I did. He couldn't get up. They carried him in the house. Have a drink?"

Instantly the men in some subtle way encased themselves in reserve. "No, thanks," said one. The group was of curious formation. Two were prominent local business men; one was the district attorney; and one was a professional gambler of the kind known as "square." But a scrutiny of the group would not have enabled an observer to pick the gambler from the men of more reputable pursuits. He was, in fact, a man so delicate in manner, when among people of fair class, and so judicious in his choice of victims, that in the strictly masculine part of the town's life he had come to be explicitly trusted and admired. People called him a thoroughbred. The fear and contempt with which his craft was regarded were undoubtedly the reason why his quiet dignity shone conspicuous above the quiet dignity of men who might be merely hatters, billiard-markers, or grocery clerks. Beyond an occasional unwary traveller who came by rail, this gambler was supposed to prey solely upon reckless and senile farmers, who, when flush with good crops, drove into town in all the pride and confidence of an absolutely invulnerable stupidity. Hearing at times in circuitous fashion of the despoilment of such a farmer, the important men of Romper invariably laughed in contempt of the victim, and if they thought of the wolf at all, it was with a kind of pride at the knowledge that he would never dare think of attacking their wisdom and courage. Besides, it was popular that this gambler had a real wife and two real children in a neat cottage in a suburb, where he led an exemplary home life; and when any one even suggested a discrepancy in his character, the crowd immediately vociferated descriptions of this virtuous family circle. Then men who led exemplary home lives, and men who did not lead exemplary home lives, all subsided in a bunch, remarking that there was nothing more to be said.

However, when a restriction was placed upon him—as, for instance, when a strong clique of members of the new Pollywog Club refused to permit him, even as a spectator, to appear in the rooms of the organization—the candour and gentleness with which he accepted the judgment disarmed many of his foes and made his friends more desperately partisan. He invariably distinguished between himself and a respectable Romper man so quickly and frankly that his manner actually appeared to be a continual broadcast compliment.

And one must not forget to declare the fundamental fact of his entire position in Romper. It is irrefutable that in all affairs outside his business, in all matters that occur eternally and commonly between man and man, this thieving card-player was so generous, so just, so moral, that, in a contest, he could have put to flight the consciences of nine tenths of the citizens of Romper.

And so it happened that he was seated in this saloon with the two prominent local merchants and the district attorney.

The Swede continued to drink raw whisky, meanwhile babbling at the barkeeper and trying to induce him to indulge in potations. "Come on. Have a drink. Come on. What—no? Well, have a little one, then. By gawd, I've whipped a man to-night, and I want to celebrate. I whipped him good, too. Gentlemen," the Swede cried to the men at the table, "have a drink?"

"Ssh!" said the barkeeper.

The group at the table, although furtively attentive, had been pretending to be deep in talk, but now a man lifted his eyes toward the Swede and said, shortly, "Thanks. We don't want any more."

At this reply the Swede ruffled out his chest like a rooster. "Well," he exploded, "it seems I can't get anybody to drink with me in this town. Seems so, don't it? Well!"

"Ssh!" said the barkeeper.

"Say," snarled the Swede, "don't you try to shut me up. I won't have it. I'm a gentleman, and I want people to drink with me. And I want 'em to drink with me now. *Now*—do you understand?" He rapped the bar with his knuckles.

Years of experience had calloused the bartender. He merely grew sulky. "I hear you," he answered.

"Well," cried the Swede, "listen hard then. See those men over there? Well, they're going to drink with me, and don't you forget it. Now you watch."

"Hi!" yelled the barkeeper, "this won't do!"

"Why won't it?" demanded the Swede. He stalked over to the table, and by chance laid his hand upon the shoulder of the gambler. "How about this?" he asked wrathfully. "I asked you to drink with me."

The gambler simply twisted his head and spoke over his shoulder. "My friend, I don't know you."

"Oh, hell!" answered the Swede, "come and have a drink."

"Now, my boy," advised the gambler, kindly, "take your

hand off my shoulder and go 'way and mind your own business." He was a little, slim man, and it seemed strange to hear him use this tone of heroic patronage to the burly Swede. The other men at the table said nothing.

"What! You won't drink with me, you little dude? I'll make you, then! I'll make you!" The Swede had grasped the gambler frenziedly at the throat, and was dragging him from his chair. The other men sprang up. The barkeeper dashed around the corner of his bar. There was a great tumult, and then was seen a long blade in the hand of the gambler. It shot forward, and a human body, this citadel of virtue, wisdom, power, was pierced as easily as if it had been a melon. The Swede fell with a cry of supreme astonishment.

The prominent merchants and the district attorney must have at once tumbled out of the place backward. The bartender found himself hanging limply to the arm of a chair and gazing into the eyes of a murderer.

"Henry," said the latter, as he wiped his knife on one of the towels that hung beneath the bar rail, "you tell 'em where to find me. I'll be home, waiting for 'em." Then he vanished. A moment afterward the barkeeper was in the street dinning through the storm for help and, moreover, companionship.

The corpse of the Swede, alone in the saloon, had its eyes fixed upon a dreadful legend that dwelt atop of the cash-machine: "This registers the amount of your purchase."

IX

Months later, the cowboy was frying pork over the stove of a little ranch near the Dakota line, when there was a quick thud of hoofs outside, and presently the Easterner entered with the letters and the papers.

"Well," said the Easterner at once, "the chap that killed the Swede has got three years. Wasn't much, was it?"

"He has? Three years?" The cowboy poised his pan of pork, while he ruminated upon the news. "Three years. That ain't much."

"No. It was a light sentence," replied the Easterner as

he unbuckled his spurs. "Seems there was a good deal of sympathy for him in Romper."

"If the bartender had been any good," observed the cowboy, thoughtfully, "he would have gone in and cracked that there Dutchman on the head with a bottle in the beginnin' of it and stopped all this here murderin'."

"Yes, a thousand things might have happened," said the Easterner, tartly.

The cowboy returned his pan of pork to the fire, but his philosophy continued. "It's funny, ain't it? If he hadn't said Johnnie was cheatin' he'd be alive this minute. He was an awful fool. Game played for fun, too. Not for money. I believe he was crazy."

"I feel sorry for that gambler," said the Easterner.

"Oh, so do I," said the cowboy. "He don't deserve none of it for killin' who he did."

"The Swede might not have been killed if everything had been square."

"Might not have been killed?" exclaimed the cowboy. "Everythin' square? Why, when he said that Johnnie was cheatin' and acted like such a jackass? And then in the saloon he fairly walked up to git hurt?" With these arguments the cowboy browbeat the Easterner and reduced him to rage.

"You're a fool!" cried the Easterner, viciously. "You're a bigger jackass than the Swede by a million majority. Now let me tell you one thing. Let me tell you something. Listen! Johnnie *was* cheating!"

" 'Johnnie,' " said the cowboy, blankly. There was a minute of silence, and then he said, robustly, "Why, no. The game was only for fun."

"Fun or not," said the Easterner, "Johnnie was cheating. I saw him. I know it. I saw him. And I refused to stand up and be a man. I let the Swede fight it out alone. And you—you were simply puffing around the place and wanting to fight. And then old Scully himself! We are all in it! This poor gambler isn't even a noun. He is kind of an adverb. Every sin is the result of a collaboration. We, five of us, have collaborated in the murder of this Swede. Usually there are from a dozen to forty women really involved in every murder, but in this case it seems to be only five men —you, I, Johnnie, old Scully; and that fool of an unfortunate gambler came merely as a culmination, the apex of a human movement, and gets all the punishment."

The cowboy, injured and rebellious, cried out blindly into this fog of mysterious theory: "Well, I didn't do anythin', did I?"

PART V

Whilomville Stories

INTRODUCTION

WHILOMVILLE—where Crane lived *for a while*—is chiefly Port Jervis, New York, where he spent three years of his boyhood (1879–82). The stories have their composite setting not only in Port Jervis but in the various New Jersey towns where the Cranes lived—Bloomington, Patterson, Jersey City, and subsequently Asbury Park, where Stephen attended school (1882–8). It is any boy's town. And Jimmie Trescott is as much Tom Sawyer as he is Stephen Crane. He is Stephen in the haircutting incident of *An Angel Child* and in the comedy of *Lynx-Hunting,* where Jimmie shoots a cow. According to Crane's niece *(Literary Digest,* March 1926), "He himself tried to shoot a cow with a toy gun my father [Willam Crane] gave him." Dr. Trescott is modeled on William, who thought that the portrait flattered him, "and we and our friends and cousins helped to supply the material for them. We were an active, healthy band of savages, keen as briars, father says, out-of-doors all day, and receiving a boy's training." It was Edmund who gave the children of *Angel Child* the money for the haircuts and (to the wrath of their mother) sheared Stephen's curls away. Later (in 1894 in Albany) Crane himself encountered two small boys with long curls and black velvet suits and lace collars, tricked out by their mothers in immitation of Little Lord Fauntleroy, and he gave the pitiful victims money: "You take this money and go down to Jake's barber shop and tell him to cut your

hair and do a good job of it." The mothers fainted, had
hysterics, wept, and denounced him, but one of the fathers
—if we can credit this legend—"averred that his son now
looked like a convict, but he was secretly pleased . . . and
sent Crane an anonymous box of cigars with a card inscribed: 'From a grateful public' " (*Bookman,* March 1927).

But if Crane is Jimmie Trescott, he is also the painter
in *Angel Child* and *The Stove,* a painter so famous that
"almost everybody in the United States who knew about
art and its travail knew about him." Jimmie falls in love
with the Angel Child, whose name is Cora—after Crane's
wife. At the tea-party in *The Stove,* "A few came to see
if they could not find out the faults of the painter's wife."
That echoes with personal undertones. Crane wrote the
thirteen *Whilomville Stories* at Brede Place, England. Published in *Harper's* starting in August 1899, and posthu-
mously in book form, with drawings by Peter Newell, in
1900, they were his last work. Another Whilomville story,
much better than these with the one exception of *The
Knife,* is *His New Mittens.* It was published in *McClure's
Magazine* in November 1898, but was not collected in the
Whilomville group until Volume V of the *Work* appeared
in 1926. It was the first Whilomville story Crane wrote,
and it was written on board the dispatch-boat *The Three
Friends* during the Santiago blockade (1898). The name
of the barber in *An Angel Child* was lifted from the name
of one of the wounded whom Crane met in the Cuban
campaign, Reuben McNab. The farmer in *Lynx-Hunting*
and the hero in *The Veteran* are Henry Fleming now
grown old, and Dr. Trescott is transposed from *The
Monster. The Veteran* and *The Knife* are not stories about
children; on the other hand, the baby sketches Crane did
in 1893, though not Whilomville stories, belong with them
—particularly *A Dark Brown Dog* and *An Ominous Baby.*
They too deal with the cruelty of childhood. *An Indiana
Campaign,* a Civil War incident, has the same mellow
humor as some of the *Whilomville Stories* and might as
well be laid in Whilomville as in a village called Wiggles-
ville. The grotesquerie of *An Illusion in Red and White,*

apparently a murder story but actually a satire on journalists, is all too violent for Whilomville, but the stonily
perverse Jones children on whom the story centers behave
not unlike Whilomville kids—"young Freddy's mind began to work like ketchup."

As Beer points out in *The Mauve Decade,* Mark Twain
had discovered in *Huckleberry Finn* that "the personality
of a child could be used to project realistic views and
pictures of a society, and that trick begins to appear in
the latter ' '90's, more and more." Twain established the
mode, not Crane, and from him Crane probably learned
also dialect and irony. It is irony that differentiates the
Whilomville Stories from Booth Tarkington's *Penrod.* It
was Mark Twain's *Roughing It* and *Life on the Mississippi*
that Crane drew upon in writing the *Whilomville Stories.*
The Stove is sheer Twain:

—Well, we ain't goin' to hurt your old stable, are we?—asked
Jimmie, ironically.
—Dat you ain't, Jim! Not so long's I keep my two eyes right
plumb squaah p'inted at ol' Jim. No, seh!—Peter began to
chuckle in derision.

So too is *The Carriage Lamps*: Jimmie is a prisoner in his
upstairs room, and Willie Dalzel attempts to rescue him
—in emulation, as it were, of Tom Sawyer and Huck Finn.
Peter Washington, the Negro, reappears again in *The Knife*
—the best of the *Whilomville Stories.*

The Knife in its theme of deception harks back to
Huckleberry Finn, where Huck learns all about social
guile. Fabrication, equivocation, deceit, the mask of the
lie—these equip man for society and protect him from it.
To lie is to be saved. In *The Knife* Alek saves Peter, the
betrayer, by lying to the white man, Bryant. This Judas
is outwitted by the all-saving lie. White against black, the
Negro's salvation lies in fidelity. The trap is set by the
white man: "I found a knife and thought it might be
yours." When Alek denies owning the knife, Bryant tries
another trap: "Is he a very close friend of yourn?" At
this Alek stutters, and his stuttering is emblematic of his
plight. "Well, seems like he *was* er frien', an' then agin, it

seems like he"—"It seems like he *wasn't?*" asked Bryant. Each equivocates, not trusting the other. Alek's only recourse is to lie: the knife belongs to Sam Jackson. Ironically, the lie is the truth, as Peter is no true friend.

Crane believed in his *Whilomville Stories* so thoroughly that he thought his best was in them, he told the editor of *Harper's Magazine*; but Crane was anything but consistent in critical opinion. Contradicting himself, he rated at one time or another some half dozen of his works as being his best and for some of these he straddled the fence. One of his inscriptions reads: "This work [*Maggie*] is a mudpuddle, I am told on the best authority. Wade in and have a swim." The answer is, it seems to me, that the Whilomville collection, sometimes charming but more often boring, is lightweight stuff. The romps and scrapes of children and the tortures their parents also suffer cannot themselves have literary interest, and their chief appeal is to readers who have experienced similar incidents in childhood and find pleasure in self-identification. To say that *Lynx-Hunting* touches "the level of *The Monster*" and that *Shame* is "a story genial, charming, and natural" sidesteps judgment with merely impressionistic opinion. To the critical point: the language is dead, the diction flat or (worse) "educated," and the point of view as well as the language badly miscalculated: the telling of these stories is directed to adults in language suitable for them but not for children. Crane was off key from the start. Furthermore, only four of the batch embody any artistic significance or attempt to embody a formed meaning: *The Knife, His New Mittens, Shame, The Fight*. The other ten stories are completely devoid of theme and design. They are a straight line with no ironic turnabout in direction, no angling downward from straight or literal progression. The others have a twist to them. But *Shame* is faulty in the suggested symbolism, and *The Fight* is not so important as a thing in itself as it is for themes of shame and flight, Johnnie Hedge being a miniature of the outcast who redeems himself—Henry Fleming in *The Red Badge of Courage*. Crane in the *Whilomville Stories* unmasks Innocence. They link thus with *The Bride Comes to Yellow Sky* and other variations on the theme: "what innocence can do if it has the opportunity." *His New Mittens* is a study of boy morals, but (as Edward Garnett remarked) "when Crane breathes an everyday, common atmosphere his æsthetic power always weakens." What saves, or almost saves, the whole thing from sheer sentimentalism is the final scene with its symbolic turnabout: "Aunt Martha turned defiantly upon the butcher, because her face betrayed her. She was crying. She made a gesture half military, half feminine. 'Won't you have a glass of our root-beer, Mr. Stickney. *We made it ourselves.*' " Our plight is what we ourselves brew. It is the same in *George's Mother*, whereas *Maggie* represents an inversion of this theme. Which theme did Crane believe in?

THE KNIFE

I

SI BRYANT'S place was on the shore of the lake, and his garden patch, shielded from the north by a bold little promontory and a higher ridge inland, was accounted the most successful and surprising in all Whilomville township. One afternoon Si was working in the garden patch, when Doctor Trescott's man, Peter Washington, came trudging slowly along the road, observing nature. He scanned the white man's fine agricultural results. "Take your eye off them there mellons, you rascal," said Si, placidly.

The negro's face widened in a grin of delight. "Well, Mist' Bryant, I raikon I ain't on'y make m'se'f covertous er-lookin' at dem yere mellums, sure 'nough. Dey suhtainly is grand."

"That's all right," responded Si, with affected bitterness of spirit. "That's all right. Just don't you admire 'em too much, that's all."

Peter chuckled and chuckled. "Ma Lode! Mist' Bryant, y-y-you don' think I'm gwine come prowlin' in dish yer gawden?"

"No, I know you hain't," said Si, with solemnity. "B'cause, if you did, I'd shoot you so full of holes you couldn't tell yourself from a sponge."

"Um—no, seh! No, seh! I don' raikon you'll get chance at Pete, Mist' Bryant. No, seh. I'll take an' run 'long an' rob er bank 'fore I'll come foolishin' 'round *your* gawden, Mist' Bryant."

Bryant, gnarled and strong as an old tree, leaned on his hoe and laughed a Yankee laugh. His mouth remained tightly closed, but the sinister lines which ran from the sides of his nose to the meetings of his lips developed to form a comic oval, and he emitted a series of grunts, while his eyes gleamed merrily and his shoulders shook.

Pete, on the contrary, threw back his head and guffawed thunderously. The effete joke in regard to an American negro's fondness for watermelons was still an admirable pleasantry to them, and this was not the first time they had engaged in badinage over it. In fact, this venerable survival had formed between them a friendship of casual roadside quality.

Afterward Peter went on up the road. He continued to chuckle until he was far away. He was going to pay a visit to old Alek Williams, a negro who lived with a large family in a hut clinging to the side of a mountain. The scattered colony of negroes which hovered near Whilomville was of interesting origin, being the result of some contrabands who had drifted as far north as Whilomville during the great civil war. The descendants of these adventurers were mainly conspicuous for their bewildering number and the facility which they possessed for adding even to this number. Speaking, for example, of the Jacksons—one couldn't hurl a stone into the hills about Whilomville without having it land on the roof of a hut full of Jacksons. The town reaped little in labour from these curious suburbs. There were a few men who came in regularly to work in gardens, to drive teams, to care for horses, and there were a few women who came in to cook or to wash. These latter had usually drunken husbands. In the main the colony loafed in high spirits, and the industrious minority gained no direct honour from their fellows, unless they spent their earnings on raiment, in which case they were naturally treated with distinction. On the whole, the hardships of these people were the wind, the rain, the snow, and any other physical difficulties which they could cultivate. About twice a year the lady philanthropists of Whilomville went up against them, and came away poorer in goods but rich in complacence. After one of these attacks the colony would preserve a comic air of rectitude for two days, and then relapse again to the genial irresponsibility of a crew of monkeys.

Peter Washington was one of the industrious class who occupied a position of distinction, for he surely spent his money on personal decoration. On occasion he would dress better than the Mayor of Whilomville himself, or at least in more colours, which was the main thing to the minds of his admirers. His ideal had been the late gallant Henry Johnson, whose conquests in Watermelon Alley, as well as in the hill shanties, had proved him the equal if not the superior of any Pullman car porter in the country. Perhaps Peter had too much Virginia laziness and humour in him to be a wholly adequate successor to the fastidious Henry Johnson, but, at any rate, he admired his memory so attentively as to be openly termed a dude by envious people.

On this afternoon he was going to call on old Alek Williams because Alek's eldest girl was just turned seventeen and, to Peter's mind, was a triumph of beauty. He was not wearing his best clothes, because on his last visit Alek's half-breed hound Susie had taken occasion to forcefully extract a quite large and valuable part of the visitor's trousers. When Peter arrived at the end of the rocky field which contained old Alek's shanty he stooped and provided himself with several large stones, weighing them carefully in his hand, and finally continuing his journey with three stones of about eight ounces each. When he was near the house, three gaunt hounds, Rover and Carlo and Susie, came sweeping down upon him. His impression was that they were going to climb him as if he were a tree, but at the critical moment they swerved and went growling and snapping around him, their heads low, their eyes malignant. The afternoon caller waited until Susie presented her side to him; then he heaved one of his eight-ounce rocks. When it landed, her hollow ribs gave forth a drum-like sound, and she was knocked sprawling, her legs in the air. The other hounds at once fled in horror, and she followed as soon as she was able, yelping at the top of her lungs. The afternoon caller resumed his march.

At the wild expressions of Susie's anguish old Alek had flung open the door and come hastily into the sunshine. "Yah, you Suse, come erlong outa dat now. What fer you— Oh, how do, how do, Mist' Wash'ton—how do?"

"How do, Mist' Willums? I done foun' it necessa'y fer ter damnearkill dish yer dawg a' yourn, Mist' Willums."

"Come in, come in, Mist' Wash'ton. Dawg no'count, Mist' Wash'ton." Then he turned to address the unfortunate animal. "Hu't, did it? Hu't? 'Pears like you gwine lun some saince by time somebody brek yer back. 'Pears like I gwine club yer inter er frazzle 'fore you fin' out some saince. G'w'on 'way f'm yah!"

As the old man and his guest entered the shanty a body of black children spread out in crescent-shape formation and observed Peter with awe. Fat old Mrs. Williams greeted him turbulently, while the eldest girl, Mollie, lurked in a corner and giggled with finished imbecility, gazing at the visitor with eyes that were shy and bold by turns. She seemed at times absurdly over-confident, at times foolishly afraid; but her giggle consistently endured. It was a giggle on which an irascible but right-minded judge would have ordered her forthwith to be buried alive.

Amid a great deal of hospitable gabbling, Peter was conducted to the best chair out of the three that the house contained. Enthroned therein, he made himself charming in talk to the old people, who beamed upon him joyously. As for Mollie, he affected to be unaware of her existence. This may have been a method for entrapping the sentimental interest of that young gazelle, or it may be that the giggle had worked upon him.

He was absolutely fascinating to the old people. They could talk like rotary snow-ploughs, and he gave them every chance, while his face was illumined with appreciation. They pressed him to stay for supper, and he consented, after a glance at the pot on the stove which was too furtive to be noted.

During the meal old Alek recounted the high state of Judge Hagenthorpe's kitchen garden, which Alek said was due to his unremitting industry and fine intelligence. Alek was a gardener, whenever impending starvation forced him to cease temporarily from being a lily of the field.

"Mist' Bryant he suhtainly got er grand gawden," observed Peter.

"Dat so, dat so, Mist' Wash'ton," assented Alek. "He got fine gawden."

"Seems like I nev' *did* see sech mellums, big as er bar'l, layin' dere. I don't raikon an'body in dish yer county kin hol' it with Mist' Bryant when comes ter mellums."

"Dat so, Mist' Wash'ton."

They did not talk of watermelons until their heads held nothing else, as the phrase goes. But they talked of watermelons until, when Peter started for home that night over a lonely road, they held a certain dominant position in his mind. Alek had come with him as far as the fence, in order to protect him from possible attack by the mongrels. There they had cheerfully parted, two honest men.

The night was dark, and heavy with moisture. Peter found it uncomfortable to walk rapidly. He merely loitered on the road. When opposite Si Bryant's place he paused and looked over the fence into the garden. He imagined he could see the form of a huge melon lying in dim stateliness not ten yards away. He looked at the Bryant house. Two windows, downstairs, were lighted. The Bryants kept no dog, old Si's favourite child having once been bitten by a dog, and having since died, within that year, of pneumonia.

Peering over the fence, Peter fancied that if any low-minded night prowler should happen to note the melon, he would not find it difficult to possess himself of it. This person would merely wait until the lights were out in the house, and the people presumably asleep. Then he would climb the fence, reach the melon in a few strides, sever the stem with his ready knife, and in a trice be back in the road with his prize. There need be no noise, and, after all, the house was some distance.

Selecting a smooth bit of turf, Peter took a seat by the roadside. From time to time he glanced at the lighted window.

II

When Peter and Alek had said good-bye, the old man turned back in the rocky field and shaped a slow course

toward that high dim light which marked the little window
of his shanty. It would be incorrect to say that Alek could
think of nothing but watermelons. But it was true that Si
Bryant's watermelon patch occupied a certain conspicuous
position in his thoughts.

He sighed; he almost wished that he was again a con-
scienceless pickaninny, instead of being one of the most
ornate, solemn, and look-at-me-sinner deacons that ever
graced the handle of a collection basket. At this time it
made him quite sad to reflect upon his granite integrity.
A weaker man might perhaps bow his moral head to the
temptation, but for him such a fall was impossible. He
was a prince of the church, and if he had been nine princes
of the church he could not have been more proud. In
fact, religion was to the old man a sort of personal dignity. And he was on Sundays so obtrusively good that you
could see his sanctity through a door. He forced it on you
until you would have felt its influence even in a fore-
castle.

It was clear in his mind that he must put watermelon
thoughts from him, and after a moment he told himself,
with much ostentation, that he had done so. But it was
cooler under the sky than in the shanty, and as he was
not sleepy, he decided to take a stroll down to Si Bryant's
place and look at the melons from a pinnacle of spotless
innocence. Reaching the road, he paused to listen. It would
not do to let Peter hear him, because that graceless rapscal-
lion would probably misunderstand him. But, assuring himself that Peter was well on his way, he set out, walking
briskly until he was within four hundred yards of Bryant's
place. Here he went to the side of the road, and walked
thereafter on the damp, yielding turf. He made no sound.

He did not go on to that point in the main road which
was directly opposite the watermelon patch. He did not
wish to have his ascetic contemplation disturbed by some
chance wayfarer. He turned off along a short lane which
led to Si Bryant's barn. Here he reached a place where
he could see, over the fence, the faint shapes of the melons.

Alek was affected. The house was some distance away,

there was no dog, and doubtless the Bryants would soon
extinguish their lights and go to bed. Then some poor lost
lamb of sin might come and scale the fence, reach a
melon in a moment, sever the stem with his ready knife,
and in a trice be back in the road with his prize. And this
poor lost lamb of sin might even be a bishop, but no one
would ever know it. Alek singled out with his eye a very
large melon, and thought that the lamb would prove his
judgment if he took that one.

He found a soft place in the grass, and arranged himself comfortably. He watched the lights in the windows.

III

It seemed to Peter Washington that the Bryants absolutely
consulted their own wishes in regard to the time for re-
tiring; but at last he saw the lighted windows fade briskly
from left to right, and after a moment a window on the
second floor blazed out against the darkness. Si was going
to bed. In five minutes this window abruptly vanished, and
all the world was night.

Peter spent the ensuing quarter-hour in no mental de-
bate. His mind was fixed. He was here, and the melon
was there. He would have it. But an idea of being caught
appalled him. He thought of his position. He was the beau
of his community, honoured right and left. He pictured
the consternation of his friends and the cheers of his enemies if the hands of the redoubtable Si Bryant should
grip him in his shame.

He arose and, going to the fence, listened. No sound
broke the stillness, save the rhythmical incessant clicking
of myriad insects and the guttural chanting of the frogs
in the reeds at the lake-side. Moved by sudden decision,
he climbed the fence and crept silently and swiftly down
upon the melon. His open knife was in his hand. There
was the melon, cool, fair to see, as pompous in its fatness
as the cook in a monastery.

Peter put out a hand to steady it while he cut the stem.
But at the instant he was aware that a black form had

dropped over the fence lining the lane in front of him and was coming stealthily toward him. In a palsy of terror he dropped flat upon the ground, not having strength enough to run away. The next moment he was looking into the amazed and agonized face of old Alek Williams.

There was a moment of loaded silence, and then Peter was overcome by a mad inspiration. He suddenly dropped his knife and leaped upon Alek. "I got che!" he hissed. "I got che! I got che!" The old man sank down as limp as rags. "I got che! I got che! Steal Mist' Bryant's mellums, hey?"

Alek, in a low voice, began to beg. "Oh, Mist' Peter Wash'ton, don' go fer ter be too ha'd on er ole man! I nev' come yere fer ter steal 'em. 'Deed I didn't, Mist' Wash'ton! I come yere jes fer ter *feel* 'em. Oh, please, Mist' Wash'ton—"

"Come erlong outa yere, you ol' rip," said Peter, "an' don' trumple on dese yer baids. I gwine put you w'ah you won' ketch col'."

Without difficulty he tumbled the whining Alek over the fence to the roadway and followed him with sheriff-like expedition. He took him by the scruff. "Come erlong, deacon. I raikon I gwine put you w'ah you kin pray, deacon. Come erlong, deacon."

The emphasis and reiteration of his layman's title in the church produced a deadly effect upon Alek. He felt to his marrow the heinous crime into which this treacherous night had betrayed him. As Peter marched his prisoner up the road toward the mouth of the lane, he continued his remarks: "Come erlong, deacon. Nev' see er man so anxious-like erbout er mellum-paitch, deacon. Seem like you jes' must see 'em er-growin' an' *feel* 'em, deacon. Mist' Bryant he'll be s'prised, deacon, findin' out you come fer ter *feel* his mellums. Come erlong, deacon. Mist' Bryant he expectin' some ole rip like you come soon."

They had almost reached the lane when Alek's cur Susie, who had followed her master, approached in the silence which attends dangerous dogs; and seeing indications of what she took to be war, she appended herself swiftly but firmly to the calf of Peter's left leg. The mêlée was short, but spirited. Alek had no wish to have his dog complicate his already serious misfortunes, and went manfully to the defence of his captor. He procured a large stone, and by beating this with both hands down upon the resounding skull of the animal, he induced her to quit her grip. Breathing heavily, Peter dropped into the long grass at the roadside. He said nothing.

"Mist' Wash'ton," said Alek at last, in a quavering voice, "I raikon I gwine wait yere see what you gwine do ter me."

Whereupon Peter passed into a spasmodic state, in which he rolled to and fro and shook.

"Mist' Wash'ton, I hope dish yer dog ain't gone an' give you fitses?"

Peter sat up suddenly. "No, she ain't," he answered; "but she gin me er big skeer; an' fer yer 'sistance with er cobblestone, Mist' Willums, I tell you what I gwine do— I tell you what I gwine do." He waited an impressive moment. "I gwine 'lease you!"

Old Alek trembled like a little bush in a wind. "Mist' Wash'ton?"

Quoth Peter, deliberately, "I gwine 'lease you."

The old man was filled with a desire to negotiate this statement at once, but he felt the necessity of carrying off the event without an appearance of haste. "Yes, seh; thank 'e, seh; thank 'e, Mist' Wash'ton. I raikon I ramble home pressenly."

He waited an interval, and then dubiously said, "Good-evenin', Mist' Wash'ton."

"Good-evenin', deacon. Don' come foolin' roun' *feelin'* no mellums, and I say troof. Good-evenin', deacon."

Alek took off his hat and made three profound bows. "Thank 'e, seh. Thank 'e, seh. Thank 'e, seh."

Peter underwent another severe spasm, but the old man walked off toward his home with a humble and contrite heart.

IV

The next morning Alek proceeded from his shanty under
the complete but customary illusion that he was going to
work. He trudged manfully along until he reached the
vicinity of Si Bryant's place. Then, by stages, he relapsed
into a slink. He was passing the garden patch under full
steam when, at some distance ahead of him, he saw Si
Bryant leaning casually on the garden fence.

"Good-mornin', Alek."

"Good-mawnin', Mist' Bryant," answered Alek, with a
new deference. He was marching on, when he was halted
by a word—"Alek!"

He stopped. "Yes, seh."

"I found a knife this mornin' in th' road," drawled Si,
"an' I thought maybe it was yourn."

Improved in mind by this divergence from the direct
line of attack, Alek stepped up easily to look at the knife.
"No, seh," he said, scanning it as it lay in Si's palm, while
the cold steel-blue eyes of the white man looked down
into his stomach, " 'tain't no knife er mine." But he knew
the knife. He knew it as if it had been his mother. And
at the same moment a spark flashed through his head and
made wise his understanding. He knew everything. " 'Tain't
much of er knife, Mist' Bryant," he said, deprecatingly.

" 'Tain't much of a knife, I know that," cried Si, in sudden heat, "but I found it this mornin' in my watermelon
patch—hear?"

"Watahmellum paitch?" yelled Alek, not astounded.

"Yes, in my watermelon patch," sneered Si, "an' I think
you know something about it, too!"

"Me?" cried Alek. "Me?"

"Yes—you!" said Si, with icy ferocity. "Yes—you!" He
had become convinced that Alek was not in any way
guilty, but he was certain that the old man knew the owner
of the knife, and so he pressed him at first on criminal
lines. "Alek, you might as well own up now. You've been
meddlin' with my watermelons!"

"Me?" cried Alek again. "Yah's *ma* knife. I done cah'e it foh yeahs."

Bryant changed his ways. "Look here, Alek," he said, confidentially: "I know you and you know me, and there ain't no use in any more skirmishin'. *I* know that *you* know whose knife that is. Now whose is it?"

This challenge was so formidable in character that Alek temporarily quailed and began to stammer. "Er—now— Mist' Bryant—you—you—frien' er mine—"

"I know I'm a friend of yours, but," said Bryant, in-exorably, "who owns this knife?"

Alek gathered unto himself some remnants of dignity and spoke with reproach: "Mist' Bryant, dish yer knife ain' mine."

"No," said Bryant, "it ain't. But you know who it be-longs to, an' I want you to tell me—quick."

"Well, Mist' Bryant," answered Alek, scratching his wool, "I won't say 's I *do* know who b'longs ter dish yer knife, an' I won't say 's I *don't*."

Bryant again laughed his Yankee laugh, but this time there was little humour in it. It was dangerous.

Alek, seeing that he had got himself into hot water by the fine diplomacy of his last sentence, immediately began to flounder and totally submerge himself. "No, Mist' Bry-ant," he repeated, "I won't say 's I *do* know who b'longs ter dish yer knife, an' I won't say 's I *don't*." And he began to parrot this fatal sentence again and again. It seemed wound about his tongue. He could not rid himself of it. Its very power to make trouble for him seemed to originate the mysterious Afric reason for its repetition.

"Is he a very close friend of yourn?" said Bryant, softly.

"F-frien'?" stuttered Alek. He appeared to weigh this question with much care. "Well, seems like he *was* er frien', an' then agin, it seems like he—"

"It seems like he *wasn't?*" asked Bryant.

"Yes, seh, jest so, jest so," cried Alek. "Sometimes it seems like he *wasn't*. Then again—" He stopped for pro-found meditation.

The patience of the white man seemed inexhaustible. At length his low and oily voice broke the stillness. "Oh, well, of course if he's a friend of yourn, Alek! You know I wouldn't want to make no trouble for a friend of yourn."

"Yes, seh," cried the negro at once. "He's er frien' er mine. He is dat."

"Well, then, it seems as if about the only thing to do is for you to tell me his name so's I can send him his knife, and that's all there is to it."

Alek took off his hat, and in perplexity ran his hand over his wool. He studied the ground. But several times he raised his eyes to take a sly peep at the imperturbable visage of the white man. "Y-y-yes, Mist' Bryant.—I raikon dat's erbout all what kin be done. I gwine tell you who b'longs ter dish yer knife."

"Of course," said the smooth Bryant, "it ain't a very nice thing to have to do, but—"

"No, seh," cried Alek, brightly; "I'm gwine tell you, Mist' Bryant. I gwine tell you erbout dat knife. Mist' Bryant," he asked, solemnly, "does you know who b'longs ter dat knife?"

"No, I—"

"Well, I gwine tell. I gwine tell who. Mist' Bryant—" The old man drew himself to a stately pose and held forth his arm. "I gwine tell who. Mist' Bryant, *dish yer knife b'longs ter Sam Jackson!*"

Bryant was startled into indignation. "Who in hell is Sam Jackson?" he growled.

"He's a nigger," said Alek, impressively, "and he wuks in er lumber-yawd up yere in Hoswego."

HIS NEW MITTENS

I

LITTLE Horace was walking home from school, brilliantly decorated by a pair of new red mittens. A number of boys were snowballing gleefully in a field. They hailed him. "Come on, Horace! We're having a battle."

Horace was sad. "No," he said, "I can't. I've got to go home." At noon his mother had admonished him: "Now, Horace, you come straight home as soon as school is out. Do you hear? And don't you get them nice new mittens all wet, either. Do you hear?" Also his aunt had said: "I declare, Emily, it's a shame the way you allow that child to ruin his things." She had meant mittens. To his mother, Horace had dutifully replied, "Yes'm." But he now loitered in the vicinity of the group of uproarious boys, who were yelling like hawks as the white balls flew.

Some of them immediately analysed this extraordinary hesitancy. "Hah!" they paused to scoff, "afraid of your new mittens, ain't you?" Some smaller boys, who were not yet so wise in discerning motives, applauded this attack with unreasonable vehemence. "A-fray-ed of his mit-tens! A-fray-ed of his mit-tens." They sang these lines to cruel and monotonous music which is as old perhaps as American childhood, and which it is the privilege of the emancipated adult to completely forget. "A-fray-ed of his mittens!"

Horace cast a tortured glance toward his playmates and then dropped his eyes to the snow at his feet. Presently he turned to the trunk of one of the great maple trees that lined the curb. He made a pretence of closely examining the rough and virile bark. To his mind, this familiar street of Whilomville seemed to grow dark in the thick shadow of shame. The trees and the houses were now palled in purple.

"A-fray-ed of his mit-tens!" The terrible music had in it a meaning from the moonlit war-drums of chanting cannibals.

At last Horace, with supreme effort, raised his head. " 'Tain't them I care about," he said, gruffly. "I've got to go home. That's all."

Whereupon each boy held his left forefinger as if it were a pencil and began to sharpen it derisively with his right forefinger. They came closer, and sang like a trained chorus, "A-fray-ed of his mittens!"

When he raised his voice to deny the charge it was simply lost in the screams of the mob. He was alone, fronting all the traditions of boyhood held before him by inexorable representatives. To such a low state had he fallen that one lad, a mere baby, outflanked him and then struck him in the cheek with a heavy snowball. The act was acclaimed with loud jeers. Horace turned to dart at his assailant, but there was an immediate demonstration on the other flank, and he found himself obliged to keep his face toward the hilarious crew of tormentors. The baby retreated in safety to the rear of the crowd, where he was received with fulsome compliments upon his daring. Horace retreated slowly up the walk. He continually tried to make them heed him, but the only sound was the chant, "A-fray-ed of his mittens!" In this desperate withdrawal the beset and haggard boy suffered more than is the common lot of man.

Being a boy himself, he did not understand boys at all. He had, of course, the dismal conviction that they were going to dog him to his grave. But near the corner of the field they suddenly seemed to forget all about it. Indeed, they possessed only the malevolence of so many flitterheaded sparrows. The interest had swung capriciously to some other matter. In a moment they were off in the field again, carousing amid the snow. Some authoritative boy had probably said, "Aw, come on!"

As the pursuit ceased, Horace ceased his retreat. He spent some time in what was evidently an attempt to ad-

just his self-respect, and then began to wander furtively
down toward the group. He, too, had undergone an important change. Perhaps his sharp agony was only as dura-
ble as the malevolence of the others. In this boyish life
obedience to some unformulated creed of manners was
enforced with capricious but merciless rigour. However,
they were, after all, his comrades, his friends.

They did not heed his return. They were engaged in an
altercation. It had evidently been planned that this battle
was between Indians and soldiers. The smaller and weaker
boys had been induced to appear as Indians in the initial
skirmish, but they were now very sick of it, and were re-
luctantly but steadfastly affirming their desire for a change
of caste. The larger boys had all won great distinction,
devastating Indians materially, and they wished the war
to go on as planned. They explained vociferously that it
was proper for the soldiers always to thrash the Indians.
The little boys did not pretend to deny the truth of this
argument; they confined themselves to the simple statement that, in that case, they wished to be soldiers. Each
little boy willingly appealed to the others to remain Indians, but as for himself he reiterated his desire to enlist
as a soldier. The larger boys were in despair over this
dearth of enthusiasm in the small Indians. They alternately
wheedled and bullied, but they could not persuade the
little boys, who were really suffering dreadful humiliation
rather than submit to another onslaught of soldiers. They
were called all the baby names that had the power of
stinging deep into their pride, but they remained firm.

Then a formidable lad, a leader of reputation, one who
could whip many boys that wore long trousers, suddenly
blew out his cheeks and shouted, "Well, all right then. I'll
be an Indian myself. Now." The little boys greeted with
cheers this addition to their wearied ranks, and seemed
then content. But matters were not mended in the least,
because all the personal following of the formidable lad,
with the addition of every outsider, spontaneously forsook
the flag and declared themselves Indians. There were now
no soldiers. The Indians had carried everything unani-

mously. The formidable lad used his influence, but his influence could not shake the loyalty of his friends, who
refused to fight under any colours but his colours.

Plainly there was nothing for it but to coerce the little
ones. The formidable lad again became a soldier, and then
graciously permitted to join him all the real fighting
strength of the crowd, leaving behind a most forlorn band
of little Indians. Then the soldiers attacked the Indians,
exhorting them to opposition at the same time.

The Indians at first adopted a policy of hurried surrender, but this had no success, as none of the surrenders
were accepted. They then turned to flee, bawling out protests. The ferocious soldiers pursued them amid shouts.
The battle widened, developing all manner of marvellous
detail.

Horace had turned toward home several times, but, as
a matter of fact, this scene held him in a spell. It was
fascinating beyond anything which the grown man understands. He had always in the back of his head a sense of
guilt, even a sense of impending punishment for disobe-
dience, but they could not weigh with the delirium of this
snow-battle.

II

One of the raiding soldiers, espying Horace, called out in
passing, "A-fray-ed of his mit-tens!" Horace flinched at
this renewal, and the other lad paused to taunt him again.
Horace scooped some snow, moulded it into a ball, and
flung it at the other. "Ho!" cried the boy, "you're an Indian, are you? Hey, fellers, here's an Indian that ain't been
killed yet." He and Horace engaged in a duel in which
both were in such haste to mould snowballs that they had
little time for aiming.

Horace once struck his opponent squarely in the chest.
"Hey," he shouted, "you're dead. You can't fight any
more, Pete. I killed you. You're dead."

The other boy flushed red, but he continued frantically
to make ammunition. "You never touched me!" he re-

torted, glowering. "You never touched me! Where, now?"
he added, defiantly. "Where did you hit me?"

"On the coat! Right on your breast! You can't fight any
more! You're dead!"

"You never!"

"I did, too! Hey, fellers, ain't he dead? I hit 'im square!"

"He never!"

Nobody had seen the affair, but some of the boys took
sides in absolute accordance with their friendship for one
of the concerned parties. Horace's opponent went about
contending, "He never touched me! He never came near
me! He never came near me!"

The formidable leader now came forward and accosted
Horace. "What was you? An Indian? Well, then, you're
dead—that's all. He hit you. I saw him."

"Me?" shrieked Horace. "He never came within a mile
of me—"

At that moment he heard his name called in a certain
familiar tune of two notes, with the last note shrill and
prolonged. He looked toward the sidewalk, and saw his
mother standing there in her widow's weeds, with two
brown paper parcels under her arm. A silence had fallen
upon all the boys. Horace moved slowly toward his
mother. She did not seem to note his approach; she was
gazing austerely off through the naked branches of the
maples where two crimson sunset bars lay on the deep
blue sky.

At a distance of ten paces Horace made a desperate
venture. "Oh, ma," he whined, "can't I stay out for a
while?"

"No," she answered solemnly, "you come with me."
Horace knew that profile; it was the inexorable profile. But
he continued to plead, because it was not beyond his mind
that a great show of suffering now might diminish his
suffering later.

He did not dare to look back at his playmates. It was
already a public scandal that he could not stay out as late
as other boys, and he could imagine his standing now that

he had been again dragged off by his mother in sight of the whole world. He was a profoundly miserable human being.

Aunt Martha opened the door for them. Light streamed about her straight skirt. "Oh," she said, "so you found him on the road, eh? Well, I declare! It was about time!"

Horace slunk into the kitchen. The stove, straddling out on its four iron legs, was gently humming. Aunt Martha had evidently just lighted the lamp, for she went to it and began to twist the wick experimentally.

"Now," said the mother, "let's see them mittens."

Horace's chin sank. The aspiration of the criminal, the passionate desire for an asylum from retribution, from justice, was aflame in his heart. "I—I—don't—don't know where they are," he gasped finally, as he passed his hand over his pockets.

"Horace," intoned his mother, "you are tellin' me a story!"

" 'Tain't a story," he answered, just above his breath. He looked like a sheep-stealer.

His mother held him by the arm, and began to search his pockets. Almost at once she was able to bring forth a pair of very wet mittens. "Well, I declare!" cried Aunt Martha. The two women went close to the lamp, and minutely examined the mittens, turning them over and over. Afterward, when Horace looked up, his mother's sad-lined, homely face was turned toward him. He burst into tears.

His mother drew a chair near the stove. "Just you sit there now, until I tell you to git off." He sidled meekly into the chair. His mother and his aunt went briskly about the business of preparing supper. They did not display a knowledge of his existence; they carried an effect of oblivion so far that they even did not speak to each other. Presently they went into the dining- and living-room; Horace could hear the dishes rattling. His Aunt Martha brought a plate of food, placed it on a chair near him, and went away without a word.

Horace instantly decided that he would not touch a morsel of the food. He had often used this ruse in dealing with his mother. He did not know why it brought her to terms, but certainly it sometimes did.

The mother looked up when the aunt returned to the other room. "Is he eatin' his supper?" she asked.

The maiden aunt, fortified in ignorance, gazed with pity and contempt upon this interest. "Well, now, Emily, how do I know?" she queried. "Was I goin' to stand over 'im? Of all the worryin' you do about that child! It's a shame the way you're bringin' up that child."

"Well, he ought to eat somethin'. It won't do fer him to go without eatin'," the mother retorted weakly.

Aunt Martha, profoundly scorning the policy of concession which these words meant, uttered a long, contemptuous sigh.

III

Alone in the kitchen, Horace stared with sombre eyes at the plate of food. For a long time he betrayed no sign of yielding. His mood was adamantine. He was resolved not to sell his vengeance for bread, cold ham, and a pickle, and yet it must be known that the sight of them affected him powerfully. The pickle in particular was notable for its seductive charm. He surveyed it darkly.

But at last, unable to longer endure his state, his attitude in the presence of the pickle, he put out an inquisitive finger and touched it, and it was cool and green and plump. Then a full conception of the cruel woe of his situation swept upon him suddenly, and his eyes filled with tears, which began to move down his cheeks. He sniffled. His heart was black with hatred. He painted in his mind scenes of deadly retribution. His mother would be taught that he was not one to endure persecution meekly, without raising an arm in his defence. And so his dreams were of a slaughter of feelings, and near the end of them his mother was pictured as coming, bowed with pain, to his feet. Weeping, she implored his charity. Would he forgive her? No; his once tender heart had been turned to stone by her injustice. He could not forgive her. She must pay the inexorable penalty.

The first item in this horrible plan was the refusal of the food. This he knew by experience would work havoc in his mother's heart. And so he grimly waited.

But suddenly it occurred to him that the first part of his revenge was in danger of failing. The thought struck him that his mother might not capitulate in the usual way. According to his recollection, the time was more than due when she should come in, worried, sadly affectionate, and ask him if he was ill. It had then been his custom to hint in a resigned voice that he was the victim of secret disease, but that he preferred to suffer in silence and alone. If she was obdurate in her anxiety, he always asked her in a gloomy, low voice to go away and leave him to suffer in silence and alone in the darkness without food. He had known this manœuvring to result even in pie.

But what was the meaning of the long pause and the stillness? Had his old and valued ruse betrayed him? As the truth sank into his mind, he supremely loathed life, the world, his mother. Her heart was beating back the besiegers; he was a defeated child.

He wept for a time before deciding upon the final stroke. He would run away. In a remote corner of the world he would become some sort of bloody-handed person driven to a life of crime by the barbarity of his mother. She should never know his fate. He would torture her for years with doubts and doubts, and drive her implacably to a repentant grave. Nor would his Aunt Martha escape. Some day, a century hence, when his mother was dead, he would write to his Aunt Martha, and point out her part in the blighting of his life. For one blow against him now he would, in time, deal back a thousand—ay, ten thousand.

He arose and took his coat and cap. As he moved stealthily toward the door he cast a glance backward at the pickle. He was tempted to take it, but he knew that if he left the plate inviolate his mother would feel even worse.

A blue snow was falling. People, bowed forward, were moving briskly along the walks. The electric lamps hummed amid showers of flakes. As Horace emerged from the kitchen, a shrill squall drove the flakes around the corner of the house. He cowered away from it, and its violence illumined his mind vaguely in new directions. He deliberated upon a choice of remote corners of the globe. He found that he had no plans which were definite enough in a geographical way, but without much loss of time he decided upon California. He moved briskly as far as his mother's front gate on the road to California. He was off at last. His success was a trifle dreadful; his throat choked.

But at the gate he paused. He did not know if his journey to California would be shorter if he went down Niagara Avenue or off through Hogan Street. As the storm was very cold and the point was very important, he decided to withdraw for reflection to the wood-shed. He entered the dark shanty, and took seat upon the old chopping-block upon which he was supposed to perform for a few minutes every afternoon when he returned from school. The wind screamed and shouted at the loose boards, and there was a rift of snow on the floor to leeward of a crack.

Here the idea of starting for California on such a night departed from his mind, leaving him ruminating miserably upon his martyrdom. He saw nothing for it but to sleep all night in the wood-shed and start for California in the morning bright and early. Thinking of his bed, he kicked over the floor and found that the innumerable chips were all frozen tightly, bedded in ice.

Later he viewed with joy some signs of excitement in the house. The flare of a lamp moved rapidly from window to window. Then the kitchen door slammed loudly and a shawled figure sped toward the gate. At last he was making them feel his power. The shivering child's face was lit with saturnine glee as in the darkness of the wood-shed he gloated over the evidences of consternation in his home. The shawled figure had been his Aunt Martha dashing with the alarm to the neighbours.

The cold of the wood-shed was tormenting him. He endured only because of the terror he was causing. But then it occurred to him that, if they instituted a search for him, they would probably examine the wood-shed. He knew that it would not be manful to be caught so soon. He was not positive now that he was going to remain away for ever, but at any rate he was bound to inflict some more damage before allowing himself to be captured. If he merely succeeded in making his mother angry, she would thrash him on sight. He must prolong the time in order to be safe. If he held out properly, he was sure of a welcome of love, even though he should drip with crimes.

Evidently the storm had increased, for when he went out it swung him violently with its rough and merciless strength. Panting, stung, half blinded with the driving flakes, he was now a waif, exiled, friendless, and poor. With a bursting heart, he thought of his home and his mother. To his forlorn vision they were as far away as heaven.

IV

Horace was undergoing changes of feeling so rapidly that he was merely moved hither and then thither like a kite. He was now aghast at the merciless ferocity of his mother. It was she who had thrust him into this wild storm, and she was perfectly indifferent to his fate, perfectly indifferent. The forlorn wanderer could no longer weep. The strong sobs caught at his throat, making his breath come in short, quick snuffles. All in him was conquered save the enigmatical childish ideal of form, manner. This principle still held out, and it was the only thing between him and submission. When he surrendered, he must surrender in a way that deferred to the undefined code. He longed simply to go to the kitchen and stumble in, but his unfathomable sense of fitness forbade him.

Presently he found himself at the head of Niagara Avenue, staring through the snow into the blazing windows of Stickney's butcher-shop. Stickney was the family butcher, not so much because of a superiority to other Whilomville butchers as because he lived next door and had been an intimate friend of the father of Horace. Rows of glowing pigs hung head downward behind the tables, which bore huge pieces of red beef. Clumps of attenuated turkeys were suspended here and there. Stickney, hale and smiling, was bantering with a woman in a cloak, who, with a monster basket on her arm, was dickering for eight cents' worth of something. Horace watched them through a crusted pane. When the woman came out and passed him, he went toward the door. He touched the latch with his finger, but withdrew again suddenly to the sidewalk. Inside Stickney was whistling cheerily and assorting his knives.

Finally Horace went desperately forward, opened the door, and entered the shop. His head hung low. Stickney stopped whistling. "Hello, young man," he cried; "what brings you here?"

Horace halted, but said nothing. He swung one foot to and fro over the sawdust floor.

Stickney had placed his two fat hands palms downward and wide apart on the table, in the attitude of a butcher facing a customer, but now he straightened. "Here," he said, "what's wrong? What's wrong, kid?"

"Nothin'," answered Horace, huskily. He laboured for a moment with something in his throat, and afterwards added, "O'ny—I've—I've run away, and—"

"Run away!" shouted Stickney. "Run away from what? Who?"

"From—home," answered Horace. "I don't like it there any more. I—" He had arranged an oration to win the sympathy of the butcher; he had prepared a table setting forth the merits of his case in the most logical fashion, but it was as if the wind had been knocked out of his mind. "I've run away. I—"

Stickney reached an enormous hand over the array of beef, and firmly grappled the emigrant. Then he swung himself to Horace's side. His face was stretched with laughter, and he playfully shook his prisoner. "Come— come—come. What dashed nonsense is this? Run away, hey? Run away?" Whereupon the child's long-tried spirit found vent in howls.

"Come, come," said Stickney, busily. "Never mind now, never mind. You just come along with me. It'll be all right. I'll fix it. Never you mind."

Five minutes later the butcher, with a great ulster over his apron, was leading the boy homeward.

At the very threshold, Horace raised his last flag of pride. "No—no," he sobbed. "I don't want to. I don't want to go in there." He braced his foot against the step and made a very respectable resistance.

"Now, Horace," cried the butcher. He thrust open the door with a bang. "Hello there!" Across the dark kitchen the door to the living-room opened and Aunt Martha appeared. "You've found him!" she screamed.

"We've come to make a call," roared the butcher. At the entrance to the living-room a silence fell upon them all. Upon a couch Horace saw his mother lying limp, pale as death, her eyes gleaming with pain. There was an electric pause before she swung a waxen hand toward Horace. "My child," she murmured, tremulously. Whereupon the sinister person addressed, with a prolonged wail of grief and joy, ran to her with speed. "Mam-ma! Mam-ma! Oh, mam-ma!" She was not able to speak in a known tongue as she folded him in her weak arms.

Aunt Martha turned defiantly upon the butcher, because her face betrayed her. She was crying. She made a gesture half military, half feminine. "Won't you have a glass of our root-beer, Mr. Stickney? We make it ourselves."

BIBLIOGRAPHY

Several Crane bibliographies have been published: in 1923 by Vincent Starrett, in 1930 by B. J. R. Stolper, and in 1948 by Ames W. Williams and Vincent Starrett: *Stephen Crane: A Bibliography* (Glendale, Calif.: John Valentine).[1] The Williams-Starrett bibliography lists 114 biographical or bibliographical writings about Crane; most of this material has to do with the life; almost nothing is represented from surveys of American literature and critical studies of modern fiction; and several important biographical pieces are neglected. The critical pieces in this bibliography consist chiefly of contemporary reviews (1893–1900), numbering 115 in all. Of these the best are George Wyndham's exposition of *The Red Badge* in the *New Review*, 14 (January 1896), 30, and the *Critic*, 24 (November 30, 1895), 363, and H. G. Wells's summary of Crane in the *North American Review* (August 1900), CLXXI, 233–42.

I Novels, Short Stories, and Poems

1893 *Maggie: A Girl of the Streets: A Story of New York*. [Written in December 1891 and published, at the author's expense, under the pseudonym "Johnston Smith," in yellow paper wrappers. Not until the 1896 edition did *Maggie* appear in regular binding and with Crane's name.]

1895 *The Black Riders and Other Lines*. [Poems.]

The Red Badge of Courage: An Episode of the American Civil War. [Published in October by Appleton and in England by Heinemann, in December—in the week of November 30, 1895. Heinemann published it in the Pioneer Series in a paper-wrapper edition and in a cloth-bound book with the title-page dated 1896. There were fourteen American printings in 1896.]

1896 *George's Mother*. [Ames Williams says that "prior to publication Crane tentatively called this work *A Woman Without Weapons*."]

Maggie. [Published by Appleton and by Heinemann. Reprinted by Heinemann in *Bowery Tales*, 1900; in *Maggie and Other Stories*, edited by Henry Hazlitt, Knopf, 1931; in a Modern Library edition, by Vincent Starrett, 1933; in *Twenty Stories*, edited by Carl Van Doren, Knopf, 1940; in *Great Short American Novels*, edited by William Phillips, Dial Press, 1946; and in *Selected Prose and Poetry*, edited by W. M. Gibson, Rinehart, 1950. *Maggie* appeared with *George's Mother* in Bowery

---

[1] In addition to these three books there are check-lists on Crane in *Stephen Crane and the Stephen Crane Association* (1926); in *Bulletin of Bibliography* (1935), check-list of Crane's short stories and essays compiled by Claude Jones; and in the *Literary History of the United States* (1948), III, 458–61.

Tales and in Hazlitt's edition: *Maggie together with George's Mother and The Blue Hotel.*]

The Little Regiment and Other Episodes of the American Civil War. [Published by Appleton and the next year by Heinemann. It was issued, like *The Red Badge*, both in cloth binding and in paper wrappers in The Pioneer Series.]

1897 *The Third Violet.* [A novel.]

1898 *The Open Boat and Other Tales of Adventure.* [Published by Doubleday & McClure Co., and by Heinemann.]

Pictures of War. [Published by Heinemann. The stories are the same as in *The Little Regiment*, but here *The Red Badge* is added.]

1899 *War is Kind.* [Poems.]

Active Service: A Novel. [Published by Frederick A. Stokes and by Heinemann.]

The Monster and Other Stories. [Published in New York and London by Harper. Reissued, with four additional stories, in 1901.]

II Work Published Posthumously

1900 *Whilomville Stories.* [Published in New York—in August—and in London by Harper.]

Wounds in the Rain: War Stories. [Published in October by Frederick A. Stokes and in England by Methuen & Co.]

1901 *Great Battles of the World.* [Published in Philadelphia by Lippincott and in London by Chapman & Hall.]

1902 *Last Words.* [Published only in England—by Digby, Long & Co.]

1903 *The O'Ruddy: A Romance.* [Coauthor: Robert Barr.]

1921 *Men, Women and Boats.* Edited with an Introduction by Vincent Starrett. [Boni & Liveright and then the Modern Library.]

1925-7

The Work of Stephen Crane. Twelve volumes, edited by Wilson Follett, with Introductions by various friends and admirers. [Alfred A. Knopf. The Introductions to Volumes II and XII by Robert H. Davis and Charles Michelson respectively are of biographical value, and the Introductions to Volumes I, IX, and X, by Joseph Hergesheimer, Willa Cather, and H. L. Mencken respectively are of critical value. The *Work*, a limited and expensive edition, has long been out of print. It omits some works such as Crane's first printed story, *The King's Favor* (*Syracuse University Herald*, May 1891), several *Sullivan County Sketches*, *The Blood of the Martyr* (a play, published by the Peter Pauper Press in 1940), *Legends* (in the *Bookman*, May 1896) and *A Lost Poem* (published by Harvard University Press, 1932, and appearing in *Golden Book*, February 1934); etc.]

1930 *The Collected Poems of Stephen Crane.* Edited by Wilson Follett. [Alfred A. Knopf. Reissued six times since 1930.]

1931 *Maggie together with George's Mother and The Blue Hotel.* Edited with an Introduction by Henry Hazlitt. [Alfred A. Knopf. Out of print in 1937.]

1933 *Maggie and Other Stories.* Edited with an Introduction by Vincent Starrett. [Modern Library.]

1940 *Twenty Stories.* Edited with an Introduction by Carl Van Doren. [Alfred A. Knopf. Reissued in 1945 by World Publishers. This edition is no longer in print.]

1949 *The Sullivan County Sketches of Stephen Crane,* edited with an Introduction by Melvin Schoberlin, pp. 1–20. [Syracuse University Press.]

1950 *Selected Prose and Poetry.* Edited with an Introduction by W. M. Gibson. [Rinehart.]

1951 *The Red Badge of Courage.* Edited with an Introduction by R. W. Stallman. [Modern Library, College Edition. Other editions with introductions include Ripley Hitchcock's (Appleton, 1900, 1917), Guy Empey's (Appleton, 1917), Max Herzberg's (Appleton, 1925, 1926; Modern Library, 1925; Pocket Books, 1942); Joseph Hergesheimer's (Volume I of the Work); Joseph Conrad's (in Heinemann's Pioneer Series, 1925, reprinted as "His War Book" in *Last Essays,* Dent, 1926); Carl Van Doren's, Heritage Press, 1944; John T. Winterich's (Folio Society, 1951); and R. W. Stallman's (Modern Library, Random House, 1951).]

III BOOKS AND ARTICLES ON STEPHEN CRANE:
BIOGRAPHICAL AND BIBLIOGRAPHICAL

1914 Hamlin Garland: "Stephen Crane as I Knew Him," *Yale Review,* N.S., 3 (April 1914), 494–506.

1923 Thomas Beer: *Stephen Crane: A Study in American Letters.* With an Introduction by Joseph Conrad. Reprinted in *The Borzoi Reader,* edited by Carl Van Doren, 1936. Knopf. Reprinted in *Hanna, Crane, and the Mauve Decade,* by Thomas Beer, 1941. Knopf.

1928 Irving Addison Bacheller: *Coming up the Road,* pp. 276–9, 292–3. Bobbs-Merrill.

1930 Hamlin Garland: "Stephen Crane," *Roadside Meetings,* pp. 189–206, 393. Macmillan.

1937 Ford Madox Ford: "Stephen Crane," *Portraits from Life,* pp. 21–37. Houghton Mifflin.

1939 Lyndon Upson Pratt: "A Possible Source of *The Red Badge of Courage,*" *American Literature,* XI, 1–10.

      H. T. Webster: "Wilbur F. Hinman's *Corporal Si Klegg* and Stephen Crane's *The Red Badge of Courage,*" *American Literature,* XI, 285–93.

1945 W. L. Werner: "Stephen Crane and *The Red Badge of Courage,*" *New York Times Book Review,* September 30, p. 4.

1948 Ames W. Williams and Vincent Starrett: *Stephen Crane: A Bibliography.* With an Introduction by Vincent Starrett, pp. 7–12. Glendale, Calif.: John Valentine.

1950 John Berryman: *Stephen Crane.* (American Men of Letters Series) William Sloane. Methuen, 1951.

1955 R. W. Stallman: "Some Additions to the Canon of Stephen Crane," *P. M. L. A.,* 70 (1955).

IV Books and Articles on Stephen Crane: Critical

1898 Edward Garnett: "Mr. Stephen Crane: An Appreciation," *Academy,* LV, 483-4. Reprinted, in expanded form, in *Friday Nights,* by Edward Garnett, pp. 201-17. Knopf, 1922; Cape, 1922, 1929.

1900 H. G. Wells: "Stephen Crane from an English Standpoint," *North American Review,* CLXXI, 233-42. Reprinted in *The Shock of Recognition,* edited by Edmund Wilson, pp. 661-71. Doubleday, Doran, 1943.

1919 Harriet Monroe: "Stephen Crane," *Poetry: A Magazine of Verse,* XIV, 148-52.

1925 Joseph Conrad: "His War Book: A Preface to Stephen Crane's *The Red Badge of Courage.*" (Pioneer Series) Heinemann. Reprinted in *Last Essays,* by Joseph Conrad, pp. 175-83. Dent, 1926.

1928 Robert Littell: "Notes on Stephen Crane," *New Republic,* LIV, 391-2.

1929 Wilson Follett: "The Second Twenty-Eight Years: A Note on Stephen Crane," *Bookman,* LXVIII, 532-7. Reprinted for the Stephen Crane Association, by Monroe F. Dreher, 1930.

Gorham B. Munson: "Prose for Fiction: Stephen Crane," *Style and Form in American Prose,* pp. 159-70. Doubleday, Doran.

1934 Harry Hartwick: "The Red Badge of Nature," *The Foreground of American Fiction,* pp. 21-44 and *passim.* American Book Co.

1935 Ford Madox Ford: "Technique," *Southern Review,* I, 20-35.

1940 Russell Nye: "Stephen Crane as Social Critic," *Modern Quarterly,* XI, 48-54.

1944 John C. Bushman: *The Fiction of Stephen Crane and its Critics.* University of Illinois dissertation (unpublished).

Jean Elizabeth Whitehead: *The Art of Stephen Crane.* Cornell University dissertation (unpublished).

1946 Horace Gregory and Marya Zaturenska: "A Note on Stephen Crane," *A History of American Poetry: 1900–1940,* pp. 133–7. Harcourt, Brace.

V. S. Pritchett: "Two Writers and Modern War," *The Living Novel,* pp. 166–78. Chatto & Windus.

1948 Robert E. Spiller: "Toward Naturalism in Fiction," *Literary History of the United States,* edited by Robert E. Spiller, Willard Thorp, and others, II, 1020–6 and *passim.* Macmillan.

1949 H. L. Mencken: "Stephen Crane," *A Mencken Chrestomathy,* pp. 496–7. Knopf.

1952 R. W. Stallman: "Stephen Crane," *Critiques & Essays on Modern Fiction,* edited by John Aldridge, pp. 244–69. Ronald Press.

STEPHEN CRANE was born in Newark, New Jersey, on November 1, 1871. From 1890 to 1895 he was a free-lance writer in New York. His first novel, Maggie: A Girl of the Streets, published in 1893, was unsuccessful. His second novel, The Red Badge of Courage (1895), made more of a mark, particularly after it was published in England in 1896. Crane served as a war correspondent in Cuba and in Greece between 1896 and 1898. He wrote numerous stories and tales and a small, but important, group of poems. Crane died of tuberculosis at Badenweiler, in the Black Forest, on June 5, 1900.

THE TEXT of this book was set on the Linotype in a face called TIMES ROMAN, designed by Stanley Morison for The Times (London), and first introduced by that newspaper in the 1930's. Composed, printed, and bound by THE COLONIAL PRESS INC., Clinton, Massachusetts. Cover design by ALVIN LUSTIG.

Vintage Books